"Kate . . ."

Jonathan's deep voice, huskier than usual, sent a delicious shiver rippling down her spine. She gazed at the tantalizing display of hard muscles that showed through his open shirt, then looked up at his face. Mesmerized by the glow in his eyes, Kate caught her breath. Jonathan wanted her and wanted her badly. The knowledge was like an aphrodisiac.

He slowly ran his hands up her arms. "Oh, my God," he whispered, closing his eyes against the soft, seductive look on her face, trying to regain control of himself.

But Kate had been widowed for five long months. Restraint was not what she wanted.

Murphy's Rainbow

CAROLYN LAMPMAN

HarperPaperbacks
A Division of HarperCollins*Publishers*

HarperPaperbacks *A Division of* HarperCollins*Publishers*
10 East 53rd Street, New York, N.Y. 10022

Copyright © 1993 by Carolyn Brubaker
All rights reserved. No part of this book may be used or reproduced in any manner whatsoever without written permission of the publisher, except in the case of brief quotations embodied in critical articles and reviews. For information address HarperCollins*Publishers,*
10 East 53rd Street, New York, N.Y. 10022.

Cover illustration by R.A. Maguire

First printing: October 1993

Printed in the United States of America

HarperPaperbacks, HarperMonogram, and colophon are trademarks of HarperCollins*Publishers*

❖ 10 9 8 7 6 5 4 3 2 1

*To Karen, Carol, Cathleen, and Trish,
who read every word, and to my family,
who let me write them.*

1

Wyoming Territory, 1869

Cholera! For Katharine Murphy it had become a living, breathing entity, a dark creature that sucked the life from Bryan's body. It hardly mattered that the wagon train had gone on without them, or that the single candle burning near at hand was almost gone. Bryan Murphy was dying, and they both knew it.

"Katie?" Bryan's voice was thin and raspy as he fought the painful cramps.

Folding his cold, dry hand into hers, Katharine swallowed the tears that threatened to overwhelm her. "I'm here, Bry. Don't try to talk. Just rest now."

"I have eternity to rest." His face was pinched and gray, the brilliant green eyes, once so full of life, now looked sunken and defeated. "Go to your uncle Matthew in Denver." He shook his head weakly as she started to protest. "I know, Katie.

But he loves you, and he'll keep you safe until you decide what to do with your life."

"Without you I have no life."

"Here now. That doesn't sound like the Katie McAnespie I married for her courage!" Bryan lifted his free hand to her face and traced the line of her cheek. "Remember every storm has a rainbow, and—"

"And there's a pot of gold at the end of it," she finished for him. "There won't be one this time, Bry."

"You're a fighter. You'll find a way to go on, and you'll find that pot of gold." He gazed at her as though memorizing her features and then smiled wistfully. "My beautiful Irish rose." His hand slipped from her cheek and fell back to the bed. "I love you, Katie."

"I love you, too," Katharine whispered, but it was too late. She was alone.

The sun was well up in the sky before Katharine finished digging the grave. The hole yawned at her feet, the raw earth stark against the green of the prairie. She lifted her head as a movement to the west caught her eye. It was a single rider coming toward her at an easy lope. From the loose-limbed way he sat in the saddle, she knew it could only be Sam Perkins, a scout from the wagon train.

When he reached her, he swung down from his horse and stared at the freshly dug grave. At last he cleared his throat. "I'm right sorry about your husband, Mrs. Murphy. Reckon I can bury him for you."

Not trusting herself to speak, Katharine merely nodded. She had already bathed Bryan and wrapped him in their wedding quilt. There was nothing more she could do. In silent agony she watched as Sam placed the man she loved in his final resting place and began the grim task of filling in the grave. Wincing as the clods of dirt struck the body below, Katharine reminded herself repeatedly that Bryan could no longer feel, that he was beyond pain.

At last the job was finished, and Sam gave her a look of sympathy. "If you know some words to say, best do it now."

Katharine stared numbly at the mound. From somewhere inside came the Lord's Prayer, which she followed with a few of her own words: "And please take my Bryan into your heart and keep him safe." With one last look, she turned away.

Avoiding her eyes, Sam twisted his hat in his hands. "If you want to collect a few things, I'll take you to that little town I saw two or three miles back."

Again Katharine nodded, not surprised that he hadn't offered to escort her west to the wagon train. Those so-called good people had already turned their backs on the Murphys. Other than Sam, only one man had shown any concern for them, by offering Katharine a revolver for protection from the riffraff that roamed the prairie. Refusing to accept money from the contaminated wagon, he had taken the team of oxen as payment.

At the time Katharine had been too worried about Bryan to think of anything else. Now she wondered if greed rather than compassion might have been the man's motivation.

She made an awkward bundle out of her extra dress, hairbrush, nightgown, and clean underwear and then dug to the bottom of the trunk to retrieve the stocking that held what was left of their life savings. It wasn't much—only a single twenty-dollar gold piece—but she wasn't about to risk someone coming along and stealing it before she could return for the rest of her belongings.

Thrusting the stocking into the center of her bundle, Katharine considered taking the handgun. No, it would only add to the already cumbersome load. She hid it in the trunk and climbed down from the wagon. Her milk cow, Suzette, was already tied to Sam's saddle horn.

"If you'll give me a hand with the chicken crate, I'll be ready," she said.

"Chicken crate! Are you crazy?"

"Well, I can't just leave them out here, can I?"

"Look, Mrs. Murphy, I've only got one horse. There's no room for a crate."

"Oh." Katharine looked abashed as she glanced at the horse. Then her face lit up. "How about if I stick them in a flour sack? I really hate to lose them after bringing them all this way."

Sam started to say something and then seemed to change his mind; he gave her a curt nod. Though the four birds complained loudly at such rough treatment, they were soon sacked up and tied to the horse.

Sam hoisted her onto the saddle and handed her the reins. "Hang on to these while I take one more look around."

Recognizing the signs of a man who had already been pushed too far, Katharine was afraid to tell him she didn't have the faintest idea how to control a horse. Not sure what else to do, she talked in a soothing voice to the animal, complimenting him on what a wonderful creature he was. Apparently the horse was not immune to flattery, for he stood perfectly still until Sam returned a few minutes later.

Katharine barely had time to wonder what she was supposed to do before Sam swung up behind the saddle and reached around her to take the reins. Without a word he prodded the horse into motion, and they took off at a jarring pace.

Katharine contemplated the possibility that Sam had lost his mind. As the chickens squawked in terror, she turned to see how Suzette was faring, and the sight that met her eyes wiped out every other thought. A thick cloud of black smoke was pouring from both ends of her wagon.

"Nooooo!" she screamed, twisting out of Sam's grasp. She jumped to the ground and stumbled, but struggled frantically to her feet and started to run, her breath coming in gasping sobs. She was still a long way from the burning wagon when Sam caught up with her. Wrapping his long arms around her, he restrained her, though she fought him with every ounce of strength she had.

"It had to be done," he said. "That wagon was full of cholera."

"I thought you came back to help us!" she cried, beating his chest with her fists. "But you just wanted to make sure we didn't catch up to the wagon train."

"No, that's not true. I came to do what I could for you both." He lifted his head to stare at the wagon now engulfed in flames. "I had no choice. I'm sorry."

"You're sorry. Everything I owned was in that wagon."

"I know," he whispered, patting her back clumsily. "I know."

He let her cry, holding her tightly until the last sob died away. "Reckon we best get a move on," he said at last.

Pulling away from him, Katharine gazed first at the new grave and then at the smoldering ruins of the wagon. "Might as well," she said dully. "There's nothing left here."

The trip was accomplished in almost total silence. Sam tried several times to start a conversation but eventually gave up when he got no response. Even the chickens were subdued, lulled by the darkness inside the sack.

Katharine had paid little attention when the wagon train had passed the town the day before. Now she saw that it was disappointingly small. Only a store, a blacksmith shop, a saloon, and a handful of houses dotted the prairie.

Sam stopped in front of the blacksmith shop and dismounted. Tying the horse to the hitching rail, he said, "I'll go see about boarding your stock."

Stock? Katharine felt a hysterical bubble of

laughter rise in her throat. Four chickens and a cow? She and Bryan had had such wonderful plans when they'd started out. They'd have a beautiful little farm where they could raise a family. But there had been no babies, and their other cows had died on the trip. Now Bryan was gone, too, along with everything from their life together. Katharine looked around desperately. And this was the pot of gold at the end of Bryan's rainbow, a dismal little town in the middle of nowhere?

Sam returned with the smith. "Mr. Jones here says he'll keep your animals for the milk and eggs."

Katharine forced a smile. "Thank you, Mr. Jones."

"Glad to oblige. The young fella told me about yer husband." He shook his head. "To die in a fire like that. Must have been awful for you."

Katharine turned shocked eyes to Sam and encountered a warning look.

Luckily Mr. Jones didn't seem to expect an answer. "You better go to Mrs. Cline over at the store," he went on. "She ain't the friendliest, but I reckon she'll take you in for a few days. Might want to leave this young feller here, though."

Katharine started to get down, but Sam grasped her around the waist and swung her to the ground. While Mr. Jones took the animals to his corral, Sam untied her things from the saddle. "I told him your husband knocked an oil lamp over in the wagon," he whispered. "Folks tend to get stirred up about cholera."

Accepting her bundle from him, Katharine replied, "I know, Mr. Perkins. I've already seen it."

Without another word she turned on her heel and walked away.

Sam stood watching her for several long moments. Then, with a shake of his head, he remounted and set out to catch up with the wagon train.

The store had an almost military neatness about it. Nowhere was there any of the friendly clutter that usually characterized such places. With a cursory glance at the only other customer in the store, Katharine approached the woman who stood ramrod straight behind the counter. "Are you Mrs. Cline?"

"I am."

"Mr. Jones over at the blacksmith shop said you might be able give me a place to stay for a few days."

"Oh, he did, did he? And who might you be?"

"I'm Mrs. Murphy."

"Mrs.?" She eyed the bundle in Katharine's hand. "Where's your husband?"

Th-there was a fire," Katharine stammered. "M-my husband d-died."

"Hmph! A likely story."

Katharine blinked in surprise at the woman's unexpected hostility. "I . . . it would just be until the stage comes in, and I can pay."

"There's some things money can't buy, and respectability is one of them. The saloon is the place for the likes of you." She folded her arms across her narrow chest. "As though I can't tell a decent woman from a piece of dance hall trash."

"But I—"

"Save your breath, Mrs. Murphy," said the other customer, a tall redhead, as she walked up to the counter and slapped down a packet of needles. "Once Mrs. Cline makes up her mind to something, she don't change it." She placed a few coins next to the needles and flashed Katharine a friendly smile. "The stage don't come to Horse Creek, but you can stay with me for a day or two."

Mrs. Cline gave an audible sniff of disdain and pushed the woman's change across the counter as though afraid of making contact with her.

The redhead gave a low chuckle as she tucked her money and the needles into her reticule. "It's always a pleasure to do business with you, Mrs. Cline." She turned and strolled out of the store with Katharine following behind.

"Self-righteous old biddy," the redhead muttered as soon as the door closed behind them. "Any fool can see you ain't from no dance hall." She gave Katharine a sympathetic look. "Looks like you've had a rough time of it, though. Heard you tell that old prune you lost your husband. I'll wager it wasn't very long ago."

Katharine nodded, barely able to speak because of the knot in her throat. "L-last night."

"You poor thing." She sighed as they started across the street toward the saloon. "Sure hope I'm doin' the right thing taking you home with me."

"If you don't have room . . ."

"Lord bless you, honey. It ain't that." She glanced at the saloon and made a face. "Most folks would say you shouldn't even be talking to me, let alone staying with me."

"Why not?"

"Mostly 'cause of the work I do."

"I don't . . ." Katharine stopped in confusion. They were no longer walking, and the redhead was studying her as though waiting for something. She suddenly realized that they were standing in front of the saloon and that her new friend was watching her closely. The revelation must have shown in her face, for the woman's expression became cold and distant.

"Well," Katharine said, "I don't guess a few nights in a saloon will damage me much. Never cared what anybody thought about me, anyway. You'd be amazed how many narrow-minded people looked down their noses at us because my husband was an Irish Catholic."

"It ain't quite the same thing," the redhead said. Then she grinned. "The name's Rosie. Welcome to the Golden Spur."

Katharine returned the smile and followed her through the swinging doors, praying that she wasn't making a mistake.

2

"*This time of day* Red's usually in the back," Rosie said over her shoulder as she led the way through the saloon. "We better go talk to him so he don't get his nose out of joint."

Katharine glanced around inquisitively as she followed her. She'd never been in a saloon before, and her curiosity was aroused. It was disappointingly ordinary, with a dozen tables and a long bar. Nowhere was there any sign of the decadence she had been told lurked in such places. Even the display of bottles behind the bar looked innocuous.

Katharine had just noticed a barber chair in one corner when Rosie disappeared through a door in the back. Before she could catch up she stopped in her tracks, her eyes riveted to a picture hanging on the wall beside the door. A lovely dark-haired woman reclined gracefully on a pale blue chaise longue while an equally beautiful blonde sat on a nearby chair playing the mandolin. The painting would have been completely unexceptional if not for the fact that both women were stark naked.

Staring at it in wonder, Katharine was suddenly called back to reality by a strident male voice coming from the back room.

"I'm not runnin' a home for lost souls."

"Since when are you so all-fired stingy you can't help out a woman in trouble?" she heard Rosie ask. "Where's that famous Irish hospitality you're always yapping about, or is that just blarney you save for the paying customers?"

"Damn it, Rosie, I've got enough problems without taking in every broke stranger that happens along. Find me somebody to replace Meg, and maybe I'll be a little more friendly." There was the sound of a match striking. "Damned ungrateful wench," muttered the man. "I still can't believe she ran off like that. Maybe this girl you found could—"

"No!" Rosie broke in. "She's a good woman, and I ain't about to let you change that."

"Servin' drinks and dancin' with a few cowboys won't do her any more harm than staying here."

Suddenly a mental inventory of her possessions flashed through Katharine's mind. Even with her gold piece and the sale of her animals, she'd have barely enough to get to her uncle in Denver. The vision of the smug "I told you so" expression he would surely wear sent her into the back room. "If you're offering me a job, I won't turn it down until I've heard what you've got to say."

"This ain't a fittin' place for someone like you to work," Rosie said.

"There's no way for me to leave Horse Creek,

and I don't have much money," Katharine said. "I need a job, and there doesn't seem to be any place else to get one. Mrs. Cline certainly wouldn't hire me."

The beefy red-haired man behind the desk raised his bushy eyebrows as he eyed her disheveled appearance. Chewing the end of a cigar, he leaned back in his chair and studied her with professional candor. At last he took the cigar out of his mouth and rolled it between his fingers. "Room, board, and fifty percent of what you make on the side."

Katharine gave him a puzzled look. "What I make on the side? You mean tips?"

"Tips?" Red gave a snort of laughter. "Where'd you find this one, Rosie, hiding behind a sagebrush?"

Rosie gave him a scornful look. "She wasn't hiding anywhere. Don't you recognize a decent woman when you see one?"

"And what would I be doing with a decent woman?" He looked at Katharine and shook his head. "I'm thinking Rosie's right, though. You don't belong here, colleen."

Katharine couldn't believe it. Mrs. Cline had turned her out because she wasn't respectable, and now this man was about to do the same thing because she was. "Look, I need a job. I can do anything you want me to," she said. "Serve drinks, dance with your customers, and . . ." Her voice trailed off as she finally realized what Red had been talking about earlier.

"And?" Red prodded.

"I—I . . ." Katharine's face turned crimson.

"Frenchie and I can handle that part of it," Rosie said quickly. "What we really need is a cook."

"A . . . a cook?"

"Everybody's got to eat. Meg always did the cooking around here, had a real knack for it. Frenchie can burn water, and I ain't much better. You can cook, can't you?"

"Oh, yes, and bake, too," Katharine said.

Rosie put her hands on Red's desk and leaned forward. "What do you say, Red? No more burned biscuits and lumpy gravy."

Red pursed his lips. At last he gave a nod. "All right. If you can turn out a decent meal, I'll pay you fifteen dollars a month to cook, but you'll have to work the floor for room and board."

Rosie gave a snort of disgust. "You're all heart, Red."

"It's a deal," Katharine said before he had a chance to change his mind. "And thank you Mr. . . . ."

"O'Leary, but I'll not be knowing who you're talking to if you call me mister." He stuck out a beefy palm. "And what might your name be?"

Bryan's face flashed across Katharine's mind, and the enormity of what she was doing hit her full force. She might shame herself, but never the man she loved. "Kate," she said, closing the door on the life of Katharine Murphy as she shook hands with the big Irishman. "Just Kate."

Rosie hustled her charge out the door before Red had a chance to protest. "Come on, Kate, I'll show you your room and maybe dig up some food for you." Rosie glanced back over her shoulder and grimaced. "If Red had his way, you'd go to work right now, even though any fool can see you're about done in."

Rosie led her to a small room at the top of the stairs and then disappeared down the corridor, leaving Kate alone in her new home. Furnished only with a bed, washstand, and dresser, the room was far from luxurious, but after the confines of a covered wagon it seemed almost spacious to Kate. A faint whiff of heavy perfume and a tattered bit of lace under the edge of the bed were all that remained of the former occupant. Otherwise the room was surprisingly clean.

Wearily dropping her bundle on the dresser top, Kate caught sight of her face in the mirror and gasped. Strands of hair had worked their way free of the bun and now hung over her ears. Touching a dirty cheek with an equally grimy hand, Kate traced the track of a tear down her face. Dark smudges of fatigue under her eyes made her look years older. It was no wonder Mrs. Cline had thrown her out.

With a shake of her head, Kate poured water into the porcelain bowl and stripped down to her corset and petticoats. Five minutes of determined scrubbing washed away most of the dirt, but there was little she could do about the wan face that stared back at her in the mirror as she brushed her hair.

The familiar task reminded Kate of the man who had watched this ritual every night, his dark eyes gleaming in the candlelight. How often Bryan had pulled her down onto the bed when she'd finished, whispering sweet words of passion as they made love in the shelter of each other's arms.

As the memories crashed in on her, Kate braided her hair, fighting the despondency that threatened to overwhelm her. With Bryan gone, she had no reason to live. He had been her whole life.

At last, unable to control the pain, Kate threw herself across the bed, sobbing her heart out into the unfamiliar pillow. Eventually exhaustion overcame her agony, and she fell into a deep sleep. Only vaguely aware of Rosie coming in and covering her with a quilt, Kate drifted along in dreamless oblivion. Even the sound of raucous laughter drifting up from the saloon below didn't disturb her.

The sun was high overhead when Kate finally awoke. Disoriented at first, she lay there for several seconds, collecting her thoughts. Then, with a startled exclamation, she jumped out of bed. Hurriedly washing her face, she pulled her hair up into a bun. Then she shook out her extra dress and put it on, smoothing out the worst of the wrinkles.

When she emerged from her room less than five minutes later, there seemed to be no one around. Downstairs, the main room was empty, though the smell of stale cigar smoke hung heavy in the air. Even Red's office was deserted. Resisting the urge to straighten the pile of papers in disorder on his desk, Kate continued her search until she found a surprisingly serviceable kitchen in the back of the building.

A heavy oak table dominated the center of the room, surrounded by half a dozen chairs. A sink full of dirty dishes was set against one wall, and a modern cookstove took up most of another. Two small windows let in light, giving the kitchen a cool, welcoming atmosphere.

Rolling up her sleeves, Kate went to work. Within an hour the kitchen sparkled. There was coffee on the back of the stove, and the room was filled with a pleasant yeasty smell emanating from a bowl of bread dough set on the table to rise. After wiping the last dish and putting it in the cupboard, Kate gave a sigh of satisfaction. With a final glance around, she untied her apron and hung it on a nail by the back door.

Since no one had yet appeared from upstairs, she slipped outside and walked the short distance to the blacksmith shop. Silas Jones greeted her with a friendly smile.

"Good morning, Mrs. Murphy." With an expert swing of his hammer, he struck a piece of hot iron. Holding it aloft with a pair of tongs, he peered at it critically before sticking it back in the forge and pumping the bellows. "Heard you got a job cooking for Red O'Leary."

"Yes, I started this morning."

A frown darkened his face. "Ain't a fittin' place for you to be working, but I reckon with Abigail Cline bein' the way she is—"

"Everyone at the Golden Spur has been very kind," she said. "Actually, I came to check on my cow."

"She's doing just fine. A little off her milk last night, but she gave almost a whole bucketful this morning." He turned the iron in the forge and pumped the bellows again. "I was thinking you might want to sell the extra. She gives a durn sight more than I can use."

"I might at that. Anyway, I can use some of it over at the saloon."

Silas chuckled. "I reckon it's been a long time since any of those folks cared to drink milk."

"Maybe, but I'll bet they'll like fresh butter on their bread."

He just grinned as he pulled the iron out of the fire and pounded it flat.

Kate spent the next thirty minutes wandering around Horse Creek. It didn't look any more promising than it had the day before.

She returned to the Golden Spur to find Rosie and a brassy blonde sitting at the kitchen table sipping coffee. An empty cup in the sink showed that Red had already been there and left. Kate blushed. "I'm sorry I wasn't here when you came down."

Rosie waved her hand. "Don't be silly. No law says you have to stay in the kitchen. Besides, looks like you've done a day's work already." She gazed around appreciatively, then nodded to the other woman at the table. "This here is Frenchie."

"Please to meet you, mademoiselle," Frenchie said in a heavily accented voice.

"Don't let her way of talking fool you. She ain't any more French than I am," Rosie said.

Frenchie grinned. "*Non,* but ze cowboys love eet." She gave a dramatic sigh and dropped the accent. "I'm going to catch me a rich rancher just like Meg did. It's only a matter of time."

Against all she'd been taught, Kate found herself liking the two prostitutes. They gossiped just like everyone else while she fixed lunch. They told Kate such outrageous stories about the people who lived around Horse Creek that she couldn't help but laugh.

Finally Rosie stood up and stretched. "Red said we're supposed to get you ready to work tonight. You sure you want to do this?"

Kate longed to tell Rosie that she'd changed her mind, but she knew she couldn't. "I don't have a choice. I need the work," she said.

And so it was, a few short hours later, that Kate found herself bathed, powdered, perfumed, and corseted tighter than she'd ever been in her life. With her back to the mirror she sat as still as she could while Frenchie deftly used a curling iron to produce long ringlets and Rosie applied rouge to her cheeks and kohl to her eyes.

Kate almost lost her nerve when she saw the dress she was expected to wear. A brilliant cherry red and trimmed in black, the garment looked as though it had been made for a much shorter person. "I can't wear that," she protested. "It's too small. I'll be falling out of it everywhere."

"That's the whole idea, honey." Rosie slipped the dress over Kate's head and pulled the laces tight. Frenchie plucked a feather headdress from the dresser and set it atop the shining brown curls, then both women stepped back to admire their handiwork. There was a moment of stunned silence. "Lordy, Lordy, who would have believed it?" Rosie said. "Your own mother wouldn't recognize you."

"Can I look?" Kate asked, already turning to the mirror. Her mouth fell open in horrified astonishment as she stared at the exotic creature reflected in the glass. It was just as she had feared: her ample breasts strained at the bodice, looking as if a single wrong move would send them spilling out of the fabric. The overall effect—décolletage, incredibly tiny waist, feminine hips, and shapely legs clad in black silk stockings—was one of blatant sexuality.

"Do you like it?" Frenchie asked.

"I—I'm not sure."

"The men will love it," Rosie assured her. "Just remember what I told you."

"I will. If they want to go upstairs, I tell them I'm indisposed and send them to one of you. But what if they ask me what's wrong?"

"Tell them it's the monthly miseries," Frenchie said with a smile. "That'll scare off most men. If it doesn't, just say you have a strange rash. They'll think it's the pox."

Rosie and Frenchie went to dress for the evening and left Kate alone with the strange new image of herself. Oh, Bry, she thought, I'm so glad you can't see what I've become. Biting her lip against the rush of pain, Kate fled the room and the vision in the mirror.

Serving drinks and dancing with lonely men turned out to be much easier than Kate had anticipated. Women were still rare enough on the frontier that even those of questionable morals were given respect. Often all she had to do was listen to the ramblings of one lonely cowboy after another while Red plied them with whiskey and Rosie or Frenchie took care of any other needs they might have.

Soon Kate's life fell into a routine of cooking by day and working in the saloon at night. She became good friends with Rosie and Frenchie and even taught them how to braid rags together for a rug. The three women spent many afternoons working on it in cozy companionship. If Kate's future looked less than hopeful, at least she was keeping herself fed and housed. Though Bryan's death was still an open wound, she slipped into melancholy reflection less and less often as the weeks went by.

A bright spot was her daily visit to the blacksmith shop. There she could be herself, unfettered by the role she was forced to play. More than once she ran into cowboys she'd danced with the night before who didn't even recognize her.

Most of the men she met at the blacksmith's were friendly, so she didn't think anything of it when a cowhand named Charlie Hobbs kept her talking for almost forty minutes. Kate might have been less complacent if she could have heard the conversation after she left.

There was a speculative look in Charlie's eye as he watched her walk away. "Who is she?" he asked Silas.

Silas glanced up. "Mrs. Murphy? She come through with a wagon train 'bout a month or so back. Her husband died outside of town and she's been cooking at the Golden Spur ever since."

Charlie's eyebrows rose. "The Golden Spur?"

"Mrs. Cline wouldn't have nothin' to do with her," Silas explained. "No place else for her to work."

Charlie rubbed his chin. "Could be that'll change."

Kate had gotten so used to men staring at her that she didn't even notice the stranger standing at the bar that night until Frenchie whispered in her ear, "If Jonathan Cantrell wants to go upstairs, send him my way."

Kate blinked in surprise. Frenchie had never made such a request before. "Who?"

"The good-looking one at the bar. He hasn't taken his eyes off you since he walked in."

Kate glanced toward the bar and caught her breath in disbelief. With dark curly hair and the bluest eyes she'd ever seen, the man was almost too handsome to be real. "Mercy sakes," she murmured.

"Ain't he something?" Frenchie sighed. "Sure seems taken with you."

Kate shrugged. Frenchie had a tendency to exaggerate. The man was probably just bored.

But as the evening progressed Kate was uncomfortably aware of Jonathan Cantrell's gaze following her around the room. Every time she looked his way he was staring at her. Finally, in an effort to disconcert him, she put her hands on her hips and stared back at him pointedly. Their eyes locked for a full thirty seconds before he quirked an eyebrow and lifted his glass in a salute.

With a gasp, Kate turned scarlet and looked away. From then on she studiously ignored him, though she could still feel his gaze on her. At last, when she could stand it no longer, she stole a glance at him.

It was as though he'd been waiting for her to do just that. Straightening, he tossed down the rest of his drink, wiped the moisture from his mustache, and started toward her.

Backing away frantically, Kate wished she could disappear through the floor. Suddenly she felt the wall at her back. She was trapped, and still he came toward her. Kate closed her eyes.

"Mrs. Murphy?"

He knew her name? Kate's eyes popped open, and she found herself staring at a very broad chest. Following the line of buttons up to his face, she swallowed nervously. The man had to be at least six feet tall.

"You are Mrs. Murphy, aren't you?"

"Y-yes . . . no . . . My name's Kate."

"I'm Jonathan Cantrell," he said, smiling down at her.

Kate stared at an unexpected dimple in one of his rugged cheeks. "How—how do you do?" she stammered.

"Is there some place we could talk?"

"I . . . n-no. I—I'm indisposed this evening."

"You're what?" He frowned.

For some reason Kate couldn't bring herself to give him the excuses she'd used so easily with other men. "I can't . . . I don't . . ." She looked down at the floor. "Frenchie will be happy to go with you," she mumbled.

There was a moment of silence before he spoke. "I don't think Frenchie can handle what I have in mind."

3

"*I—I'm sure* Frenchie will be more than happy to accommodate you," Kate said, aware of how this man's spectacular looks were adding to her nervousness.

"I doubt it." A twinkle appeared in his blue eyes. "I have a business proposition for you."

"No, thank you."

"You haven't heard what I have to say yet."

"I don't think I want to."

"Oh, come now, Mrs. Murphy. What harm can there be in listening? That is your job, isn't it?"

Jonathan Cantrell was enjoying himself. If he regretted it later, it wouldn't be the first time his sense of humor had gotten him in trouble. The temptation to tease her was more than he could resist. She had such an adorable way of blushing, with the color traveling over her chest and up to her face. It was quite a show.

"Shall we sit down?" He nodded toward a

nearby table. Watching her lead the way, looking as though she were being forced into something very unpleasant, Jonathan found it difficult not to grin as he followed her to the table and pulled out her chair. Women didn't usually mind his company so much.

"W-would you like a drink?" she stammered.

"No, I've had plenty, thank you." He took a chair opposite her. "What I'd really like is to sit and talk for a while." This time he couldn't help but chuckle in response to her horrified expression. "I promise it won't be too painful."

"N-no, of course not. What would you like to talk about?"

"I'd like to offer you a job."

"I have one."

"I think the one I have in mind is better suited to you."

"You know nothing about me," Kate snapped.

Jonathan watched her eyes turn darker. He had come to town because his partner, Charlie Hobbs, had met a young widow at Silas Jones's shop and insisted she was the answer to their problems. From Charlie's description Jonathan had expected a drab but respectable young lady who'd jump at the chance to leave her seamy surroundings. Instead he'd discovered a woman with a body to make a man's mouth water.

It had soon become obvious to Jonathan as he'd observed her that Mrs. Murphy was no ordinary saloon girl. Though she got her share of admiring glances, no man was allowed to touch her, and she never went upstairs. Then, when he'd offered a blatant invitation that would have brought either of her coworkers to his side in a moment, she'd turned the color of her bright red dress and ignored him altogether. It appeared that Charlie was right after all.

"Do you like children, Mrs. Murphy?"

"Children?" Kate gave him a startled look. "I . . . yes, of course."

"Good, I was hoping you'd say that." He sat back and stroked his mustache absently. "I need someone to take care of my two sons."

"Your sons?" It was the last thing Kate had expected him to say.

"I can't be a mother and father both. They're good boys, but they need a woman's touch." He sighed. "I guess we all do. I'll pay you forty-five dollars a month plus room and board to be our housekeeper."

Kate couldn't believe her ears. "Is that why you came here tonight, to hire me as your housekeeper?"

"Well, I—"

"Yes or no?"

Jonathan shifted uncomfortably. "Yes."

"Then why didn't you just come out and ask? Why all that nonsense of watching me?"

"I had to be sure."

"Sure of what?" Kate glared at him. "That I wouldn't corrupt your boys?"

"Not exactly." Jonathan shrugged. "More like whether you could handle the job."

"And after watching me serve drinks for three hours you're sure I'd make a good house-keeper?"

"Maybe not," he said softly, "but I do know you don't belong here."

Kate looked away. He was right, of course. She didn't belong here. Jonathan Cantrell was offering her a way out, and at three times what Red paid her. It would be stupid to turn him down just because he made her nervous. "What exactly would I be doing?"

"Taking care of the boys, cooking, cleaning. You know, woman things."

"Does that include anything of a . . . personal nature for you?"

He looked surprised. "Well, I might ask you to sew on a button now and then or darn my socks, but . . . oh." His dimples appeared, and the sapphire eyes twinkled at her across the table. "No, Mrs. Murphy. I assure you, I won't require your 'personal' attention."

Suddenly Kate felt silly for asking, and she looked down at her hands in embarrassment. "I—I'm sorry, that was a stupid question."

Watching in fascination as a flush once again climbed to her face, Jonathan resisted the urge to tell her otherwise. "Why don't you try it for a week or two? If it doesn't work out, you can always come back here." His voice took on an almost pleading tone. "I'll pay you a full month's salary no matter how long you stay."

"You seem awfully anxious to hire someone you know nothing about."

"To be honest with you, Mrs. Murphy, I'm desperate. There just isn't enough time to do everything that needs doing, and it's the housework that gets neglected. My boys are going to grow up without any real idea of civilized behavior, or even what it's like to have regular meals and clean clothes."

An image of two motherless little boys rose in Kate's mind. Could she turn her back on them? "I'd need one day a week off."

"Of course."

"And a certain amount of privacy."

"You'll have your own room."

"I'd have to bring my cow with me."

Jonathan gave her a startled look. "You have a cow?"

"And four chickens."

He laughed, a deep rich sound that made more than one head swivel their way. "I hire a housekeeper and get fresh milk and eggs in the bargain. If I give your animals a home, will you take the job?"

Kate couldn't help thinking what a nice laugh he had. "When you put it like that, how can I refuse?"

Packing her things the next morning, Kate wasn't so sure. What did she know about Jonathan Cantrell, after all? Only what he'd told her and Frenchie's ecstatic response to what she considered Kate's good fortune. Rosie had been far less enthusiastic, but only because she thought Kate was going to a life of domestic drudgery.

Kate looked into the mirror above the dresser. In the month she'd spent at the Golden Spur little had changed. She still had the same brown hair and hazel eyes. Only the faint lines that were starting to form around her mouth and the deep shadows under her eyes were any different.

Suddenly she grinned at her reflection. A glance in the mirror might have convinced her of Jonathan Cantrell's sincerity last night. Though far from homely, she'd been described as plain more often than pretty, and her grief for Bryan had etched itself into her face. With a shake of her head, Kate picked up her bundle and turned away. How silly she'd been. As if a man who looked like Mr. Cantrell would be attracted to her. The thought was strangely comforting.

Without any real regrets, Kate walked down the stairs and out the door. She had said her good-byes last night, with hugs and a few tears from Rosie and Frenchie. Even Red had been surprisingly understanding, saying gruffly that she'd always have a job at the Golden Spur. As she followed the now familiar path to the blacksmith shop, Kate hoped fervently she'd never have to take Red up on his offer.

She recognized Charlie Hobbs right away. Though the name had meant nothing when Jonathan Cantrell told her his partner would come get her this morning, Kate remembered the tall, lean cowboy she'd met only the day before.

"Morning, Mrs. Murphy." Charlie gave her a friendly grin and tipped his hat. "Already got your cow tied to the wagon and your chickens loaded. Is there anything you need before we leave town?"

"No." Kate returned his smile. "I'm as ready as I'll ever be."

Charlie nodded and put her bundle in the back

of the wagon before helping her up to the seat. They headed out of town toward the rugged blue mountains that rose majestically to the north. At first Kate relaxed and enjoyed the scenery and Charlie's conversation, but the longer they traveled the worse the butterflies in her stomach became. Perhaps if Jonathan Cantrell were more like his partner, she'd be less nervous. Finally she looked up at her companion timidly. "How far out do you live?"

"About six miles or so. Jonathan's place is a mite closer, though. You can travel it in twenty minutes on a good horse. Usually takes about an hour in the wagon."

"Good gracious! I had no idea it was so far."

"It was a durn sight farther to town before folks settled in Horse Creek." He smiled. "Reckon you'll get used to it."

"I suppose. So you don't live with the Cantrells?"

"Nope. Got my own claim a coupla miles up the creek."

"I thought you were partners."

"Yup. Reckon we are, but ol' Jon's a clever one. He figures on takin' advantage of the government's offer of free land. With both of us homesteading, we can get twice as much land legal like. Jon seems to think folks will start comin' pretty fast now that the war's over, and it won't take 'em long to find this place."

"I see," Kate murmured, but she was far more concerned with the realization that, other than the children, she'd be totally alone with Jonathan Cantrell miles from anywhere. It was a disconcerting thought, but once again the picture of two little boys rose in her mind, images of sun-kissed faces and tousled mops of hair. At last she'd have little ones to tuck into bed, to cuddle, to love. It was a cherished dream she and Bryan had once shared.

Finally they arrived at a small log cabin. Kate's eyes were drawn immediately to the cactus that bloomed in yellow profusion among the clumps of grass on the sod roof. From the freshly peeled logs of the corral to the raw framework of a new barn, the place exuded a kind of restless energy, like a dream impatient to become reality.

"I mighta known it," she heard Charlie mutter under his breath as he tied the reins to the brake lever and jumped down. For the first time Kate noticed the two boys rolling around in the dirt at the side of the house. Though one would occasionally throw a punch at the other, it looked as though their fight had degenerated into a wrestling match.

With a hand on each collar, Charlie pulled them up from the ground and drew them apart. "Thought your pa told you two to behave."

"It was Levi's fault." The smaller combatant glared at his brother. "He said he was going to show the new housekeeper around just 'cause he's older."

The other boy swiped at the blood running from his nose with the back of his hand. "Well, I am almost thirteen and you're still just a kid."

"That's enough." Charlie gave them both a shake. "You keep this up and Mrs. Murphy will turn tail and run 'fore she even gets unpacked."

Both boys gave her a guilty look. "Sorry, Mrs.

Murphy," Levi mumbled, and then gave his brother a meaningful nudge.

"Oh, yeah, sorry."

"Apology accepted."

Kate felt a sinking in the pit of her stomach as she looked from one to the other. Her image of two little boys who needed tucking in at night disappeared. Why hadn't she thought to ask Jonathan how old his sons were? These two were nearly as tall as she was.

"I'm Bernie Cantrell, and this here's my brother, Levi," the younger boy said before Levi had a chance to say anything.

"It's very nice to meet you both. I wonder, could one of you take care of my cow?" She glanced at Suzette, who was still tied to the wagon, swishing her tail from side to side.

The words were barely out of her mouth before Levi was headed toward the wagon. "Sure thing, Mrs. Murphy."

"And do you suppose you can find a place for my chickens, Bernie?" She was rewarded with a nod and a wide grin.

"Are they always like that?" she asked, watching them walk away together as though nothing had happened between them.

"Yup." Charlie reached into the back of the wagon and retrieved her things. "Most times they're best friends, but when they get to scrappin' . . ." He shook his head.

When they reached the house, he opened the front door and stepped aside, allowing her to pass. "Jon said you could have the room in the back."

Kate gazed around in amazement. Two large curtainless windows, covered with dirt and fly specks, flooded the room with light. With a wide variety of items scattered here and there, it was obviously the main living area of the house. A saddle, some bridles, saddle blankets, and various building tools covered most of the floor, though Kate could see flashes of dingy floorboards here and there.

A good-size table stood near the windows, buried under a pile of dirty dishes. Pots and pans filled a large dishpan, overflowing onto the hoosier on one side and a rusty old stove on the other. Articles of clothing of various sizes were flung about carelessly, and a thick layer of dust covered the few surfaces that remained uncluttered.

When Jonathan Cantrell had told her how desperately he wanted a housekeeper, Kate had thought he was exaggerating. Now, she saw it had probably been a gross understatement. She'd never seen such a mess, nor had she ever felt so needed. For the first time in four weeks, Katharine Murphy really felt like smiling.

4

"*Jon was plannin'* on straightenin' up some before you got here," Charlie said apologetically as he moved past her through the kitchen. "Something must have come up." He kicked a pile of clothes out of the way.

Kate ran a hand along the window ledge and absently rubbed her gritty fingertips against her thumb. She didn't think anyone had "straightened" the place in a good long time.

She followed Charlie through a low door and blinked. The tiny room was flooded with sunshine from a window that seemed to take up nearly half of one wall.

"Good gracious! It's so bright in here."

Charlie nodded as he set her bundle on the bed. "This time a day it's a mite overpowerin', but it ain't so bad later on. You can always close the shutters if you want."

For the first time, Kate noticed the wooden

structures on either side of the window. Split across the middle like a Dutch door, they were unlike any shutters Kate had ever seen. Before she had time to wonder about them, however, Charlie was turning to leave.

"Bein' as how it's your first day and all, Jon said not to worry 'bout a noon meal today, and the garden can wait till tomorrow. We'll be in for supper long about dark." He paused just inside the door. "Almost forgot. If you want to make a list of supplies you'll be needin', Jon said he'd give it a look-see when he comes in tonight."

"Did Mr. Cantrell leave any other messages for me?" Kate asked with a tinge of sarcasm. If Jonathan had so darn much to say to her, why hadn't he been here when she arrived?

"Nope. Just make yourself at home." He tipped his hat and was gone.

Kate looked around the brightly lit room. Unlike the rest of the house, it was uncluttered. Of course it was so small the bed and washstand nearly filled it. There was a strangely familiar odor in the air—turpentine? How odd. This overgrown closet must have had some other use before today, though what it could have been eluded her.

After walking back into the kitchen Kate stood uncertainly in the doorway. It was hard to know where to start, with everything in such a shambles. A quick inspection behind doors in the east wall revealed two bedrooms. The first obviously belonged to the boys, as it was filled with a con-fused collection of dirty clothes, pieces of rope, and odd bits of indistinguishable paraphernalia. There was even a bird nest among the clutter on the dresser.

Then she moved on to the other bedroom, which she found herself reluctant to enter after a cursory glance inside. The sight of Jonathan's rumpled bed gave her a curious feeling of intruding, almost like taking an intimate peek at a stranger. She decided Mr. Cantrell would probably want to keep his own room in order and closed the door with a sense of relief.

Back in the kitchen she rolled up her sleeves and began stacking dishes. It was going to take a while, but if she worked fast, she would have the worst of the chaos straightened out by the time Jonathan Cantrell returned home.

Kate had just built a fire in the stove and was putting water on to boil when Levi and Bernie appeared at the door. "Pa said we're supposed to stick around and help you today," Levi said.

Kate looked at her two charges and swallowed a sigh. Even disregarding the blood and dirt from their fight, it didn't look as if either one had touched water in a week. Teaching these two civilized behavior might turn out to be the biggest challenge of her life. "I'd be glad of your help just as soon as you wash up."

Twin expressions of shocked dismay crossed their faces. "Ain't no woman gonna tell me to wash," Bernie muttered.

Kate turned back to her work with a shrug. "Suit yourself, but no man sits down at my table with a dirty face or hands." She resisted the urge to cross her fingers as she heard their mutters behind her. The next few minutes would establish her either as a figure of authority or as a silly woman to be ignored.

"She can't starve us . . . can she?" Bernie asked his brother. "Pa would never let her, would he?"

"I'm not so sure. Pa said we had to do what she told us to, or we'd have to deal with him. You know what that means."

"Yeah, he'll give us a good talking to. I'd rather have a whipping."

"Me too."

"You think she's a good cook?"

"I dunno, but she's got to be better than Pa."

There was a moment of silence, then Levi sighed. "Well, heck, washing your hands and face ain't so big a deal, I guess."

"All right," Bernie said, moving to the door. "But last one to the well is a cross-eyed range cow!"

Bernie ran out, but Levi lingered in the kitchen for a moment and touched her arm. She looked down into his serious blue-gray eyes.

"Bernie ain't . . . that is, he hasn't been around women much and doesn't know how to act. He's not bad or nothin', he just doesn't know any better."

Levi's expression was so anxious that Kate couldn't help but smile. "I'll keep that in mind. We'll all have some adjusting to do, I expect." She picked up the empty water bucket and handed it to him. "Since you're headed that way, could you please fill this for me?"

Levi left with the water bucket and a relieved smile on his face.

Kate was still congratulating herself on how

well she'd handled her first opposition from the gruesome twosome, when they came back. "Gracious sakes!" she said incredulously, admiring their shining faces and slicked-back hair and ignoring the occasional rivulet of dirty water that trickled past an ear or down a neck. "I had no idea you two were so grown-up. When I first saw you I thought I had two little boys to take care of, but I can see now I was dead wrong. You're practically young men."

Bernie's chest expanded visibly. "I'm eleven, Levi's twelve."

"Almost thirteen."

Kate raised her eyebrows. "You look older."

Levi nodded. "We're both tall for our age. Pa says it's 'cause our Grandpa Colburn was nearly a giant."

"He must have been." Grandpa Colburn aside, she could see that they resembled Jonathan Cantrell a great deal. Both were already showing the beginnings of their father's broad-shouldered, muscular build and his square-jawed profile, though each had his own features.

The sapphire blue of Bernie's eyes was more startling than the softer blue-gray of his brother's, but Levi's twinkled in a most appealing way. While Levi had inherited his father's chestnut-colored hair, Bernie's black locks had the wave.

"Here's your water." Levi carried the bucket over to its place by the stove. "Now what do you want us to do?"

"How about taking these bridles and things outside?"

"You mean the tack?" Bernie was clearly horrified by the idea. "What if it rains?"

"I hadn't thought of that." Kate looked at the saddle pensively. "There must be some place else we can put them where they'll be safe. Didn't I see a shed when we rode up?"

There was a pause. "You mean that little shed out back?" Levi asked.

"Yes. That's the one."

He exchanged glances with Bernie. "I'm not sure Pa would like us to put his saddle in there."

"Why? Is it full?"

"No . . . I'd say it's a long way from full. Wouldn't you, Bernie?"

"Oh, yeah," Bernie said quickly, his eyes dancing. "Pa was just talking about how glad he was he'd built it so big. It doesn't fill up near as fast."

Kate smiled brightly. "Good, then I don't see any reason we can't store the saddles and bridles in there until the roof is on the barn."

"You'll tell Pa it was your idea?" Bernie asked.

"If he asks, certainly."

Kate was unable to shake the feeling that they were playing some joke at her expense as she turned back to her dishes. Her suspicions dissipated, though, as the morning passed and nothing happened. In record time the boys dispensed with the tack, and they continued to work without complaint no matter what she gave them to do.

Kate swept up the loose dirt on the floor and prepared to scrub off the rest. "Would you two mind moving the table for me?" she asked, carrying her bucket of water to the far side of the room and kneeling on the rough plank floor.

"Sure." Bernie smiled brightly. "Where do you want it?"

"Over by the door for now, I think." Kate's eyes narrowed as both boys jumped to do her bidding. There was definitely something afoot.

As Kate worked her way toward the door, she began to imagine what Jonathan Cantrell would say when he came home. As more and more dirt disappeared, her confidence grew. Surely he would be pleased with the changes she had wrought already.

She only hoped that his spectacular good looks wouldn't be so intimidating in the bright light of day and she wouldn't be so tongue-tied around him. Of course he couldn't be as handsome as she remembered. It would be a relief to have reality replace the incredible picture she had of him in her mind.

Kate had scrubbed her way nearly to the door when a small, furry shape dashed through the opening and ran between her hands. With a scream, she scrambled to her feet and watched the prairie dog skid across the wet floor.

"Catch him!" yelled Levi, diving after it.

Bernie jumped up and ran toward his brother even as Levi's hands closed over the frightened creature. "Look out, you're gonna get bit."

"Ouch!" With a yelp Levi let go, and his captive darted under the hoosier. "Damn," he mumbled, sucking on his injured finger.

"I think it's one of yours," Bernie called out. Intent on cutting off the prairie dog's escape, he paid no attention to the slick, wet floor. With a cry of surprise, he slipped and landed in a heap against the hoosier. The dishpan teetered precariously for a moment or two and then crashed to the floor, showering Bernie with dirty dishwater.

Terrified, the prairie dog headed in the opposite direction, with Levi hot on his heels. Determined to catch it, Levi grabbed a dish towel to protect his hands. As he dashed by the woodbox, his foot caught the edge, tipping it over and sending him sprawling. Kindling and pieces of firewood scattered all over the room, sprinkling a layer of sawdust onto the damp floor.

Still moving as fast as its little legs could carry it, the prairie dog scurried toward the door, right under the edge of Kate's skirt and across her feet. For one brief heart-stopping moment she pictured the creature becoming tangled in her petticoats and climbing up her leg. With a shriek she jumped back and tripped over the mop bucket that was directly behind her. As she tried to catch her balance she hit the flour bin she had set on the table for safekeeping. In what seemed like slow motion, she felt herself falling and saw the flour bin toppling over. A large white cloud billowed toward the door and right into the astonished face of Jonathan Cantrell.

"What the hell?" he roared.

As she landed on the floor, Kate closed her eyes in horrified embarrassment. Sitting there in a welter of soaked skirts and petticoats, she wished she could sink right through the floor.

There was a long moment of silence, then

Jonathan cleared his throat. "Would someone mind telling what's going on here?"

Both boys began talking at once.

"It was a prairie dog, Pa . . ."

"It was one of Levi's . . ."

"He bit me so I let him go . . ."

"The floor was slick . . ."

"I tripped over the woodbox . . ."

"The dishpan spilled . . ."

"Mrs. Murphy screamed. . . ."

"He got away . . ."

"Do you mean to tell me this entire debacle was caused by one of those misbegotten rodents of yours?" Jonathan's voice was low and ominous.

Kate's eyes popped open in surprise. Curses she might have expected, but certainly not a string of words more suited to an orator than a rancher.

"Uh-oh, he's really mad," one of the boys whispered. "Listen to all those big words he's using."

Kate stared up at Jonathan in trepidation, but he was glowering over her head at his sons.

"I beg your pardon?" Jonathan said in a voice as cold as steel.

"We didn't do it on purpose, Pa. He just came in."

"We tried to catch him, honest we did."

"Yes, I can see that." Brushing flour off the front of his shirt, Jonathan suddenly transferred his gaze to Kate, who was still sitting in a puddle of mop water on the floor. "I hope you're not seriously injured."

"No," Kate began, "I—"

"Good, because I don't have a lot of time to

waste right now." He ignored Kate's indignant gasp and glared at his sons again. "The reason I came up here in the first place was to find out why the extra saddle and all the tack is in the outhouse."

"What?" Kate gave the boys a startled look. That big shed was the outhouse? Her eyes narrowed with sudden understanding. No wonder they'd been so compliant. It was so predictable, she felt stupid for not having figured it out sooner.

"We put it where she told us to."

"But I . . ."

Before Kate could decide how to handle the situation, Jonathan grasped her hand and pulled her to her feet. A small part of her mind registered the fact that she hadn't exaggerated Jonathan Cantrell's attractiveness. Even angry, he was breathtaking.

"You told them to put my saddle in the privy?"

"Well, I . . ."

He released her hand. "I hired you to make our lives more comfortable, not turn my house inside out."

"I didn't mean—"

"Last night you managed to convince me you had a good head on your shoulders." He looked around at the chaotic mess. "I must have been crazy. What kind of fool sticks a saddle in the outhouse, for God's sake?"

Jonathan's words rubbed salt in the wound to Kate's dignity. Anger boiled up inside her like hot water in a geyser. "At least the horse smell won't bother anyone there," she snapped. "As for turning your house inside out, I doubt if a tornado could do that! I've never seen such a pigsty."

Her temper thoroughly roused, Kate advanced on her startled employer, fists firmly planted on her hips. "How dare you come in here and accuse me of being a fool? Maybe the outhouse isn't the best place for your saddle, but neither is the kitchen. From what I saw of it, you should be able to put your tack somewhere in that barn you're building fairly soon. In the meantime, your precious saddle will be safe enough in the privy."

With that, she turned and stomped across the kitchen. The sight of Bernie and Levi still sitting on the floor reminded her of the scene Jonathan had walked into. She whirled around and faced him again. "And that's another thing. Your sons had nothing to do with that prairie dog coming in here. I'm the one who left the door open. The boys were only trying to catch it." Leaving behind a stunned audience, Kate stalked into her bedroom and slammed the door.

Flopping down on her bed, Kate glared out the window for several seconds before she realized what she'd done. In a moment of uncontrolled anger she'd thrown away the only respectable job she could hope to get. She could almost hear Bryan chiding her for losing that fiery temper of hers. With a sinking feeling, she knew she'd left herself no choice: she'd have to return to the Golden Spur. Jonathan Cantrell was right . . . she was a fool.

Kate was still sitting there motionless when someone knocked on the door. "Who is it?" she asked, knowing full well it was Jonathan Cantrell coming to tell her she was fired. She could still see the incredulous expression on his face as she'd told him off. It was quite obvious that the man was not used to being crossed.

"It's us, Levi and Bernie." The small voice was almost inaudible.

Kate stared at the door in surprise. "Come in."

The door opened slowly, and the boys stood hesitantly on the threshold. "Pa said to tell you the tack can stay in the outhouse for now, but he wants you to ask him before you move anything else outside."

"Is that all he said?" Kate couldn't quite believe she still had a job after her outburst.

There was a moment of uncomfortable silence. "No." Levi looked miserable. "He said we'd have to figure out how to hang the saddle on the wall in the outhouse."

"And if our prairie dogs cause any more trouble, we're going to have to get rid of them like he told us to in the first place," Bernie added.

"Why do you keep saying *your* prairie dogs?"

Levi and Bernie glanced at each other. "Well, when we first got here they were all over the place, and Pa set us to trapping them," Levi said.

Bernie nodded. "Their holes are dangerous for the horses, you know."

"We caught ten right away," Levi went on, ignoring his brother's interruption. "Then we decided to see who could catch the most. Trouble was, the cage wouldn't hold very many, so after a while we had to let some of them go. Of course, then when we caught one we couldn't tell if we'd had it before."

"That's when we started to brand them."

Kate's eyes widened. "You branded prairie dogs?"

"Yup," Levi said. "We made little branding irons from some of Pa's nails. Charlie thought we were pretty smart. He said we had the makin's of good cowhands."

"I think Pa was impressed, too, even if he did act mad. He let us keep the ones we had already branded." Bernie sighed. "Charlie got rid of most of the rest, though, so they're lots harder to catch now."

"You mean you're still branding them? Oh, never mind, I don't want to know." She stood up and shook out her damp skirts. "You two best go take care of your pa's saddle, while I finish up the kitchen." As she watched them scurry out the door, she realized they really were going to be a handful.

But she couldn't help thinking that their father might prove to be even more of a challenge. Jonathan might have the face of an angel, but he had the devil's own temper. It was interesting that the boys had seemed more concerned about a lecture from him than a beating. And he'd let them keep their prairie dogs, after all.

Doing up the buttons on a clean dress, Kate glanced at the window. Whatever else the man was, Jonathan Cantrell was original. Even his home reflected it. Both the palatial outhouse and the overabundance of hard-to-come-by windows were surprises out here in the wilderness.

Though he'd apparently forgiven her spurt of

temper, Jonathan's impression of her couldn't be very good. On her first day she'd already shown him that she had the housekeeping skills of a cyclone and the personality of a shrew.

5

"Is supper ready?"

Setting the last plate on the table, Kate looked up and smiled at Levi's eager expression. "It'll be on the table by the time you get washed up."

"Again?" Bernie said.

"I'm hungry." Levi disappeared back out the door. "Hurry up, Bernie. It's time to eat."

It sounded as if a good-natured argument ensued between the two outside the door, but Kate paid little attention until she heard Charlie and Jonathan join them.

"Well, well, I see you two finally figured out what the washbowl is for," she heard Jonathan say.

"Mrs. Murphy said we have to."

"Good for her. Now get a move on. Charlie and I want to wash up, too."

Kate's hands shook slightly as she cut thick slices of cornbread. Jonathan might still decide to send her packing, especially when he saw what she'd fixed for supper. With the flour nearly gone, she'd been hard-pressed to find anything at all. A pot of beans and a pan of cornbread were the best she could do with the ingredients she had to work with.

"You better wash your neck, Pa," Bernie said. "Mrs. Murphy said she wouldn't let you eat unless you did."

The splashing noises stopped abruptly. "What?" Jonathan's deep voice sounded threatening. He obviously thought she'd mentioned him specifically.

"She said no man would sit down at her table with a dirty face and hands," Levi pointed out, "but she didn't say anything about necks."

"Ah." There was another moment of silence, then the sounds of washing resumed. "Well, since I don't want to be turned away from my supper, I don't think I'll take any chances."

Struggling against the desire to run and hide in her bedroom, Kate set the cornbread on the table and turned back to dish up the beans. The menfolk trooped in and were seated by the time she was finished. Making every effort to smile, she set the bowl of beans on the table and took her place next to Bernie.

"Good evening, gentlemen," she said.

Charlie and the boys returned her greeting, but Kate saw only Jonathan's enigmatic stare.

After a long moment he raised a eyebrow and said, "Well?"

"P-pardon?"

Jonathan tilted his head, exposing his neck for her inspection. "Is it clean enough?"

Color crept up her cheeks, but she raised her

chin defiantly. "It's fine for tonight. I'm sure you'll do better next time."

To Kate's surprise, Jonathan answered with a deep chuckle. "Touché, Mrs. Murphy." At her look of bewilderment, he smiled. "It's a fencing term that means you won this round."

"I wasn't aware we were having a contest." As she picked up a large pitcher Kate pretended a serenity she didn't feel. "Would you rather have milk or coffee?"

The meal passed without further disturbance. In fact, everyone was so busy eating, Kate's fears about the plain supper seemed ludicrous. They acted as though she had served them a sumptuous feast. After they'd gobbled up all the beans, they poured milk and molasses over the leftover cornbread and polished it off as dessert. Kate watched them in amazement. Bryan had always appreciated her cooking, but never like this.

At last Charlie pushed back his chair with a contented sigh. "Mighty fine vittles, Mrs. Murphy." He patted his stomach. "I reckon she'll do, Jon."

Jonathan took a sip of his coffee and looked at Kate over the rim of his cup. "If she learned to control that temper and bite her tongue, she'd be just about perfect." The twinkle in his eye belied the harshness of his words. "Somehow I don't think that's likely to happen any time soon, so I guess we'll just have to be content with her good cooking."

"If that was meant as a compliment, thank you . . . I think." She gave Jonathan a direct look. "And I'll have you know I never lose my temper without cause."

"Reckon we'd best get used to it, then," Charlie said as he stood up and stretched. "If Jon don't git you goin', the boys will." He plucked his hat from a peg by the door. "'Course, I don't know but what you can handle all three of 'em. Might be you got more'n you bargained for, Jon," he said on his way out the door.

Jonathan just grinned and took another swallow of coffee. Actually, he was fairly pleased with his new housekeeper. Feeling content after his first hot meal in weeks, he relaxed in the well-scrubbed comfort of his home. Thanks to Kate Murphy, the house looked better than it ever had. Even the boys seemed to be responding to her, though he suspected some of it was due to the gratitude they owed her for not revealing who had really been responsible for stowing his saddle in the outhouse. He figured they must have had something to do with it.

Idly watching the respectable Mrs. Murphy move about the kitchen, Jonathan found it difficult to see the voluptuous saloon girl he'd met the night before. Only her sensuous walk remained, and he was certain she wasn't aware of that. Perhaps it was just as well.

He set down his cup and turned his attention to his sons. "We've got about an hour or so before bedtime. Might as well spend it on your lessons."

"Oh, Pa. Can't we skip it tonight? It's Mrs. Murphy's first day here."

"I'm sure she won't mind."

Pouring hot water into the dishpan, Kate couldn't help smiling at Levi's predictable reaction.

She was pleased to find Jonathan Cantrell was not allowing his sons to grow up uneducated just because they lived on the frontier. Bryan had valued book learning, too, and had taught himself to read and write. He used to always tell Kate that the educated men of the world would prevail.

Expecting reading or arithmetic to be the subject of the evening's instruction, Kate nearly dropped the plate she was washing when she heard what came next.

Bernie groaned. "Why do we always have to start with Latin, Pa? Nobody talks it."

"Speaks it," Jonathan corrected him, "and I've told you over and over, it's the language of science. Besides, it gets your mind working so you can learn other things."

"But we're going to be ranchers, not scientists," protested Levi.

Jonathan unfolded a pair of spectacles and put them on with a nonchalance that suggested he'd had this conversation before. "You might decide to do something else."

"You're a rancher."

"Yes, but I had a choice. You do want to leave yourself with other options, don't you?"

"We could always break horses to sell to the army," Bernie said.

"You'd make more money training them to sell back east." Jonathan opened a book and ran his finger down the page. "Wealthy men are always in the market for a good horse, but they only respect someone who appears to know as much or more than they do."

From Levi's and Bernie's sighs, it was obvious that their father had won. They went to work without further complaint. By the time Kate had put away the last of the dishes and dried her hands, Bernie and Levi had moved on to mathematics, though it was totally unlike the arithmetic she was familiar with.

Looking up from his books, Jonathan put down his pen and sat back in his chair. "If you have a moment, Mrs. Murphy, I'll take a look at that list I asked you to make."

"Goodness," she said, reaching into her pocket. "I nearly forgot."

Adjusting his glasses, Jonathan ran his eyes down the list. "Stove black? What do we need that for?"

"I think it's fairly obvious." Kate pointed to the rust along the top of the kitchen range. "That cookstove is in shameful condition."

Peering over his spectacles, Jonathan gazed at the rust as though he'd never seen it before. He rubbed his mustache as he returned to the list.

"Buttons, thread, and fabric? Are you planning on making yourself a new wardrobe?"

Kate was indignant. "The buttons and thread are for mending your clothes. I was going to make curtains for the windows with the material, but they really aren't necessary until winter."

Jonathan stared at her for a long moment and then removed his spectacles. "All right. As long as they don't look like something out of a lady's boudoir. When you go to town tomorrow you can get everything on the list. Just tell Mrs. Cline to put it on my bill."

"Me?" Kate was horrified. "I thought you'd go."

"I don't have time."

"But how will I get there?"

"Take the wagon," he said. "You do know how to drive a team, don't you?"

"Well . . . not exactly."

"It seems to me you either know or you don't. Which is it?"

"I drove our oxen part of the time, but I don't think it's quite the same thing."

Jonathan sighed. "No, it's not the same. I suppose one of the boys will have to go with you, then."

"I will," Levi and Bernie both said at once.

"I said it first."

"No, I did."

"I'm the oldest."

"So what? I can beat you any day of the week."

"Can not."

"Can too."

"Let's settle this without bloodshed." Kate retrieved the broom from the corner and pulled a straw from it. Breaking the broom straw into two uneven pieces, she arranged them in her hand. "Now then," she said, holding her hand out to the two boys, "whoever picks the long straw gets to drive me to town."

Silently they made their choices and compared straws. Bernie crowed with delight when his turned out to be the longest.

"Fine." Jonathan collected the books and rose

from the table. "Bernie can drive Mrs. Murphy to town while Levi helps me haul logs for the barn."

Levi grimaced. "Oh, Pa."

"I'm sorry, son. Somebody's got to do it." Jonathan stretched and gave a big yawn. "Time for bed."

Levi was still wearing a disgruntled look when Bernie and Kate left for town the next morning. On the other hand, Bernie's grin seemed to stretch clear across his face.

"You're certainly in a good mood this morning," Kate said.

"Sure am."

"I'll bet it has a lot to do with you going to town and Levi staying home."

"Yup." Bernie grinned mischievously. "And he's madder'n a badger in a pig wallow."

"You don't very often get the upper hand, do you? It must be hard when you're almost the same age."

"It's because of my name. That's why they treat me like a baby."

Kate was startled. "Why do you say that?"

"Pa's grandfather was Levi, so everybody thinks of it as a man's name. Did you ever know a grown-up named Bernie?"

"Well, no. I don't guess I ever have."

"That's because there aren't any. When I'm a man everybody will laugh at me because I have a little boy's name."

"So why don't you change it?"

"What?"

"Change your name. That's what I did. My name is Katharine, you see, but my whole family called me Katie. When I turned fourteen I decided Katie was just too childish for someone my age. So I announced I wouldn't answer to Katie anymore. If they wanted to talk to me, they had to call me Katharine. It didn't take long for people to realize I was serious."

"And nobody ever called you Katie again?"

The memory of Bryan's lilting Irish voice saying, "You'll always be my beautiful Katie," brought a lump to her throat. She closed her eyes against sudden tears. "Not unless I wanted them to."

Oblivious of her pain, Bernie sighed. "I wouldn't want anybody to call me Bernie. I don't think Pa will let me change it, though."

"Why not?" Kate pushed away her memories and tried to concentrate on Bernie.

"'Cause it's my ma's family name."

"I see. What's your full name, then? Bernard?"

"No, it's worse. Colburn."

"Hmm. How about Cole?"

"Cole?"

"It's not a common name, but it does sound very grown-up. In fact, I think Cole Cantrell has a rather nice ring to it."

Bernie's eyes narrowed as he thought about it. Finally he nodded. "So do I. From now on that's my name, Cole Cantrell."

Kate smiled, and the rest of the trip to town passed pleasantly. When they pulled up in front of the store, Kate climbed out and looked up at her companion. "Aren't you coming in, Ber . . . er, Cole?"

"Nope. Old Lady Cline can't stand me."

"Why not?" She ignored the derogatory nickname for the moment.

"Beats me."

"Never mind. Just wait for me here." Wondering what the little rapscallion had done, Kate couldn't help grinning as she walked into the store.

"Good morning." She greeted Mrs. Cline with composure, hoping the woman wouldn't remember her from the one and only time they had met. "Here's a list of the things I need." She handed the paper to the storekeeper and looked around for the sewing goods. "I'll just pick out my notions while I'm waiting."

Mrs. Cline gave a disapproving sniff, then turned to fill the order. Kate spent a quarter of an hour browsing. Since Horse Creek was so far from civilization, there wasn't a great deal of selection, but it had been a long time since Kate had been in any kind of a store.

"Will there be anything else?"

At the sound of Mrs. Cline's cold voice, Kate set down a pretty china cup she'd been admiring and walked to the front of the store. "Why, yes." She placed her buttons and thread on the counter and pointed to the bolts of fabric stacked against the far wall. "I'd like five yards of that light yellow calico and a length of white muslin."

"Not until I see the color of your money."

"I beg your pardon?"

Mrs. Cline crossed her arms and glared at Kate.

"You already have over ten dollars' worth of merchandise here. I'm not cutting any material until I'm sure you can pay for it."

Kate drew herself up indignantly. "You may put this on Jonathan Cantrell's bill, except for the white muslin, which I'll pay for myself."

"I'll do no such thing! As if Mr. Cantrell would let a harlot from the saloon put things on his account."

Kate blushed. "I don't work at the saloon anymore. Mr. Cantrell hired me as his housekeeper yesterday."

"A likely story. Mr. Cantrell never said a word to me about you being able to charge."

Kate suddenly realized that she didn't have any actual proof that she did indeed work for Jonathan Cantrell. But she could just imagine what he'd say if she came home without the supplies. After yesterday's disaster he'd think she was the most incompetent woman in the world.

"Very well, then." She pulled out her precious twenty-dollar gold piece and slapped it on the counter. "There's the money. Now please cut my material."

Though Kate experienced a certain amount of satisfaction at being able to put Mrs. Cline in her place, her stomach knotted in trepidation as the other woman took the money. Kate had only brought it along in order to buy some muslin for aprons. Surely Jonathan would pay her back, wouldn't he? She wondered what he was going to say when she presented him with a bill for thirteen dollars.

At the other end of the counter, Mrs. Cline

pulled down the two bolts of material. Measuring out the cloth, she muttered just loudly enough for Kate to hear, "Someone else might be misguided to give a person like her a job, but never Jonathan. A handsome man like that wouldn't want someone as plain as dirt and as dull as ditchwater in his house."

Kate stiffened. The old biddy was badly in need of a set-down. There must be some way to prove she worked for Jonathan. . . . Then an idea struck her. With a wicked gleam in her eye, she said, "Pardon me, Mrs. Cline. I hate to interrupt, but would you mind if I get my driver, Cole, to help carry out the supplies?"

"Suit yourself."

Kate opened the door and called loudly enough for Abigail Cline to hear as well, "Cole, tie up the horses. I need your help carrying out supplies."

"But Mrs. Cline . . ."

"Mrs. Cline said it was all right."

Cole was skeptical. "Are you sure?"

"Certainly. I asked her specifically if you could come in and help me."

When Abigail Cline saw whom Kate had brought into the store, her face turned quite purple. Since she uttered not a single word, Kate never knew if the near apoplexy was caused by Cole himself or by the obvious proof that Kate worked for the Cantrells.

Once Cole had the wagon loaded he went to wait outside, where Mrs. Cline's angry glare couldn't reach him. Kate smiled as she gathered up the last of her purchases. "I'll tell Jonathan to stop by next time he's in town to straighten this out. With any kind of luck he'll find it all quite humorous." Despite her smile, Kate's tone was far from encouraging.

For once Abigail Cline was speechless.

6

"*A bath?*"

"That is what a bathtub is for, isn't it?" Kate asked, ignoring Levi's horrified tone. "I thought we'd start as soon as supper's over. Would you like to be first?"

Levi shook his head vehemently. "It's Bernie's turn."

"Nobody around here named Bernie," his brother said. "Don't guess he'd mind if you took his place, though."

"Just 'cause you changed your name doesn't mean—"

"What are you two arguing about now?" Jonathan asked. His low chuckle produced a ripple of alarm in Kate's stomach.

Drat the man, anyway. That handsome face of his was hard enough to get used to without his incredibly bad timing. Couldn't he, just once, come into the house when she had things under control? "We were just discussing who gets the first bath. I guess we'd better draw straws."

"Levi's older."

"It's Bernie's turn."

"And I already told you, there's nobody here named Bernie."

"Pa . . ."

Jonathan held up his hand. "I think Mrs. Murphy had the right idea. We'll get a couple of straws and—"

"Better get three," Kate said, bending over to take a loaf of bread out of the oven. "You haven't had a bath in the two weeks I've been here, either."

There was a moment of stunned silence, broken only by Charlie's laughter. "Reckon she's got ya there, Jon."

"Would you care to join them, Mr. Hobbs?" Kate looked up from the pan and smiled sweetly.

Charlie took an involuntary step backward, his grin disappearing. "No, ma'am."

"You do bathe, don't you?"

"Sure . . . but . . . ah . . ." Turning his hat in his hands, Charlie glanced toward the curtain Kate had rigged across one corner of the kitchen. "Well . . . I just ain't real comfortable takin' off my clothes with a woman around."

Jonathan gave a snort of laughter. "That must be pretty awkward at times."

Inadvertently Charlie's and Kate's eyes met in an embarrassed glance. Equally discomfited by Jonathan's off-color innuendo, they pretended not to notice the blush staining each other's cheeks.

"Land sakes." Kate turned back to the stove in

an attempt to change the subject. "I nearly forgot the stew."

Though a twinkle still lurked in the sapphire depths of his eyes, Jonathan behaved remarkably well until it came time to draw straws after supper. With a flourish he pulled two straws from the broom and pointedly broke them into four uneven pieces. "Short straw goes first, longest last."

Cole watched with interest. "Who's the extra straw for, Pa?"

Jonathan's telltale dimples appeared as he arranged the straws in his hand. "We can't forget Mrs. Murphy, can we?" He caught her eye and grinned. "Ladies first."

Trapped in her own clever scheme, and uncomfortably aware of the boys' scrutiny, Kate had no choice. She stepped forward and took a straw, trying to ignore the near smirk on Jonathan's face. He certainly had a bad habit of getting even. After Cole and Levi had drawn their straws, Jonathan held his up. "Who's the lucky winner?"

Levi looked at the straws and groaned. "How come I only win when I don't want to?"

"Guess we'd better get started, then," Kate said briskly. Secretly relieved that she'd be the last to bathe, she filled the tub with the first three buckets of water. Now she knew exactly how Charlie felt. The thought of undressing with Jonathan Cantrell on the other side of the curtain was unnerving. She sent Cole out after more water and handed Levi a small bar of soap. "Go easy on this. It's all we have until I have time to make some more."

Jonathan looked surprised. "Didn't you get some when you were at the store?"

"Store-bought soap is far too expensive," Kate told him. Other than a raised eyebrow and one of those darn dimples peeping out at her, she hadn't gotten much of a reaction from him when she'd explained why she'd had to spend her own money on supplies. He'd paid her back right away, and the incident had not been mentioned in the week and a half since. She'd been hoping that he leave it that way.

Jonathan shook his head. "No, I didn't mean that kind of soap. Abigail says she always makes more than she can use, so she puts a bar or two in my order."

"She probably would have if you'd done your own shopping," Kate said. "Mrs. Cline was too busy trying to put me in my place to think of anything else."

Leaning back in his chair, Jonathan put his hands behind his head. "You must have done something to get her back up. Abigail Cline is one of the most amiable woman alive."

"Most amiable . . . are you out of your mind? She's a miserable old witch!"

"I'm surprised at you," he said. "I never thought you'd be so unkind to someone less fortunate than yourself."

"Less fortunate . . ." Kate had a momentary vision of Bryan's grave next to her burning wagon and nearly choked on the unfairness of Jonathan's statement.

"I don't know, Pa." Cole came to Kate's defense,

surprising himself almost as much as he did her. "Mrs. Cline doesn't seem real friendly to me. She won't even let Levi and me in her store."

"Can't say that I blame her after what you two did with that skunk." Charlie chuckled.

"Abigail Cline," Jonathan continued as though no one else had spoken, "doesn't have your ability to take what life gives and make the best of it, Kate. If she'd been left alone like you were, she'd have never had the courage to survive, and she certainly couldn't have performed the miracle you have with this house."

At the warmth in Jonathan's gaze as much as his startling words, Kate was speechless, even breathless. She watched the familiar twinkle suddenly appear in the sapphire depths. "Of course, Abigail isn't one to lose her temper, either," he added.

"Personally, I don't think the Widda Cline shows you the same old prune face the rest of us see, Jon," Charlie said. "She's got her eye on you sure as shootin'. With a sweet woman like that, I reckon it'd be real easy to find yerself in a parson's mousetrap."

Jonathan regarded his partner through narrowed eyes. "I'll bet we could squeeze another bath in tonight if we tried."

Grinning, Charlie unfolded his long legs and rose to his feet. "Appreciate the offer, Jon, but it's time I headed home."

"Funny, I was just thinking the same thing," Jonathan said.

With a chuckle, Charlie retrieved his hat and was gone.

Much to Kate's relief, Jonathan seemed content to sit at the table and work on his ledgers while she washed the supper dishes. She'd had enough of his biting wit for one evening, though the memory of his unexpected compliment lay soft and warm in the back of her mind. Not only was it the first time he'd ever said a word about all the work she'd done, he'd called her Kate. Smiling to herself, she admitted she liked the way it sounded.

By the time Cole and Levi had finished their baths and dumped the water, Kate was working on the large pile of mending. Not for the first time she marveled at how many missing buttons, frayed cuffs, and tears the three Cantrells could generate. She glanced up as Jonathan rose from the table and stretched.

"Looks like you survived the ordeal," he said, ruffling Cole's damp hair. "Just in time for bed, too."

"Oh, Pa. It's hardly dark outside."

Jonathan looked out the window. "By gosh, you're right. There's probably even time to read some Latin."

Levi jumped up and gave an exaggerated yawn. "I'm real tired. Guess I'll go to bed."

Cole looked longingly toward the window, then shrugged and followed his brother into their bedroom. With a wink at Kate, Jonathan went in to say his usual good night. The ritual must have started when the boys were toddlers and their father tucked them in. Though he no longer kissed them good night, he spent at least ten minutes with them every night, discussing the events of the day.

By the time he was finished, Kate had filled the bath with fresh water for Jonathan. He closed the door behind him and grinned.

"It's amazing how fast the mention of Latin will send them off to bed." He took the towel she handed him and draped it over the back of a chair. "Thanks." Pulling out his shirttails, he said, "You look pretty tired yourself."

"I am, a little."

He paused in the act of unbuttoning his shirt and looked at the steaming tub. "Why don't you go first, then? I don't mind waiting."

Gazing at the dark curly hair exposed in the open V of his shirt Kate parted her lips unconsciously. "No," she murmured, "you go ahead. I'll take mine later." Mesmerized, she wasn't even aware that she was staring. She'd never seen hair on a man's chest before, as Bryan's had been completely bare. It was surprisingly attractive.

After a moment Jonathan's fingers continued their slow journey down his shirtfront. "We could always share it," he said softly.

Kate gave a shocked gasp.

He went on. "We might find it a bit small, but with a little ingenuity I think we could manage." The dark glow in his eyes held her spellbound as he dropped his shirt over the back of a chair. In the lamplight his muscles looked powerful beneath his golden skin, and the furring of masculine hair emphasized his broad chest and flat stomach.

"What do you say, Kate?" His voice was a husky, teasing caress as he reached for his belt. "Shall we scrub each other's backs?"

The words suddenly jolted her out of her stupor. "I . . . I . . ." Face flaming, Kate backed away. "Oh—"

She broke off with a horrified cry and ran to her room, slamming the door after her.

Jonathan stood still for several moments and then ran an unsteady hand through his hair. When he'd caught her staring at him, he couldn't resist the temptation to tease her a little. He knew perfectly well that she hadn't meant to entice him, nor had he intended for things to go quite so far. Though she was hardly the first woman to admire his body, those enormous eyes of hers had gotten to him somehow.

As he'd reached for his belt, an image of the tempting curves that lay beneath her demure dress had suddenly materialized in his head, and he'd been hit with a wave of desire so strong it left him weak.

Shedding his pants, Jonathan stepped into the tub and slid into the hot water. He felt like a fool for embarrassing her that way. Kate hadn't realized that he was teasing, nor, it seemed, had his body. Leaning back, he closed his eyes. Too bad the water wasn't cold.

Kate expected breakfast to be strained, but Jonathan once again surprised her. His nonchalance convinced her that he didn't share her embarrassment—at least until he was ready to leave. After sending the boys on ahead, he stopped at the door, hat in hand, and stared outside as though afraid to look at her.

"We'll be working on the barn all morning, so it might be a good time to take your bath," he said. Settling his hat on his head, he turned and met her eyes. "I'll make sure no one disturbs your privacy." With that he was gone, leaving Kate more confused than ever.

Pouring water into her dishpan to wash the breakfast dishes, Kate wondered which she'd imagined, his discomfort or his nonchalance. Both couldn't be real. Determined not to think about her employer anymore, she finished the dishes and prepared her bath.

The water steamed invitingly as she slipped out of her clothes and into the tub. Easing herself into the water, Kate sighed in pleasure. How Jonathan Cantrell had come by a hip bath out here on the frontier she had no idea, but she intended to fully enjoy the luxury.

With her body relaxed, Kate's mind relentlessly drifted back to Jonathan. The man was incomprehensible. One minute he was a charming rogue, far too attractive to ignore, and every inch the self-assured male. The next, those dimples would appear and he'd say or do something so much like one of his sons that he was impossible to take seriously. Oddly enough, those were the times Kate found him the most appealing. She much preferred the rogue, as he was far easier to resist.

Irritated by the thought, Kate turned her attention to washing her hair and taking the first unhurried bath she'd had in a long time. She stayed in the tub until the water grew too cool for comfort and her skin began to wrinkle. Then, wrapped in the robe Frenchie had given her, she sat in front of the window and began to brush her hair dry.

The knock at the door startled her. *Jonathan* . . . Her heart leapt to her throat, and then she shook her head. No, he'd promised her privacy. It was one of the boys, no doubt.

Tossing her hair back over her shoulder, she adjusted the belt on her robe, walked to the door, and threw it open.

"I thought your fa—" The rest of her speech died in her throat as she gazed up at the startled face of a total stranger. For several seconds they simply stared at each other.

In spite of the heat, he was dressed in a suit of superfine, complete with matching coat and vest. Tall, slender, and handsome, he was the epitome of a wealthy gentleman. Looking at him, Kate was sickly aware of her own dishabille and of the damp hair curling around her face.

"Pardon me," he said, removing his low-crowned hat. The soft southern drawl was like warm honey in the late summer. "I was looking for Jonathan."

"He . . . he's working on the barn," Kate said, staring at the thick silver hair his hat had hidden. Though the color seemed to indicate he was past middle age, his face looked much younger.

"I'll go find him, then." The skin around his eyes crinkled at the corners when he smiled. "Thank you, Miss . . ."

"It's Mrs. . . . Mrs. Murphy."

"And I'm Clayton Langton, Clay to my friends."

"How do you do, Mr. Langton."

"Delighted, Mrs. Murphy. I assume I'll have the pleasure of making your husband's acquaintance this morning as well?"

"I'm a widow."

"Oh. I'm terribly sorry to hear that."

Kate nodded slightly in acknowledgment.

He put his hat back on and smiled before he turned away. "It was nice meeting you."

Kate nodded again, then watched as he mounted his horse and turned toward the barn with another horse in tow. Somehow she wasn't surprised to find he rode a beautiful white stallion.

"Jonathan?" Clay Langton called, looking up at the half-finished barn. A dark head soon appeared in the doorway.

"It's Mr. Langton, Pa," Levi called over his shoulder.

A few moments later Jonathan himself came outside with a smile on his face. "Morning, Clay."

"Good morning, Jonathan. I brought your mare back."

Jonathan stepped over and took the lead rope. "Thanks. Do you think she took?"

Clay laughed and patted his horse on the neck. "If you don't get yourself a fine foal, it certainly won't be because Gallahad didn't try."

"Good." Jonathan grinned. "Let's hope it's a good strong filly."

Clay nodded, then glanced toward the house. "Speaking of fillies, who's that bewitching creature you have hidden away in your cabin?"

"You mean Kate? She's our housekeeper."

"Ah, I see. Do you have any claims there?"

"She's only been with us for a couple of weeks."

"Good, then you won't mind if I pursue our acquaintance?"

"Why should I?" But deep down inside, Jonathan was surprised to find he did. He minded a great deal.

7

Was it possible?

Kate excitedly counted the days again. She hadn't had her monthly flow since the first of May, nearly three and a half months ago! With all that had happened, she hadn't even thought about it until this morning when she had woken up sick to her stomach for the third day in a row. She tried to stay calm as she cataloged her symptoms: tender breasts, upset stomach in the early morning, occasional bouts of dizziness, and no monthly miseries. She was pregnant! It couldn't be anything else. Still sitting in bed, Kate hugged the joyous news to herself, almost afraid to believe it.

"I'm going to have Bryan's baby!" she whispered. She felt a stab of pain that the child would never know its father. Biting her lip, Kate closed her eyes and reminded herself that when this baby was born, part of Bryan would live on. She hadn't lost him completely. This incredible thought kept running through her head the whole time she dressed and then as she fried eggs for breakfast. Though the lively crew at the table distracted her, the warm glow stayed with her just below the surface. The hard knot of grief she carried around didn't seem quite so painful now.

It was that same feeling of well-being and happiness that gave her the courage to face the one job she'd been putting off . . . cleaning Jonathan's room. She'd been waiting patiently for three weeks, and so far he hadn't touched a thing himself.

Pausing in the doorway, Kate looked around. Since the door was always kept closed, this was the first time she'd actually seen the whole room. The rumpled bed in the middle was hardly noticeable in the chaotic mess. A tall wooden secretary stood against the wall next to the door. Kate was dumbfounded. A secretary? What next? Jonathan must have come west with a Conestoga wagon and a mule train. He certainly had brought along all the amenities.

The secretary's glass-doored bookcase was empty and the desk overflowing with papers. She shook her head in disgust. Here was a perfectly good bookcase, and Jonathan left his books stacked in piles all around it on the floor. Honestly, the man was impossible. He seemed to go out of his way to be untidy.

Making the bed and removing the clutter on the washstand, Kate felt a small glow of contentment. She remembered her granny saying that she was never happier than when she was doing for her family. The Cantrells could wear you out "doing" for them, Kate thought.

With a guilty start she realized where her thoughts were leading. No matter how much she enjoyed making a home for Jonathan Cantrell and his sons, they were not her family. Her husband lay in a lonely grave, and her baby's future was uncertain. She wondered how Jonathan would react when she told him of her impending motherhood.

When she opened a drawer in the bureau to put away some socks she'd darned the week before, her eyes were drawn to a gilt frame tucked under the clothing. Curiosity overcoming her scruples, Kate pulled out the picture. It took her only a second to realize she was looking at the boys' mother. The blue-gray eyes and friendly smile were Levi's, and the thick black hair was Cole's.

Kate had expected Jonathan's wife to be a striking beauty and was surprised to find that she was not. Though she was rather pretty, her most noticeable feature was her size. Even in a painting, it was obvious that she had been tiny and delicate.

After carefully replacing the picture where she'd found it, Kate closed the drawer. She couldn't help wondering why it was hidden there instead of sitting out in plain view. If she had a picture of Bryan, it would certainly be out where she could see it.

Then she turned her attention to the secretary.

She opened the glass doors of the bookcase and bent to retrieve the books from the floor. As she arranged the leather-bound volumes in the bookcase, she noticed that they included a smattering of everything—literature, philosophy, mathematics, science, even poetry. His interests were obviously as varied as they were extensive.

After picking up the last of the books from the floor, she glanced curiously at a wooden crate on the floor behind them. She closed the doors of the bookcase and carefully opened the lid, only to be assailed with a strong odor of turpentine. Her eyes grew wide as she realized what the box contained: brushes, paints, rags . . . Good heavens, he was an artist, too! Suddenly she knew what her bedroom had been: not an oversize closet, but Jonathan's study. The huge windows and odd shutters were meant to regulate the light for his painting. That was why the books had been on the floor; he hadn't gotten around to putting them away.

Replacing the lid to the box, Kate wondered if there was anything Jonathan Cantrell couldn't do. Then, instantly ashamed of herself for such a thought about the intelligent, attractive man who had given her so much to be thankful for, Kate tackled the overflowing desk with renewed vigor. Afraid of losing something of great importance, she carefully stacked the papers more or less where they lay.

An oversize piece of parchment drew her attention as she straightened the last pile. It was partially concealed by the cubbyholes as though it had been shoved out of the way. She pulled out the document and peered at it curiously, then carried it over to the window where she could see it better.

It appeared to be a certificate of some sort, but since it was written in Latin she was unable to decipher much of it. Only the words *Princeton University* arched across the top and Jonathan's name in the center had any meaning for her at all. Even then there was a word in front of his name that she couldn't figure out. Scrutinizing the ornate script, Kate slowly spelled out the illegible word. "P-r-o-f-e-l-l"—no—"s-s-o-r." Professor. *Professor?* Jonathan Cantrell? How could that be?

Her mind whirling, Kate numbly replaced the document. No wonder he taught his sons Latin and higher mathematics.

"Kate?"

She started guiltily at the sound of Jonathan's voice and closed the front of the desk. "I'm in here."

"Is there any coffee?"

Taking a deep breath in an effort to calm her pounding heart, Kate assumed what she hoped was an innocent facial expression. "In the pot on the back of the stove. I was just straightening your room. Hope you don't . . ." Kate's voice died in her throat as she walked into the kitchen and found herself face to face with Clay Langton.

He swept his hat from his head. "Good morning, Mrs. Murphy."

"Mr. Langton," Kate said with a slight inclination of her head.

"You'll find we aren't so formal here in the West. Call me Clay."

His perfect smile lacked the appeal of Jonathan's dimples, but Kate couldn't help thinking that his soft southern drawl had a magic of its own. "Then, of course, you must call me Kate."

"Clay just got a package from his sister." Jonathan held up a handful of newspapers. "He brought these over."

Clay grinned. "I know how much Jonathan likes to keep in touch with the world. He's so anxious to get started reading, he invited me in for a cup of coffee so I wouldn't hold him back. I hope you don't mind."

"Of course not." Kate walked over to the stove. "I was just about to take a huckleberry pie out of the oven. Do you have time for a piece?"

Clay's smile was warm. "I always have time for a piece of huckleberry pie, especially when it gives me the chance to visit with a lovely lady."

Surprised by the unexpected flattery, Kate blushed as she turned away to take her pie out of the oven.

Jonathan was already putting on his glasses as she set down his pie and coffee next to him. Mumbling his thanks, he picked up a paper and was soon deeply engrossed, leaving Kate to entertain Clay on her own.

"What do you think of Wyoming so far, Kate?" Clay asked her.

She thought of how horribly unprotected she'd felt traveling across the near desert with its hot dry weather and incessant wind, but she'd never seen the likes of the majestic mountains or the incredibly beautiful sunsets. "It's not a place for the faint-hearted," she said, "but I'm beginning to like it."

Neither Kate nor Clay was aware of the sidelong glance Jonathan gave them. "Well, I'll be damned." Jonathan's muttered exclamation drew their attention. "The Mexicans finally got rid of Maximilian." He peered at the date on the paper. "God, this is over a year old."

"The rest are more recent." Clay turned back to Kate. "The West does have its drawbacks, though. Sometimes the news is a trifle stale by the time we get it, and there aren't many women around to bring us the gentler side of life." He took a bite of his pie and closed his eyes as he chewed. "Sheer heaven. I haven't had pie like this since before the war."

"I see the Union Pacific hooked up with the Central Pacific in Utah," Jonathan said a trifle loudly as he looked up from his second paper. "Charlie owes me six bits on that one." His eyes fell to the paper again. "It says here the trip from New York to California takes less than a month now."

"Land sakes! What next?" Kate couldn't help thinking of her own tragic journey west. If they had waited a few more months, they could have traveled most of the way by train, and Bryan would probably still be alive.

"What do you say, Kate?"

With a start Kate realized she had no idea what Clay had asked her. "I . . . I'm sorry. I was wool-gathering."

If Clay was irritated by her inattention, he was far too much of a gentleman to let it show. "I asked if you'd care to go riding one day soon."

"Oh!" Kate blinked in surprise. "I . . . I don't ride."

"If it's a proper lady's horse you're worried about, I'll be glad to lend you one of mine. I have a pretty little mare that's as sweet a goer as I've ever seen."

"Oh, no, it's not that," Kate said. "I don't ride because I don't know how. I grew up in the city, you see."

Clay looked slightly nonplussed, but only for a moment. "Well, then perhaps you'd care to go for a carriage ride with me?"

Kate shook her head. "I don't thi—"

"That's a great idea, Clay," Jonathan said, looking up from his paper. "It may be kind of hard to arrange, though. Kate's always so busy."

Kate snapped her mouth shut. If Jonathan Cantrell thought he could dictate how she spent her free time, he had another think coming. "I'd be pleased to go buggy riding with you, Clay, and I have one day a week off." She glared at Jonathan. "It's this Sunday."

"Splendid! Shall we say this Sunday, then? I'll have my cook pack us a picnic lunch, and we'll make a day of it."

"That sounds fine," Kate said.

"I'll pick you up about ten-thirty, then." Clay finished off the last of his pie and sat back with a satisfied sigh. "Delicious. Jonathan is lucky to have found you. A good cook is worth her weight in gold in the territory. You know, Kate, I'd be happy to teach you to ride."

"Oh, I—"

"That's mighty neighborly of you, Clay," Jonathan broke in, taking a sip of his coffee, "but it's too much to ask of such a busy man."

Clay shrugged. "I don't mind. I expect to be spending some time around here anyway." The warm look he sent Kate left no doubt as to what would be bringing him to the Cantrell ranch.

Jonathan's jaw hardened. "Nevertheless, I must insist—"

"Actually, the boys have promised to teach me how to drive," Kate interrupted, noticing the challenging look in Clay's eyes. "I'm afraid I wouldn't have time to do both."

"Ah. Perhaps later, then."

Kate nodded. "Perhaps."

Clay pulled out an ornate gold watch and opened the cover with an expert flick of his thumbnail. "Well, it's time I was going." He stood and picked up his hat. "Thank you so much for the pie and coffee."

"You're welcome. Stop by again," she replied.

"You can count on it." He glanced at Jonathan. "Keep the papers as long as you like."

"Thanks, Clay. I appreciate your thinking of me." His dark expression was at odds with his words.

"Anytime." Clay walked to the door, then turned back to Kate. "Until Sunday, then." Settling his hat on his head, he gave her one last smile; then he was gone.

Except for the rustle of a turning page, silence reigned in the kitchen as Kate picked up the empty plate and cup. She was nearly at the stove when Jonathan spoke.

"I'd be careful about flirting with Clay Langton if I were you."

Kate whirled around. "Flirting?"

"Clay's a man of the world," he said, ignoring her indignance. "He'd have a sweet little thing like you for breakfast before you even knew you were on the menu."

"Of all the . . . in spite of what you think, Mr. Cantrell, I wasn't born yesterday." She slammed the dishes down on the hoosier. "I spent a month at the Golden Spur spurning the advances of cowpokes who were far less gentlemanly than Clay. I know how to take care of myself."

"Yes, by simpering and fawning over the first dandified idiot that comes calling. I tried to warn you, but you were far too enamored to listen."

She set her fists on her hips. "That's another thing. How dare you refuse an invitation that was meant for me? I'm fully capable of making my own decisions, enamored or not. What I do on my own time is none of your business."

"Going off for an afternoon with a man you hardly know seems rather ill advised to me."

"Oh, for pity's sake. What in heaven's name do you think he's going to do to me on a buggy ride?"

"You don't know what men of Langton's ilk are like."

"You're right." She untied her apron and

tossed it onto the table. "I've met very few gentle-men in my life. There certainly aren't any in this house."

"Where do you think you're going?" he asked as she stomped to the door.

"For a walk. Any objections, Mr. Cantrell?"

"Only one." The almost wistful note in his voice brought her to a stop. "It seems to me if you can call a virtual stranger by his first name, you can call me by mine."

For a moment the only sound was that of a bird chirping right outside the open window.

"I'll think about it," she said at last, and flounced out, slamming the door.

As she expected, her anger cooled rapidly as she walked away from the house toward the creek. Jonathan Cantrell was insufferable, yes, but he had a point. If he hadn't gotten her temper going, she would have refused Clay's invitation herself. It was too soon after Bryan's death for her to be going for a buggy ride with anyone, let alone a stranger. And perhaps Jonathan had reason to warn her. What did she know about the debonair Mr. Langton, after all?

Of course, she didn't know much about Jonathan Cantrell, either. During Clay's unsettling visit, the discoveries she had made in Jonathan's bedroom had slipped to the back of her mind. Now they came flooding back with a dozen unanswered questions. Though she didn't really know how one became a college professor, Kate was sure it was not easily accomplished. Why would a man just walk away from it? And why was his wife's portrait hidden from view?

From bits and pieces of conversation she'd heard between Charlie and Jonathan, Kate knew that Jonathan had brought west with him a herd of rare and probably very expensive Hereford cattle. He spent hours poring over his breeding records and keeping meticulous notes on his animals, but until the railroad came through, there was no way to get the cattle to market. Kate knew that there had been little or no income for the last four years, yet the ranch was prosperous. Jonathan had to have money from some other source.

Why would such an intelligent, handsome man be living on the frontier, where he couldn't even make a living off his precious cattle? Could Jonathan Cantrell be running from something? Kate suddenly wondered about the implications for herself and her unborn child.

She was so deep in thought that she didn't hear the brush crackling behind her. She had no inkling of danger until a large callused hand closed over her mouth and a strong arm clamped around her waist. Though she fought with all her strength, Kate was unable to stop her assailant from dragging her back into the trees. Kicking and flailing her arms wildly, she heard a grunt of pain when her elbow connected with his midsection.

Taking advantage of her attacker's momentary weakness, she tried to twist out of his grasp. She succeeded only in turning halfway. Looking up at the darkly bearded face above her, Kate froze, her eyes widening in disbelief.

8

"*Shhh.*" *Kate's abductor* raised his head to listen. In the distance they could hear Levi yelling curses at the mule. Deciding that the sound posed no threat, the man looked down at Kate's face. "Will you promise not to scream if I take my hand away?"

With tears swimming in her eyes, Kate nodded, and he released his hold. "Darn you, Patrick McAnespie. How dare you scare me that way?" she cried as she threw her arms around him. "And where have you been the last seven years?"

"Is that any way to greet your baby brother?"

"After what you just did to me, I ought to kick you. The very idea, dragging me off into the woods instead of coming up to the house like a normal person." Kate buried her face against his chest. "Oh, Patrick, we thought you were dead."

"Aw, Katharine, don't cry." Ill at ease with her

tears, he patted her back and spoke softly. "Katie did, Katie cat, ate a bug, caught a rat."

"Wh-what?"

Patrick gave her a lopsided grin. "You heard me."

"My name isn't Katie." She straightened and wiped her eyes. "And you promised you'd never say that again."

"Only because you were sitting on me at the time. Besides, it worked, didn't it?"

"You still haven't told me where you've been."

"How could I with you bawling all over me?"

"Well, I'm not crying now."

He shrugged. "I've been all over. Kansas, Nebraska, Oklahoma, Missouri. I got here by way of Texas. Came north with a herd of longhorns for the colonel."

"The colonel?"

"Colonel Langton. He was short of hands, so I stayed on after we delivered the cattle." Patrick glanced toward the house. "I thought you knew him. He was in there long enough."

Kate blinked. "How long have you been out here?"

"A couple of hours today. I was here yesterday and the day before, too, but you never got very far from the house."

"Patrick, are you in trouble?"

"Trouble?" He gave an artificial laugh. "Me? Whatever gave you that idea?"

"I wonder."

Avoiding her eyes, Patrick took off his hat and ran his fingers along the top crease nervously. "Aren't you curious how I found you?"

"Now that you mention it . . ."

"I found your burned-out wagon. Didn't think too much about it at first, then I recognized what was left of the bureau. Not too many like it around, and it's the only one that has my initials carved into the bottom side of the middle drawer. That's how I was sure it was yours." He hesitated. "I found the grave, too. Bryan?"

Kate nodded, tears filling her eyes as she looked down at her hands. "Cholera."

"Jesus. I'm sorry, Katharine. He was a good man." Patrick stared into the past for a moment and then sighed. "Anyway, I asked around town, and they said you lived out here with a man named Cantrell."

Kate blushed at her brother's choice of words. They made it sound so sordid. "I'm Jonathan Cantrell's housekeeper," she said. "I don't live with him."

"Guess I wouldn't blame you if you did. He's a good-looking son of a gun."

"Patrick! Bryan's barely cold in his grave!"

Her brother had the grace to look sheepish. "I know, but he'd be the last one to hold it against you. Bryan believed in living life to its fullest." His eyes narrowed. "Is this Cantrell good to you?"

"Yes, even when he's mad at me, but this is all entirely beside the point. You still haven't told me why you're acting so strangely."

Patrick wandered toward the edge of the thicket and silently contemplated the creek. "I couldn't take the chance of running into you somewhere," he said at last.

"Why not?"

"I figured you'd cry all over me." He turned and gave her a crooked grin. "Just like you did."

"You were afraid I'd embarrass you?"

"No, not exactly. I didn't want anyone to hear you call me Patrick. I go by Tom Fielding now."

There was a moment of silence. "You're running from the law, aren't you?"

He gave a humorless laugh. "If it were that simple, I'd just turn myself in."

"Oh, for heaven's sake, Patrick." Kate made no effort to hide her exasperation. "Quit all this shilly-shallying and tell me what's going on!"

"All right. I suppose you already figured out I ran off to join the army?"

Kate nodded. "We weren't sure, but we suspected as much."

"Well, I wasn't much of a soldier. I was captured during my first battle and wound up at Andersonville."

"Andersonville!" Kate was horrified. Like everyone else, she'd heard about the atrocities that had taken place in the Confederate prison camps during the war, and Andersonville had reputedly been the worst.

"I'd never have survived if it hadn't been for a man named Frank Johnson. I never really knew why he helped me, but he saved my life a couple of times. Then he got sick, and I nursed him through it. He was the closest friend I ever had other than Bryan. After a couple of months we managed to escape and make our way to Kansas, where we joined up with Frank's brother, Bullwhip."

Kate raised an eyebrow. "Bullwhip? What kind of a name is that?"

"The man's a genius with a whip. When he's driving a four-horse hitch he can take a fly off the leader's ear and never have his team miss a step."

"A most useful skill, to be sure."

"It impressed me at the time. Besides, he was Frank's brother. Looking back on it now, I realize how incredibly stupid and naive I was, but it never occurred to me to question Frank about what was going on. For the first month or so I mostly stayed around camp, still a little sickly from Andersonville and too weak to do much but take care of the horses and cook. Then one day Bullwhip decided to take me along."

Patrick stopped talking and stared off into space. He looked almost ill. Apparently the memory still had the ability to reach over the years since and affect him.

"Patrick?" Kate said softly when the silence had gone on too long.

"What?" Patrick seemed disoriented, and then his eyes refocused on her face. "Oh, sorry. Have you ever heard of Quantrill's Raiders?"

"Yes."

"Bullwhip Johnson had the same philosophy, only on the opposite side of the fence. He called himself a Yankee Jayhawker and claimed as long as a person supported the South, they were enemies of the United States. In his mind that gave him license to do anything he wanted. That day he'd planned raids on two small towns that were known to have Confederate sympathizers. Fool that I was,

I didn't have any notion of what was going on until we rode in and opened fire.

"They were animals, Katharine, and it didn't have a damned thing to do with politics. I saw a man I thought I knew well rape a young girl, then shoot her point-blank." He rubbed a hand over his eyes. "I ran. Don't even know if I was aware of where I was going or not, but suddenly I was in the next town. I warned the sheriff that Bullwhip was coming. By the time they got there, the whole town was waiting for them. Frank . . ." Patrick closed his eyes and swallowed convulsively. "Frank took a bullet in the chest. He . . . he died almost at my feet."

"Oh, Patrick."

"Bullwhip and a few others escaped, but I truly thought it was over with. I was wrong. It didn't take Bullwhip long to catch up to me. When he did, they tied me to a tree, and he used that damned whip on me."

Horrified, Kate put her hand to her mouth. "Oh, no."

Patrick seemed almost to have forgotten she was there as his eyes stared past her unseeingly. "Sometimes I almost wish he'd finished it that night, but somebody came along and scared him off. He's been after me ever since. Six long years I've been running, but he always shows up eventually."

"But why? I mean, six years is an awful long time to hold a grudge."

"It's more than a grudge, it's vengeance. He holds me responsible for his brother's death." Patrick sighed. "I guess I do, too."

Kate touched his arm lightly. "I'm sorry things have been so hard for you."

Patrick blinked and looked down at her. "Oh, it hasn't been so bad, really. I've seen lots of country I wouldn't have otherwise." He gave a shrug, and the haunted expression disappeared from his face. "Besides, keeping ahead of Bullwhip has turned into a challenge." A glimmer of mischief entered his brown eyes. "This time he's going to find it hard tracking me down. The last place he'll think to look is right under the nose of a Confederate war hero."

"But, Patrick . . ."

"Here now, Katharine, don't you be worryin' none. I've been takin' care o' meself for a long time."

She smiled. "It's funny how that Irish brogue of yours comes and goes." Then she sobered. "But you will be careful?"

"I'll not be lettin' the likes o' him catch me!" He dropped his teasing brogue and gave her a brotherly hug. "I'll get word to you somehow if I have to leave."

"Well, be sure you—" She broke off suddenly as Cole's panicky voice rang through the air.

"Mrs. Murphy . . . Mrs. Murphy . . ."

"Oh, no, something's happened. I have to go." Kate gave Patrick a quick squeeze before lifting her skirts and running toward the sound of the mule's angry braying.

With an irritated sigh, Jonathan folded the paper and slapped it down on the table. He'd been looking at the same page for the last fifteen minutes and still didn't have the faintest idea what it said. All he could think of was Kate and how she'd stormed out of the house.

He'd only tried to give her a word of advice. There was certainly no reason for her to fly off the handle like that. It wasn't as though he'd done anything bad. Heck, he'd even invited Clay in because he knew the other man wanted to "further his acquaintance" with Kate.

Taking his last swallow of coffee, Jonathan tried unsuccessfully to ignore his conscience. He couldn't really explain what had come over him as he and Clay had walked into the pie-scented kitchen and Kate had come out of his bedroom. Suddenly Clay hadn't seemed quite so presentable. What Jonathan had always thought of as Clay's natural sophistication seemed a bit too polished, too slick. If he hadn't been there to keep Clay under control, poor Kate would have found herself in way over her head, if she wasn't already.

Uncomfortably aware that Kate had been less than pleased with his intervention, Jonathan told himself that he'd only been protecting her from a man whose practiced charm was clearly beyond her experience. In spite of her sojourn at the Golden Spur, she wasn't anywhere near as worldly as she thought she was. If she had any kind of sense at all, she'd listen to someone older and wiser instead of blowing up and stomping off in a snit.

He scooted back his chair, stood up, and ran his fingers through his hair. As he turned to go, the dirty dishes on the table caught his eye. With some vague notion of placating Kate, he scooped up his plate and cup and carried them to the dishpan. If Charlie could see him doing such a thing, he'd probably think Jonathan had lost his mind.

Jonathan himself couldn't help wondering why he was acting the way he was. Was he afraid that Clay would sweep Kate off her feet and take her away? Blast the woman, anyway. In the few short weeks she'd been there, he'd gotten damn used to having her around.

He liked coming home to a clean house and a hot, tasty meal. He had to admit that he even enjoyed her cheerful chatter and the way her beautiful hazel eyes reflected her mood. Watching them change from flashing brown when she was mad to green when she was happy was almost as much fun as watching her blush.

"Mrs. Murphy! Mrs. Mur . . . Pa!" Cole burst through the door, his eyes wide and his face pale. "Pa, come quick. Jughead dumped Levi in the creek. I drug him out, but he ain't moving."

Jonathan dropped the dishes with a crash and ran out the door with Cole. Kate was already near the creek, her skirts hiked far above her ankles as she ran toward Levi's prone form. Jonathan reached them seconds after Kate had dropped to her knees beside the unconscious boy.

"Levi . . . oh, please, Levi, open your eyes." Tears were streaming down her face as she desperately chafed his hand. She looked up as Jonathan arrived. "Thank God you're here! We need a wet rag of some kind."

Jonathan jerked his handkerchief out of his pocket and dipped it in the icy water of the creek.

With a quick twist, he wrung out the excess and began tenderly to bathe Levi's face.

Panting from trying to catch up with his long-legged father and fearing the worst, Cole couldn't quite keep the quaver from his voice. "I . . . is he d-dead?"

Kate sent the younger boy a reassuring glance. "No, he's breathing, and his heartbeat is strong. I just wish he'd wake. . . ."

Levi moaned, and his eyes fluttered open. He stared uncomprehendingly up at Kate and Jonathan for a moment, then shut his eyes again. "Damn mule," he muttered. "He threw me over his head on purpose."

"How you feel, son?" Jonathan asked, dipping the rag in the water again.

"Like that miserable mule stomped me into the mud. At first he wouldn't go at all. Then he took off and ran like a demon till he got to the creek."

Relieved, Kate pulled the boy into her arms and gave him a hug. "Thank heavens you're all right. You scared us half to death."

Jonathan laughed shakily. "Maybe more than half."

As he reached out to grip his son's shoulder, his hand brushed against Kate's arm, and their glances collided in an exchange that was as unexpected as it was revealing. Their relief over Levi was obvious, but there was something more, something neither of them had anticipated. Neither was prepared for the impact of the other's gaze, and both drew back as though they had been burned.

9

"*Looks like we* might get some rain today," Jonathan remarked.

Charlie's eyes narrowed. "Could be, but I don't reckon it's real likely."

"Maybe not, but you better make sure you have your slicker just the same."

"Always do."

Kate glanced at the bright sunlight streaming in the window and went back to her breakfast dishes. Only the thinning of her lips gave any indication that she'd heard the conversation at the table. She was going on that buggy ride today even if Jonathan said there was going to be a tornado precisely at noon!

Charlie took another swallow of coffee. "Saw the boys over by my place a little after dawn this morning. Young scamps said they was huntin'."

"They were. They've been after me to let them

go for a couple of weeks now. I finally said as long as they got their chores done and were back in time to start work, they could go first thing in the morning. Figured they'd never make it out of bed in time." Jonathan rubbed a finger across his mustache. "Don't know how they managed to get themselves going, but I heard them leave about an hour before daybreak."

As if on cue, the sounds of raised voices wafted in on the morning breeze.

"I say she'll make stew."

"No, stew's for winter. She'll roast 'em."

"Unless I miss my guess, the hunters have returned," Kate said.

Moments later Levi and Cole burst through the door, each carrying a dead jackrabbit.

"You're going to fix rabbit stew for lunch, aren't you?"

Kate draped the dish towel over the edge of the hoosier. "No."

"See," Cole said. "I told you she'd roast 'em."

Kate shook her head. "I'm not going to roast them, either."

Levi couldn't believe his ears. "You aren't going to cook our rabbits?"

"Not for lunch, anyway." Kate untied her apron and hung it on a peg by the window.

"But Pa says you have to eat what you kill."

"Yeah," Cole said. "Otherwise you've taken a life for nothing."

"If you skin it and clean it first, I'll gladly cook any animal you bring in," Kate said, "but not today."

Levi gave her a pleading look. "As hot as it is, these rabbits will spoil before tomorrow."

When Kate glanced toward Jonathan for support she could see that he would be no help at all. In fact, she thought she could detect a certain amount of smugness in his innocent shrug. Her jaw tightened and then relaxed into a smile.

"Heavens, we couldn't have that, could we? You don't think they'll last until supper?"

Both boys shook their heads emphatically.

Kate sighed. "Well then, I guess there's no help for it. You'll just have to cook them yourselves. But don't worry, I'm sure your pa'll be glad to help you. Now, if you'll excuse me, I have to get ready for my drive with Mr. Langton."

The sight of Jonathan's incredulous expression before she closed her bedroom door nearly made Kate giggle. There wasn't so much as a glimmer of smugness left. Good! Maybe that would teach him a much needed lesson. As she slipped out of her dress, Kate wished she could understand the murmur of voices just beyond her door. Unfortunately the thick log walls made it impossible.

It took her very little time to wash, put on her only other dress, and brush her hair. By then the kitchen was deserted. She cleared Jonathan's and Charlie's cups from the table and settled herself by the window with her mending.

The shirt she pulled out of the basket brought a smile to her face. Jonathan had been wearing it the day he and Charlie had successfully tangled with a range cow that needed doctoring. When they had come in afterward, Kate's breath had caught in her throat at the sight of Jonathan with one shoulder hanging out and the buttons missing nearly to his waist. Even in torn, dirty clothing, no one could match him for sheer masculine beauty. Charlie's shirt had been just as tattered, but he hadn't made her heart pound.

A knock at the door made Kate jump. Embarrassed by her improper thoughts, she thrust the shirt back into the pile of mending. Smoothing the front of her dress nervously, she hurried to the door.

Clay assumed that the becoming flush staining Kate's cheeks was for him, and he smiled. "Good morning, Kate. You're looking lovely." Though there wasn't a speck of flirtation in her manner, her murmured thanks and downcast eyes reminded him of the young women he had courted before the war. The memory of happier times only endeared her to him. He held out his arm. "Shall we go?"

Trying to convince herself that she wasn't doing anything improper by going on a perfectly innocent picnic, Kate took his arm and stepped through the door. "I'm quite looking forward to our ride. I haven't really had time to do much exploring."

"Good. I thought we'd drive over to my place, unless you had somewhere else in mind."

"Oh, no," she assured him. "I'd love to see your ranch."

He led her to the buckboard. "I must apologize. I don't have a buggy yet."

Kate glanced at the short-boxed vehicle as Clay helped her climb aboard. Its bright red wheels and shiny black paint added a touch of elegance to the strictly utilitarian conveyance. "Actually, I think it looks quite nice."

"Perhaps, but it's hardly the appropriate carriage for such a beautiful lady," he said as he climbed up beside her and took the reins.

"I wish you wouldn't do that."

He quirked an eyebrow as he started the horses. "Do what?"

"Make such outrageous remarks. I've never cared for flattery, especially when it has no basis in fact."

"You think I'm flattering you when I call you beautiful?"

"I have a mirror," she said, "and even if it were true, I'd hardly need to be told every other minute, would I?"

After several moments of silence Clay laughed and shook his head. "You are an amazing young woman. I know, you probably consider that flattery also. Never mind, I shall endeavor to admire the view instead of my delightful companion."

Clay spent the next half hour pointing out interesting landmarks and generally being good company. An amusing escort, he soon put Kate at ease. She found herself enjoying her outing far more than she had anticipated.

At last they came to a stop on top of a windswept hill, and Clay sat back as Kate surveyed the scene below. "Well, that's home, such as it is."

A few buildings sat huddled in the center of a wide, grassy valley with cattle and horses dotting the landscape. Kate knew the animals were almost certainly only a small part of Clay Langton's stock.

The rest were probably out on the open range or even on top of the nearby mountains. "Most impressive," she said, and glanced at Clay in admiration. To her surprise, his face was set in a melancholy frown.

"It still seems so primitive." He spoke softly, almost as if to himself. "And it will never be Golden Oaks."

"Golden Oaks?"

"My home in Georgia. It's gone now, of course, burned to the ground by the Yankees, the land bought up by carpetbaggers for back taxes." His hands tightened on the reins. "If I'd been there, I might have stopped the destruction somehow."

Kate had the distinct feeling the Yankees had destroyed more than his home. She couldn't help wondering what had happened to the family he'd left behind when he'd marched off to war. Swallowing a knot in her throat, she laid her hand gently on his arm. "I'm sure no one blamed you for not being there. As a colonel, you had to go where your orders sent you."

His head swiveled around. "How did you know I was a colonel?"

"I . . . I don't know," she stammered, realizing her blunder. "Jonathan must have said something."

"He couldn't have. Jonathan and I both feel the war is best forgotten. We've never discussed it."

"W-well, maybe I heard it in town." She tried desperately to think of a way out that wouldn't expose Patrick. "I met a lot of people when I worked at the Golden Spur."

He was clearly startled. "What?"

At his horrified expression, Kate removed her hand from his arm and fought down a hysterical bubble of laughter that rose in her throat. She'd successfully diverted his attention all right. "I thought you knew. There was nothing left after my husband died. I . . . I had no choice but to find work. Horse Creek doesn't have a lot to offer in the way of employment."

"But surely Abigail Cline . . ."

"Mrs. Cline took instant exception to me. If it hadn't been for Rosie, the woman would probably have thrown me out into the street. Rosie whisked me away and convinced Red O'Leary to hire me as a cook."

"Ah." Clay sounded relieved. "You cooked for Red and his girls, then."

Kate raised her head and stared him in the eye. She had nothing to be ashamed of, and she wouldn't lie. "Yes, I cooked, and I also served drinks and danced with the customers."

To her surprise, Clay nodded. "And then Jonathan came along and rescued you. I wish I'd been there first."

"Jonathan Cantrell did not rescue me. Red and I had an understanding. I worked the floor but never went upstairs with anyone. Frenchie and Rosie took care of that part of it. I was perfectly safe at the Golden Spur. I left only because Jonathan offered me a better job."

To her amazement, Clay chuckled. "And I'll wager he got more than he bargained for with that Irish temper of yours." Watching her lips thin, he added hastily, "No, no, don't take my head off. I meant it as a compliment." He pulled out his watch and flicked open the cover. "It's nearly noon. What do you say we go have our picnic and forget all this past history?"

At Kate's nod, he turned the buckboard around and drove back down the hill. By the time they reached the picnic spot he had chosen, they were on the best of terms again.

They spread a blanket on the ground beneath a huge cottonwood tree, and Clay began unpacking the food.

Left with nothing to do but watch, Kate leaned back against the tree with a sigh. "It's been a long time since I went on a picnic."

Clay nodded. "For me too." He popped the cork on a bottle of red wine and poured her a glass. "There hasn't been much opportunity." He filled a glass for himself, set aside the bottle, and smiled. "Shall we drink a toast to the day?"

"Oh, yes, let's." Her eyes sparkling, she straightened and held her glass up to his. "To beautiful summer days and new friends."

"Especially to new friends," he said softly, clicking the glasses together. The warmth in his voice made Kate blush, but she found herself unable to look away. Their gazes remained locked for a long moment, and then the sound of pounding hooves drew their attention away. "Now who's this?" Clay said, looking back over his shoulder.

Kate thought she had a pretty good idea. But if Jonathan thought he could ride in here and interrupt their picnic, he was in for a nasty surprise. She'd had it with being treated as though she were fifteen years old, and she fully intended to tell him so.

The rider who came into view was not Jonathan or even one of the boys, however. Kate's heart gave a lurch as she recognized Charlie and saw the grim expression on his face. "What happened?" she cried.

"We need you back at the ranch. There's been an accident."

"Oh, no." Kate sprang to her feet and practically ran over to his horse. "Is it Jonathan or one of the boys?"

"It ain't so bad you need to git all riled up, now. Ain't nobody gonna die, but I reckon it'd be a good idea if I was to take you home."

"You were right to come for me." Kate turned to Clay. "I'm sorry to have to go, but—"

"Don't apologize. I completely understand." His face filled with concern, Clay looked over her head to Charlie. "I'll follow you back."

Charlie shrugged. "I don't reckon it's that serious. You know how them boys are with their bumps and scratches."

Charlie took his foot out of the left stirrup and held his callused palm down to Kate. "Put your foot in and give me your hand. When I count three, bounce a little and I'll pull you up behind the saddle."

Kate complied and was soon perched behind Charlie on the rump of the horse.

"Are you sure you don't need my help?" Clay asked again.

Charlie shook his head. "Mighty neighborly of

you to ask, but I don't reckon we ought to put you
to such a bother."

"I don't mind."

"I'll remember that, thanks." Charlie reached
down and shook the other man's hand. "If we need
you later, I'll send one of the boys."

Then it had to be Jonathan who was hurt, Kate
thought, her stomach twisting into a painful knot.
She was so worried she forgot to be afraid of the
horse. Caught up in her dire forebodings, she was
hardly aware of the ground so far below or even of
her skirts hiked up almost to her knees.

That all changed the moment Clay was out of
sight and Charlie spurred his horse into a run. Suddenly Kate's arms clenched around Charlie's waist
in a death grip. The cantle at the back of the saddle
jabbed into her belly every time she bounced up,
and her bottom collided with the horse's hard
backbone every time she came down. "Charlie,"
she managed to say after only a few moments, "I
can't do this."

He slowed the horse immediately and peered
over his shoulder at her.

"I'm sorry, but I don't know how to ride." Kate
felt as though the bouncing of the horse were making her words unintelligible, but Charlie brought
the animal to a full stop.

"Dang, I plumb fergot. Reckon if I get on the
back, you could sit in the saddle?"

"Well, maybe. Will I still bounce around?"

"Some, but not so much. Are you one of them
folks it makes sick?"

"No, but . . ." She hadn't wanted to tell anyone yet,

but it didn't seem as though she had much of a choice. "I . . . I don't think it's very good for my baby."

Charlie turned as far around in the saddle as he could. "Baby?" At Kate's nod, he took off his hat and ran his fingers through his hair. "Does Jon know?"

"No. I didn't want to tell him yet."

Charlie stared off across the prairie as he pondered this. "Don't see any reason for you to say anything till you're good and ready," he said at last. "I sure won't say nothin'."

"Thank you. Ah . . . Charlie, don't you think we'd better hurry?"

"Huh?" He seemed to have forgotten the urgency of his errand. Then he slapped his hat on his head and turned back around. "Yeah, we'd better. Ya kinda threw me for a loop there. Will you be all right if I go slow?"

"I think so."

"All right, then, you let me know if it's too much." He started off at a brisk pace that was still considerably faster than what Kate considered slow.

"Who's hurt, Charlie? Is it Jonathan or one of the boys?"

He was silent so long that she thought he wasn't going to answer. "Truth is, it ain't any of 'em. I just said that so you'd come with me."

"What? You mean you scared me half to death and dragged me away from my outing with Clay when everybody is fine?"

"Didn't say that. Just that Jon and the boys ain't hurt."

"Charlie, what's going on?"

He sighed. "Don't reckon I know a whole lot more'n you do."

Charlie seemed disinclined to say more, and Kate was too busy trying to hang on to question him further. At last they rode into a clearing in front of a small cabin.

"Where are we?" Kate asked, looking at the unfamiliar homestead.

"My place." Charlie helped her slide to the ground and then swung down behind her. After cautiously opening the door of the cabin, he peered inside for a long moment as though not quite sure it was safe. Finally he stepped aside to allow Kate to enter.

With an uncertain glance at Charlie, she moved hesitantly toward the open door.

10

"*Ain't sure bringin'* you here was right, but I didn't know what else to do," Charlie said.

It took Kate a few moments to scan the small room as her eyes adjusted to the dim interior. The tiny, sparsely furnished cabin seemed incapable of concealing any menace, yet Charlie's unease made her decidedly nervous. A movement from the bed made her jump. What she had dismissed as a pile of blankets and clothing suddenly took on human form.

Cautiously Kate moved closer. One look at the battered face was all it took. Her own fear completely forgotten, she knelt by the bed. The face was a mass of lumps and bruises, swollen almost beyond recognition. Kate winced as she took in the split lip and the cut over one eye that was still oozing. "Charlie, get me a clean rag and some water." She rolled up her sleeves. "I'll need hot water, too, just as soon as you can get it for me."

The stained buckskin dress and beaded, calf-high moccasins on the body, which was drawn into a tight ball, were a complete surprise to Kate. An Indian woman! Her attention shot back to the woman's face. Even with closer scrutiny, she couldn't see the brown undertone of the woman's skin, for there were few places that weren't bruised or bloody. "Who is she, Charlie?"

"Don't know." Charlie set the bowl of water on the washstand. "Found her hidin' in some willows down by the creek. Acted plumb scared of me, but she was too stove up to do much more'n whimper." He gently lifted a lock of hair away from the woman's face. A muscle in his jaw clenched angrily. "Looks like somebody done beat her half to death."

Kate dipped the rag into the cool water and wrung it out. "I wonder who."

"If I find out, reckon I'll be mighty tempted to give him a taste of his own medicine," Charlie said, standing up and moving away.

Kate glanced over her shoulder at him as he started to build a fire in the fireplace. It was the first time she'd ever seen him angry. Turning back to her patient, she began the difficult task of cleaning the wounds. Though as careful as possible, Kate knew she was causing the woman a great deal of pain. Even so, with eyes closed, the patient lay unmoving beneath Kate's gentle hands. After sponging away the dirt and blood, Kate felt carefully along the woman's arms and legs for broken bones. Fortunately there didn't seem to be any.

With a sigh, Kate stood up and took the bowl of dirty water outside to dump it. When she returned, she found Charlie standing over the bed, staring down at his guest. As if she knew her benefactor was there, the woman's dark brown eyes opened and gazed up at him.

"Not sure you can understand me, but you're safe now," Charlie said softly. "Ain't nobody here gonna hurt you." He reached toward her in a reassuring gesture, but the woman cringed, her eyes scrunching shut in obvious fear. He stood there another moment or two before turning away. "If I ever catch that son of a bitch, I'll kill him," he muttered.

In spite of her horror at the way the Indian woman had been brutalized, Kate was a bit shocked to hear such a statement from the normally taciturn Charlie.

"Your hot water'll be ready soon," he said, apparently oblivious of her startled expression. "Reckon you'll both be wanting me outta here." He reached over and plucked his hat from a peg by the door. "I'll go take a look around and be back in a coupla hours."

"You're leaving us? What if somebody comes?"

"If you put out the fire and shut the door, nobody's gonna know you're here." Charlie put on his hat and pointed to the gun rack on the wall over the bed. " 'Sides, I plan on leavin' my rifle behind. You can shoot, can't you?"

Kate nodded. "My husband taught me because he was afraid we'd have trouble with wild Ind . . ." Her voice trailed off in embarrassment.

"Look, Kate, if this don't set easy with you . . ."

"Well, of course it doesn't. What this poor

woman must have gone through. . . ." Something in Charlie's expression made her realize he was not referring to the woman's injuries or the fact that he was leaving them.

"Most folks ain't real comfortable with Injuns, so if you want to go home, I'll take ya."

"Now see here, Charlie Hobbs. You needn't be thinking I'm like most folks! I've always been one to make up my own mind, and I don't plan to change now. You just run along and do whatever it was you were going to do."

There was a long moment of silence, and then he nodded and left. Slightly offended by Charlie's obvious assumption, Kate stalked to the fireplace. As if she'd turn her back on someone who needed help, just because of their race! Nobody knew better than she what it was like to fall on hard times and have people turn away.

Though the fire was burning brightly, the water was still tepid. Glancing toward the window, Kate wondered uneasily how long it would be before she could douse the fire. Pulling the cabin's one and only chair over to the bed, she settled down to wait.

Unused to sitting idly, Kate looked around for something to do almost immediately. Charlie probably had a needle and thread as well as a pile of torn clothing tucked away somewhere. Glancing back toward the bed, she was startled to find the Indian woman watching her with her one uninjured eye. "Do you want some water?" Kate asked, pointing to the bucket.

The woman nodded slowly, and Kate went to get

a dipper full of cool water. With Kate's arm supporting her, the woman drank about half a dipper and then indicated that she was finished.

Easing the woman back onto the bed, Kate gave her a friendly smile before returning the dipper to the bucket.

"He is not your man?" The words were slurred and hesitant, but understandable all the same.

Kate turned around and gazed at her in amazement. "You speak English?"

Once again the woman nodded slowly and fixed Kate with that unblinking stare. "The man," she repeated. "You not belong to him?"

"Good heavens, no." Kate came back to the bedside and sat on the edge of the chair. "Charlie and I are friends. After he found you he came to get me, hoping I could help. Are you feeling better?"

"The hurt is not so much now."

"I'm glad." Kate smiled. "What's your name?"

"In your tongue it is Moonflower. By what you called?"

"Katharine Murphy, but mostly people just call me Kate. Where did you learn to speak English?"

Moonflower was silent for so long, Kate was beginning to think she wasn't going to answer. Finally she closed her eye. "My husband is of your people."

"Who hurt you?"

This time Moonflower was silent. She lay still for so long that Kate thought she had fallen asleep.

The water came to a boil at last and splashed over the side of the kettle, hissing as it spilled into the fire. Kate jumped to her feet and rushed to the fireplace. After carefully wrapping the handle with a towel, she pulled the kettle from its iron hook and set it on the hearth.

Charlie took most of his meals with the Cantrells, but Kate managed to find some cornmeal and soon had a small pan of mush steaming next to the kettle. Then she smothered the fire with ashes.

Feeling somewhat less vulnerable without smoke going up the chimney, Kate returned to the bed. She was surprised to find Moonflower awake and watching her closely.

"I thought you might be more comfortable if we got you cleaned up some," Kate said, indicating the mud crusted on Moonflower's arms and clothing. "After that, some cornmeal mush will surely make you feel better."

Moonflower stared at her for a long time before nodding. Kate carried the washbowl over to the table and poured in some of the hot water. She tested the temperature with her elbow and kept adding small amounts of cold water from the bucket until she was satisfied. When she turned toward the bed, she nearly dropped the bowl on the floor.

Standing unsteadily by the bed, Moonflower was slowly and painfully removing her dress. As an only daughter, Kate had been raised with a great deal of modesty. Only Bryan had ever seen her naked as an adult, and she'd certainly never seen another woman so. Nearly as shocking as Moonflower's unabashed nudity was the realization that she wore no underwear.

Only when Moonflower's face turned a sickly yellow color and she began to waver did Kate snap out of her immobility and rush forward. She set the bowl on the washstand and helped Moonflower lie back down on the bed. Averting her eyes from the other woman's body, Kate busied herself with the washbowl.

"I . . . if you'll turn over, I . . . I'll wash your back," Kate stammered, trying to stifle her embarrassment as she wrung out the rag. Moonflower did as she was told, and Kate closed her eyes, praying for strength before attending to her patient.

The sight that met her eyes wiped away all self-consciousness and replaced it with righteous, burning anger. Moonflower's entire back was covered with bruises. Some were still dark purple, but a great many showed the green-and-yellow coloration associated with healing. Crisscrossing the bruises were weals of all sizes and shapes, some still raw, others puckered scars.

Kate felt the bile rise in her throat. Moonflower hadn't been beaten once but many, many times. It had to have taken place over a long period of time, and by someone close to her. Suddenly a thought clicked into place. "Good heavens! It was your husband, wasn't it?" Kate asked in a horrified whisper. "What kind of a monster is he?"

But Moonflower didn't answer.

By the time Charlie was due to return, Kate had done her best to convince Moonflower to stay at the cabin. It seemed the safest place for now.

Moonflower had been reluctant, but Kate had assured her over and over that Charlie wouldn't harm her. The knowledge that she would quite possibly die if she left was the only thing that made Moonflower consider it.

Kate had thought of taking Moonflower home but rejected the idea immediately. Even if Jonathan were willing to take the Indian woman in, which was by no means certain, there was a much stronger chance of her being seen there. Anyone traveling through the area stopped at the Cantrells'. On the other hand, Charlie rarely got any visitors. People either saw him at Jonathan's or caught up with him in town.

Bathed, fed, and dressed in one of Charlie's shirts, Moonflower had allowed herself to be tucked into bed and now lay sleeping peacefully while Kate did her best to clean the stains from her buckskin dress. The sound of the door opening brought Kate to her feet in an instant. She couldn't quite stifle her sigh of relief when she saw it was Charlie.

Putting her finger to her lips, she motioned him back outside, where she joined him. Somehow she wasn't surprised to see Jonathan with him. Charlie had probably asked his partner to help look for Moonflower's attacker.

"She's sleeping," Kate said softly as she shut the door behind her. "You can't imagine what's been done to that poor woman." She proceeded to tell them everything she had discovered. "And I think I've convinced her to stay here, but I don't know for how long."

Charlie nodded. "Good. We didn't find a sign of anybody bein' around, but that don't mean nothin'. Could be he's hidin' out somewhere. You sure it was her husband?"

"She didn't deny it. Be kind to her, Charlie. She's been through so much."

He sighed. "Don't reckon I know any other way to be with a woman." He smiled down at her. "Thanks for your help, Kate. I didn't have an idea in he . . . er, heck what to do."

"I'm glad you found me."

"Are you ready to go home, Kate?" Jonathan asked.

"Yes, I think so. I can't do anything more for Moonflower right now. I'll bring some salve over in the morning and see how she's doing."

It wasn't until Jonathan swung up onto his horse that Kate realized he hadn't brought the wagon. With a sinking feeling she noted the relaxed way he sat in his saddle. He made it look so easy. Still, she knew that the minute she was up behind him, she'd be hanging on for dear life. Should she tell him about her baby now or wait and see what kind of pace he set?

She was still trying to decide, when strong arms scooped her up from behind, and she was deposited sideways in front of Jonathan. A chuckle sounded somewhere near her left ear.

"From the look on your face I'd venture to guess you weren't expecting a boost from Charlie."

Kate discovered that Jonathan's dimples were particularly devastating at close range. "I think his aim was off," she said.

"How so?"

"I'm supposed to be behind you." She fought the feeling that she was drowning in the sapphire pools of his eyes. "I don't know how to get there from here."

"Charlie said you didn't do too well behind the saddle." The dimples deepened. "I think he was afraid you'd fall off."

"I didn't do so bad," Kate mumbled, but she knew this was Charlie's way of protecting the baby without giving away her secret. Uncomfortably aware of the saddle horn against her right hip and the warmth of Jonathan's muscular body on her left, Kate stared at her hands. She'd almost rather take her chances on the back of the horse.

"Kate?" There was a humorous note in Jonathan's voice. "You'll be more comfortable if you relax."

"I'm perfectly fine."

"You're as stiff as a board."

"It doesn't matter. This is the way I want to ride."

"All right, if you say so." Jonathan put his arms around her and nudged the horse with his heels.

Kate's mouth opened in shocked indignation. "What do you think you're doing?"

"I'm going home."

"That's not what I mean." She pushed his arm. "How dare you . . . embrace me!"

"Kate, I have to hold on to the reins." He held them up for her inspection. "Why don't you just relax. I've never molested a woman on horseback, and I have no intention of starting now."

Suddenly she felt very foolish. Jonathan probably thought she was a complete idiot. He was getting her home the only way he could, and here she was acting like a silly schoolgirl. With a sigh, she relaxed and leaned against him. It felt just as nice as she'd been afraid it would.

Jonathan grinned as he watched bright color climb Kate's neck. She really did have the most adorable way of blushing. When she settled her body into his, though, the grin disappeared. He hadn't really thought about how a warm female body sitting on his lap would feel. It was going to be a long ride home.

11

Cole wrinkled his nose as he looked down at the bucket in his hand. "How come you want all the fat from Pa's elk?"

Kate took it from him and set it next to her kettle of lye water. "I'm going to make soap."

"With ashes and fat?"

"That's what it takes."

Cole gave her a disbelieving look. "But it doesn't make sense."

"It does seem kind of silly, doesn't it? Still and all, it's the way my granny taught me to make soap before I was even as old as you are."

"How come you have to do it outside?"

"It smells."

"Glad I ain't a girl." Cole dismissed the whole mysterious process of making soap with a shrug of his shoulders. "Pa told Levi and me we could go with him to check for strays. We may have to go clear to the mountain, so he said we might not make it back by noon."

"Do you want me to throw a lunch together for you, then?"

"Thanks, Mrs. Murphy." Cole took off toward the barn. "I'll go tell Pa."

"I take it that means yes," Kate called after him. Shaking her head, she went into the kitchen. She placed thick pieces of elk roast between slices of her homemade bread and wrapped the sandwiches in a clean dish towel. Adding a few carrots from the garden and three hard-boiled eggs left over from breakfast, she put it all in a flour sack and tied the top. "That should be enough to hold them until supper."

Trying to quell her anticipation, she set out to find Jonathan. When she rounded the corner of the house, her eyes widened in surprise. Jughead was headed toward the garden at a high lope, with Levi and Cole chasing after him. Intending to slow the beast's headlong flight or at least keep him out of her garden, Kate ran to the edge of the corn patch and waved her arms. She might as well have been invisible for all the attention Jughead paid her. He just kept on going . . . straight at her.

On his way to the house, Jonathan had stopped to fill the canteens from the well. Now he stood in dismay, watching the mule bearing down on Kate. The damn fool woman obviously didn't know what kind of danger she was in. Once Jughead got started, nothing would stop him. That blockheaded mule was going to trample Kate into the mud without missing a step.

"Kate!" Tossing aside the canteens, he sprinted toward her. With a flying dive, Jonathan grabbed her and rolled them both out of the way, his elbows and knees taking the brunt of the fall. Tucking her face under his shoulder, he ducked his head just as the deadly hooves thundered past, spraying them with dirt and bits of corn stalk.

"Pa"—Cole's voice was breathless as he ran up to them—"what happened?"

"Mrs. Murphy just tried to outstubborn Jughead. Get that depraved nuisance under control before he destroys the whole ranch."

"We will, Pa. Levi's right behind him with the rope."

"For God's sake, don't rope him!" Jonathan yelled, scrambling to his feet and staring after his sons.

Shaken, Kate struggled to sit up. "Do you think he could?"

"I doubt it, but with those two you never . . . Lord, Kate, are you all right?"

"Yes, I think . . . oh!" Kate gasped as Jonathan hoisted her to her feet. She wavered, and he caught her in his arms.

"You're hurt." His deep voice was filled with concern as he pulled her closer and gazed down into her face.

"N-no," she murmured, vaguely surprised that her air supply suddenly seemed inadequate. "Just a little d-dizzy, that's all." She breathed in the strangely wonderful aroma of leather, horses, and Jonathan.

Instead of catching her balance, Kate felt her

knees weaken. With her heart pounding, she raised her hands to push him away, but they came to rest on his chest, and she lacked the strength to do more. His skin, warm and vibrant through the thin cotton of his shirt, seemed to pull the energy from her fingers, leaving her helpless to resist him.

It was as if an invisible force held them together as their eyes locked for a timeless moment. Then he lifted his hand to brush a streak of dirt from her cheek. "Kate?" he whispered softly.

She was incapable of reply. Her lips parted slightly, and she melted closer into his embrace. With a soft sigh, her eyes drifted shut as his mouth closed over hers in a gentle kiss. The hard strength of his body and the unexpected softness of his mustache flowed through her in a warm surge of pleasure. Sensations she'd thought never to feel again stirred to life deep within her.

"Pa!" Cole's voice from the back of the house struck them both like a bucket of ice water. Jerking apart, they stood staring at each other in disbelief.

Both boys rounded the corner of the cabin, Cole leading Jughead by the reins of a halter and a glowering, disheveled Levi stomping along beside him. "We caught him, Pa."

"I see that. How did he get out in the first place?"

"I went to saddle him like you said, only when I opened the gate he ran over me." Levi glared at the now docile animal. "I hate that damn mule."

"Levi, a gentleman never swears in front of a lady."

"Sorry, Mrs. Murphy."

"Oh, Levi," Kate said, touching a long scratch on his forearm, "are you hurt?"

A little embarrassed by her concern, Levi brushed some of the dirt off his pants. "Nah, I bumped the fence a little is all."

"What do you want me to do with Jughead?" Cole asked.

"He only gets frisky when he has too much freedom. Guess we haven't been working him enough lately." Jonathan bent over and retrieved his hat from among the squash vines. "Take him back to the corral and tie him to the fence. He should be calmed down by the time we get home this afternoon."

With a self-conscious glance at Kate, Jonathan went to pick up the canteens he had cast aside in his mad dash to rescue her. How did one apologize for an impetuous kiss? he wondered. He'd never felt the need to do so before.

"Jonathan?"

Reluctantly he turned back to her. "Kate, I don't—"

"Your lunch," she said, holding out the flour sack with an uncertain smile.

Their eyes met, and a flash of understanding passed between them. Kate had no more wish to discuss what had happened than he did.

Jonathan took the bag. "Thanks." He gave her a long look before he turned away. "We'll be back by late afternoon."

For once Kate was glad of the tedium of making soap. She had so much to think about. What in the world had possessed Jonathan to kiss her like that? No doubt he'd been overcome by her great beauty. Adding the melted fat to the boiling lye, she smiled at the ridiculous notion. More likely he'd been prompted by a surge of lust. Men tended to give in to their baser instincts without thinking.

Her own actions were of more concern. She still felt married to Bryan, so why had she melted so easily in Jonathan's arms? It didn't make sense, even if Jonathan was one of the handsomest men she knew. She sighed. Who was she fooling? Jonathan Cantrell was the best-looking man she'd ever seen, and for a long time she'd been wondering what it would be like to kiss him. Still, there was a big difference between wondering and actually doing. It felt like betrayal.

Closing her eyes, she wondered how to tell him she was pregnant. Surely he'd let her stay. She might not be able to do her full load of work for a while after the birth, but he'd understand . . . wouldn't he? Jonathan's very presence there was mysterious, yet she had no reason not to trust him. Even Clay seemed to, though they'd obviously been on opposite sides in the war.

Clay. What was she going to do about him? He'd been to see her four times since their aborted picnic and was more attentive with each visit. She liked him well enough, enjoyed his company, even, but she felt uncomfortable with the idea of being courted by anyone.

Then there was the problem of what to do about her brother. Kate hadn't seen Patrick since that day nearly three weeks ago by the creek, but she knew he hadn't left the area. The last thing he'd said was that he'd get word to her somehow if he had to go. Opening her eyes, she peered into her kettle of thickening soap and wondered why her life was so very complicated.

A slight movement to her left drew her attention and very nearly a scream. Four Indian braves stood there, watching her silently. Dressed only in breechclouts and moccasins, with their long black hair loose around their shoulders, they looked terrifying fierce. Frozen in fear, Kate stared at them, her spoon suspended in midair over the kettle. Her heart slammed in her chest as she remembered dozens of horrible stories she'd heard about what Indians did to white women.

A long moment passed, and the Indians' enigmatic expressions did not change. Kate had never been so close to any before, except for Moonflower. Moonflower! Could these be her people? Though Kate had been to see her almost every day for the last two weeks, the Indian woman had avoided every question about her past. As Kate looked at the four braves, she became convinced they'd come looking for Moonflower. They might even be her brothers. A little bit of her fear dissipated at the thought.

Finally one of the men gestured to the kettle and spoke some words in a guttural language.

"I . . . I don't understand."

The brave pointed to the kettle again and put his fingers to his mouth as though he were eating.

"You're hungry?"

He gestured once again.

"Oh, no." Kate shook her head. "You can't eat this."

Not understanding her words, the Indian repeated his demands, and again Kate refused him.

Apparently tired of the selfish white woman, one of the others stepped forward and wrested the spoon from her hand. Dipping it into the thickening mass, he took a bite. His expression didn't change as he passed the spoon to the next brave.

"No, no. You don't understand, it's not to eat," Kate said desperately as the second Indian took the spoon and tasted the lye soap.

With sudden inspiration she dashed into the kitchen and grabbed a loaf of bread. She returned to the kettle just as the last Indian had taken a spoonful from it. Like his companions, his face remained impassive as he handed Kate her spoon.

"Here," she said, holding out the crusty brown loaf. "Eat this instead."

All four men looked at the bread, then at each other. As one, they turned and walked away.

"No, wait," Kate called, running after them. "I know where Moonflower is."

Ignoring her, they mounted their horses and headed out onto the prairie.

Helplessly she watched them ride away, certain that she had spoiled Moonflower's one chance of being reunited with her people. Suddenly an idea sprang to life in her mind. If she could ride Jughead to Charlie's place, she might get there in time for Moonflower to catch the four men.

Dashing into the garden, she grabbed a handful of carrots and headed for the corral. What if the

Indians caught her away from the house and she couldn't make them understand about Moonflower? The thought of what could happen to her made her stomach clench with fear. No, that was cowardly thinking. Moonflower needed to know. Kate tried to squelch her fear as she arrived at the corral.

Jughead looked sound asleep. A carrot held under his nose got his attention immediately, however, and he munched it down. Praying that Jonathan had been right about the mule calming down, she untied the halter reins from the fence and led him over to the gate. Once they were through, she climbed up the rails and swung her leg over Jughead's back. Leaning forward, she held another carrot out to him. The mule swiveled his head around and took the offering in his teeth, then started off down the trail to Charlie's.

Kate tried not to think about what would happen if Jughead decided to run away with her, or even that her soap was ready to go into the molds. Her priority was reuniting Moonflower with her people.

Despite her fears to the contrary, the trip went without mishap. Every time Jughead stopped, Kate gave him another carrot, and they would be on their way again. Though it seemed like hours they reached Charlie's cabin within thirty minutes. Kate slid to the ground and tied Jughead to a tree.

"Moonflower," she called, running to the open door of house. After finding the cabin empty, Kate scanned the clearing. "Moonflower, where are you?" Around the side of the house, Kate saw

Jonathan's elk hide staked out on the ground to dry. Moonflower's work, of course, but where was she?

As soon as she saw Kate was alone, Moonflower stepped out from behind a tree. "Something has happened?"

"They've come for you," Kate said breathlessly.

Moonflower's face paled. "Who?"

"Your brothers. Well, I'm not positive about that, but I'm sure they were your people." Kate told Moonflower of her visitors. When she finished the Indian woman shook her head.

"Not my people," she said. "I am Blackfoot, this not their land."

Kate's mouth dropped open. "But . . . but couldn't they have come looking for you?"

Moonflower turned away. "To my people I am dead."

"Your family thinks you're dead?"

"I run from husband. Family turn away."

Kate was aghast. "But he beat you! Doesn't that matter?"

Moonflower shrugged. "It his right."

Kate started to say how unfair she thought such an attitude was, but Moonflower's closed expression stopped her. Perhaps the subject was better left alone. "If they aren't your brothers, I rode that stupid mule all the way over here for nothing."

Moonflower laid a hand on Kate's arm. "We hide," she said urgently. "Horses come."

"Horses? Where?"

Moonflower tugged on her sleeve. "They come, hurry."

Some of the other woman's panic seeped into

Kate. With a frightened glance over her shoulder, she picked up her skirts and ran to the trees. Moonflower pulled her down and under a bush.

"Make no noise," Moonflower whispered as she lay down on the other side.

Within seconds Kate could hear the pounding of hooves on the road. Someone was approaching very rapidly, but who? Maybe the Indians? Biting back a whimper, she cowered even farther under the bush.

"Charlie!" Jonathan's frantic voice rang through the trees. "Charlie, we've got trouble!"

"It's Jonathan and the boys," Kate said, scrambling out from her hiding place. "Something's wrong." She reached the front of the cabin just as Jonathan turned away from the open door. "What happened?" she cried.

"Kate! Thank God!" He swiftly closed the distance between them and swept her into a fierce hug. "You're all right."

Before Kate had a chance to respond, he thrust her away and glared down at her. "What in the name of sanity do you think you're doing?"

"What am I doing?"

"Don't you know any better than to go wandering off by yourself?"

Kate stared at him. Had he lost his mind? "I come here all the time by myself."

"You could have at least left a note."

"Oh, for pity's sake," Kate snapped. "Since when do I have to tell you where I go?"

"Since I saw twenty Indians less than a mile from the house!"

"Twenty? What an exaggeration. Those 'twenty' Indians looked more like four to me."

"What?" Jonathan roared. "You knew there were Indians around and you still walked over here?" Kate winced as his fingers dug into her shoulders. "Where there's one there's usually more. We ran into a whole damn hunting party!"

"Of course I knew there were Indians. That's why I came, to tell Moonflower!" she replied angrily. "And if you'd take time to look around, you'd see I didn't walk. I rode Jughead."

"You rode Jughead!" Jonathan's face turned an alarming shade of red, and blue sparks seemed to shoot from his eyes. "Of all the moronic . . . That intractable brute nearly ran you down less than two hours ago." He shook her. "What in God's name were you using for brains?"

Kate had had enough. With an angry jerk, she wrested herself out of Jonathan's grip. "Let go of me, you big bully. I'm your housekeeper, not your wife. I go where I want, when I want, and have no intention of asking your permission to do so. You have no right to treat me this way, and I won't tolerate it. If you can't control yourself, you can find someone else. You're setting a terrible example for your sons." She stepped back and folded her arms across her chest. "Do I make myself clear?"

Jonathan blinked. He had been thwarted so seldom in his life that he didn't know how to react. A movement near the cabin drew his attention. The sight of Charlie with a milewide smile on his face didn't help matters. Where the devil had he come from?

"I said, do I make myself clear?"

"Abundantly," he said. "Now, if you're finished telling me off, do you suppose we could go home?"

Ignoring Jonathan's sarcastic tone, Kate glanced toward Moonflower and was surprised to see Charlie standing there. She'd been so involved in her argument that she hadn't even noticed him ride up. Since Charlie was home, there was no reason for her to stay. "Yes, I'm finished here."

"Fine. Levi, you lead Jughead, Kate will ride with me," Jonathan ordered.

She whirled around and glared at him. "No, I won't. I rode Jughead over here. I'll ride him back."

"If he runs away—"

"I didn't have any trouble before, and I don't think I will now. If I do, I'm sure you can catch him on that monster you ride." Kate knew she was being reckless but didn't really care. Jonathan Cantrell was far too used to getting his own way. She untied Jughead and led him over to a stump. Before she could mount, however, Jonathan lifted her onto the mule's back.

"I just have one question," he asked. "How did you get rid of the Indians?"

She smiled mysteriously. "I fed them."

12

"*Lunch about ready?*" Jonathan asked, taking off his hat.

His mournful tone made him sound so much like Levi or Cole when they imagined themselves starving that Kate couldn't help grinning. "Pretty close. Are you hungry?"

"Yup. It's been a long morning, but we've got the roof on the barn."

"Great. Are you going to have enough shingles to cover it?"

"I don't know. Charlie's got the boys working on it, but even with all four of us making them, we may not have enough before the snow flies. How was your visit with Moonflower?"

"Fine." Kate jumped when Jonathan's sleeve accidentally brushed her cheek as he reached past her to get a cup from the cupboard. His nearness always had a disturbing effect on her. "I came back a different way and found a deserted cabin down by the creek," she said, hoping the innocuous topic would calm her pounding heart. "It doesn't look like it's been empty very long."

"It hasn't." Jonathan poured himself a cup of coffee. "A German named Hofflemeir homesteaded there a year or so ago. He made it through one winter, then pulled up stakes and left. Seemed awfully anxious to get out of here."

"Oh. I suppose that's why he left the cookstove behind."

"Probably."

Kate watched Jonathan sit down at the table. She knew it was past time to tell him of the baby. If she didn't get on with it, he'd know pretty soon anyway. It obviously wasn't something she could hide forever. Setting aside the churn, she cleared her throat. "Jonathan, there's something I've been meaning to talk to you about."

"Oh?" Jonathan's heart sank. He'd known he couldn't avoid this conversation forever, but so much time had passed that he'd begun to think Kate had forgotten about the stolen kiss. "The boys haven't been acting up, have they?"

Kate shook her head. "No more than usual. This isn't about them. It's more personal."

"You want a raise?"

"No, er . . . that is, I'd take one, of course, but that's not what I wanted to discuss."

Resisting the urge to grab his hat and run for the door, Jonathan took a sip of coffee and eyed her over the rim of his cup. "What is it, then?"

"Well, you see . . . er, that is . . . I—"

A sharp knock at the door interrupted her. As she went to answer it, she didn't know whether to be relieved or irritated.

"Clay!" Kate was surprised to find him standing on the doorstep. He rarely visited in the middle of the day.

"Good afternoon, Kate."

Even as she welcomed him, Kate couldn't help wishing he'd waited ten minutes.

"Is Jonathan home?"

"He's just having a cup of coffee before we eat. Would you like to stay for lunch?"

"I don't mean to intrude."

"Nonsense. We have plenty, and it's always nice to have company. It won't take but a minute to set another place."

"Then how can I refuse?"

Feeling as though he'd been given a stay of execution, Jonathan greeted his guest with real pleasure. "It's good to see you, Clay, but you might want to reconsider staying to lunch. She's been known to feed visitors lye soap, you know." His eyes twinkled, and he pretended to ignore Kate's outraged gasp.

"That's what I heard," Clay said with a smile, "but I'll take my chances. Actually I came to tell you the news."

"Oh?"

"Just got word from Cheyenne that Governor Campbell's territorial census is finished."

"It's about time," Jonathan said. "They've been working on it since May."

"True, but it's a big territory. Campbell divided it

up according to population, with five counties and three council districts. Our district gets to send three representatives to the legislature next month. Are you willing to run?"

"Lord, no. I've had enough politics to last me a lifetime. What about you, Clay? You'd be a natural."

Clay grimaced. "You forget. I fought on the wrong side of the war."

"Seems to me the war is over and best put behind us. There's no shame in a man fighting for what he believes in."

Clay gave a humorless laugh. "Unfortunately, most people aren't so open-minded. In case you've forgotten, Governor Campbell was a good Yankee. I doubt he'll be as complacent as you."

"I met John Campbell when I was in the army. He didn't strike me as the kind to hold a man's past against him." Jonathan shrugged. "Besides, representatives are elected, not appointed. Most people around here don't give a tinker's damn about Confederates or Yankees either one. If you run as a rancher instead of a southerner, I'd say you have good a chance of winning."

"You'd have a better chance," Clay protested.

"I doubt it. Even if I wanted to go, it might be spring before the legislature gets everything ironed out. I couldn't very well leave Kate and my boys here to take care of things. But your operation pretty much shuts down in the winter. A foreman and a few men could handle anything that comes up."

"God, Jonathan, you almost make it sound like I have an obligation to go!" Clay gave Kate a rueful grin. "And he thinks I'd be a better legislator. I swear, that silver tongue of his could talk the moon out of the sky."

"Does that mean you're going to run?" Kate asked as she refilled their cups.

"I suppose so." Clay sighed. "There are just too many important issues to be decided. Taxes, water rights, and there's even some talk of giving women the right to vote."

Jonathan nearly choked on his coffee. "You're joking!"

"From what I hear, Esther Morris is already bending the ear of every prospective legislator within a twenty-mile radius of South Pass City."

Jonathan gave a snort. "She'll never get any man to introduce such a ludicrous bill."

"Ludicrous?" Kate repeated. "Why do you say that?"

Jonathan shrugged. "No woman ever took the time to find out what the issues are, let alone investigate the merits of one candidate over another."

"I'd like to know how you can be so sure of that," Kate burst out. "I've never met a man yet who would listen to a woman's opinion on anything, including politics." Her fists planted firmly on her hips, she glared at Jonathan. "Maybe if you took time to ask, you'd find out a thing or two."

"With all due respect, Kate, I think you're wrong." Jonathan gave her an infuriating smile. "If women's suffrage ever comes to pass, they'll vote for whoever their husbands tell them to."

"Of all the dunderheaded, close-minded . . . You mark my words, Jonathan Cantrell. There will come a time when women have the same rights as men, and the world will be a better place for it."

"Well, if they do, it'll be long after I'm dead. For that I'm heartily thankful."

Kate turned her glare to Clay. "How do you intend to vote, Mr. Langton?"

"I . . . ah . . ." Nonplussed by the unexpected attack, Clay was grateful that Charlie chose that moment to come in for lunch. Kate left to get him a cup of coffee, but when she returned, it was obvious she still expected a reply.

"Well . . ." He cleared his throat. "If I ever had the chance, I guess I'd have to say yes." Jonathan made a disgusted sound, and Clay gave him an apologetic shrug. "Thanks to Abraham Lincoln, ex-slaves are able to vote. It's hard for me to see them given a right my mama and sisters are denied."

"I'm sorta curious," Charlie said. "If you was given the choice, Jon, would you let womenfolk vote or not?"

"I'd vote no on a bill like that, but I don't suppose it would matter much if it did pass. Once women got the right to vote, they'd undoubtedly settle down and we wouldn't hear another word from them."

"That's all you know about it!" Kate muttered to herself.

Just then the boys came trooping in for lunch, and the question of suffrage was lost in their excited chatter.

"We saw a big old rattlesnake just layin' out on a rock down by the creek, Pa." Levi's eyes sparkled with excitement as he held out his freshly washed hands for Kate's inspection. "I thought they didn't like the hot sun."

Jonathan was happy for the change of subject. "They don't during the summer. The one you saw was probably soaking up the last of the warm sunshine before fall really hits."

"Do you call these clean?" Kate frowned over Cole's hands.

"Aw, Mrs. Murphy, they ain't that bad."

Raising her eyebrow, Kate pointed to the door. With a sigh, Cole turned to go wash his hands again.

Charlie ignored Cole's theatrics. "Them snakes show up in some mighty strange places this time of year. Can't stand the cold."

"That's true," Jonathan said, settling back in his chair. "During the round-up last fall, I woke up one morning and found a bullsnake curled up in my bedroll with me. I was lucky it wasn't a diamond-back."

"My friend Dan had a run-in with a rattler a coupla years back right in his own cabin," Charlie said. "First cold day he lit a fire and was warmin' himself in front of it when he heard this kinda slithery noise behind him. Turned around and found himself face to face with the biggest rattler he'd ever seen. Jumped clean out the window. Reckon he didn't cotton to sharin' his fire."

Smiling at what she was sure was another of Charlie's tall tales, Kate dished up lunch.

It wasn't until after Cole and Levi went to bed that night that Kate had another opportunity to tell Jonathan of her impending motherhood.

Jonathan closed the boys' bedroom door and joined Kate at the table. "They're still talking about that snake. I think I convinced them not to try trapping him, but I hope the snake has enough sense to be somewhere else tomorrow morning."

Kate looked up from her mending. "With those two after him, I almost find myself feeling sorry for the snake."

"So do I." Jonathan chuckled as he put on his glasses and opened his ledger. For several minutes the scratch of his pen was the only sound in the kitchen.

At last Kate laid aside her mending. "Jonathan?"

"Hmmm?"

"About the conversation we had this morning."

He glanced up with a twinkle in his eye. "Don't tell me. You're going to start wearing bloomers, smoking cigars, and marching with that Anthony woman."

"What?"

"Weren't we discussing suffrage?"

"No, not that conversation, the one we had before."

"Oh." The twinkle disappeared.

"I don't know a polite way to tell you this."

He sighed. "I've been expecting you to bring it up."

"You have?"

He took off his glasses and rubbed the bridge of his nose. "Look, Kate, sometimes I do things without thinking."

"Jonathan—"

"No, let me finish. I should have apologized when it happened, but—"

"Jonathan, I'm with child."

"I thought it might be easier if . . . Wh-what?"

"I'm going to have a baby."

"A baby?" His face paled. "Good Lord."

"I should have told you before, but I didn't quite know how. . . ."

"When?"

"W-well," she stammered, startled by his reaction. "I'm not really sure, but I think February."

Jonathan winced. February wasn't all that far away. "Then it's your husband's?"

Kate's mouth dropped open in surprise. "Of course it's Bryan's. Who else . . ." Suddenly she realized what was going through his head. With a cry of outrage she jumped to her feet. "You thought it happened at the Golden Spur?"

Embarrassed to admit that she was right, Jonathan rose from his chair and held out his hand. "Now, Kate . . ."

"You honestly thought I was a whore." Her voice wasn't much more than a whisper, but it quivered with anger and pain. "Is that why you kissed me? Because you thought one kiss more or less would hardly matter to a prostitute?" Her voice cracked on the last word and she turned away, angrily brushing the tears from her cheeks.

"Kate, for God's sake." Jonathan reached out to touch her shoulder. Then, thinking better of it, he curled his hand into a fist and let it drop to his side. "I never thought you were a whore," he said quietly. "I did think something might have happened to you at the Golden Spur that . . . well, some men don't take no for an answer. I didn't really mean to question the parentage of your child."

There was a long, tense moment of silence. When Kate finally spoke, Jonathan had to strain to hear her words.

"Then you don't mind about my baby? I can stay?"

"Can you stay? Good Lord, Kate. Did you think I'd throw you out? I don't know how we'd ever get along without you."

"I . . . thank you." She didn't know what else to say. "I think I'll go to bed. I'm rather tired."

Jonathan watched her go, cursing softly when the door shut behind her. He'd certainly handled that poorly. A baby! God! He closed his eyes, remembering when his wife, Mary, had told him she was pregnant for the second time. She'd been so excited. He stood for there for several minutes looking into the past.

It was well past midnight when Kate awoke. Disoriented at first, it took her a minute to realize what had wakened her. Then she heard it again—a low cry, almost like a moan. Thinking that one of the boys must be sick, she climbed out of bed and tiptoed to the door.

The sight of Jonathan seated at the table with his head resting on his crossed arms came as something of a surprise. The moan came again, and she quickly went to his side. "What is it, Jonathan?" she asked, touching the back of his head.

"Kate?" He raised his head and peered at her through bleary eyes.

For the first time she noticed the empty bottle sitting on the table next to the open ledger and the heavy, sweet odor of whiskey in the air. "You're drunk!"

"S'pose I am. God knows I tried hard enough." He leaned back in his chair with a sigh. "Didn't help, though. Whiskey ran out too soon."

"Good heavens, if you drank any more, you'd pass out."

"That's what I wanted."

"What on earth for?"

His head wavered back and forth slightly as he looked up at her. "To forget, of course. Don't you ever miss Bryan so bad you can't stand it?"

"Yes, but I don't try to drink myself into a stupor." Her expression softened. "It's your wife, isn't it?"

"Sweet little Mary." His eyes closed, and his face scrunched up in pain. "God, how I miss her."

"I know, Jonathan, I know," she said. "But sitting here won't help things. I think it's time you went to bed."

His eyes popped open and focused on her nightgown. "It's late?"

"Very."

With a weary sigh, he heaved himself to his feet and swayed as he stood.

"All right," Kate said. "Put your arm around my shoulders and I'll help you to bed." She slipped one hand around his back and nearly staggered under his weight when he put his arm around her and sagged against her side.

His warm breath against her ear caused an odd

little twist in her middle. "Ah, Kate, what a delightful armful you are," he said softly, his lips brushing her hair in a light caress as they stumbled toward his room.

Kate wasn't the least bit impressed. "And you are very drunk!"

"Can't deny that." As she tried to navigate through the door, he bumped against the wall and nearly knocked them both to the floor. "But I was stone sober the first time I ever laid eyes on you. The way you looked in that red dress . . . Damn, if ever a woman was built for loving . . ." He collapsed on his bed. "Your Bryan was a very lucky man."

Squelching the surge of pleasure his words gave her, Kate tugged on his boot as his eyes drifted closed and his head lolled to the side. Realizing that he'd fallen asleep, Kate smiled as she pulled off his other boot and spread the quilt over him. In the half-light of the moon he was breathtakingly handsome, but there was a vulnerability there, too. Unable to resist, she brushed a lock of hair from his forehead with her fingers.

"I'm sorry, Mary," he murmured in his sleep. "Forgive me."

Startled, Kate stared down at him for a moment, then reached out and touched the side of his face. "Mary loved you, Jonathan. I'm sure she forgave whatever you did."

"She couldn't have. I killed her."

13

Thoughts of Jonathan's confession kept Kate awake all night. It explained why Mary's picture lay hidden in the bureau, why Jonathan had feelings of guilt so intense that he had drunk himself insensible, even why he and his sons were living out here in the middle of nowhere. So why couldn't she believe it?

Heaving a sigh, she climbed out of bed when the sky outside her window paled with the early light of dawn. After splashing water on her face, Kate frowned at the dark circles under her eyes. Then she turned away from the tiny mirror and slipped into her dress. Who would notice, anyway?

She was building the fire in the cookstove when the boys came out of their room, already dressed and whispering between themselves. They came to a halt when they saw Kate.

"Mrs. Murphy! You're awake."

"I couldn't sleep. Where are you two headed so early?"

"Ah . . . we're just going out to hunt for a little while before breakfast," Levi said, sidling toward the door.

"With no gun?"

The boys exchanged glances. Then Cole flashed her an uneasy smile. "We left it in the barn yesterday."

Kate's eyes narrowed. "What are you up to?"

"Up to?" Two pairs of eyes widened innocently. "We're just going hunting."

"Yeah, but we'll be back in time for breakfast."

"All right, but if I find out you've been up to mischief . . ."

"Don't worry, Mrs. Murphy," Levi called back over his shoulder. "See you later."

"Don't worry," she muttered, turning back to the stove. They had probably decided to shoot something really obnoxious like a skunk or a porcupine. Ever since she'd promised to cook any meat the boys brought in, there'd been a steady stream of game. Considering some of the strange things that had found their way into her kitchen so far, Kate had a suspicion the boys were testing her.

On her way back from milking Suzette, Kate met Cole and Levi halfway to the house.

"Done milking?" Cole asked with just a shade too much innocence.

"Why else would I have a bucket of milk?" she asked sardonically. "I thought you were going hunting."

"We did."

"And you're back already?"

Levi shrugged. "We changed our minds."

"Good," Kate said. "Then you won't mind gathering the eggs for breakfast, will you?"

"Aw, Mrs. Murphy . . ." Cole began.

"Be glad to," Levi put in quickly as he delivered a sharp pinch to his brother's arm. "Anything else you want us to do for you?"

"No." Kate gave them an odd look. "Just bring the eggs in before you do the rest of your chores."

"We'll be back in a flash."

Kate turned back toward the house with a shake of her head. No doubt she'd find out what was going on soon enough.

Inside, she set the milk on the hoosier and put on her apron. Unable to do anything about the boys' scheme, whatever it was, Kate turned her mind to the day ahead. First breakfast, then she'd set some bread to rise before she finished harvesting the garden.

They'd been lucky that the frost had held off this long. Soon the leaves would change colors, the geese would fly overhead on their way south, and the cold autumn winds would blow. Mornings were already uncomfortably cool.

She stoked the fire and bent over to pick up another piece of wood. It fell from her fingers as a terrified scream froze in her throat. A huge rattlesnake lay in the woodbox, coiled and ready to strike.

Run! her mind yelled, but her body was paralyzed by fear. Only her breath moved, whistling in and out with ever-increasing speed.

A shred of sanity remained aloof from the panic. It was this small part of Kate's conscious mind that noticed the rattles weren't moving, and then that the snake's head wasn't even attached to its body. The creature was dead! She staggered to a chair and collapsed with a whimper of relief. Feeling dizzy, she sank her head into her hands and closed her eyes.

This time those two hellions had gone too far. They needed to be taught a lesson. As her heart slowed and her breath calmed, a plan began to form in her mind. She lifted her head and gazed at the window, now bright with the morning sun. What she was thinking was truly rotten. In fact, she ought to be ashamed of herself for even considering such a thing. A slow grin spread across her face. It was perfect.

If Kate's conscience told her Charlie and Jonathan would become victims of her revenge on the boys, she reminded herself they both deserved it as well. The men's snake stories had no doubt given the boys the idea for the prank in the first place.

By the time Cole and Levi came in with the eggs, Kate was standing at the hoosier calmly mixing biscuits for breakfast. She looked up with a smile. "Thanks." Pretending to ignore their surreptitious glances toward the woodbox, Kate went back to her stirring. "Say, if it isn't too much trouble, Levi, would you fill the water bucket for me?"

"Sure."

"Oh, and, Cole, I could really use another armload of wood if you've got time."

"Wood? You mean in the woodbox?"

Kate glanced up. "Well, of course in the woodbox. Is something wrong?"

"Ah . . . no, but Pa likes me to feed the horses before—"

"Go get Mrs. Murphy her wood, Cole, and no more back talk," Jonathan growled from his bedroom door. All it took was one glare, and both boys were out the door in a second.

Still dressed in the same clothes he'd been wearing the night before, Jonathan seemed as oblivious of his rumpled condition as of the dark stubble on his face. It was impossible to imagine this pathetic creature killing anyone, let alone someone he loved as much as Mary. Kate watched him sympathetically, but her words were hardly encouraging as she set a cup of coffee in front of him. "Feeling a little under the weather this morning?"

"A little." He peered at her through bloodshot eyes. "Did you by chance put me to bed last night?"

"Yes, but it wasn't by chance." Kate went back to the hoosier and began dropping biscuit dough onto the pan. "You couldn't even stand up by yourself, much less make it all the way to your bed."

Jonathan watched her silently for several moments. "Do I have anything to apologize for?"

"No."

"But you don't approve, do you?"

"It's not my place to approve or disapprove of anything you choose to do."

"If it were your place, I'm sure you'd lecture me on the evils of drink."

"That depends."

"On what?"

"On how often this happens."

"Very seldom. I'll admit I used to do it quite regularly, but that was years ago. Now I usually have more control." He sighed when she made no reply. "Go ahead. I can see you're bursting to give me a piece of your mind."

Kate walked over to the table and studied him. "I'll admit the temptation is strong, but I doubt I could improve on what Mother Nature has already done." Her lips twitched slightly as she turned away. "It appears you understand the evils of drink quite well this morning."

"Here's your water, Mrs. Murphy." Levi set the brimming bucket next to the stove just as Cole came in with the wood. Kate had a difficult time keeping a straight face while the boys carefully arranged the wood so as not to bury the snake too deeply.

"Thank you," she said when they had finished. "I appreciate it."

"Mrs. Murphy's going to need extra help for a while, boys," Jonathan said. "From now on it's your responsibility to fill the woodbox and the water bucket. I'll take over the milking."

"Oh, Jonathan, that's hardly necessary," Kate began, but he cut her off with a shake of his head.

"Don't be stubborn, Kate. You have no business lifting heavy buckets or swinging an ax, and you know it. I'd better not see you trying to ride that stupid mule again, either."

"Are you sick, Mrs. Murphy?"

"Good heavens, no. It's just that . . . I . . . ah . . ."

"She's going to have a baby." Jonathan finished for her.

"A baby," Levi said in awe.

Cole was, as usual, less easily satisfied. "How is she going to do that?" he asked suspiciously.

"We'll discuss it later," Jonathan said, the barest hint of a blush visible beneath his tan. "It's time the three of us had a talk anyway, I suppose. Go finish your chores so Mrs. Murphy can put breakfast on the table."

When Cole and Levi returned, Kate found herself unable to resist teasing them a bit. Seemingly picking them at random, she put several more pieces of wood in the stove. She could almost hear the boys holding their breath as she came closer and closer to the snake without uncovering it.

Much to Levi and Cole's disappointment, breakfast passed without incident. It wasn't long before Charlie arrived and the meal ended. Cole and Levi each cast one last look at the woodbox before following the men out to work.

As soon as the door closed behind them, Kate grinned. "And now, my fine friends," she muttered, rolling up her sleeves, "you'll find out what my brother has known for many years. I always get even!"

By the time lunch rolled around, there was a cold wind blowing from the north, and dark gray clouds covered the sky. "Reckon it's a mite early for this kind of weather," Charlie remarked as he sat down at the table. "Feels like snow."

"It does at that." Jonathan looked out the window. "I never heard of it snowing this early in September, though."

"You keep forgettin', Jon. This here ain't the East. Knew an old trapper who said he'd seen it snow in every month of the year. In fact, he told me about a killer blizzard they had in the middle of July."

"Really?" Cole and Levi asked in unison.

Their wide-eyed attention was all the encouragement Charlie needed. It wasn't long before he was spinning an incredible tale of horses growing winter coats in a matter of hours and flocks of geese walking south because their babies were too young to fly.

Hanging on Charlie's every word, Cole and Levi hardly noticed when Kate filled their bowls for the second time. Jonathan, however, spent a good part of the meal watching Kate with a worried expression on his face.

"Kate, are you feeling all right?" he finally asked in a low voice.

"Why, yes. I'm fine."

"Are you sure? You've hardly touched your food, and there are dark circles under your eyes."

"I'm just not very hungry," she lied, blushing guiltily. His unexpected solicitude surprised and embarrassed her. Stifling a stab of remorse, she reminded herself that he deserved this trick as much as anybody else.

At last Charlie's story came to an end, and the boys sat back with satisfied grins on their faces. After polishing off his third bowl, Charlie scooted back his chair and patted his stomach. "Them was mighty fine vittles, Mrs. Murphy. Don't know as I ever tasted anything quite like it before."

"Why, thank you, Charlie. I wasn't quite sure what to do when I saw what the boys had brought me to cook this morning." She smiled benignly as the boys' eyes widened in horror and they glanced at the woodbox.

"Oh?" Jonathan said. "And just what is this new creation of yours?"

"Well," Kate said, taking a sip of coffee, "I guess you'd call it rattlesnake stew."

14

"Who ever heard of a blizzard in the middle of September?" Kate grumbled, looking out the window at the thick blanket of snow.

Jonathan grinned as he buttoned his coat. "Sometimes I forget how green you are. In a blizzard the wind blows, and the snow piles up in drifts. This was nothing more than an early snowstorm."

Kate stared at him incredulously. "You call that a simple snowstorm? Good heavens, there must be two feet of snow out there. I spent half the night listening to the tree limbs break under the weight of it."

"I know, and that probably wouldn't have happened in a blizzard. The wind would have kept the snow off the trees. It was the combined weight of the snow and the leaves that did the damage. But don't worry. We may have lost a little of our natural windbreak, but we'll have plenty of firewood this winter."

"I suppose so. Do you think Charlie will make it over today?"

"It's hard to say." Jonathan's eyes twinkled. "Might be afraid of having leftover stew for lunch."

"There wasn't any left. The four of you ate it all."

Kate turned back to the window, hiding a grin. The reaction to her stew had been all she could have wished for. None of them actually got sick, but they all thought about it. "I was just wondering if Charlie would brave the snow today."

"He's been spending a lot more time at home lately."

"I've noticed." She glanced at him questioningly. "Do you think it's because of Moonflower?"

Jonathan's dimples appeared. "Well, it's not because he suddenly developed a taste for his own cooking."

Kate sighed. "I was afraid of that. Moonflower seems quite taken with him, too."

Jonathan's smile faded. "What's wrong with that?"

"Have you forgotten her husband?"

"No, I haven't forgotten. It just never occurred to me that it was any of my business. They're both adults, and no one forced Moonflower to stay. She made that choice of her own free will." There was an ominous note in his voice that Kate had never heard before. "Charlie may have taken Moonflower to his bed without benefit of clergy, but he's a hell of a lot better than the animal that beat her half to death."

Kate was shaken by the sudden disgust in Jonathan's voice. "Oh, I didn't mean—"

"I never realized you were such a self-righteous prig," he continued, ignoring her protest.

Kate shook her head. "That's not what I meant. It's nothing to me if Charlie and Moonflower spend all their time . . . together. But what if her husband comes back? They both might be hurt, or even killed."

There was a long silence. Finally Jonathan took his hat from the peg and set it on his head. "Don't underestimate Charlie Hobbs. He was living by his wits when you were still playing with dolls." He turned to go. "I'd better get the milking done."

Kate fought back unexpected tears as he stomped out and slammed the door behind him. Why did Jonathan's opinion mean so much to her? she wondered. Pregnant women were supposed to be overly emotional. Perhaps that was why she felt like crying.

Giving her eyes an angry swipe, she set to work fixing breakfast. What did she care what Jonathan thought? The last thing she wanted was a close relationship with him, especially if he'd killed his wife. As usual, the thought brought a surge of denial from her heart, and she shoved it away in disgust. Why was it that she couldn't believe anything bad about him? He certainly didn't have any problem thinking the worst of her.

Actually, Jonathan Cantrell's opinion was the least of her worries this morning, she thought as she mixed dough for biscuits in the big enamel bowl. Winter had arrived, and all she had to wear outside was a thin shawl. She'd fully intended to make herself a warm coat long before the first snowfall, but there were so few women around Horse Creek, and Abigail Cline didn't stock much in the way of fabric. Reluctant to make her new coat out of one of Abigail's ugly gray blankets, Kate had waited, hoping another shipment of supplies would arrive before winter. But, as usual, whenever she procrastinated she wound up paying the price one way or another.

Kate felt like a fool as she stripped the blanket from her bed and wrapped it around her body. If she had to wear a blanket, at least she should have sewn it into a proper coat first. Of course, with Jonathan milking and the boys God knew where, there was very little chance anyone would see her as she went to gather the eggs for breakfast anyway.

As she stepped through the door, Kate squinted in the almost painful brightness of reflected sunlight. Cole's and Levi's tracks broke the pristine surface of the knee-deep snow. Unfortunately, there was nothing resembling a usable path.

Hiking her skirts as high as she could, Kate attempted to keep to Jonathan's footprints, but his strides were too long for her to match. Within four steps she realized the futility of it and gave up trying to minimize the discomfort as she plowed ahead.

By the time she reached the side of the outhouse she was cold, wet, and decidedly grumpy. Any vestige of guilt left for serving them all rattlesnake stew the day before had disappeared. In fact, she was beginning to wish it had given them all a good case of indigestion instead of just a moment or two of squeamishness.

Kate jumped as a masculine voice hissed into her ear, "Ssst! Katharine."

She sagged in relief when she saw who it was—Patrick. Her irritation and fright were forgotten as she hugged him. "I've been so worried about you." Then she tilted her head back in sudden fear. "Bullwhip found you. That's why you're here, isn't it?"

He chuckled. "You're still the same, always worrying over nothing and thinking the worst."

"Nothing! That man has been trying to kill you for the better part of six years."

"True, but I've always managed to stay ahead of him. Besides, I'm safe for now."

"Just because you're working for Clay Langton doesn't mean Bullwhip won't be able to find you."

He grinned down at her. "That's what I came to tell you. Bullwhip has already been here and left."

"What?"

"A drifter came through a couple of days ago. Turns out he'd ridden with Bullwhip and his gang for a month or so but quit when they headed up to Montana."

"Montana? Are you positive?"

"That's what the man said. Something about a woman, I guess. Anyway, Bullwhip should be gone at least until spring."

"You think he'll be back?"

"It's hard to say." Patrick shrugged nonchalantly. "He's never left before. Maybe I finally lost him."

Kate looked skeptical. "Why did this drifter tell all of this to a stranger?"

"He didn't tell me. It came out at a poker game in the bunkhouse. Everybody thought I was asleep already, so I know it wasn't a setup."

"I don't know, Patrick. It seems a little too coincidental to me."

"See what I mean? You always think the worst. Besides, I didn't say I wasn't going to be careful anymore. I'm not that stupid."

"I don't see why you don't just go to a United States marshal and tell him what's going on."

Patrick stared into her face sadly for a few moments. "I didn't tell you everything, Katharine. While I was still with the gang one of them was captured and thrown in jail. To escape execution he gave a description of everyone he'd ridden with, including me." Patrick was silent for several seconds. "As far as anyone knows I'm still part of the gang and as guilty of their crimes as the worst of them. If I go to the law, I'll hang."

"Oh, Patrick." Kate grasped the lapels of his coat. "There must be something someone can do. Jonathan's a powerful man. Maybe he could . . ."

"Could what? Katharine, he doesn't know me. He'd have no reason to believe my innocence."

"But I know you couldn't have done those things. Surely I could convince him."

"Katharine, Katharine." Patrick's voice held a note of gentle admonishment. "You haven't seen me for almost seven years. The first thing your Jonathan would tell you is that you couldn't possibly know what I have or haven't done."

"If he met you, he'd know."

Patrick sighed. "Would you trust this man with my life?"

Two days ago Kate might have answered yes, but things had changed drastically since then. How could she vouch for a man who admitted to killing his own wife?

"Neither would I," Patrick said, taking her silence as a negative answer.

"Well, what about Clay Langton? He knows you well enough to realize you're not a criminal."

"The colonel doesn't know spit about me, Katharine. I'm just a cowhand. He doesn't spend a whole lot of time with his hired help. Besides, you forget what I'm accused of. How do you think Colonel Langton would react if he knew I was wanted for murdering innocent women and children? Southern women and children."

"Clay will listen to reason. I'll go with you. . . ."

"Oh ho, so it's Clay now, is it?" Patrick's grin had a touch of admiration as he looked down at her. "I'll be damned. It is you he's sparking after all. The men have been talking about it, but I didn't believe them. Figured you and that Cantrell fella had something going."

Kate's face turned fiery red. "I don't have anything going with anybody," she said. "I work for Mr. Cantrell, and Mr. Langton has been kind enough to take me for a buggy ride now and then. That's all there is to it."

"Sure, and just who do you think yer foolin', Katie gal?" The Irish brogue rolled off Patrick's glib tongue with ease. "Is this the same colleen who used to worry about no man wantin' to marry her? Here she is leadin' not one, but two of the poor devils on."

"I don't have time for your nonsense, Patrick." Kate glanced toward the barn, half expecting to see Jonathan or one of the boys. "If you insist on staying hidden, we'll have to find another place to meet. You take an awful chance every time you come here."

"Got any ideas?"

Kate bit her lip pensively. "If I talked to Rosie, I'll bet she'd let us use a room at the Golden Spur."

"At the saloon?" Patrick was clearly shocked by the suggestion. "It's not a fit place for you."

"Oh, for pity's sake, Patrick, I worked there for most of a month. Do you have any better ideas?"

He thought for a moment. "No, I guess I don't, but when?"

"I have to go in for supplies once a month. I'll just make sure I always go on the second of the month around, oh, say, two o'clock. No one will be suspicious of my going to visit Rosie and Frenchie."

"Can you trust them?"

"I won't tell them you're my brother."

Patrick was aghast. "But they'll think . . ."

"So what if they do. If I know Rosie and Frenchie, they'll probably be pleased I found a man."

"You missed me, you missed me!" Levi's singsong voice wafted to them from somewhere near the barn.

"That's my signal to leave," Patrick said, giving her a quick kiss on the cheek. "The colonel said he was going to need a few hands all winter, so it looks as though I'll be staying. If anything comes up before the second, I'll get word to you." With another hug, he was gone.

Sighing, Kate turned and trudged through the snow to the small pen where the chickens were kept. She wasn't even aware of the sapphire eyes that had watched the entire encounter from the dark interior of the barn.

Jonathan had finished milking and was just getting ready to leave the barn when he saw Kate step out into the bright sunlight. Setting the steaming bucket on the floor, he pulled on his gloves as he watched her contemplate the deep snow at her feet. Unwilling to face her so soon after their argument, he crossed his arms and leaned against the wall brace.

He knew if he looked into her eyes and saw pain, he'd feel horribly guilty. He had realized that he'd misunderstood her as soon as he'd mentioned Moonflower sharing Charlie's bed. The shocked look on Kate's face told him she hadn't even thought of it before, but by then he'd dug himself in so deep he didn't know how to get out gracefully.

Vaguely embarrassed by the whole situation, Jonathan told himself he wasn't hiding in the barn. Rather, he was saving Kate the discomfort of coming face to face with him so soon. Watching her hop from one of his footsteps to another, he couldn't help but grin. Nothing ever seemed to throw her, not even knee-deep snow without a trail to follow.

His smile faded when he noticed she was wearing a blanket wrapped around her body for warmth. It hadn't even occurred to him that Kate didn't have proper winter clothing. Damn the woman, anyway. Didn't she have wits enough to ask for the things she needed? It wasn't as if he'd ever—

Jonathan's thoughts suddenly skidded to a halt. He'd been so intent on Kate, he hadn't even noticed the man hiding behind the outhouse until Kate was almost there. He had just opened his mouth to call out a warning when Kate turned and saw the man. Instead of screaming in panic, she threw herself into his arms and hugged him.

Openmouthed, Jonathan watched in stunned amazement as the two carried on what appeared to be an animated conversation. Whoever the stranger was, Kate seemed to know him quite well, even allowing him to touch her cheek in such a familiar manner that Jonathan gritted his teeth in anger.

Just as Jonathan was about to make his presence known, Kate glanced toward the barn with a worried expression on her face. Could it be she didn't want him to know about her visitor? Stepping farther into the shadows, Jonathan scowled. Who was this stranger, and why was Kate acting this way? What was she hiding?

If Jonathan had any doubts about his reading of the situation, they disappeared as soon as Levi started taunting Cole from the back of the barn. The strange man gave Kate a quick kiss and melted back into the trees.

Before Kate had even passed the barn door, Jonathan had slipped out the back into the corral. With a few curt words he ended his sons' snowball fight and sent them to the house with the bucket of milk. In less than five minutes he'd saddled his horse and set out after Kate's mysterious visitor.

The trail was easy to see but difficult to follow. Jonathan's horse floundered more than once in the deep snow. It wasn't long before his quarry came into view, riding along a high ridge. Keeping out of sight as much as possible, Jonathan became more puzzled than ever. Rather than trying to hide, the man seemed to be gathering cattle.

After nearly an hour, Jonathan rode to the top of a rise and looked down on Clay Langton's ranch. Far below he could see the man he had followed drive the small herd of cattle to the creek, then turn his horse toward the ranch house. After riding nonchalantly into the corral, he dismounted, unsaddled his horse, and walked into one of the many outbuildings. The mysterious stranger obviously worked for Clay Langton.

Turning toward home, Jonathan tried to put the puzzle pieces together. In spite of Kate's obvious affection for the man, Jonathan didn't think he was simply one of her suitors. Though Kate was very open about her relationship with Clay, her actions with this man had been furtive, as though she didn't want anyone to see him. Suddenly an unwelcome suspicion entered his mind. Could Clay be involved, too?

Before he could reject the ridiculous notion out of hand, he suddenly remembered an incident at the beginning of the war. He and five others had been assigned to transport a secret shipment of gold bullion. About an hour from their destination they were attacked by men in Confederate uniforms. The first shot grazed Jonathan's temple, and he was knocked unconscious.

When he came to he was lying on the ground in a puddle of blood. Disoriented at first, he thought it was his own but soon realized it belonged to one of his fallen comrades. Apparently the attackers had thought him dead, too, for a nearby figure in gray was digging through the wagon, oblivious of any threat.

By the time Jonathan realized he was lying on his rifle, the soldier was holding the strongbox with a triumphant smile on his face. Supporting himself unsteadily on his elbows, Jonathan took aim and shot. There was a cry of anguish from his intended target, and then everything went dark once more.

When Jonathan awakened again, he was in an army hospital. That was when he met Matt McNesby, the head of Union espionage, and became a spy. The gold was never located, and though the Union army cleared him of any implication, it had never been offical. The shadow of suspicion had been part of his cover during the war.

For the first time it occurred to Jonathan to wonder why Clay Langton had chosen to settle so close to him when he had his choice of land. And what about Kate Murphy? Had she and Clay really met for the first time a few months ago? They had certainly gotten chummy in a hurry. Jonathan wondered if he had walked into a trap by hiring Kate Murphy as his housekeeper.

Were they after the sensitive information still locked away in his mind? Could the Confederacy have traced the missing gold shipment to him? With a feeling very much like nausea, Jonathan realized he couldn't discount either possibility, no matter how remote. Nor could he trust the woman he called Kate.

15

"*You're not in trouble*, are you, Kate?" Rosie's eyes were filled with concern.

"No. I just need a place to meet my . . . friend."

"If he's a friend, why can't you meet him at home?"

Kate blushed. This was turning out to be harder than she had anticipated. "Jonathan can be . . . difficult. Besides, P—uh, Tom and I can't be alone there."

"If he's just a friend, you don't need to see him alone."

"Rosie, please. I can't explain right now, but I promise you it's nothing for you to be concerned about."

Rosie's face relaxed into a grin. "Somehow I can't imagine you doing the sort of thing that would concern me."

"Then you'll help us?"

"I'll have to clear it with Red, but as long as it's during the day I can't see any problem."

Kate closed her eyes in relief. "Thank you, you're a true friend."

"I'm not so sure about that, but I guess you're old enough to know your own business."

"Kate!" Frenchie's high squeaky voice was Kate's only warning before she was enveloped in a perfumed hug. "You aren't coming back to work here, are you?"

"No, I just stopped in for a minute," Kate said, hugging her back. "It's good to see you both."

"Do you have time for a cup of coffee?" Rosie asked. "It isn't as good as you used to make, but it's hot."

Putting her hands on the small of her back, Kate stretched to ease the ache that had settled there. It might feel good to rest for a few minutes. "Well, maybe a quick one. I have to get over to the store, then right home."

Frenchie made a face. "If I had to go see Abigail Cline, I'd have a shot of whiskey instead of a cup of coffee. After that I'd think of some good reason to put it off until later."

Kate laughed. "That's why I have to go today. I've already put it off too long. As it is, I got caught without a coat last week when it snowed, because I didn't want to make one out of those ugly gray blankets she has in stock. I still don't, but I doubt she's got anything better."

"Wait a minute." Frenchie gave Rosie a look. "Isn't that cloak Meg left behind still upstairs?"

"That's right. I'd forgotten all about it." Rosie shook her head as Kate began to protest. "You might as well have it. Meg ain't coming back, and it's better than one of Crabby Abby's blankets. It won't take me a minute to fetch it."

Frenchie took Kate by the arm and led her back to the kitchen. "Now what's this I heard about you and Clay Langton?"

Glad she had mastered the skill of driving, Kate climbed onto the wagon seat and slapped the reins on the horse's rump. It had been so nice to sit and visit with her friends, though Rosie and Frenchie had given her a hard time about both Jonathan and Clay. Grinning to herself, Kate headed the wagon out of town. It was kind of fun to pretend she had two handsome men madly in love with her.

Then she sobered. Jonathan certainly wasn't. He didn't act as if he even liked her anymore. In the five days since they'd had their misunderstanding about Charlie and Moonflower, he'd barely spoken to her. The few times she'd caught him staring at her, his expression had been odd, almost as if he didn't quite trust her. With a shrug, Kate tried to tell herself it didn't matter, but she was miserably aware that it did.

A few ruts and an occasional puddle were all that remained of the unseasonably early snowfall, but they made the going rough. By the time she reached home, her backache had intensified from all the bouncing around. She climbed down stiffly and stretched before starting to unhitch the horse from the wagon.

"Want me to put the horse away for you, Mrs. Murphy?"

"Why, yes. Thank you, Levi. I am a little tired. I'm not used to driving, I guess."

"Did you already drop the supplies off at the house?" Jonathan asked, stepping out of the shadows near the back of the barn and peering into the empty wagon.

"I didn't get any this trip."

"Then why did you go to town?"

"I . . . I needed something warmer to wear this winter." Feeling distinctly dishonest for not telling him the whole truth, Kate felt herself blushing uncomfortably.

Jonathan glanced suspiciously at the garish yellow wool of her new cloak. In spite of the huge black buttons and rows of heavy braid, the garment was obviously not newly made. "Abigail sold you this?"

Kate noticed his accusing tone and suddenly forgot her dismay at the slight vulgarity of the cloak. "No. Mrs. Cline doesn't stock much in the way of women's clothing. Frenchie and Rosie gave me an old cloak of Meg's until I can find something more suitable. Now if you'll excuse me, it's getting late, and I need to go start supper."

Jonathan watched her flounce off to the house. He was almost certain she was hiding something. That telltale blush of hers was a dead giveaway. Yet he could think of nothing nefarious that she could have done in town. Actually, it was hard for him to imagine Kate Murphy doing anything underhanded.

*   *   *

Kate was setting the table for supper when the first cramp hit her. "Oh, no," she whispered, gripping the back of a chair until the pain passed. Her back pain had continued to worsen all afternoon until her whole body ached. Headachy and nauseated, she had promised herself an early bedtime. Now she closed her eyes and prayed that it was simply exhaustion and that a good night's sleep would take care of it.

The second pain hit, with double the intensity of the first. "Oh, please, God, no," she whimpered, her throat working convulsively as she tried to deny what was happening.

"Kate?" From the doorway Jonathan took in her pasty complexion and her whitened knuckles gripping the chair. In three strides he was at her side. "What's wrong?"

Still fighting the agony of the second contraction, Kate opened her eyes and stared up at him. "Jonathan?"

"I'm here, Kate."

"Help me!" she cried, grabbing the front of his shirt. "Please don't let my baby die."

"Your baby? Oh, Christ." He caught her in his arms as she crumpled toward the floor. "Levi, Cole," he called over his shoulder as he carried Kate to her room. "Catch up with Charlie and tell him to get Moonflower over here as fast as he can. Kate needs her."

He laid her on the bed and stared at her helplessly. "Wh . . ." He swallowed hard, then forced the words past the knot in his throat. "What do I do, Kate?"

"I don't know. Just don't leave me."

"I won't," he said hoarsely. Sinking to his knees, he took her hand in his and held it tightly. "I'm right here."

When Cole and Levi came to say that they'd found Charlie, Jonathan nodded and sent them outside again. True to his word, he never left Kate's side, though he suffered a thousand agonies she never knew about. Ignoring the impropriety of the situation, he helped her out of her dress and under the blankets. Then he gently bathed her forehead with cool water and murmured encouragement. Never once was she aware of the hell he was going through as she gripped his hand for comfort.

"Jon?"

Jonathan raised his head and breathed a sigh of relief when he heard Charlie's voice at long last. "In here," he called. "Did you bring Moonflower?"

"Yup. Soon as she heard Kate was needin' help, I had a hard time keepin' up with her. What's the trouble?"

Jonathan continued to hold Kate's hand as Moonflower pushed past Charlie and moved to the bedside. "I'm afraid she's losing her baby," he said quietly.

Moonflower glanced at him, then back at Kate. "Her man not needed here. You go now."

Jonathan nodded and gave Kate's hand a squeeze before he released it.

"Jonathan?" Kate's voice quavered.

"I'll be right outside, Kate."

Moonflower gave the two men a meaningful

look that sent them both out the door with no further delay.

Charlie gripped his friend's shoulder reassuringly. "I reckon Moonflower knows what to do."

Jonathan nodded. "She's bound to know more than I do." He glanced toward the stove and sighed. "Guess I better feed the boys or Kate'll have my head for neglecting them."

Supper was subdued. Jonathan told the boys Kate was very ill and left it at that. They had just started to clear the table when Moonflower appeared with a tiny hide-wrapped bundle in her hands. Without a word she closed Kate's door and went outside. Jonathan and Charlie exchanged a glance and then went back to the dishes.

When Moonflower returned a short time later, she went straight to the stove and began to pour hot water from the kettle and cold from the bucket into the washbowl; she kept on combining the two until she seemed satisfied with the temperature. Then she took the bowl and returned to the bedroom.

The dishes had been washed and the boys sent to bed before Moonflower came out again. "She sleeps now," she said, "but her spirit very sad." Wrapping herself in her blanket, she walked out into the night without another word.

"Reckon that means it's time to go," Charlie said, rising from the table and putting on his hat and coat.

"Tell Moonflower thanks for me, Charlie."

Jonathan sat in the kitchen for several long minutes after the door had closed behind his partner. Then, with a deep sigh, he removed his glasses and

rubbed the bridge of his nose. He closed his
ledgers, laid the glasses next to them on the table,
and cleaned his pen. The familiar task was soon
completed, and he rose.

Lantern in hand, he walked to Kate's door and
stood staring at the sleeping woman. Breathing a
sigh of relief, he saw that Moonflower had cleaned
up all signs of the miscarriage. A part of him had
been afraid of what he would find in the tiny room.

The nightmare was over, and the heartbreak-
ing reality of the last time he'd been involved in
a birthing was reduced, once more, to an old
memory. Unbidden, his mind had blended past
with present. As he'd held Kate's hand it had
become Mary's, too. As he'd sponged the feminine brow, his words of loving comfort had been
for his wife as well as Kate. But now the memories of Mary's terrible cries in the throes of childbirth were fading from his mind, leaving only
concern for Kate.

Even against the white of her nightgown, Kate
looked pale and drawn, with dark circles clearly
visible under her eyes.

Under the light of the lantern her eyelids fluttered and opened. Vaguely disoriented, she tried to
focus on the familiar silhouette in the doorway.
"Jonathan?"

"I'm sorry. I didn't mean to wake you."

"That's all right."

"How do you feel?"

"A little weak, I guess."

He nodded. "Well, I'll let you go back to sleep,
then."

"No!" she said quickly. "Please. I . . . I don't want to be alone."

Jonathan paused and then came into the room. He hung the lantern on the wall hook and gazed down at her. "Do you want some supper?"

Kate shook her head. "No. I'm not hungry."

"A drink of water?"

"No, thank you." Kate reached a self-conscious hand to her hair. The normally tight bun hung halfway down the back of her head in disarray. "Would you mind handing me my brush?" she asked, fumbling weakly with the pins.

With a crooked smile, he shook his head and picked up her hairbrush from the washstand. If that wasn't just like a woman. Here it was the middle of the night, she had just gone through hell, and all she could think of was her hair.

Having removed the last of the pins, Kate took the brush from him with shaky fingers and began to pull it against the snarls.

Jonathan watched her awkward attempts for several minutes, then gently removed the brush from her grasp. "Here, let me give you a hand with that. Can you turn on your side?"

Kate stared up at him with huge brown eyes, then silently offered him the brush and rolled to her side.

He settled himself on the edge of the bed and began to brush her hair. It took only a few strokes to remove the snarls, but he continued as he felt her relax under the rhythmic motion. Pulling the bristles through the thick mass, Jonathan was amazed that he'd never noticed what pretty hair she had. Curling softly around his hand, the brown strands felt like silk. It was much like Kate herself. Its beauty was hidden unless one took the time to look beneath the surface.

He began to hope Kate would fall asleep, soothed by the gentle strokes.

"It was a boy," she said quietly, "the son we always dreamed of."

"Kate . . ."

"Bryan and I had such plans. A farm, children, growing old together . . . all my dreams died with him. Nothing mattered anymore until I discovered I carried his child. Suddenly life was worth something, I had a reason to go on." She paused. "This baby was my last little bit of Bryan, and now it's gone, too."

"Kate . . ." Jonathan gently turned her face toward him. "Don't torture yourself like this. It's all right to grieve. Let it out, scream, cry . . . do whatever it takes, but don't hold it all inside."

For a full minute she stared at him, and then her eyes filled and she burst into tears. "Oh, God, Jonathan. It hurts so bad."

Pulling her into his arms, Jonathan closed his eyes and held her tightly as she sobbed against his shoulder. "I know, Kate. I know."

16

"We'll be out on the range most of the day. Is there anything you need before we go?" Jonathan asked from the doorway.

Kate picked at the blanket covering her. "No. I'm fine. Thank you."

With a nod he turned to leave, and Kate gazed listlessly at her shuttered window. For the past three days Jonathan had been wonderful. From letting her sob out her heart in his arms to keeping the boys outside and telling her not to get out of bed until she felt fully recovered, he had been kindness itself. So far all she'd felt like doing was sleeping. Perhaps there was something very wrong with her, she thought as her eyes descended slowly. Perhaps she should . . .

The sun was well up in the sky when she awoke again. Blinking against the brightness, she realized that Moonflower was standing in front of the open window shutters, looking down at her. "Moonflower?"

"You get up."

Kate shook her head. "No, I'm sick, I—"

"You not stay here anymore," Moonflower said, reaching down and pulling the blankets away from Kate's body.

"Oh, I don't think—"

"No, think too much." The Indian woman produced a pair of soft moccasins and slipped them onto Kate's feet. "Body fine. Spirit sick." Pulling insistently on her arm, Moonflower forced Kate to get up.

Kate tried to protest as Moonflower threw a blanket around her shoulders and pushed her into the kitchen. "Why are you doing this to me, Moonflower?" Kate muttered. "I thought we were friends."

"You make me well. Now I help you."

In her weakened condition, Kate found it impossible to resist Moonflower's determination, even when the other woman pulled her through the front door and down to the creek.

They continued downstream until they came to a small pool formed by a long abandoned beaver dam. Willows grew in profusion along the grassy bank. Wondering why Moonflower had brought her here, Kate gazed around the pleasant little clearing. A strange dome-shaped structure sat nestled between two huge clumps of willows. Somewhat less than chin high, the whole thing was covered with animal hides with a flap over what appeared to be the door. A thin plume of smoke curled up from a hole in the roof.

"What is it?" Kate asked.

"A sweat lodge. I make for you."

"For me? I don't understand."

"When Kate help me, I not know her ways, but my hurts heal."

"You mean this will somehow make me better?"

Moonflower tapped her heart. "It make well here."

Kate's eyes traveled from her friend to the sweat lodge. Building the odd little structure must have taken a lot of work, and Moonflower had done it for her out of friendship. "What do you want me to do?"

Following Moonflower's cryptic instructions, Kate soon found herself seated inside the dark sweat lodge, stark naked and more than a little uncomfortable. In the middle of the floor was a pile of heated stones over which Moonflower sprinkled water. Steam rose up around the two women in a dense cloud. At first Kate had trouble breathing the heavy, moist air, but she soon found herself almost enjoying the sensation of pulling it into her lungs.

"How will this help?" she asked.

My people do this to . . ." Moonflower made a gesture with her hand. "Not know the word . . . take away unclean things. . . ."

"Purify?"

Moonflower nodded. "Yes, to purify spirit so it heal." With that she began to chant in an unfamiliar language as she swayed back and forth.

Kate watched her for several minutes. Then she closed her eyes and let herself drift as Moonflower's chants surrounded her, weaving in and out of her mind with the wisps of steam. Kate could not tell how much time passed, but the black curtain slowly lifted from her heart.

At long last Moonflower motioned for Kate to follow her outside. Expecting to dry off and get dressed, Kate was surprised and then alarmed when Moonflower grabbed her arm and ran toward the beaver pond.

At first the cold water on her hot, sweaty skin made her lungs contract in an agonizing gasp. Then, almost as quickly, her body adjusted to the temperature, and the water felt like liquid silk against her skin. The sensation was like nothing she had ever experienced before, the pure sensual pleasure of water caressing her limbs.

The two women swam in the cool water until Moonflower indicated that it was time to leave. Drying off and dressing in her nightgown, Kate was amazed at the difference the sweat lodge had wrought. Though the heat had sapped her strength somewhat, she actually felt renewed and invigorated.

When they returned to the cabin, Kate tried to thank Moonflower, but the other woman just shook her head. "Moonflower's spirit heal, too." With that she was gone, leaving Kate to wonder what she had done to deserve such a remarkable friend.

Several hours later Jonathan returned, creeping softly into the house to keep from disturbing Kate. Inside, he came to an astonished halt. No longer was Kate languishing in a darkened room, as he had expected. Not only was she out of bed and dressed, she was pulling a loaf of bread from the oven.

"Should you be up?"

Kate looked up in surprise. "Oh, Jonathan, I didn't hear you come in." She straightened and set the bread on the table. "Actually I'm feeling much better. Moonflower built a sweat lodge for me and took me down for what she called a healing sweat."

"And it cured you?"

"Well, it certainly helped. Land sakes, what are those two fighting about now?" Kate asked as Cole's and Levi's voices floated through the open door.

Jonathan stepped out of Kate's way as she hurried outside. Hanging up his hat, he smiled when he heard her breaking up the fight. Damn, it felt good to have things back to normal again.

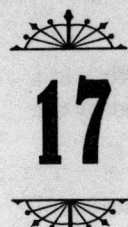

17

"*Good afternoon, Kate.*"

"Clay! Come in."

"Actually, I was hoping you'd go for a ride with me," he said with a smile. "I brought my buckboard."

"Well . . ." Kate glanced at her spotless kitchen. Jonathan had gone to town, and the boys were out with Charlie, so she didn't need to start supper for a while. "Sure, why not. Just let me get my wrap."

After throwing her cloak around her shoulders, Kate shut the door and took Clay's arm. "Any news on the election?" she asked as he handed her up into the buckboard.

"That's one reason I came over." Clay climbed into the driver's seat and picked up the reins. "I wanted you to be the first to hear the good news."

"News?" Her eyes widened. "Good heavens, do you mean you won?"

He gave her a boyish grin. "You're looking at a full-fledged territorial delegate duly elected by the people."

"Oh, Clay, that's wonderful!"

"I guess Jonathan was right about the election." He snapped the reins across the horses' rumps. "Although I can't say I'm very comfortable about being a politician."

"You'll do a fine job," Kate said. "When do you leave?"

"By the end of next week, I hope."

"So soon?"

"I should be able to to get my affairs in order at the ranch by then. Luckily I have a good foreman and a couple of hands I can trust to take care of things this winter."

"This winter!" Kate looked at him in surprise. "How long are you planning on being gone?"

Clay shrugged. "It's hard to say, but with all that has to be done I imagine it will take us most of the winter, if not longer."

"Good heavens. I thought Jonathan was exaggerating when he said it would take so long." Kate felt a twinge of regret. "I'll miss you," she said, touching his arm.

Clay put a hand over hers. "I'm glad, Kate, because I'll miss you, too."

The warmth of his gaze and his fingers gently caressing hers made Kate decidedly nervous. "Oh, Clay, look." She pulled her hand from his grasp and pointed toward the trees by the creek. "Did you see the deer?"

Accepting the change of subject gracefully, Clay

directed his attention to the animals as they bounded away.

Their conversation ran to small talk until they reached the top of the hill overlooking his place. "I have to check in at the ranch. Do you mind?"

"Of course not. I'd like to see it anyway."

"Good. It won't take long, and I have something I'd like to ask your opinion about."

As they drove into the yard, Kate couldn't help noticing how different Clay's ranch was from Jonathan's. The large two-story house was far more imposing than the Cantrells' modest log cabin, with its sod roof and leather hinges, but Jonathan's barn was more than twice the size of Clay's.

Jonathan had once told Kate that his Hereford cattle were not as hardy a breed as the Texas longhorns Clay owned. Perhaps that was why he felt he needed so much more barn space, even though the Langton herd was considerably larger.

"Here we are." Tying the reins to the brake lever, Clay jumped out and walked around to Kate's side to help her down. "I thought you might like to see my latest addition," he said, leading her into the barn.

After the bright sunlight, Kate's eyes took a few minutes to adjust to the dim interior of the building. It smelled of hay and horses, and she realized it was more of a stable for horses than a barn for cows. The white stallion, Gallahad, snorted as they walked by his stall, but Clay only patted the magnificent animal in passing and continued on until he reached a good-size pen against one wall.

At first Kate saw only a dark brown horse; then

the mare lowered her head to nuzzle a small white form on the floor. When the tiny creature staggered to its feet, Kate gasped in surprise, for there was another foal still lying in the straw. "Oh," she breathed, "twins!"

Clay beamed at her obvious delight. "I thought you might like to see them."

"Oh, yes, they're beautiful, and both of them look just like Gallahad. I would have thought at least one would be a bay like their mother."

"Actually, I'd thought so, too. I didn't think the color would carry through, and I certainly never expected to get both a filly and a colt. These two are even better than I had hoped for. We bred champion racehorses at Golden Oaks, you see, and Gallahad is the last of the line."

Kate could detect the pride in Clay's voice. Jonathan talked about his Herefords in much the same way.

They stayed a few more minutes, admiring the wobbly youngsters, and then walked up to the house. They had barely entered when a door at the end of the hall opened, and Patrick McAnespie came out with some papers in his hand.

"Ah, Fielding. Just the man I was looking for," Clay said, helping Kate remove her cloak and hanging it on the hall tree. "Did you check over those contracts from the cattle buyers?"

"Yes, sir, and everything is in order just as you . . ." Patrick stopped dead in his tracks as Clay stepped back and Kate came into view. "Sorry, Colonel," he mumbled. "I didn't realize you had company."

"That's quite all right. I just stopped by to see if you'd had a chance to sort through the contracts."

"Yes, sir, and they're ready for your signature."

Realizing that Clay had no intention of making Patrick known to her, Kate took matters into her own hands. "Clay, aren't you going to introduce us?"

"Oh . . . ah . . . certainly. Kate Murphy, may I present Tom Fielding? Mr. Fielding works for me."

For the first time Kate found herself wondering if Clay was a social snob. "How do you do, Mr. Fielding?" She held out her hand, smiling mischievously at her brother as he shook it. "I didn't realize Clay had a secretary."

"Actually, I'm mostly a cowhand," Patrick said, grinning.

"I discovered Mr. Fielding had trained extensively at his uncle's bank," Clay said. "His expertise has been most helpful on occasion."

"How interesting," Kate said, watching her brother's face turn red. They both knew he'd run away and joined the army to get away from his uncle's bank.

"I'll just leave these contracts with you, Colonel." Patrick turned to Kate. "It was nice to meet you, Mrs. Murphy."

Kate nodded. "Mr. Fielding."

Clay took the papers from Patrick's hand and guided Kate toward the door at the end of the hall. "Thank you, Fielding."

"He seems like a capable young man," she remarked as Clay closed the door behind them. "Is he one of the men you're going to leave here when you go to Cheyenne?"

"Yes." Clay set the papers on the desk and smiled. "But I didn't bring you here to discuss my cowhands. As I said before, I want to ask your opinion about something."

"Certainly. I'd be most happy to help." She settled herself on a chair by the desk and looked around the room as Clay pulled a key out of his watch pocket and unlocked the desk drawer. This was obviously the library, though very few books lined the many shelves.

Unbidden, the image of Jonathan Cantrell sitting at the kitchen table poring over one of his many well-thumbed volumes flashed into her mind. The differences between the men had never been more apparent than today. Irritated with herself for comparing the two, Kate turned her attention entirely to Clay and the rectangular wooden box he was pulling out of the drawer.

"These are the last of my mother's jewels. She sold the rest to help me build this place." He rubbed his fingers over the polished wood sadly. "I wish she had lived to see it."

"Oh, Clay . . ."

He blinked as though he'd forgotten, for a moment, that she was there. With a sigh he walked around the desk and perched on the edge of it in front of her. "Enough of old regrets. It's time to look toward the future." He flipped open the lid and held out the box for her to see.

Kate's eyes widened. On a bed of black velvet lay the most beautiful necklace she had ever seen. Four strands of diamonds and sapphires came together and connected to one large sapphire in the center. Dangling from it was a small but exquisitely cut diamond.

"It has always been given to Langton brides on their wedding day." Clay touched the single diamond with a finger. "I'm considering having this stone made into the wedding ring. What do you think?"

Dazzled by the jewels, Kate found it difficult to look at the stones objectively. "I'm hardly an expert, but I think the diamond would make a lovely ring." She covered it with her hand and studied the effect. "And really, the necklace is just as pretty without it."

She paused and then looked up at Clay. "You're getting married soon?"

"I haven't asked her yet." He closed the box and set it on his desk. "She's still in mourning for her husband, you see."

"Oh." Kate felt an odd tingle in her stomach.

He grasped Kate's hands and pulled her to her feet.

"Clay, I can't—"

"Shhhh," he said, drawing her into his embrace. "I know it's too soon, and I promise I won't say anything more until spring." Stroking her cheek with the backs of his fingers, he gazed down at her. "You're a very special woman, Kate."

Kate knew that he was going to kiss her, she could see it in his eyes. "I don't think—"

"Good," he whispered against her lips. "I only want you to feel."

Clay's kiss was warmly caressing, a truly pleasant sensation but one that stirred her blood not at all. When it was over, he kissed her forehead lightly. "I don't intend you to forget me while I'm gone, Kate."

Kate felt a lump form in her throat. Why couldn't Clay's kiss have overwhelmed her the way Jonathan's had? She really liked this man, and he obviously cared for her. He was someone a woman could build a future with. If she had any sense at all, it would be his face that haunted her dreams at night, instead of one with blue eyes and dimples.

Holding the letter at arm's length, Jonathan managed to read it without the aid of his glasses. As he deciphered the contents, a slow smile spread across his face.

"Good news?" Abigail Cline asked, peering up at him from behind her counter, her eyes alive with curiosity.

"The best!" Jonathan folded the letter and stuck it in his pocket. "And unexpected, too." He looked up and scanned the shelves. "Did Ox Bruford bring any axle grease in his last trip?"

"Yes, but I'm not sure I have any left," Abigail said. Disappointed that he was not going to tell her anything more, she went to check the supplies left by the freighter a week ago.

While he waited, Jonathan wandered around the store. Though he'd never noticed before, it didn't take him long to realize that Kate had spoken the truth when she'd said that Abigail didn't stock anything for women. No wonder Kate never seemed to buy anything for herself.

"There's one bucket of axle grease left, Jonathan," Abigail called from the back of the store. "Do you want it?"

"Yes." He joined her at the door of her store-room. "Just put it on my bill and I'll settle up with you next week."

"Don't you have time for a cup of coffee and a piece of pie?" Abigail asked as he bent over to pick up the heavy bucket of grease.

"Sorry, I have to be getting home." He managed to look regretful as he said, "Maybe next time."

"If you wanted to answer your letter right away, you could write it here and save yourself a trip to town."

"Thanks, but I don't need to answer it." He tipped his hat. "Good afternoon, Abigail. Thanks again for all your help." He turned and walked out of the store, unaware that Abigail was staring after him.

Climbing onto the wagon seat, he thought of the letter in his pocket again and smiled. His cousin Daniel had just returned from his business trip to England, and he'd brought back the purebred Hereford bull Jonathan had asked him to purchase while he was there. Now both were awaiting him in Chicago. With a slap of the reins, Jonathan drove the wagon out of town, his mind busy with the implications of his cousin's letter.

Daniel must have completed his business early to be back home so soon, Jonathan thought; he really hadn't expected to hear from his cousin until spring, and he certainly hadn't thought about making such a long trip so late in the year. With the new transcontinental railroad, it would take only a few weeks to make all the necessary preparations and travel clear to Chicago and back. Even though it was already the first of October, he could surely be back by November. Winter didn't usually didn't hit hard until a week or two later.

Even so, he was reluctant to leave the boys and Kate alone for such a long time. So many things could happen. Charlie had told him of a man in Dakota Territory who'd intended to leave his wife and daughter alone for only a few weeks, but heavy winter snows had kept him away. Without a rifle and unable to hunt, the woman and child had died of starvation before spring.

Then, too, those Indians could still be around somewhere. Nor had Jonathan forgotten the stranger he'd seen Kate embrace. Who knew what she'd do while he wasn't there to keep an eye on things? It was enough to make him consider taking Kate and the boys along.

Maybe that wasn't such a bad idea, he mused. It would be very educational for his sons, and he would feel much better if Kate were where he could watch her. Besides, the trip would probably do her a great deal of good. Even though she seemed better now, a month after her miscarriage, he'd watched her eyes turn from a happy green to a sad brown on more than one occasion.

Jonathan felt his heart lighten at the prospect of taking his family to Chicago with him.

18

"Is this where we're going to camp tonight?"

Levi and Cole eyed the big rocks lining the stream with undisguised delight. They had been traveling since early morning and were more than ready to put an end to the first day of the trip.

"Don't go wandering off," Jonathan warned them. "You both have chores to do."

"Oh, Pa," Cole groaned. "I thought we were supposed to have fun this trip."

Jonathan appeared much struck by his son's statement. "You know, I'd forgotten that! I guess that means I won't need to set up the lean-to and Mrs. Murphy can skip fixing supper. Oh, and you'd better go tell Mr. Langton he doesn't have to picket the horses for the night. I'm sure he'll enjoy a rest before he gets down to the legislature."

The boys exchanged defeated glances. "What do you want us to do?" Levi asked finally.

"Mrs. Murphy needs a couple buckets of water

and some wood for the fire." Jonathan pulled the canvas cover loose from the sides of the wagon. "If you get a move on, you'll still have time to do some exploring before supper."

Levi grabbed a bucket and took off at a high run. "Last one to the creek is an old cow's tail!"

"That's not fair," Cole yelled, racing after his brother with the second pail. "You cheated."

"Did not."

"Did so."

"Did not. . . ."

Kate shook her head. "Do you suppose those two will ever change?"

"I doubt it." Jonathan grinned. "Makes you wonder what they'll be like as adults, doesn't it?"

Thinking of some of the things Jonathan had said and done in the time she had known him, Kate didn't have to wonder. She already had a pretty good idea what Cole and Levi would be like when they grew up: incorrigible.

"What do you need out of here tonight?" Jonathan asked as he flipped the canvas off the load.

"Just the grub box for now," she said, rolling up her sleeves and adjusting her shawl. "Though I'll need some other things later." She pulled a large pan out from under the seat and lifted the lid to check on the beans inside. Satisfied that they were ready to cook over the campfire after soaking all day, Kate watched Jonathan convert the back of the wagon into a traveling kitchen. "I'm glad Clay was ready to leave when we were."

"So am I." After releasing the tailgate, Jonathan gave it a sharp jerk, and the hinges squealed in protest as he lowered it. "I'll feel a lot better with an extra man along." Supporting the wooden tailgate with his leg, Jonathan fastened it to the chains dangling from the sides of the wagon and then let it drop the last few inches into place. "You never know what kind of trouble you might run into along this trail," he said as he leaned on the board to make sure the chains would hold when Kate used it for a work surface.

"Pa!" Cole rushed back into camp, completely ignoring the water that sloshed over the sides of his bucket. "There's a giant fish in the creek."

Levi was no less excited. "You ought to see it, Pa. It's at least two feet long!"

"Two feet?" Raising his eyebrows, Jonathan looked over the boys' heads. "What do you say, Kate? After they gather enough wood for the fire, do you think you could spare these two? A monster fish like that doesn't come along every day, you know."

Rubbing her chin pensively, Kate pretended to consider his words. "Well, this once, I suppose. . . ."

"Thanks, Mrs. Murphy."

"You won't be sorry when you see that fish."

"Just don't forget the wood," she called after them. She carried the beans to the work space Jonathan had made for her. "Much good it would have done me to say no."

Jonathan grinned. "They knew you wouldn't. You're too much of a sweetheart for that." Startled, Kate looked up at him but he'd already turned away and was busily arranging large rocks for a fire ring. "Of course, with all their yelling and carrying on, that fish is probably halfway to the Missouri by now."

"If he has any sense, he is."

Kate leaned against the wagon and soaked up the sunshine. She hoped that the warm days of Indian summer would stay with them. Casually watching the play of muscles in Jonathan's back as he moved the heavy rocks, Kate imagined herself running her hands across that broad expanse, caressing the golden skin she knew lay beneath his shirt, and winding her fingers through the curls on the back of his head. The sudden realization of what she was thinking brought the daydream to a screeching halt. Horrified by the images she had created in her mind, Kate turned away, a blush of shame flooding her face.

"The horses are all picketed for the night," Clay said as he joined the two by the wagon. "But I think we'd better post a sentry."

Jonathan placed the last rock and stood up, brushing his hands. "I suppose so. There probably aren't any Indians in the area, but there's no sense taking a chance."

Clay smiled. "It's been a while since either one of us had guard duty."

His choice of words brought Jonathan's attention into sharp focus. Was Clay's statement as innocent as it sounded, or did he know about a certain missing Union gold shipment and the one guard who had survived?

"Indians! D-do you think I should call the boys back?" Kate asked.

"Nah, they know not to get out of sight of camp."

As if on cue, Cole and Levi tore around the side

of the wagon, each dropping a load of wood next to the fire ring.

"Is that enough, Mrs. Murphy?" Cole asked eagerly.

"Hmm. I'm not sure. . . ."

"We'll be right down by the creek," Levi said. "Just yell if you need some more." Before the words were out of his mouth he and Cole were on their way out of camp.

"Don't go too far," Kate yelled after them. "Remember to stay close to the wagon." She glared at the two grinning men. "I'm surprised you aren't going with them. I never knew a man yet who could resist a fish."

Jonathan grinned. "Actually, I was planning on it as soon as I get your fire started. What about you, Clay? According to my boys there's a big trout down in that creek just waiting to be caught."

"I haven't been fishing for a long time," Clay said with a gleam in his eye. "Let's get that lean-to up."

In the end, nobody caught the big fish, but there were enough smaller ones to fry for supper. After a satisfying meal of beans, fish, and cornbread, Clay brought out his guitar. His tenor blended beautifully with Jonathan's bass, and they sang every song they could think of. Kate found the combination of male voices oddly moving and was disappointed when Jonathan announced that it was time for bed.

Jonathan and Clay took turns watching the horses, and the night passed uneventfully. They were on their way again shortly after daybreak. The rest of the trip passed in much the same way as they made their way south to the Oregon Trail and then southeast.

Since everyone took turns driving the wagon, Kate never lacked for someone to talk to. She tried to tell herself that it was only a coincidence that both Jonathan and Clay always seemed to be close at hand when the other was driving, but she was female enough to be delighted by the attention of two such handsome men.

On the fifth day they crossed the Platte River bridge, and Jonathan regaled his sons with the story of Lieutenant Caspar Collins, the brave young officer who had given his life holding off Red Cloud's hordes long enough for his men to escape back across the bridge to the safety of the Platte River station. Cole and Levi stared in wide-eyed fascination as they passed the burned-out ruins of the fort that had been renamed Fort Caspar in honor of the twenty-one-year-old lieutenant and then abandoned two years later.

The story found great favor with Levi and Cole, but Kate spent the next five days glancing over her shoulder looking for the Indians who she was sure must be following them. The only times she was truly comfortable were the nights they spent first at Fort Fetterman and then at Fort Laramie.

It wasn't just fatigue that caused Kate to greet the sight of Cheyenne with heartfelt relief. At last, they would be in civilization again. But the feeling lasted until she saw what Cheyenne was like. Though there were quite a few permanent buildings among the many tents, most of them seemed to house establishments of questionable virtue. Chaos was everywhere. Men and horses crowded the streets as the sound of piano music mixed with raucous laughter and drifted through the open doors of the many saloons and bawdy houses.

How Jonathan managed to locate a decent hotel Kate never knew, but she was immensely grateful. After seeing his family settled safely in the hotel, Jonathan went to make arrangements for the train trip east. Clay stood in the lobby with Kate, preparing to take his leave.

"I'll be back to check on the wagon and horses tomorrow," Clay told Kate, taking her hands in his, "but I may not get a chance to see you before you leave."

"I . . . I'm so glad you came with us."

"So am I." He lifted one of her hands to his lips and pressed a kiss on the back of it. "I only wish I were going the rest of the way with you. I won't feel completely at ease until I know you're safe at home again."

"Your responsibility here is too important to spend time worrying about us. We'll be fine."

"Nevertheless, I plan to spend a great deal of time thinking of you, Kate, and looking forward to next spring." Smiling tenderly, he bent down and brushed her forehead with his lips. Then he dropped her hands and walked to the door, where he turned and smiled at her one last time. "Remember me fondly," he said softly, and then he was gone.

With a sigh, Kate stared at the door. Why

couldn't she seem to feel anything but relief as he walked away? They said absence made the heart grow fonder. Maybe it would work for her.

"Are you going to marry him, Mrs. Murphy?" The sound of Levi's shocked voice brought her out of her reverie with a jolt.

Turning, she found both boys looking at her with twin expressions of amazement.

"I thought you were going to marry Pa."

Kate shifted under their scrutiny. "I'm not planning on marrying anyone right away."

"Mr. Langton kissed you," Levi said.

"For goodness' sake, it was only a friendly kiss on the forehead," she said, attempting to dismiss the significance of what they had seen. "Now, let's go look at the rooms and get washed up for supper before your father comes back."

Thinking that she had allayed their fears, Kate turned away. It was just as well for her peace of mind that she missed the look that passed between them.

19

Noon the next day found the four of them standing on the rough-planked platform at the Cheyenne train station. Shifting her feet nervously, Kate clutched the basket of food and smiled in an effort to reassure the boys. She needn't have bothered, as neither Levi nor Cole shared her trepidation.

"Here it comes!" Levi shouted, pointing to a puff of smoke in the distance.

To Kate it seemed as though only a few seconds had passed before the shiny black locomotive arrived amid the hiss of escaping steam and the screech of metal wheels upon the rails. The heavy smell of coal smoke permeated the air. The crew began the task of refilling the huge boilers with water, and the conductor swung down from one of the passenger cars. Kate gazed up at the mechanical monster fearfully.

"Is this your first time on a train?" Jonathan's warm breath fanned her ear as he bent down to make himself heard.

She nodded. "It's silly I know, b-but they go so fast. We'll get to Chicago in half the time it took us to get here."

"I know, I felt the same way my first time." He lifted one of her hands from the handle of the basket and gripped it reassuringly. "Don't worry, Kate, I'll be right here."

Kate tried to force herself to calm down. Though Jonathan's grip on her hand was comforting, it wasn't slowing the pace of her heart any.

All too soon it was time to board, and she found herself being lifted to the bottom step by Jonathan's strong hands at her waist. Following Levi and Cole into the passenger car, she almost welcomed the distraction caused by the inevitable argument that erupted between the two brothers.

"I get to sit by the window."

"No, sir, I'm older."

"So what? I can still beat you."

"Can not."

"Can too."

"Can—"

"Stop that right now," Kate said, "or neither one of you will sit by the window." She pointed to an empty pair of facing seats about midway through the car. "We'll sit there. That way you can each have a window seat."

"I get to ride backwards."

"No, I do."

"Oh, for pity's sake," Kate snapped. "You'll

take turns. Levi, you get the backwards seat to the first station and then you'll switch with Cole."

"How come he always gets everything?" Cole asked.

Levi gave him a smug look as he settled himself on the choice seat. "Because I'm older."

Rolling her eyes, Kate sighed.

"Are you one of those who get sick riding backwards?" Jonathan asked her.

"I have the constitution of an ox. I've never been carriage sick in my life."

"Good, because it does bother me."

Kate turned in surprise. It was the first time the man had ever shown the slightest weakness. Her motherly instincts were instantly aroused by the slightly shamefaced look he gave her.

"Well then, I can take the backwards seat without feeling guilty," she said. "I always like to see where I've been when I'm in a carriage, but I don't like to be selfish about it."

The warmth of his smile instantly melted any guilt she might have felt over the little white lie, and she settled herself next to Levi with a pleasant feeling of well-being.

It wasn't until the train started with a loud whistle and an unpleasant jerk that it occurred to her Jonathan's difficulty had made her forget all about her own anxiety. He answered her suspicious look with a bland smile and turned his attention to his sons' innumerable questions.

Kate never knew if Jonathan's malady was real or invented merely to distract her, for he never mentioned it again. Still, he took care always to sit on the forward-facing seat and seemed a bit pickier about his food than usual.

The boys soon lost their curiosity about their fellow passengers and gazed in awe out the windows at the scenery they were passing with incredible speed. Kate had a little more difficulty adjusting to the cross section of humanity that surrounded them in the smoke-filled car.

Richly garbed gentlemen, strolling through from the first-class section, rubbed elbows with roughly dressed farmers and dangerous-looking individuals with revolvers strapped to their hips. There were few other women, and almost without exception they gave Jonathan more attention than Kate thought seemly. Although none of them did more than give him an appreciative glance as they passed, Kate's lips thinned in irritation every time it happened.

In the middle of the afternoon, the train came to a sudden stop. Nearby rifle fire echoed all the way down the train as an odd thundering noise filled the air.

Terrified that they were being attacked by Indians, Kate reached across and grabbed Jonathan's arm.

"It's all right," he said, patting her hand. "Look."

Peering out the window nervously, Kate gasped in surprise. A large herd of buffalo pounded across the tracks in front of the train, creating a living wave of shaggy hides and gleaming horns as far as the eye could see. As they watched from the train, one of the hulking beasts stumbled and fell to the ground, downed by a sharpshooter's bullet.

Cole turned to Jonathan. "Why are they killing them, Pa?"

"Mostly because the railroad considers them a nuisance, I guess. It does seem an awful waste, though."

Kate was sickened by the senseless slaughter, but by the time all the buffalo had passed in front of the train, she was beginning to understand the railroad's attitude. They had lost the better part of an hour waiting for the animals to move on. Still, she hoped the engineer wouldn't try to make up for lost time by coaxing the locomotive to go even faster.

When they started out Kate was unable to discern any increase in speed, and the rest of the afternoon passed uneventfully. As twilight settled over the landscape, Kate passed out the sandwiches she had prepared before they'd left the hotel that morning. Their hunger satisfied, both boys soon succumbed to the soothing rhythm of the wheels clacking along in the darkness and slept.

When Cole sagged against her, Kate instinctively put her arm around him to keep him from slipping to the floor. At first the position was comfortable, but it wasn't long before her shoulder started to cramp. Moving slightly to ease the strain, she closed her eyes in an attempt to sleep, but soon her back began to hurt.

"Damn," Jonathan muttered from the opposite seat. It looked as if Levi were about to push him off of their seat. "Kate, this isn't going to work."

"I know, but what can we do? There just isn't enough room."

Jonathan was silent for a moment as he considered all the possibilities. "Let's put Cole and Levi together," he said at last.

It took quite a bit of persuading to get the two sleepy boys arranged on the backward seat. Using their coats as pillows, they rested their heads on opposite ends of the seat. "Sleep well," Jonathan whispered, covering them with his coat.

Kate felt her heart expand as she watched. Jonathan might have some dark secrets, but the love he had for his sons was as bright and warm as the sun on a summer day. She couldn't help smiling tenderly at him as he sat down next to her.

"Now for us. If you take your cloak off, we can use it for a blanket," he said, pulling her shawl out of the basket and folding it into several layers. As Kate stood up to unbutton her cloak, Jonathan turned slightly on the seat, leaned his shoulders against the window, and stretched his long legs out toward the aisle. "There," he said, tucking the shawl behind him. "All right, Kate. Come here."

Kate stared down at him in confusion. "I don't understand what—" Just then the train rounded a curve, and she was thrown off balance by the unexpected sway. If Jonathan hadn't caught her, she'd have fallen across his lap.

"Careful," he said, settling her back against his chest. "I'd hate to have you knock yourself unconscious."

"What do you think you're doing?" she gasped, struggling to sit up.

"Trying to get some sleep."

"We can't sleep this way."

"Why not?"

Her face burned with embarrassment. "Because it's not . . . we aren't . . ."

"Aren't what? Married?" She thought she detected a note of amusement in his voice. "Nobody on this train knows that, and probably wouldn't care if they did. We won't get to Chicago for another four days. What do you suppose we'll be like without any sleep?"

Suddenly Kate felt silly. What did she think he was going to do in front of his sons and thirty strangers? "I . . . I guess you're right," she murmured, leaning back against him and allowing him to spread her cloak over them both.

Surrounded by the warmth of his body she fell asleep far sooner than she would have thought possible. She awakened only once, when they made a stop at a tiny station.

"Shh," Jonathan whispered as she stirred against his chest. "Go back to sleep."

With a sleepy smile she snuggled closer. She was on the edge of oblivion once more when a startling thought drifted through her mind: Her foolish heart had betrayed her; she'd fallen in love with Jonathan.

20

"Next stop Big Springs."

The sun glinted off the brass buttons of the conductor's coat as he walked through the car, rousing the passengers.

Kate became aware of the solid comfort of Jonathan's arms around her and the hard warmth of his chest under her cheek. Sometime during the night she must have turned, for now the top of her head lay nestled into the curve of his neck, and her body was stretched out along the length of his. Embarrassed by such an intimate position, she struggled and sat up.

Jonathan opened his eyes and blinked several times before stretching. "Good morning, Kate," he said with a smile. "Did you sleep well?"

I love him! The thought burst into her consciousness with equal amounts of excitement and dismay. "Pretty well. What about you?"

"Not bad." Considering he'd spent the night

with a desirable woman in his arms and couldn't do a thing about it, he added mentally. He pulled the shawl from behind his back and peered out the window. "Looks like we're almost to the station."

"Do you think we'll stop here very long?"

"Long enough to use the facilities, at least, I hope." He rubbed the dark stubble on his face wistfully. "I don't suppose I'll have time to shave, though."

Self-consciously reaching up to touch her hair, Kate gasped when she realized how much of it had worked loose and was hanging around her face. "Gracious sakes, I must look a sight." She blushed deeply as she felt Jonathan's eyes upon her. He was probably embarrassed to death to be seen with such an untidy female, she thought, digging her comb out of the bottom of the basket.

She was a sight all right, Jonathan thought, resisting the urge to touch her delicately flushed cheeks, though how she managed to look so damnably appealing when most women would be at their worst was beyond him.

Looking away from the tempting picture of Kate with her hair down over her shoulders, Jonathan reached over and shook his sons gently. "Come on, sleepyheads. Time to wake up."

He doesn't even realize my whole world's turned upside down, Kate thought in vexation as she pulled on a stubborn snarl with the comb.

The rest of the trip to Chicago was bittersweet for Kate. She knew that loving Jonathan was ill advised and told herself so repeatedly. Yet at night, nestled in his arms, she felt as if she had come home, and it was impossible to stop her heart from turning over when he grinned at her. Through it all, Jonathan treated her with a friendly detachment that had her gritting her teeth in frustration. Though part of her didn't want the interlude to end, Kate breathed a sigh of relief when they finally arrived in Chicago.

"Look, Pa, isn't that Uncle Daniel?" Cole was bouncing up and down in excitement.

Jonathan put his hand on Cole's shoulder to hold him down and looked out the window. "Sure is, and it looks like he brought Cassandra with him."

"Cassandra?" Cole was bewildered. "Who's that?"

Levi gave his brother a look of disgust. "Cassie, you idiot."

"Oh." Cole squinted at the young girl standing next to his uncle on the loading dock. "She looks different."

"I'm sure you do, too," Jonathan said with a grin. "It's been five years, you know. Now grab Mrs. Murphy's basket and your coats. Your uncle Daniel is waiting for us." Both boys were on their feet and halfway down the aisle in less than a minute. With a weary shake of his head, Jonathan stood up and offered Kate his hand. "I hope Daniel is prepared to be knocked down by his nephews."

"I thought he was your cousin."

"He is, but his wife and mine were twin sisters."

Kate's eyes widened, and Jonathan grinned. "You don't need to look so surprised. We all grew up together and were the best of friends." Putting his hand at the small of her back, he guided Kate toward the open door of the railway car. "Of course, it did take Mary and Belle a while to convince Daniel and me it was time to get married."

As she stepped down from the train, Kate wondered suddenly how long Mary had been gone. Was this the first time Jonathan had been with his family since her death? There was certainly no restraint between the two men as they greeted each other warmly. Standing back, Kate couldn't help smiling at their exuberance.

"Daniel," Jonathan said, grasping his cousin's hand and slapping him on the shoulder. "I see you're as short and fat as ever."

"And you're as ugly."

As they grinned at each other, Kate looked in vain for a family resemblance between them. Though Daniel was several inches taller than Jonathan, he was slender rather than muscular and didn't have a speck of Jonathan's flamboyant good looks. It wasn't until Daniel turned toward Kate that she realized he had the same brilliant blue eyes as Jonathan and Cole.

"And this must be Mrs. Murphy," he said.

"But how . . . ?"

"Jon's telegram yesterday said there were four of you. Belle figured the extra person had to be either you or Charlie Hobbs." Daniel grinned. "You're obviously not Charlie."

Kate looked at Jonathan, who shrugged a trifle self-consciously.

"I might have mentioned you once or twice in my letters."

"Once or twice! My wife is already a great

admirer of yours. She's convinced you've single-
handedly saved Jon and the boys from death by
starvation and neglect, at the very least."

"Oh, I hardly think—"

"Pa," Cole broke in, "Cassie says Uncle Daniel
might let us ride some of his horses."

Daniel nodded seriously. "Actually you'd be
doing me a big favor, but first you have prove to
me I wouldn't be endangering my stock."

"We wouldn't, would we, Levi?"

Levi shook his head. "Oh, no. We're always real
careful."

"Papa's teasing you," Cassie said. "He's already
picked out the horses for you."

"What's mine like?" Cole wanted to know.

"Good Lord," Jonathan murmured as he got his
first good look at his niece.

"I know," Daniel said. "Your son gave me quite a
turn, too."

Though Cassie was not as tall as Levi and her
hair was a slightly darker hue, the two cousins
looked like opposite halves of the same coin. From
the animated conversation the three youngsters
were carrying on, it was apparent that they had
accepted the astonishing likeness and moved on to
more interesting topics.

"Spitting image of their grandpa Colburn,"
Daniel said. "Well, I suppose we'd better get moving if we're going to be home in time for you to
dress for dinner." He grinned. "I hate to say it, Jon,
but you look like something the cat dragged in."

Jonathan rubbed the untidy growth of whiskers
on his face. "I know. That's one thing I didn't like

about the train trip. I haven't had a chance to shave since we left Cheyenne."

Amid much friendly banter they set out, with Kate between Jonathan and Daniel on the front seat of an elegant surrey while the children shared the backseat with the luggage. The incredible likeness between Cassie and Levi made Kate feel strangely out of place. No matter how important the three Cantrells had become to her, these people were family. She was not.

"I hope you're planning on staying for our annual horse sale next Thursday," Daniel said as soon as they pulled out onto the road. "Looks like we'll have buyers coming from all over the country this year, and Belle's planning on turning it into the social event of the season."

Jonathan grinned. "I hope she hasn't done away with the horse race."

"Nope. We still have that before the auction, but she's added a huge buffet afterwards. This year she's decided to end the evening with a dress ball and a late supper."

"Just the sort of thing I moved out west to get away from." Jonathan made a face. "I don't suppose I really have a choice in this, do I?"

Daniel chuckled. "Afraid not. Belle's already figured out her seating arrangement."

"Then I suppose we'll stay."

As the men's conversation went on, Kate realized that Daniel had increased his already substantial fortune by raising Thoroughbred racehorses. Discovering that Jonathan's relatives were wealthy made Kate feel even more like an intruder. Her expectation of a small comfortable home in a respectable part of Chicago faded, and she was not particularly surprised when they arrived at a large, sprawling house surrounded by prosperous green pastures worthy of a gentleman's country estate.

Kate's sense of alienation lasted until she met Belle Dayton. The woman was like a friendly whirlwind, kissing Jonathan's cheek, exclaiming over Cole and Levi, remarking on the look-alike cousins, and enveloping Kate in a warm hug of greeting all within seconds of their arrival. Before Kate had time to catch her breath, she found herself whisked upstairs and into a spacious bedroom.

"I was really hoping Jonathan would bring you along," Belle said, crossing to the window and opening the heavy curtains. "There are so many things I want to ask you. I can't wait to have a long, long chat, but if I know Jonathan, you're probably exhausted. That man thinks the only way to travel is at full speed." Pulling back the counterpane on the bed, she smiled at Kate. "I'll send up Elisa with water for a bath and then you can rest until dinner. We eat unfashionably early, but I imagine you're used to that. If you need anything else, just ask Elisa."

In less than fifteen minutes Kate was climbing into a tub of hot water. Though the Daytons hadn't yet installed the new indoor plumbing that had become the rage in the East, there was a separate room for bathing off of the bedroom. A door in the opposite wall indicated that the room probably had more than one use, but Kate didn't want to show her ignorance by asking the maid, Elisa, to explain.

After assuring Elisa that she truly didn't need any help, Kate relaxed in the steamy luxury. The scented soap felt like satin on her skin and made the task of scrubbing away two weeks' worth of trail dirt a pleasure. The water was on the verge of turning cold when Kate finally climbed out and dried herself with the big fluffy towel.

She rang for the maid to take away the bathwater, put on her robe, and settled onto an overstuffed chair by her bedroom window. Brushing her hair dry, she delighted in the warm sunshine. It wrapped her in a golden glow as it warmed her damp skin, and she felt herself drifting. . . .

Kate awakened with a start. A glance out the window assured her that her nap had not been a long one. Relieved that she hadn't committed the unforgivable sin of missing dinner, Kate stood up and stretched. It was probably time she started getting ready. Glancing at the dressing table, she frowned. What in the world had she done with her hairpins? A moment of reflection reminded her she'd taken her hair down in the bathing room and laid the pins on a small table there.

Pulling the brush through her hair, Kate entered the bathing room and stopped in surprise. Filled with steaming water, the tub had been prepared once again, and a fresh towel lay on a stand next to it. Puzzled, she picked up the bar of soap. It was similar to the one she had used, except it was not perfumed.

She was just beginning to wonder if someone had made a mistake when the other door opened and Jonathan walked in. He froze in the act of unbuttoning his shirt cuffs and stared at her. Kate looked past his open shirt to the room beyond his shoulder and gasped. It was obviously another bedroom, his. With a flash of insight, she realized that Belle had put them in adjoining rooms, thinking they were lovers.

Dropping the soap from her nerveless fingers, she turned and fled back to her room, slamming the door behind her. Unsure as to whether to throw herself on the bed in a flood of tears or die of mortification where she stood, Kate was still in the middle of the room with hands pressed to burning cheeks when she heard Jonathan enter the room behind her.

"Kate, it doesn't mean anything."

"B-but your sister-in-law thinks . . . thinks . . ."

"Knowing Belle, she's had these rooms ready since she got my letter. She probably intended this one for the boys and changed plans when she got my telegram from Omaha. Even then she was expecting Charlie."

Kate dropped her face into her hands. "You know that isn't true. She could have changed things when we got here."

"Kate." Jonathan turned her gently to face him and, with a finger under her chin, forced her to look up at him. "It doesn't matter what Belle thinks. You and I know the truth. Besides, our bedrooms are closer than this at home."

"I know, but—"

"Look, if it will make you feel better, I'll find the keys to both doors and keep them locked. I don't have any need for a dressing room anyway."

Kate shook her head. "No, it isn't that. I know I'm perfectly safe with you." She lowered her gaze once more, carefully avoiding his tantalizing bare chest. "I just . . ."

"You don't want my family thinking I share your bed." He touched the heavy curtain of hair surrounding her face. "Don't give it another moment's thought. I'll take care of it."

"Wh-what will you do?"

"I'll just tell Belle and Daniel that we aren't sleeping together."

Kate's eyes flew to his in startled dismay. "Oh, Jonathan, you wouldn't. How embarrassing."

"Don't worry. It won't be the first time one of us has made an error of judgment." He grinned. "Besides, it's more embarrassing for you if they think you're my mistress, isn't it?"

Kate's face flamed. "Yes."

"There, you see? Now, I'd better go take my bath before the water gets cold and I have to explain to Belle why I was late for her carefully planned dinner."

When he turned and walked to the door, Kate suddenly remembered why she'd gone into the room in the first place. "Oh, dear. Jonathan, wait, I need my hairpins."

She darted into the room, scooped up the pins, and came back into the bedroom. "Jonathan?" she said as he stepped past her. "I . . . I . . . thank you. It was silly of me to be so upset."

Nodding, Jonathan closed the door and sighed. If she had any idea what the sight of her in a robe with her hair down around her shoulders had done to him, she would be far more upset than she was now. In fact, if she could see the erotic images going through his mind this very minute, she'd probably lock the door and push the armoire in front of it for good measure.

21

"*My goodness but* you're an early riser!" Belle exclaimed as she swept into Kate's bedroom early the next morning and found her guest fully clothed. "I thought I'd catch you still in bed so we could have our morning coffee together, and here you are already hard at work with a needle. Ah, well, no matter. We'll just have it here by the window instead. There on the table, I think, Elisa."

Setting a tray on the small table, Elisa gave Kate a shy smile, then turned to Belle. "Anything else, Mrs. Dayton?"

"No, that's all for now. Run along." Belle seated herself on the chair across the table from Kate and picked up the delicate teapot. "Oh, and give my best to Samuel."

Elisa blushed. "I will, Mrs. Dayton."

"I expect I'll be losing her within the year," Belle said with a sigh as the door closed behind the young maid. "But I suppose she'll be happier taking care of her own family." She poured coffee into one of the dainty cups. "Daniel says I shouldn't try so hard to find them husbands. Elisa will be the third one in two years."

Kate couldn't help laughing as she laid her sewing aside. "I'm sure they appreciate your efforts."

"Oh, I have no doubt of that. I have no less than eight godchildren, and four of those are named Arabelle in my honor."

"Arabelle?"

Belle filled the other cup and set the pot back on the tray. "It was my father's notion. He thought twins should have sound-alike names. I think he must have been exceedingly tired or drunk, because Marybell and Arabelle were the best he could come up with. Daniel and Jonathan were the first ones we were able to convince to call us Belle and Mary. We fell in love with them on the spot. Do you use cream or sugar?"

"Neither, thank you," Kate said with a smile, thinking that holding a conversation with Belle was rather like following a trail through the woods. You never knew where each little twist or turn was going to take you, but it was sure to be interesting.

Belle peered into the cream pitcher and made a face. "Daniel thinks I should learn to drink it plain, but I never could stand the taste." With a sigh she poured a generous amount of cream into her cup, added a spoonful of sugar, and stirred. Then she took a sip of the light brown mixture and closed her eyes in appreciation. "Mmmm. That's ever so much better than plain coffee."

JOIN THE
TIMELESS ROMANCE READER SERVICE AND GET FOUR OF TODAY'S MOST EXCITING HISTORICAL ROMANCES FREE, WITHOUT OBLIGATION!

Imagine getting today's very best historical romances sent directly to your home — at a total savings of at least $2.00 a month. Now you can be among the first to be swept away by the latest from Candace Camp, Constance O'Banyon, Patricia Hagan, Parris Afton Bonds or Susan Wiggs. You get all that — and that's just the beginning.

PREVIEW AT HOME WITHOUT OBLIGATION AND SAVE.

Each month, you'll receive four new romances to preview without obligation for 10 days. You'll pay the low subscriber price of just $4.00 per title — a total savings of at least $2.00 a month!

Postage and handling is absolutely free and there is no minimum number of books you must buy. You may cancel your subscription at any time with no obligation.

GET YOUR FOUR FREE BOOKS TODAY ($20.49 VALUE)

FILL IN THE ORDER FORM BELOW NOW!

YES! *I want to join the Timeless Romance Reader Service. Please send me my 4 FREE HarperMonogram historical romances. Then each month send me 4 new historical romances to preview without obligation for 10 days. I'll pay the low subscription price of $4.00 for every book I choose to keep – a total savings of at least $2.00 each month – and home delivery is free! I understand that I may return any title within 10 days without obligation and I may cancel this subscription at any time without obligation. There is no minimum number of books to purchase.*

NAME_____

ADDRESS _____

CITY_____STATE_____ZIP_____

TELEPHONE_____

SIGNATURE_____

(If under 18 parent or guardian must sign. Program, price, terms, and conditions subject to cancellation and change. Orders subject to acceptance by HarperMonogram.)

GET 4 FREE BOOKS
(A $20.49 VALUE)

.

Kate picked up her cup. "It's all what you're used to, I expect."

"I suppose." Belle gave Kate a look over the top of her cup. "It seems I owe you an apology," she said. "Jonathan informed me I had jumped to the wrong conclusion entirely. He was actually quite severe." Tactfully ignoring Kate's dismayed expression, Belle scrutinized the plate of golden-brown scones and chose one near the bottom of the pile. "Of course, I didn't let that bother me. He's mostly bluster, anyway. Do have a scone. My cook has a special touch with them."

"N-no, thank you." Kate looked down at her hands, feeling as if her stomach had sunk to her toes.

"I was disappointed at first. I had so hoped . . ." Belle hesitated. "But perhaps it's better this way. Jonathan is entirely too attractive for his own good. You wouldn't believe how many foolish women have fallen victim to those darn dimples of his." She sighed. "I'm afraid he's been terribly spoiled by all the attention. Don't you find him rather arrogant at times?"

"Well . . . uh . . . there have been a few times . . ."

"There, I knew it!" Belle nodded in satisfaction. "You're the first one who hasn't been blind to his faults. I knew you were exactly what he needed when he wrote that you'd banished his saddle to the outhouse and informed him that he could do a better job of washing his neck."

Kate's face turned red. "He told you about that?"

"Yes, and several other times you've set him on

his ear. Oh, don't look like that. He wasn't complaining. Besides, Jonathan's been left to his own devices long enough. It was high time someone took that family in hand, and you've done an admirable job of it."

Kate nervously clenched her hands in her lap. "I'm afraid I'm not as much in control as you think," she admitted.

"Why, because you've fallen in love with Jonathan?" She smiled as Kate's eyes widened with shock. "I'm not surprised. In spite of his imperfections, he's quite irresistible. Just don't let your heart rule your head. That man needs a firm hand, not someone who will pander to his slightest whim."

"I'm only the housekeeper."

"I think you underestimate your influence." Belle set down her cup. "Now, I think I've embarrassed you quite enough. I came to apologize, not dig myself a deeper hole."

"I . . . I don't know what to say."

"That my apology is accepted, of course, and then we can move on to more important things, like where we're going shopping today." She met Kate's eyes. "I truly am sorry, you know. I wouldn't have insulted you for the world."

"I wasn't insulted," Kate assured her. "It was just that—"

"Just that you didn't want me thinking you were living in sin with my brother-in-law," Belle finished for her. "Well, now I know, even though it wouldn't matter to me if you were. Don't worry, I'll try not to stick my nose into your romance."

That shouldn't be difficult, Kate thought, since

there was no romance. "I accept your apology, then," she said with a smile. Belle's openhearted friendliness was hard to resist.

Belle beamed at her. "Good, that's settled. Now then, Jonathan said we could take the boys to the city and buy them whatever they need. And I'll bet you're just dying to do some civilized shopping yourself."

"Well, yes," Kate admitted, "I do need a few things."

"Then let's plan our attack."

Kate discovered that Belle did indeed approach shopping like a military campaign. Ignoring Cole's and Levi's complaints about being dragged away from watching their uncle train horses, she whisked them into Chicago and had them outfitted with new winter coats, trousers, shirts, and boots long before lunchtime. When Kate protested that she could make everything but the boots, Belle just smiled, saying that Jonathan could well afford it and that Kate should sew because she wanted to, not because there was an urgent need.

At first both women thought Cassie had come along out of boredom, but it soon became obvious that she had another reason entirely. Cole. Every time she looked at him, her eyes grew soft and dreamlike. She followed him around like a puppy dog, hanging on every word, trying to anticipate his every need and providing it for him.

Cole seemed oblivious of the attention she was showering on him, though Levi gave her an occasional odd look. She even offered Cole her cherished seat by the carriage window, which he blithely accepted. Cassie sat staring at him with a particularly fatuous expression while Kate and Belle exchanged grins.

"Just like his father," Belle whispered to Kate.

"Heaven help the women of Horse Creek in a few years!"

"What are you whispering about, Aunt Belle?" Levi asked suspiciously. "We aren't going to a barber, are we?"

"Why, no. We're on our way to Madame Blanchard's. Mrs. Murphy and I have time to do a little shopping before your father and Uncle Daniel meet us for lunch."

Kate contemplated the boys for a moment. "Now that you mention it, though, you two could use a haircut."

"Look!" Cole cried, trying to divert her attention. "A monkey!"

While all three children crowded to the window to see the organ grinder and his pet, Kate winked at Belle over their heads. "We'll have to tell your father you want a haircut. I'm sure he won't mind taking you."

Suddenly Cole and Levi couldn't get enough of the sights. Apparently awed by the unfamiliar city, they asked dozens of questions about anything that came across their line of vision. Their strategy was so transparent that both adults had a difficult time keeping straight faces.

When they finally arrived at Madame Blanchard's, the boys walked into the feminine establishment smiling angelically. "We'll just sit over there and wait for Pa," Levi said, nodding toward a window seat nestled in one corner of the store.

"That's right," Cole added as he pushed an unprotesting Cassie toward the embrasure. "Go ahead and enjoy yourself, Mrs. Murphy. You won't even know we're here."

"That'll be the day," Kate said to Belle under her breath. "I should have thought of the haircuts earlier."

Belle chuckled. "If you work it right, you could get as much as a day of good behavior out of it."

A tiny birdlike woman appeared from the back of the store and smiled when she saw who her customer was. "Mrs. Dayton! What a nice surprise. I wasn't expecting you until the day after tomorrow." Suddenly her smile faltered. "Oh, dear, your ball gown isn't quite finished."

"No matter. I'm here to order a new riding habit anyway."

"What did you have in mind?"

"Oh, I think something in a pale blue this time." Belle pulled off her gloves and removed her hat. "This is my friend Mrs. Murphy. Kate, meet Madame Blanchard herself, Sybil Jones."

Madam Blanchard chuckled at Kate's confused expression. "Jones is my married name. Mrs. Dayton thought my maiden name sounded more professional. Is there anything we can do for you today?"

The minute they'd entered the posh showroom, Kate had realized it was far too expensive for her meager budget and reconciled herself to spending her money on fabric and making her own clothing.

Now she shook her head regretfully. "Oh, no, I just—"

"I think Mrs. Murphy might be interested in looking at those dresses you were telling me about the other day," Belle interrupted. "It seems someone's husband canceled a rather large order after most of it was finished," she explained to Kate. "You'd be doing Sybil a big favor if you could take some of them off her hands. You'll be amazed how reasonable her prices are."

Sybil nodded eagerly. "Oh, yes, most reasonable. Ready-made clothing is so difficult to sell, you see."

Unable to resist the temptation of trying on new clothes, Kate capitulated. "Well, perhaps I might look at some of the more simple things."

Sybil clapped her hands together in delight. "Wonderful. It won't take a minute to prepare the fitting room. I'll have one of the girls bring you refreshments while you're waiting. She can keep an eye on the children for you, too."

"Sybil was my very first personal maid after Daniel and I were married," Belle whispered to Kate as Madame Blanchard scurried away. "She's so incredibly talented with a needle that I felt guilty keeping her to myself. Setting her up in this shop is probably the best thing I've ever done for the city of Chicago."

Kate raised her eyebrows. "What? You didn't find her a husband?"

"Oh, yes." Belle grinned mischievously. "Mr. Jones was my doing, too. He's a very open-minded, scholarly, gentleman who doesn't care one wit that his wife owns the most prosperous modiste shop in Chicago. Actually, I'm not sure he ever comes out of his books long enough to realize that she's gone most of the day. He's a trifle absentminded, but he's truly devoted to her."

When the girl brought them a tray of tea and biscuits, Kate glanced at the children still ensconced in the window seat. All three heads were bent together in conversation. Kate wondered what nefarious scheme they were planning now.

She was starting to turn back to Belle when she noticed a beautiful full-length coat hanging on a dress form. It was an eye-catching combination of red wool and black braid. Cut to fit the figure, the garment dipped in at the waist and then flared gracefully to cover the wearer's skirts. Thin black braid trimmed the cuffs of the full sleeves, circled the high-necked collar, and followed the straight line of buttons down the front clear to the floor.

Knowing full well that the price was probably way beyond her means, Kate couldn't resist asking Madame Blanchard's assistant anyway. The figure the girl named was as dear as Kate had expected it to be, and she regretfully put the notion of buying the coat from her mind.

Her disappointment was soon forgotten in the pleasure of trying on dozens of outfits. Most were far too fashionable for her simple life-style, but there were several appropriate day dresses. After the high cost of the coat, Kate was pleasantly surprised by how inexpensive they were. Feeling reckless, she chose four—more dresses than she had owned at one time in her entire life.

"The blue or the yellow will be very nice for the horse auction Thursday," Belle said as Sybil set Kate's selections aside to be altered, "but we still need something for the ball."

"You know, I think I have just the thing," Sybil said. With that she disappeared through a door in the back.

Kate's heart sank. She'd been dreading the affair ever since she'd heard about it. "Another dress really isn't necessary, Belle. I won't be going to the ball."

Belle's eyebrows shot up. "And why is that?"

"It's not the sort of thing a servant goes to."

There was a moment of stunned silence. "I beg your pardon. I didn't realize I had treated you so shabbily that you feel like a servant."

"Oh, no! You've been wonderful, but the fact remains I'm Jonathan's housekeeper."

"What you are to Jonathan is his business," Belle said. "To me you are an honored guest whom I wish to thank for taking care of my family."

"You don't understand. I don't know how to dance."

Belle's expression cleared as if by magic. "Oh, is that all? We have three days, plenty of time to teach you to dance well enough to get by. Please, Kate, it would mean so much to me."

Kate sighed. "When you put it like that, how can I refuse?"

"You can't." Belle's eyes widened as Madame Blanchard returned with a dress. "Oh, yes, Sybil. That's exactly what we need."

Any objections Kate had died as she gazed at the

gorgeous creation. Instinctively she knew that the maroon velvet was perfect for her. Trimmed with only a small amount of delicate white lace, it was deceptively simple and beautifully elegant. It would cost too much, of course, but Kate had spent very little of the money Jonathan had paid her over the last four months. Protesting halfheartedly that she'd never have any place else to wear such a dress again, she allowed Sybil to help her into it.

"Don't be silly, Kate," Belle said, walking around her and admiring her in the gown. "This is the sort of dress that never goes out of style. Eventually there will be some sort of civilization, even in the wilds of Wyoming. Besides, from what I understand, women don't stay single very long in the West. You'll probably be needing a wedding dress before too long."

Kate gave her a sharp look, but Belle just smiled and shrugged.

It took only a few minutes for Kate to slip out of the dress and into her own drab clothing again. "I'd better go see how the children are faring," she said as Sybil and Belle sat down with the fashion plates to decide on the style of the new riding habit.

The three children and the assistant were all sitting in the window seat, sharing the stereoscope that Madame Blanchard provided for the bored husbands and children of her customers. "Mrs. Murphy!" Cole said. "Come look at this."

Though Kate had seen a stereoscope several times before, she obediently fitted her brow into the curved box and peered through the lenses at a three-dimensional picture of a gigantic waterfall. Suitably awed by the incredible invention, she handed it back to Levi and left them to their explorations.

She wandered over to the red coat and gazed at it longingly. Perhaps she could copy the design.

"Would you like to try it on?" the assistant asked. "Madame Blanchard doesn't mind."

It took the woman only a moment to unbutton the row of shiny black buttons and remove the garment from the dress form. After slipping it on, Kate stepped over to the looking glass to assess the effect.

The coat might have been made for her. Hugging her contours perfectly, it fell in a smooth line from her waist to about four inches above the floor. Staring critically at her reflection in the mirror, Kate doubted that she'd be able to match the perfect tailoring, but maybe she could get close enough. . . .

"Pa!" Levi called out. "Can we get a stereoscope like Madame Blanchard's?"

Startled, Kate looked toward the door and encountered Jonathan's sapphire gaze. The look in his eye held her immobile for a breathless moment.

"If you want my opinion, Kate," Daniel said from behind his cousin, "I think you should buy it."

"A stereoscope would be very educational for us," Cole said. "Please, Pa, please."

Blinking, Jonathan looked away from Kate and turned his attention to his sons. Within seconds he was engrossed in a heated discussion about whether or not he should buy them a stereoscope.

With her heart pounding, Kate removed the coat

and handed it to the assistant, wondering if she had imagined the flare of interest she'd seen in Jonathan's eyes. Probably. He'd no doubt spent the morning admiring and being admired by beautiful women. Suddenly she was very glad that she had bought the maroon ball gown.

22

"One, *two, three,* one, *two, three* . . . No, no, Kate. Don't look down at your feet," Belle admonished her pupil. "Smile at your partner."

"If I smile at him while I tromp all over his toes, he'll think I'm doing it on purpose."

Belle raised her eyebrows. "A gentleman would never be so impolite as to notice when a lady stepped on his foot. Anyway, it's much easier to waltz with a man. You feel like your feet never touch the ground."

"Which they don't if you spend all your time treading upon his toes," said a deep voice.

"Oh, good, you two are exactly what we need." Ignoring Jonathan's snide remark, Belle unceremoniously pulled her husband and brother-in-law into the room. "Now then, which of you wants to play the piano for us?"

Jonathan shook his head. "I'd like to help out, but

I haven't been near a piano in ten years. I imagine I've forgotten all I ever knew."

"Which wasn't much to begin with." Daniel winked at Kate. "Jon's piano-playing talents are legendary. Rumor has it his first teacher is still doing penance for introducing him to the instrument."

"At least I had the good sense to quit before anybody called me a sissy."

"That's all very fine and good," Belle interrupted them, "but who's going to play for us now?"

Giving his cousin a grin, Daniel bent to kiss his wife on the cheek. "I'll be glad to play for you, dear, just as I'm sure you had planned all along."

"Wonderful. That means Jonathan can be my partner and show Kate what the waltz is supposed to look like."

"I knew I should have stayed in the barn," Jonathan muttered. Then he gave Belle an innocent look when she glared at him.

Listening to the three, Kate shook her head fondly. Their affectionate banter seemed inexhaustible, and she couldn't help wondering what things had been like when Jonathan's wife was alive. The four must have been inseparable.

If Belle and Daniel knew of the circumstances surrounding Mary Cantrell's death, they certainly didn't seem to hold it against Jonathan. It was all very curious.

With a dramatic flare, Daniel pounded out the first few notes of the "Blue Danube" waltz, and Jonathan swept Belle into the dance. "*One* two, three . . . look at my feet, Kate," Belle instructed. "*One,* two, three . . ."

Watching Jonathan and Belle glide around the room, Kate sighed wistfully. They made it look so easy, so graceful. Jonathan was still twirling Belle with effortless style when Kate heard voices from the hallway.

"Ah, come on, Cassie." Levi said. "Cole can go talk to Pa by himself. Let's go riding without him."

"It won't take that long, Levi. Besides, Cole's right. You have a better chance if you both ask."

They entered the room moments later and came to a halt next to Kate. The boys stared at the couple swaying in time to the music.

"I didn't know Pa could dance." It was obvious that Cole wasn't sure such a skill was an asset.

"Your father probably has a great many talents you aren't aware of," Kate said.

As Daniel played the last few bars, Jonathan waltzed Belle off the floor and gave a deep bow. "This has been a truly great pleasure, madam." His eyes twinkled merrily. "I can only remember once when I enjoyed dancing with you more."

"The time you stuck the frog down the back of my dress, no doubt." Belle gave him a playful slap on the wrist with an imaginary fan. "Since you still show no sign of repenting that evil deed, you can postpone whatever you and Daniel had planned long enough to help Kate master the waltz."

Cole's face fell. "Oh, Pa. You promised you'd go buy us a stereoscope today."

"I said we'd talk about it, and there's plenty of time for that later. And actually, it wouldn't hurt you two to learn how to dance."

"Why?" they asked in unison.

"Dancing is a very handy skill to have. You never know what important people you might meet at a party."

Levi looked doubtful. "Like who?"

"Oh, perhaps a rich man who's interested in buying some of your cattle. Or maybe even the president of the railroad who lets his friends ship their stock at half price."

"Pa, we wouldn't dance with anybody like that. They're men!"

"Yes, but men have daughters. By dancing with the daughter you may meet the father."

The boys exchanged a skeptical glance, but Cassie suddenly became animated. "Oh, yes, let's try it. Mama will show us how."

It took some persuading, but eventually Levi and Cole gave in, and the lessons began in earnest. At last Belle deemed her four pupils ready for music and sent Daniel back to the piano.

Kate nervously rubbed her sweaty palms against the skirt of her dress.

"Don't worry." Jonathan's voice held a note of humor as he took her hand and led her out onto the "floor." "I won't put a frog down your back. Belle screamed so loud last time, I swore I'd never do it again."

"Don't be silly. I wasn't worried about that."

"Ah, then it's your toes." He nodded wisely as he pulled her into his arms. "Can't say as I blame you for that."

Kate smiled at his teasing. "My toes are perfectly safe, but yours are in grave danger, I'm afraid."

"I promise not to notice." With that he swept her away, and she forgot everything else.

Belle was right, the waltz was totally different in a man's arms, but Kate still felt clumsy and unsure of herself. Uncomfortably aware of how well Jonathan danced in spite of her, she took too big a step and tripped over the hem of her skirt. One moment she was falling, the next she was crushed to Jonathan's chest as he caught her.

"Are you all right?"

Telling herself it was only the near accident that was making her heart pound so hard, Kate nodded. "Y-yes. I'm sorry."

"I'm not noticing, remember." Grinning, he set her at the proper distance again. "Now then, forget your feet and concentrate on relaxing. If you let it, your body will just naturally follow mine."

With Jonathan's strong hand at her waist to guide her, Kate began to feel far more adept. Before long she was whirling around the floor with nary a stumble, though she suspected it was due more to Jonathan's expertise than to her own ability.

All too soon the practice session ended and Belle pronounced them all ready for the coming ball. With a feeling very much like disappointment, Kate reluctantly stepped out of Jonathan's embrace.

After lunch Levi and Cole finally prevailed on Jonathan to take them out in search of the coveted stereoscope. Daniel and Cassie went along, too, leaving Kate and Belle alone to finish the last-minute preparations for the upcoming festivities. By the middle of the afternoon even indefatigable Belle was beginning to droop.

"If you need us, Elisa, we'll be in the morning room," Belle said as she led Kate to a room toward the back of the house.

Kate's first impression was one of light, for the sun shone brightly even through the lacy curtains covering the French doors. The room was as immaculate as the rest of the house but had an air of being lived in.

"This is my hideout," Belle explained, dropping onto an overstuffed chair and kicking off her shoes. "It's called the morning room, though I've never really figured out why. The sun doesn't come in until afternoon. Sit down and make yourself comfortable," she said, rubbing the arch of her foot. "Not even Daniel has the courage to follow me in here without an invitation."

Seating herself on the curved settee, Kate looked around Belle's inner sanctum. It was filled with a fascinating collection of items as unusual as their owner. Suddenly Kate's attention was riveted to a painting on the wall next to the door. It was a portrait of Jonathan and Mary Cantrell. They were young and, if the artist was to be believed, very much in love. Both glowed with the radiance unique to newlyweds.

"That was done shortly after they were married," Belle said, following Kate's gaze.

"She was so tiny."

"Mary had rheumatic fever when she was thirteen and stopped growing. It affected her heart, too. She was never strong afterward." Belle smiled sadly. "It's a very good likeness of them both. Jonathan gave it to me right after she died."

"They must have loved each other very much."

Belle sighed. "They did, but I'm not so sure they were good for each other. Mary was perfectly content being married to a college professor, you see, but Jonathan yearned for adventure. He never even considered going west while she was alive. Her health was too delicate to survive the trip, let alone building a new life in the wilderness. If she hadn't died, I'm sure he'd still be a stodgy old mathematics professor."

"Mary was your only family?" Kate asked.

"We had a younger brother, too. Ben died at Gettysburg."

"Oh, I'm so sorry. I didn't realize. . . ."

"No need to apologize. I'm not the only one who lost a loved one in that infernal war." A shadow crossed Belle's face. "I guess that's why Jonathan and the boys are so important to me. Other than Daniel and Cassie, they're all the family I have left."

Uncomfortably aware that she had unwittingly caused her hostess pain, Kate greeted Elisa's entrance with heartfelt relief.

"Madame Blanchard's assistant has arrived with a pile of boxes, ma'am. Where would you like them?"

Belle's melancholy lifted as if by magic. "Oh, good. Shall we take them all to your room, Kate? You'll need to try everything on to make sure the alterations are correct." Without waiting for an answer, she bounced to her feet and began searching for her shoes.

Belle's excitement was contagious. By the time they had reached her room, Kate could hardly wait to open the boxes on her bed.

It soon became obvious to her why Madame Blanchard's establishment was so popular. Though the garments had originally been made for a slightly larger woman, Sybil had expertly taken in the waistlines, let out the bosoms, and shortened the hems. The results were stunning.

Kate purposely left the ball dress for last, knowing instinctively that the others would fade into insignificance once she saw it. She wasn't disappointed. It was exquisite. Even Belle's emerald-green gown was no prettier. Standing in front of the looking glass, the two women gazed at their reflections with pleasure.

"We're going to outshine them all, you know, Kate."

Touching the delicate lace at her breast, Kate smiled wistfully. There was only one person she wanted to impress.

"Here's one you missed."

Kate turned as Belle pointed to one last box on the bed.

"That's odd. I only ordered the five dresses. Are you sure it isn't yours?"

"Positive. It has your name on it." Belle beckoned her over. "Come see what it is."

Kate crossed to the bed and lifted the top off the box. "Oh, no," she gasped. "There's been a mistake. I didn't buy this." She reached out and touched the collar of the red coat regretfully. "I can't imagine how this happened."

"Look, here's a note." Belle pulled the card out of the box and read it. "I should have known," she said, handing it to Kate.

> *Wyoming winters are cold.*
> *Jonathan*

Kate looked up in surprise. "Jonathan! But how . . . ?"

"They probably stopped by Madame Blanchard's in town today. Oh, Kate, how lovely!" Belle lifted up the coat and shook out the folds. "It's perfect for you."

"But I can't accept it."

"Why not? Don't you like it?"

"I love it, but . . ."

"Good, then you'll tell Jonathan that when you thank him, and that will be the end of it."

"Oh, Belle, it just isn't proper."

"Hmph. I've never had much use for propriety, especially when it calls for needless sacrifice. If you send it back, you'll hurt Jonathan's feelings terribly, you know."

"I . . . I hadn't thought of that."

When Kate thanked Jonathan that evening, he simply shrugged. "It looks much nicer on you than the other one."

In fact, he hadn't been able to resist buying it for her. Not only was it beautiful on her, he hated her yellow cloak with a passion. Every time she wore it he wanted to rip it from her back. She was far too good to be wearing the cast-off of a whore.

Kate gazed up at him with luminous eyes. "It's the nicest coat I've ever owned."

"I'm glad you like it," he said with a pleased smile. "Red's my favorite color, you know."

His eyes locked with hers for a long moment. A wealth of emotionally charged energy flowed between them. No words were spoken, yet the exchange left them both with a soft, warm feeling that something special had happened.

23

"*Look, Mrs. Murphy,* they're getting ready to start."

Pulling Levi back off the racetrack, Kate craned her neck to see the horses lined up at the starting line. There was the sound of a gunshot, and the Daytons' annual horse race was on.

"I can't see," cried Cole, darting forward.

Kate grabbed his arm and dragged him back just as the horses thundered by in a cloud of dust. Then she released both boys and stepped out with the rest of the crowd, trying to see which horse would win.

"Papa's horse is ahead," Cassie yelled, jumping up and down. "He's winning!"

"Uh-oh. Here comes the black one."

"Go, Uncle Daniel, go!"

"They're across the finish line."

"Who won?" Kate asked, stretching above the three youngsters.

"I can't tell."

"Come on, let's go find out."

Before Kate could stop them, all three had taken off across the center of the oval horse track. Knowing that they'd never hear her call them back amid the roar of the crowd, she decided it was a lost cause and went looking for Belle. Kate found her in the kitchen deep in conversation with the cook.

"I've got the extra people you hired working on the tables right now, Mrs. Dayton. I expect you'll be wanting to supervise the setting up?" the cook asked.

"Oh, heavens, no. We'll take a peek at the tables, but I'm quite sure you have it well in hand. If you need me for anything, I'll be over at the auction. I'll send someone back about half an hour before the end so you can start putting the food out."

The cook looked quite gratified as she assured Belle that everything would be taken care of.

"You know, a positive word now and then makes such a difference with people," Belle said to Kate as the kitchen door closed behind them. "How did you manage to escape the children?"

"I didn't. They escaped me. The last I saw, they were headed across the paddock at a high run to see who had won the race."

"Good. If they get into trouble, their fathers can deal with it. Shall we check on the tables and then go on over to the auction?"

The army of extra servants was already hard at work in the huge room that would serve as a dining room now and a ballroom later. Belle moved among them, giving directions here and a word of encouragement there, always with a smile on her face. It was obvious that she was well acquainted with many, for she would often ask after some family member or other.

Belle was soon satisfied that all was progressing well in the dining room and guided Kate through the open French doors. "I wish you didn't have to leave the day after tomorrow. It's been so nice having you all here."

"Jonathan's worried about getting back before winter sets in. We'll be into November as it is."

Belle sighed. "I just wish Wyoming wasn't so far away. The last time we saw Jonathan and the boys was when they stopped in Chicago on their way west five years ago. Who knows how long it will be before any of you get back this way again?"

"He went to Wyoming five years ago? I thought Jonathan fought in the war."

"He did for most of it. After being wounded at Gettysburg, he was discharged from the army and headed west almost a year before the war ended." A shadow crossed Belle's face as she and Kate entered the crowd in the paddock. "I don't know what happened on that battlefield, but Jonathan's never been quite the same since. When I asked what was wrong, he said it was best I didn't know." She shook her head. "I've never asked again, either. He seemed . . . well . . . anguished. I haven't seen him in that kind of pain since—"

"Mrs. Murphy, Aunt Belle." Both women's heads swiveled toward the sound as Cole rushed to meet them. "Pa just bought us some horses!"

"Yeah, quarter horses!" Levi chimed in as he

and Cassie joined his brother. "Uncle Daniel says they'll be better for working cattle than his Thoroughbreds."

"What in heaven's name is a quarter horse?" Kate asked.

"It's like a Thoroughbred, only it's shorter and heavier," Cassie explained. "Papa says they're almost as fast over a short distance but can start and stop better."

"Mine's named Lightning, and Cole's is Thunder," Levi added. "And they'll be perfect for working cattle."

"At least Uncle Jonathan thinks they should be, anyway," Cassie said.

Cole gave her an indignant glare. "You think my pa's wrong?"

"Oh, no. But he . . . he did say it was an experiment."

"I guess we'll just have to wait and see, won't we?"

Jonathan's voice made Kate's heart hammer in her throat. Though she'd known he was somewhere in the crowd, she had thought he'd be occupied with the sale.

"Why don't you three go make sure our new horses get put into the right stalls in the barn?" he added. The cousins exchanged a look and then disappeared into the throng. Shifting his attention to Kate and Belle, he grinned. "It took you two long enough to get out here. I've been watching for you ever since the terrible trio showed up after the race."

Kate's breath caught as she looked up at him.

Blue eyes, dimples, the tanned chest exposed by the open collar of his shirt—she'd never get used to his masculine beauty. Had he really been watching for her? Kate felt the oddest tingle as his gaze scanned her from head to toe.

"You look very pretty today, Kate. That of blue suits you."

Fighting down her blush, Kate smiled shyly. "Thank you."

"Are you enjoying yourself?"

"Oh, yes. I've never been to a horse race or an auction before."

"There you are, Jonathan." A sultry female voice cut through Kate's pleasure like a shard of ice. "And I see you found Belle for me."

"I told you she'd show up sooner or later," Jonathan said.

Kate didn't see the flash of irritation cross Jonathan's face. She was aware only of the tall, willowy blonde who emerged from the crowd and latched on to his arm. The woman's trim figure, emphasized by her beautifully tailored clothing, made Kate feel suddenly dowdy in spite of her new dress.

"Good morning, Elizabeth. I see you've already met my brother-in-law," Belle said.

"Daniel introduced us," Elizabeth said, moving closer to Jonathan. "I was so surprised. You didn't tell me you were going to have company, Belle."

"Of course I did. Just two weeks ago, in fact. I invited you to dinner, but you said you didn't like family parties," Belle reminded her.

"As a general rule I don't." Elizabeth smiled up

at Jonathan. "But I had no idea your brother-in-law would be so . . . interesting."

With a jolt Kate realized that Belle had intended to introduce Jonathan to her beautiful friend all along. Suddenly feeling like an intruder, she forced a smile as Belle introduced her to Elizabeth as a friend who had come east with Jonathan. "How do you do?" Kate said in a surprisingly calm voice.

"So nice to meet you, Miss Murphy," Elizabeth said. "How fortunate for you to have found someone to travel with. Will you be staying on after Jonathan leaves?"

For some reason Kate felt a surge of anger. "It's *Mrs.* Murphy, and no, I'll be leaving the day after tomorrow, too. Mr. Cantrell pays me to take care of his sons, you see. Now, if you'll excuse me, I'd like to get a closer look at the auction." Kate turned and stomped off through the crowd. Though her outburst was probably unjustified, at least she'd made it clear that she had no claims on Mr. No-Woman-Can-Resist-Him Cantrell. Far be it from her to stand in the way of any amorous adventures he might have on his last two days in Chicago!

Kate made her way to the middle of the paddock, where the sale was taking place. The smell of horses mixed with the pungent odor of fallen leaves tickled her nose as the auctioneer's litany rose above the murmur of the crowd. In a surprisingly short time she found herself caught up in the activity. Watching the horses being led one by one to the auction block, Kate shared the excitment of the people around her. She was disappointed when the last of the magnificent animals had been sold and the crowd began to move toward the house for Belle's luncheon buffet.

Kate was considering sneaking off to her bedroom when Belle's cheerful voice stopped her flight. "There you are, Kate. I've been looking all over for you. Would you mind helping out with the luncheon? I know it's horribly impolite to ask it of you, but I'm in something of a bind." Linking her arm with Kate's, she began walking toward the house, chattering incessantly about some sort of mishap in the kitchen that had thrown everything into a pelter. Kate wasn't fooled for a minute.

"Belle, this isn't necessary, you know."

"Of course it is," Belle said. "You were planning on slipping away for the rest of the afternoon."

"Would that be so terrible?"

Belle looked shocked. "You can't be serious. Levi and Cole on the loose with only their father and me to keep track of them?"

Kate couldn't help the laughter that bubbled up in her throat. "All right, you win. I'll stay."

"Good." Belle whisked them both through a side door and into a stillroom off the kitchen. "This is where the extra food will be. If you could just make sure the servants keep the tables full, it would be a great help. She's not Jonathan's type, you know."

"What?"

"Elizabeth. Oh, I know I wanted to introduce them, but only because she's one of the few unmarried friends I have. It was silly, of course. The last thing Jonathan needs is help with women." Belle shrugged. "Anyway, Elizabeth will drive him crazy before the day is over."

"He didn't look bothered to me."

"No, but then he never does. It's an odd quirk he has, one I've always found rather endearing. Women were throwing themselves at Jonathan's feet before he was old enough to shave. He's become horribly cynical, I'm afraid, but he's developed a way of putting distance between himself and his admirers without hurting their feelings. When he walks away from a woman, he makes her think it was her idea. You watch. Elizabeth will move on to someone else before the day's out."

Kate tossed her head. "Frankly, I couldn't care less."

Belle grinned. "And that's exactly why Jonathan likes you so much. He isn't used to a woman he can't wind around his little finger with a smile. Just keep pushing him away. He won't be able to resist."

"But I don't want . . ." Kate's words were lost in the hum of the crowd as Belle hurried away without waiting for an answer.

As the day progressed, Kate realized that much of what Belle said seemed to be true. Elizabeth clung to Jonathan like lichen to a rock for most of the afternoon, and then she just drifted away. Of course, there were at least four others who quickly took her place. Kate finally turned away in disgust and went up to get ready for the ball.

Since the servants already had more than they could handle, Kate carried her own bathwater up the back stairs, knowing full well that Belle would have a fit if she knew. It took several trips, but the physical exertion kept her mind off the rapidly approaching dance.

The bath helped her relax enough to greet Elisa with equanimity when the maid came to help with her hair. Three-quarters of an hour later, Kate stood staring into the mirror, amazed by what she saw.

The dress was even more beautiful in the lamp-light. It displayed her hourglass figure enticingly without being vulgar. The deep maroon velvet gave her skin a delicate, almost translucent quality and turned her eyes a brilliant green. Her dark, shining curls were piled high on her head and swept down to long ringlets draped gracefully over her shoulder.

Kate was pleased by the transformation, but Belle was ecstatic.

"Look at you!" Belle cried as she swept into the room. "Just wait till Jonathan sees you."

"Don't be silly," Kate said, blushing. "With all the beautiful women there tonight, he'll hardly notice me."

"We'll see." Belle smiled enigmatically. "Anyway, we'd better go. Daniel gets so fidgety if he has to wait a minute longer than he thinks is necessary. Jonathan will no doubt make it worse."

But when Kate and Belle swept into the drawing room, Daniel was sitting on a comfortable chair, calmly discussing the sale with his cousin. Swirling a snifter of brandy, Jonathan leaned against the mantel as if he had all the time in the world. So much for fidgeting, Kate thought.

At that precise moment, Jonathan glanced up

and straightened in surprise. Here was the exotic creature he had glimpsed so briefly the night he'd first met Kate. In the candlelight she looked for all the world like an exquisite cameo created from warm flesh and bone. Enchanted by the vision in maroon velvet and lace, he found himself strangely breathless.

Kate thought she had grown used to Jonathan's attractiveness, but she'd never seen him in full evening attire before. He was magnificent. The perfectly tailored black jacket and trousers emphasized his tall, muscular frame and set off the sapphire color of his eyes to perfection. She wondered how many female hearts he would break tonight.

How long they stood there gazing at each other in mute appreciation neither of them knew. It wasn't until the butler came to tell Belle and Daniel that the first of their guests were arriving that Kate and Jonathan returned to reality.

"That's our cue," Belle said as she set her husband's brandy snifter on the table and pulled him to his feet. "Jonathan, you bring Kate in, and for heaven's sake don't scowl at anyone. My guests aren't used to men like you. You'll frighten them to death." Winking at Kate, she swept out the door with Daniel at her side.

"It's amazing no one has strangled her," Jonathan said pleasantly as he set his drink on the mantel and crossed to Kate's side. Wondering if he could span her tiny waist with his hands, he offered her his arm. "Shall we?"

24

"*Here you are,*" Kate's companion said, placing a glass in her hand.

"Thank you." Kate smiled at him as he sat down next to her and tried to remember his name. Belle had introduced her, but there had been so many pleasant young men that their names and faces had begun to blur together. No matter. She'd discovered that it wasn't necessary to know who they were to dance or carry on a polite conversation with them. Smiling at him and nodding occasionally, she allowed her mind to wander.

As far as she was concerned, her first ball had been a great success. She'd have been content just to sit and take in the beauty of it all. Elegantly dressed men and women twirled around beneath gleaming crystal chandeliers to the sound of a full orchestra, as ornate mirrors on the walls reflected back a dozen images of splendor. It was the stuff dreams were made of. Even the centerpiece on the refreshment table, a running horse carved from a solid block of ice, was a piece of whimsy that Kate knew she would never forget.

Much to her surprise, she hadn't lacked for partners. At first she'd suspected that Belle was responsible but soon realized that her friend had done no more than introduce her to them. So much male attention was a novel experience for Kate, and she was enjoying it.

Though her eyes scanned the room frequently, she told herself it was mere curiosity, not because she wondered where Jonathan was. He wasn't difficult to find, anyway. Taller than most of the men in the room, he would have been easy to locate even without the bevy of beautiful women surrounding him whenever he wasn't dancing.

"Is there something wrong with your drink?"

"Hmm?"

The young man nodded to the glass in her hand. "You're not drinking your champagne."

"Oh." Embarrassed to have been caught not paying attention, Kate smiled yet again. "I was just so fascinated by what you were saying. . . ." She let her voice trail off as she took a gulp and nearly choked on the unexpectedly strange taste.

He gave her a gratified look. "Most women aren't that interested in my hobby. What is it you like about it?"

"Ah . . . well . . ." She took another sip as she desperately searched her memory for some inkling of what he'd been talking about. "I . . . I'm not really sure."

"I suppose coming from the West, you probably

know as much about it as I do." He leaned forward eagerly. "Tell me, what's it really like when you're right there?"

Kate recklessly drained the rest of her champagne. "You know, I really am thirsty." She handed him her glass. "Would you mind?"

"No, of course not." He was just starting to rise when a footman came by with a tray. "Oh, good. We need another glass of champagne here."

Kate had the irrational desire to kick the footman as he handed her a full glass, bowed, and walked away.

"Now then, you were saying?"

Taking another gulp of the champagne, Kate was surprised to find that it no longer tasted so strange. In fact, the bubbles were becoming quite pleasant. Unfortunately, her admirer was still waiting for an answer.

"Actually . . ."

"I believe this is my dance," said a familiar deep voice.

Kate could have hugged Jonathan. If ever there was a timely interruption, this was it. "Why, yes, I think you're right." After draining her glass once again, she placed it on a nearby table and stood up with an apologetic smile at her companion. "Will you excuse me?"

"Yes, of course, but I do hope we get a chance to finish our conversation before the evening is over."

Placing her hand on Jonathan's arm, she nodded pleasantly before walking away.

"What was that all about?" Jonathan asked, leading her clear to the other side of the room.

"To tell the truth, I haven't the faintest idea," she said as the orchestra struck up the first few notes of a waltz and he pulled her into his arms.

Whirling her into the dance, he chuckled when he heard her explanation. "I knew there was something wrong when I saw you toss down that glass of champagne."

"I think that was a mistake. My head feels a little fuzzy."

"It doesn't seem to have impaired your dancing ability," he said with a soft smile.

"I just hope I can keep away from him until the ball is over."

"That shouldn't be too difficult. If he gets too close, just tell him you have to go powder your nose or something."

Suddenly Kate became aware of Jonathan's warm hand against the small of her back, guiding her through the steps of the dance. Her social faux pas was all but forgotten as she reveled in the intimate contact. The movement of the dance was nearly erotic as they waltzed together in perfect rhythm. Kate wondered if she looked as starry-eyed as she felt.

It may have been her newly acquired taste for champagne that gave the rest of the evening a fairy-tale quality in her eyes. Though she had many different partners, Jonathan was never far away, and he claimed her for every waltz. It was a night of magic, filled with splendor, beautiful music, and Jonathan. Kate didn't ever want it to end, for she knew she would change from the enchanted princess back into plain, unexciting Kate Murphy.

When the last note had died away and the orchestra began packing up their instruments, Kate found herself commandeered by Belle to help bid the last of the guests good night. Heaven only knew what had happened to Daniel and Jonathan, though Belle suspected that their disappearance during the last set had a great deal to do with an expensive bottle of Kentucky bourbon Daniel had hidden away.

At last, arm in arm, the two women wearily climbed the stairs. Smiling apologetically, Belle stopped at Kate's door. "I told Elisa not to wait up for us. Would you like me to come in and unhook the back of your dress?"

Kate nodded. "If you wouldn't mind. Shall I do yours, too?"

"Oh, no, that's Daniel's job." Grinning, Belle shut the door and began to unfasten the tiny hooks that closed the back of Kate's dress. "You'll probably think I'm horrid, but that's why I send Elisa to bed early. There's a lot to be said for a long row of difficult hooks!"

Though Kate was a bit shocked that Belle admitted such an intimate detail of her married life, she couldn't help smiling at her friend's audacious wink. With a warm hug Belle was out the door, and Kate was left alone to finish undressing.

She slipped out of her dress, draped it carefully over the back of a chair, and rubbed her fingers over the soft velvet regretfully. Petticoats and corset soon followed the dress, and Kate drew a deep breath of relief before seating herself in front of the mirror. She removed the pins and shook her hair free, enjoying the sensuous feel of it across her back. Too much champagne, she thought with a grin. Granny would probably have apoplexy if she could see her well-brought-up little granddaughter right now.

The familiar task of brushing took little thought, and Kate let her mind drift. Lost in a pleasant daydream of Jonathan lovingly unhooking the back of her dress, she didn't realize he had returned to his bedroom until she heard a muffled crash.

When a string of curses came through the wall, Kate paused midstroke. If he were truly angry, he'd be using big words, not curses. The only time she'd ever know him to swear this way was when he was in pain. Laying down the brush, she stood and walked to the door between their rooms. "Jonathan?"

When she got no answer, she opened the door and tried again. "Jonathan?"

"Damn. Did I wake you, Kate?" His voice came through the bathing room from his open doorway.

"No, I hadn't gone to bed yet. What happened?"

"I dropped the goddamn warming brick on my foot!"

"Oh, no." Instantly concerned, Kate was through the bathing room and into Jonathan's bedroom. "I hope you didn't break it."

"Pretty hard to break a brick," he muttered, looking up. His breath froze in his throat as he saw Kate.

Crouching next to the bed he sat on, she ran expert fingers over his injured foot. "I can't tell if anything's broken without probing deeper. I'll try not to hurt you."

But Jonathan had ceased to worry about his foot. He was far more interested in watching the lace at the top of Kate's camisole and the creamy flesh that swelled against it. The bottle of bourbon he and Daniel had shared blunted the pain in his foot but did nothing to slow the racing of his heart or make the vision before him any less tempting.

"I think the bones are all right, but you're going to have a nasty bruise on the top." She tenderly massaged the sole of his foot. "I wonder if there's any ice left from Belle's centerpiece."

"Kate . . ."

His deep voice, huskier than usual, sent a delicious shiver rippling down her spine, and she glanced up in surprise. She gazed briefly at the tantalizing display of hard muscles and enticing skin that showed through his open shirt and then looked up at his face. Under his smoldering blue gaze, she suddenly had difficulty breathing, as if there weren't enough air in the room.

Folding her hands in a warm grasp, he gently rubbed his thumbs across her knuckles as he pulled her onto his lap. Kate was mesmerized by the glow deep in his eyes. Had she been a young innocent, she would have been terrified by the naked desire she saw there, but Bryan had taught her to enjoy the physical side of marriage. Though her saner self would never admit it, she had missed it a great deal.

Jonathan wanted her and wanted her badly. The knowledge was like a strong aphrodisiac.

He slowly ran his hands up her arms, gently kneading the delicate flesh. "Oh, my God," he whispered, closing his eyes against the soft, seductive look on her face. He lifted one hand to the nape of her neck and rested his forehead against hers as he tried to regain control of himself.

But Kate had been alone for five long months. Restraint was not what she wanted. Cupping his face in both hands, she kissed his brow, then the bridge of his nose, then his lips.

For a moment Jonathan was stunned by her unexpected aggression. Then, with a groan, he pulled her tightly into his embrace, and they fell back on the bed. They kissed hungrily—champagne, bourbon, and lust effectively destroying all inhibitions.

Jonathan deftly slipped one hand beneath her camisole and gently massaged her ribs with the circular motion of his thumb while the fingers of his other hand unfastened the row of buttons that held the delicate garment closed against him. He tossed it to the floor and turned her to her back. With his heart hammering in his chest, he trailed kisses of fire down her neck to the generous breasts that had fascinated him for so long.

Running her fingers through his hair, Kate moaned as he lavished attention first on one breast and then the other, driving her to such distraction that she hardly noticed when her drawers went the way of her camisole.

He returned to the sweetness of her mouth and

plundered it eagerly. Rolling to his back, he pulled her onto his chest, where he had easier access to her supple curves. With an increasing sense of wonder, he allowed his hands to linger on the soft, sensuous skin of her shoulder blades before following the indentation of her spine down to her enticing small waist and firm derriere.

Having been married to a man who expected full participation, it didn't occur to Kate to remain passive. Glorying in the feel of his naked chest against her aching breasts, she squirmed a bit, trying to get even closer. The soft masculine hair that grew there was a new experience, one she decided she liked very much. She proceeded to investigate every muscle, every hollow—in fact, every square inch of warm, vibrant skin she could.

When she ran her tongue around the shell of his ear, Jonathan suddenly gave an agonized shudder, rolled out from under her, and rose from the bed. She opened her eyes in bewilderment. What had she done?

Devouring her with his fiery gaze, Jonathan swiftly shed the remainder of his clothes. Then he stood there, looking at her, the smoldering heat in his eyes mixed with a kind of awe. "My God, you're beautiful," he murmured as he lay down beside her and ran his hand across her midsection. "You take my breath away." The words were whispered against her neck, as he pulled her to him.

For a brief, agonizing moment the memory of another man who had thought her beautiful intruded. Then there was only Jonathan, his lips and hands driving all other thoughts into oblivion as he worshiped her body. The hot pleasure he created within her was so intense, she wondered how much more she could stand before bursting into flames. Her fingers encountered a hard ridge of scar tissue over his ribs, but it was soon forgotten as her need overwhelmed her.

When they finally joined, their bodies moved together in perfect rhythm, the seething fires building within each until they seemed to melt together as the final conflagration consumed them both.

It was like nothing Kate had ever known before. Drifting back to earth, she wondered if it would always be that way with Jonathan. She ran her fingers across the plane of his cheek and kissed him lightly before snuggling against his chest and relaxing into sleep.

Jonathan pulled the blankets over them both and kissed the top of her head. What an incredible experience! Though he'd made love to his share of partners, this was the first time a woman had ever made love to him at the same time. Who would have thought the proper, even prudish, Kate Murphy would be so uninhibited in bed?

Though he was stunned by the discovery, he found himself quite pleased. Here was yet another facet of her unique personality. What a special woman Kate was. Satiated and content, he folded his arms more closely around her and fell asleep with a smile on his face.

Filled with sweet languor, Jonathan drifted along in pure sensual pleasure. With a soft sigh, he pulled the woman in his arms closer. "Mary," he murmured.

The second Kate stiffened in his arms, Jonathan jerked awake. "What . . ."

"Oh, Lord, what have we done?" she cried, trying to struggle out of his arms.

"Kate, don't—"

"Let me go, Jonathan," she whispered, in such pain that he couldn't refuse. She grabbed her underthings and headed for the door.

He caught up with her in the bathing room. Grabbing her shoulders, he stopped her flight. "For God's sake, Kate, it's all right."

"No, it isn't. This should never have happened."

Wrapping his arms around her, he pulled her back against his body. "How can you say that? What we shared was very special."

"It was wrong. It's not supposed to happen this way."

"Kate . . ." He turned her to face him. "There wasn't anything wrong with what we did."

"Wasn't there?" Kate looked directly into his eyes. "Do you love me, Jonathan?"

Her question came as a complete surprise. "L-love you?" he stammered.

"No, I didn't think so. You're not ready to put Mary behind you. She's still the one you call out to in your sleep."

"My wife has nothing to do with this."

"Doesn't she? Bryan does." Kate twisted her wedding ring nervously. "The love I shared with him was my whole life. I won't sully it by indulging in a tawdry affair."

"Tawdry . . ."

"I'll be your housekeeper, a mother to your

boys, even your friend, but I can't be your mistress."

"Damn it, Kate. I didn't mean to hurt you."

"I know, but I think it's best if we forget this ever happened."

Running his hand wearily over his face, he sighed. Forget it? How could she even ask it of him?

"I'm sorry if that's not what you want, Jonathan, but I can't change." Bowing her head, she hid behind a curtain of hair, but her pain came through very clearly in her voice. "It's late, and I'm tired." She stepped into her room and shut the door firmly in his face.

Staring bleakly at the wooden barrier, he heard the unmistakable sound of a key grating in the lock.

Jonathan struck the door frame with the side of his fist and then dropped his forehead to his upraised arm, his eyes closed in frustration. He felt guilty and small, as though he had carelessly crushed a delicate butterfly beneath his boot.

25

"*Is this everything,* Kate?" Belle eyed the modest pile of luggage in the entryway skeptically. "It doesn't look like much."

Kate smiled. "It's twice as much as we came with, not to mention all the animals."

"Well, thank heaven Jonathan rented a special car for his stock and all the paraphernalia that goes with them. At least you won't have to deal with that mess until you get back to Wyoming."

"I can't imagine how he can afford it."

Belle laughed aloud. "I see Jonathan has you completely fooled."

"What do you mean?"

"My brother-in-law is quite disgustingly well off, though he does his best to hide it. The man is a financial wizard." She waved a hand at her home. "We have all of this because Jonathan convinced Daniel to invest in several ventures with him at the beginning of the war. He's also Daniel's silent partner in the horses, though he always puts his half of the profits right back into the business."

"I had no idea."

"Well, he keeps quiet about it. Before he went west he seemed almost driven to make money, as though it were the only challenge available to him. If he had stayed in the East, he would no doubt be a millionaire, but when he moved he left that part of his life behind."

"His house is very ordinary," Kate said. "It has huge windows, but everything else is very simple and plain."

"Money isn't particularly important to Jonathan anymore. I think he's much happier in his little cabin carving an empire out of the wilderness." Belle grinned. "Jonathan is a terrible tightwad until he wants something. That bull cost him a small fortune. Then he paid a bundle to have it shipped back to the United States. Over half his herd came the same way. He could easily afford to have someone travel with the animals all the way back to Wyoming. But if I know Jonathan, he'll spend the whole trip running back and forth to check on them."

Sighing, Kate thought how uncomfortable the trip home was going to be for them both.

Belle gave her a sharp look. "Are you sure you're all right, Kate? You still look a little peaked."

"I'm fine. A little tired, maybe, but otherwise healthy as a horse." Kate forced a smile. "Believe me, I've learned my lesson about too much champagne."

"A case of overindulgence doesn't last for two days."

Only if it's Jonathan Cantrell you overindulge in, Kate thought. "Maybe it's worse if you're not used to strong spirits. Those little bubbles are deadly. I think every one of them is loaded with gunpowder."

Belle laughed. "Oh, Kate, I'm going to miss you. I always knew I'd like you, I just didn't know how much."

"I'll miss you, too." Kate's smile was real this time. "You've been wonderful. I can't even begin to thank you for everything. I trust Madame Blanchard won't suffer unduly because of the special low prices she gave me?"

Belle didn't bat an eye. "Of course not, it's already been taken care of. Daniel has decided to give me a whole new winter wardrobe." She looked pensive for a moment. "I wonder if I've told him yet. Oh, well, no matter. Elisa, will you please fetch someone to take these bags to the carriage?"

"You are coming to the station, aren't you?" Kate asked as she put on her coat.

"Certainly. Otherwise Cassie might very well stow away with the horses. I'm afraid she's quite smitten with her cousin Cole."

"And he's completely oblivious. I overheard Levi telling his brother to stop being so mean to her, but I honestly don't think Cole had the faintest idea what he was talking about." Kate looked around. "Where are they, anyway?"

"Didn't Jonathan tell you? The three of them went with Daniel and Jonathan to load the stock."

Kate suddenly became very busy buttoning her coat. "It must have slipped his mind." In truth, she hadn't even seen him since she'd left him standing stark naked in the bathing room night before last. Yesterday she'd been very grateful for his absence, but the longer he avoided her, the more she dreaded their first meeting. She smoothed her red coat nervously, hoping she'd been right to put it on. By wearing his gift she was trying to send the message that she wanted to bury the hatchet and have everything be the same as before.

Kate's first contact with Jonathan turned out to be anticlimactic. When she and Belle arrived at the station, the others were already waiting, and Jonathan greeted them with a teasing remark about being late. He handed Kate three tickets for herself and the boys, telling her he'd decided to stay with the animals to make sure they were going to travel all right.

In a flurry of hugs and a tear or two, they said their good-byes and boarded the train. Kate and the two boys waved through the window until the platform disappeared from sight.

"By the time we see Cassie again she'll be all different," Levi said dejectedly. "She probably won't be any fun anymore."

Cole looked surprised. "Why not?"

"She's already starting to get . . . strange. Pa says girls do that."

"I didn't notice anything."

"That's because you're stupid."

"Am not!"

"Are so!"

"Oh, look," Kate said, "they're hooking cars up to that locomotive."

Both boys were instantly glued to the window, and Kate sat back with a relieved sigh. Chicago had the largest switching yard in the world. Watching all the comings and goings should keep them occupied long enough to forget their argument.

If only she could find such a distraction for herself. Far too frequently during the past two days she had been haunted by bittersweet memories of her encounter with Jonathan. Now, with nothing else to occupy her mind, they became almost unbearable. As in her experience with champagne, effervescent images rose to the surface of her consciousness, only to burst painfully as they spun around in her head.

Yet in spite of everything, she couldn't bring herself to wish that she'd never entered Jonathan's room that night. Deep within her heart, embarrassment and shame warred with the feeling of how very right it had seemed at the time.

By the time they reached the first stop, Kate had decided to quit wallowing in misery. Pulling a sock out of her mending bag, she attacked a hole in the toe with a vengeance. Before long, the familiar task soothed her jangled nerves and put life in perspective again.

How clearly she remembered her wedding night, when Bryan had taught his eighteen-year-old bride about the mysteries of sex. Holding her close to his heart, he'd explained that the good Lord had intended for married couples to share their love with each other in every way. That was why, in His infinite wisdom, God had given mankind the need to join physically and celebrate the love He had gifted them with.

Kate wasn't naive enough to think that everyone shared Bryan's views, but it certainly explained why she had allowed lust to cloud her judgment this time. She hadn't meant to fall in love with Jonathan and certainly hadn't intended to seduce him. If she'd been sober and taken a moment to think about it, she never would have entered his room.

In her heart the sweet memory of Jonathan's touch battled with feelings of guilt. Though Bryan was gone, Kate felt as though she had somehow betrayed him. Of course what was done was done, and nothing could be changed now. As Charlie always said, there wasn't any use crying over spilled milk.

Kate had fully expected Jonathan to join them in the passenger section of the train at the first stop. When he didn't, she decided that he must be having some problem with the animals. No doubt he'd come in later. By late afternoon she was becoming quite concerned. At the tenth stop, when she still hadn't seen hide nor hair of him, Kate convinced the conductor to check the boxcar to see if he was all right.

Within a short time the man returned. "Mr. Cantrell said he's going to stay with the animals."

Kate was dumbfounded. "For the whole trip?"

"He didn't say."

"Well, thank you for checking," she said.

Kate felt as if she had been punched in the stomach. He was purposely staying away from her. Suddenly she saw the image of herself dressed only in her underwear, sitting on his lap, kissing him while he struggled for restraint. Even more damning pictures of her wanton behavior flashed through her mind. Then, after he'd given in to her blandishments, she'd run away like some frightened schoolgirl. It wasn't surprising that he was avoiding her.

"What's wrong, Mrs. Murphy?" Levi was watching her with concern. "Your face turned red."

Cole nodded. "Yeah, and now it's all white. Is something wrong with Pa?"

"Oh, no, he's just making sure the animals are riding comfortably. He'll probably join us later."

But he didn't—not when the train held up for ten-minute refreshment stops, not at suppertime, not even when it was time to go to sleep for the night. By Omaha, Kate was devastated. Jonathan must be thoroughly disgusted with her behavior. He probably thought that she belonged back at the Golden Spur.

By Grand Island she was irritated. It wasn't all her fault. He'd given in pretty easily.

By Willow Bend she was angry. Jonathan had enjoyed her body just as much as she had enjoyed his. Everything had been fine until she'd made it clear that she wasn't about to become the mistress of a man who didn't love her.

By Ogallala she was furious. He hadn't checked on his sons once in the three days since they'd left Chicago. How dare he treat her like this? Did he think that by punishing her this way she'd give in and invite him to share her bed? Well, if he did, he had another think coming!

She told the boys to stay put, climbed down from the passenger car, and stomped to the back of the train. Oblivious of the early morning hour, she pounded on the door of the boxcar. "Jonathan!" she yelled. "Jonathan Cantrell, open this door!"

"Huh . . . wha . . . ?" Jonathan's sleepy voice came through the slats. "Kate?"

Kate could hear the sound of rustling straw and imagined him crawling out of his bedroll. Seconds later the door slid back, and he peered down at her. "What's wrong?"

"I want you to stop this nonsense right now."

Jonathan blinked in confusion. "What are you talking about?"

"You know very well what I'm talking about. Ever since we left Chicago you've been acting like a spoiled little boy, and I'm tired of it. You ought to be ashamed of yourself, a man your age pouting for four days because you didn't get your way for once."

"Pouting! In case you don't realize it, these animals are extremely valuable. I'm back here protecting my investment."

"Horsefeathers! That bull crossed the Atlantic Ocean without you, for goodness' sake. As for the horses, if they can't stand up to this trip, how in heaven's name do you expect them to survive your sons?" Kate eyed his dishevelment with disgust. "Just look at you. I've seen tramps more presentable than you are right now."

"You're overstepping yourself, Mrs. Murphy," he warned her through clenched teeth.

"No, you're overstepping yourself. How dare you expect me to take care of Levi and Cole with no help? You know how restless they get when they can't get outside and run around. Did you know they brought a snake onto the train? If I hadn't been on my toes, there would have been a terrible ruckus. I get paid to be your housekeeper, not their governess."

"I thought you said you didn't mind being a mother to my boys."

"If I really were their mother, I'd have dragged you out of here by your ear three days ago. It takes two people to control those two and you know it."

"Board!" The conductor's voice echoed up and down the train.

"When we stop again, I'll expect you to join us."

His blue eyes flashed. "And if I don't?"

"Then you can find yourself a new housekeeper when you get to Cheyenne!" With a swish of her skirts, she turned and marched back to the front of the train.

Fuming, Jonathan watched her until the conductor helped her back into the passenger car and the train jerked into motion once more. He slid the door shut with a crash. Who the hell did she think she was, anyway?

He kicked at a pile of straw, stomped over to his bedroll, and threw himself down on it angrily. Pouting! He'd generously given her time to get over her embarrassment, and she accused him of

acting like a spoiled little boy. That was gratitude
for you.

*She was probably over being embarrassed by
noon the next day, but you haven't been near her
since she said she didn't want you to make love to
her anymore,* his conscience reminded him. *Admit
it, you were hoping that if you ignored her for a
while, she'd change her mind.*

But what was wrong with that? It wasn't like she
wasn't willing. Hell, she's the one who came in
half-dressed!

*And you loved every second of it. That's the
whole problem. You can't wait to get her in bed
again, but you're not willing to do it on her terms.*

She wanted love, and I don't have that to give
anymore.

*Then you shouldn't have slept with her. Kate is
a special woman. She deserves better than a casual
toss in the hay. Stop being so selfish.*

Jonathan kicked a pile of straw in frustration.
"Damn it all, anyway."

Disturbed by the angry voice, the bull snorted
and stamped his foot.

"Oh, shut up," Jonathan muttered.

When the train pulled into the station at Big
Springs, Kate glanced out the window and then
calmly resumed her sewing. To the casual observer
she was the epitome of serenity. Inside she was a
screaming mass of nerves. What had possessed her
to deliver such an ultimatum to Jonathan Cantrell?
With his temper he'd probably fire her just on prin-

ciple. There was nothing like burning your bridges before you got to them, she thought.

The ten-minute stop seemed to go on forever. At last the conductor called for the passengers to board, and the train started to move. Jonathan hadn't appeared. Fighting her tears, Kate ducked her head and swallowed hard. That was that.

"Pa!" Cole and Levi shouted in unison.

Kate's head jerked up just as Jonathan slid onto the seat next to Cole. His wet hair was plastered to his head, the curls just starting to reappear after what had obviously been a good dousing. Though his shirt was still rumpled and he was badly in need of a shave, it was obvious that he had tried to clean up some. It must have taken the entire ten minutes of the stop. That's why he'd been late.

"Will the horses be all right without you, Pa?" Levi asked anxiously.

"Oh, I think so." Jonathan gave Kate a meaningful look. "Since we'll make Cheyenne today, Mrs. Murphy suggested I come finish the trip with all of you."

Kate complacently resumed her sewing. "I'm glad I was able to persuade you."

"My conscience got the better of me." He grinned at her. "I'd never be able to live with myself if I cast a woman penniless upon the world."

"Humph. More like you didn't relish the idea of finding a replacement."

Cole looked back and forth between them anxiously. "Pa, you weren't going to fire Mrs. Murphy, were you?"

"Of course not. The thought never even crossed my mind. Now what's this I hear about a snake?"

It was late afternoon when they reached Cheyenne. Though both Kate and Jonathan had had some uncomfortable moments, they managed to treat each other with casual friendliness. As soon as they disembarked, Jonathan and the boys went to unload the animals while Kate collected all the baggage with the help of the porter.

Surrounded by the pile that had seemed so small in Belle's large entrance hall, Kate settled herself on the bench in front of the station. She was soon engrossed in observing the wide variety of people milling about the station platform.

"Katharine Murphy? Good Lord, Katie, it is you!"

With a start, Kate turned toward the voice. Her eyes widened with dread when she saw the man coming toward her.

26

"*Katie, I can't believe* it's really you!" Clasping her hands in his own, the well-dressed gentleman beamed at her.

"Uncle Matthew! I certainly never expected to see you here."

"Ah, Katie, if you aren't a sight for sore eyes."

"My name is Katharine," she said automatically. Dispassionately, Kate noted how much he had aged in the years since she'd seen him. His hair was completely gray now, and there were many new wrinkles in his face. "How have you been?"

"Never better." He glanced around. "Is Murphy still with you?"

"No."

"Ha! I always said you'd live to regret marrying that damned scoundrel. Deserted you, didn't he, just as I always said? I tried to tell you how irresponsible he was."

Any hope that her uncle had changed evaporated.

"Bryan didn't leave me, Uncle Matthew. He caught cholera last summer and died."

"Eh? I'm sorry to hear that, but that's the way they are. You can't trust the Irish."

"You seem to forget you're Irish, too."

"I was born and raised in the United States. Murphy was straight off the boat, and a Catholic to boot."

"You liked him well enough when he worked for you. In fact, you're the one who invited him home to dinner."

"That's beside the point. He betrayed my trust by kidnapping my one and only niece. I can never forgive the man for that."

"Bryan Murphy didn't kidnap me, Uncle Matthew," Kate snapped. "I went with him willingly, and for your information, I never regretted it for an instant."

Glaring up at him, Kate suddenly remembered Bryan on his deathbed telling her to go to her uncle. Until Bryan had come between them, she and Uncle Matthew had been close. If only he hadn't tried to control her life. . . . Kate sighed.

"What brings you to Cheyenne, Uncle?"

"Business. We're thinking of opening a new bank." He gave her a sharp look. "And what are you doing here? Last I knew, you and Murphy were headed out to Oregon."

"We were on the trail when Bryan died. I was lucky enough to find a job."

"Doing what?"

Kate bristled at the tone of his voice. "I'm the housekeeper for a wealthy family."

"What family is that?"

"Probably no one you've ever heard of," Kate said, hedging. "They own a big ranch." There was a slight chance that he'd recognize the name Cantrell, and if he knew that she was living in an isolated cabin with a handsome widower, he'd probably drag her back to Denver with him.

"I make it my business to know anyone with money in this territory, including all the cattle barons. I'm likely well acquainted with this family of yours."

"All aboard!"

He glanced at the conductor in irritation. "That's my train."

Before Uncle Matthew could continue his line of questioning, Kate stood up and gave him a kiss on the cheek. "Then I won't keep you. It's been wonderful seeing you again." She gave him a slight push toward the train. "Hurry now, or you'll miss it."

"You don't have to earn your living," he said. "There's always a place for you with me."

"Thank you, Uncle Matthew. I won't forget."

"You're all I have left." He paused a moment. "I always loved you and Patrick, you know. An old bachelor doesn't know much about being a father, but I did the best I could." He touched her cheek one last time before hurrying off to catch his train.

She watched the train pull out of the station, waving when she saw her uncle's face in the window. Would she ever be able to forgive him for the things he'd done to Bryan? Kate sighed. Maybe one day, but not yet.

"Who was that, Mrs. Murphy?" Levi asked, coming to stand beside her.

Kate looked down at him in surprise. "Who?"

"That man you were waving to."

"Oh, just a man I met while I was waiting for you."

Kate ignored her conscience. Since she'd disowned her uncle in a fit of anger, it had always given her satisfaction to deny their relationship. Besides, deep inside, she wasn't completely sure that Jonathan had been joking when he'd said that he wouldn't fire her because she had nowhere to go. "Do you have a message for me from your father?"

"Oh, yeah. He and Cole went to get the wagon. They'll be back pretty quick."

"Did they take the new animals with them?"

"Yup. Pa said they'd leave them at the same place we left the others."

Jonathan and Cole returned a short time later. The baggage was soon loaded, the boys tucked into the back of the wagon, and Kate safely ensconced on the seat next to Jonathan.

They were able to get rooms in the same hotel they had stayed in before, and Kate soon found herself overseeing the distribution of the baggage. Already anticipating a hot bath, she hardly noticed when the desk clerk handed Jonathan a folded piece of paper.

Jonathan took out his glasses to read the message and then looked up at Kate. "Clay wants to meet us for supper tonight. Is that all right with you?"

"Yes, of course, but how did he know we were back?"

"I sent him a message from the train depot," Jonathan said, returning his glasses to his pocket. "I thought I'd better let him know, since he's been keeping an eye on the horses and the wagon."

"What time?"

"Seven-thirty."

"Fine. I assume you gentlemen can take care of yourselves?" Kate included all three of them in her glance. "Good, then I'll meet you all here at seven twenty-five."

Kate climbed the stairs and closed the door to her room behind her, unable to suppress a grin. That would teach him to leave her all alone on a train with his sons for three days.

Kate's act of revenge was not lost on Jonathan. He was forced to admire her tactics as he tried to convince his sons that a bath wouldn't do them the least harm. Neither of them seemed at all concerned that they wouldn't have a chance to take another for a week or more. At last, while Cole sat in a steaming tub with a scowl on his face, Jonathan lay back on the bed with a sigh.

"Pa?" Levi asked. "Why would Mrs. Murphy lie to me?"

Jonathan opened his eyes in surprise. "What makes you think she did?"

"When you sent me to get her I saw her kiss a man and wave good-bye to him when he got on the train. When I asked her who he was she said it was just a man she met while she was waiting."

"What did this man look like?"

"Old."

"How old? My age?"

"Oh, no, Pa. This guy was really old. He had white hair and everything."

"Hmm, that does sound strange. Did she hug him?"

"No, just kinda touched his cheek with her mouth."

Jonathan smiled to himself. Most likely an elderly gentleman had stopped to ask Kate directions and she'd leaned forward to shout something to him over the roar of the nearby steam engine. From a distance it must have looked as though she'd kissed his cheek. "I wouldn't worry too much about it. It probably wasn't what it looked like."

Clay was already there when Kate came downstairs at the appointed time. She had regretfully decided that the maroon ball dress was too formal, but there was an appreciative glow in Clay's eyes as he took in her new blue dress.

"Hello, Kate," he said softly, taking her hands and pulling her forward. "I've missed you."

Turning her head at the last moment, Kate managed to deflect his kiss to her cheek. "It does seem like we were gone forever," she replied. "How is the legislature going?"

"It took a while to get started, but once we finally did, things have been going rather well, I think." Clay led her to a pair of chairs next to the wall. "We've already passed several bills to regulate mining, and we're working on the location of a penitentiary now."

"It must be difficult to get everyone to agree."

Clay chuckled. "That, my dear, is a terrible understatement." He took her hands once more. "But I haven't told you the big news. As of yesterday, you will quite probably be one of the first women in the entire world to have the right to vote!"

She stared at him in astonishment. "It passed?"

"It did indeed. When William Bright first introduced his bill, most people thought it was a joke. In fact, it caused a great deal of hilarity, but we passed it yesterday. Now it goes to Governor Campbell."

"I . . . I hardly know what to say." Like many women, Kate hadn't given a great deal of thought to what women's suffrage might mean to her if it became law. "I can help elect the president," she said in an awestruck voice.

"You might even be able to run for president someday." Clay squeezed her fingers. "Not only that, there's also a bill on the floor to give married women the right to own their own property."

"Do you think that will pass, too?"

"I think there's a good chance of it."

"A good chance of what?" Jonathan asked, coming down the stairs.

"Oh, Jonathan, the suffrage bill passed!" Kate said. "As soon as the governor signs it, women will have the right to vote."

Jonathan looked over her head at Clay. "You can't be serious."

Clay nodded. "It's sitting on Governor Campbell's desk right now."

"Good Lord! Surely the man will be smart enough to veto it."

"Well, that's what a great many of my fellow legislators believe, but I'm not so sure he will."

Kate stood up angrily. "What difference does it make, Jonathan? You don't think any of us have the intelligence to make a decision on our own, anyway. Didn't you say women would just vote the way their husbands told them to?" Her eyes flashed. " 'If we give them the right to vote, they'll settle down and we'll never hear another word out of them,' " she added, mimicking his deep voice. She grabbed her coat from the back of her chair and stomped to the door. "Cole, Levi, get your coats on and let's go."

As the boys meekly followed her out the door, Clay and Jonathan exchanged a look of pure astonishment.

"Whew!" Clay pretended to wipe the sweat from his brow. "I'm glad I wasn't the one to make her mad."

Jonathan gave him a rueful smile. "Actually it's the second time today she's blasted me like that. We'd better get going. I'm afraid I might not survive a third."

By the time they reached the restaurant, Kate had calmed down and felt a little foolish for her outburst. Still, there was no way she was going to back down from Jonathan. The man had enough arrogance to choke a buffalo.

During the meal the men carefully avoided politics, and the conversation turned to the price of cattle and Jonathan's new bull, Sampson's Supreme. It wasn't long before Kate's mind began to wander.

A bath and a shave had made a distinct difference in Jonathan's appearance. It was the first time since the ball that she'd seen him cleaned up. He looked wonderful. Watching him dreamily, she ate her food without tasting it. Her gaze traveled from his chestnut curls to his dark eyebrows and stunning blue eyes. He truly did have a beautiful masculine face. Even his neatly trimmed mustache was memorable. In fact, she had vivid memories of its soft silkiness against her breasts, her hip, even the underside of her knee.

"What do you say, Kate?" Jonathan asked as the men turned toward her expectantly.

Returning to reality, she blushed. "I'm sorry, what did you say?"

Jonathan grinned. "I thought you learned your lesson about woolgathering with that look on your face. It seems to me it's gotten you into trouble before."

Turning even redder, Kate turned to Clay. "I'm sorry, I didn't hear what you said."

"One of my men brought some important documents down for me yesterday. I thought I'd send him back with the lot of you. I'd feel a whole lot safer if you had an extra man."

"Oh. That sounds fine to me." With a final glare at Jonathan's wide grin, Kate changed the subject, and the rest of the evening passed pleasantly.

*   *   *

The next morning they bought supplies and had the wagon loaded by ten-thirty. The white-faced bull, whose name had been shortened to Sampson, was tied to the back with Jonathan's horse. Coming down the steps in front of the hotel, Kate smiled at the boys mounted proudly on their new horses. "My, my. Those horses will be the envy of every cowboy between here and Horse Creek."

Jonathan eyed the yellow cloak she was wearing with disapproval. "Where's your new coat?"

"Packed away. I didn't want to ruin it with trail dust," she said as he helped her climb up into the wagon. Settling herself on the seat, she missed the smile that crossed his face.

"Pa, isn't that Mr. Langton again?"

"Sure looks like it," Jonathan replied as he tightened the canvas covering over the load and checked Sampson's lead rope.

"Good morning, Clay," Kate called out.

"Good morning. Thought I'd ride over with Tom to see you off."

Looking past Clay, Kate found herself staring into the dancing brown eyes of her brother, Patrick.

27

"I wish we'd brought Cassie back with us and left you in Chicago with Aunt Belle and Uncle Daniel!" Levi yelled at Cole. "She'd be more fun as a sister than you are as a brother."

Cole balled his fists. "Oh, yeah? Well, anybody'd be more fun than you, even a girl who likes dolls."

"Be glad you have a brother. I'd have happily traded my sister for one, or even a good dog, for that matter," Patrick said, pouring himself another cup of coffee and settling back against a log by the campfire. "Has your brother ever told you to wash your hands or wipe your feet?"

"No!" Cole and Levi both looked horrified by the thought.

"My sister did. In fact, after our parents died, she decided it was her job to keep me clean. She was a horrible nag. Worse than that, she was plumb stupid when it came to important things. She didn't even like presents."

"She didn't?"

"Nope. I gave her my best snake, and all she did was scream. Then I found a toad about the size of this tin cup. I put it out in plain sight so it wouldn't scare her, but she screamed louder about the toad on her plate than she did about the snake on her pillow. My granny put me on bread and water for two whole days." He shook his head. "Your brother wouldn't scream his head off over a toad, would he?"

Cole and Levi exchanged a look.

"I'm sure your sister didn't see it quite the same way," Kate snapped from the back of the wagon where she was washing the supper dishes.

"That's true. We didn't see eye to eye on most things, but then she was a lot older than I was." Patrick grinned as Kate glared at him across the campfire. "And mean . . . I can't tell you how many times she sat on me and tortured me until I cried uncle."

Jonathan was amused in spite of himself. "This sister of yours must have had some redeeming qualities."

"Oh, sure. On her eighteenth birthday, she ran away and got married."

"And you never saw her again?" Cole asked.

"No, I saw her all the time. She wouldn't come to the house because she was mad at my uncle, but Granny and I used to go to her house a lot. My brother-in-law was a lot more fun than my sister."

Levi was agog with curiosity. "How did your sister torture you?"

"A hundred different ways." Patrick lowered his

voice to a sinster tone. "I can tell you things that will freeze your blood."

Listening to the clearly embellished stories the young man launched into, Jonathan had to fight the urge to like him. The bitter taste of betrayal was strong as he watched Tom Fielding and Kate pretend to be casual acquaintances. Two months ago they'd been hugging behind the outhouse, and now they didn't know each other? Any doubts he'd had about Kate's duplicity had died this morning.

When Clay had arrived with Tom Fielding, Jonathan had felt as if a giant fist had slammed into his gut. Then he'd remembered the chummy way Kate and Clay had been talking when he had come downstairs the night before. Had they really been discussing politics?

If he had a lick of sense, he'd have denounced all three of them this morning and left them behind. Staring glumly into the fire, Jonathan wondered why he hadn't.

"What's she like now?" Cole asked Patrick.

"That's the funny thing. My sister turned into a pretty decent person. In fact, she's one of my favorite people. I wouldn't be at all surprised if you feel the same way about each other when you grow up." He dumped his coffee and stood up, stretching. "Well, guess it's time to take my watch." He put his hat on his head and sauntered off into the darkness.

Walking to where he'd left his bedroll by the side of the wagon, Jonathan avoided looking at Kate. "Guess I'll turn in." Though he could sense her gaze following him, he shrugged off the feeling.

He didn't owe her a thing, he reminded himself.

Jonathan could hear Kate moving around camp long after he'd crawled into his bedroll. Even with his eyes closed he could see her emptying the dishpan, banking the fire, doing a dozen little tasks he usually helped her with. At last she finished, and he heard her leave camp. Assuming she'd gone to visit the bushes before she went to bed, he lay there for nearly ten minutes before he realized that she wasn't coming back.

He crawled out of his bedroll and hurriedly slipped into his clothes. It took him very little time to find Kate, and when he did he almost wished he'd remained ignorant. She was seated on a rock next to Tom Fielding, her head bent next to his in quiet conversation. Straining to hear, Jonathan could just make out their words.

"I saw him at the train station in Cheyenne yesterday," she was saying.

"What was he doing there?"

"Business, he said."

"I wish I had seen him."

"What for? He hasn't changed, you know."

"I didn't figure he had," Fielding said with a slight smile. "Lately I've kind of wondered if I made a mistake by leaving him."

"You're not serious."

Fielding shrugged. "I've really enjoyed the work I've been doing for the colonel, and it's the same sort of thing."

"Clay Langton has a completely different personality."

"Not really. You only think so because he's sweet

on you." He grinned as she glared at him. "Anyway, when this is all over I think I might mosey on down to Denver."

"What do you mean when this is all over?"

"When Bullwhip comes back I'm going to end it one way or another. I'm tired of it, Katharine. The lying, the hiding—I can't even admit I know you." He sighed. "Do you think Cantrell suspects anything?"

"Jonathan? No, why should he?"

"I don't know, but he seems pretty cool toward you."

Kate looked down at her hands. "He's angry because of something I did."

"Lost that sweet little temper of yours, did you?"

"No . . . well . . . yes, but that's not why he's mad." She twisted her gold wedding band. "I did a stupid thing, one I don't think he'll ever forgive me for. Anyway, it has nothing to do with you." She leaned forward and kissed him on the cheek. "I'm glad you're here, Patrick. I've missed you."

Jonathan didn't wait to hear the details of their intimacy as he turned and made his way back to camp. The man's name wasn't even Tom, it was Patrick, and he was obviously Kate's lover. Feeling as though he had lost something very precious, Jonathan undressed and crawled into his bedroll.

Kate straightened and looked off into the darkness as she heard something move through the brush. "Did you hear that?"

"Just an animal." Patrick gently took his sister's hand. "So you don't want Langton, and you don't want Cantrell. Katharine, Bryan's dead, and you're too young to spend the rest of your life as a widow."

"I know, but I can't put it behind me yet. Don't ask me to give up Bry before I'm ready."

He stared at her silently for a moment and then shook his head. "Just don't wait too long."

The next day Jonathan was even more remote and Kate more miserable. When he spoke to her at all, it was to bark out orders. As the afternoon progressed Kate sank farther and farther into her misery, her heart wrapped in a cocoon of unhappiness. She knew she couldn't stand much more of this.

Jonathan followed Kate again that night, eavesdropping on her conversation with Fielding without a single twinge of guilt.

"Oh, I wish I'd stayed in Cheyenne."

"What for?" Patrick asked in surprise.

"I don't know if I can work for Jonathan anymore."

"I thought you liked your job."

"I do, or rather I did, until Jonathan decided to punish me. I can't live with his hatred."

"You're in love with him, aren't you?" Patrick asked softly.

"Don't be silly."

"He's a handsome man."

"Yes, but he's also arrogant, opinionated, hotheaded, and lately downright mean. Jonathan's my employer, Patrick, nothing more." Kate stood up and pulled her shawl closer. "I need to be getting back. Thanks for listening." She leaned forward to kiss him on the cheek as she had the night before. "I love you."

Jonathan couldn't believe his ears. A sharp pain

stabbed him when Kate passed close to his hiding place on her way back to camp. He imagined her hazel eyes softening to green as she leaned forward to kiss him.

What a consummate actress she was. He'd thought their unforgettable night of shared passion was real, but now he knew what she really thought of him. Had it just been a ploy to get close to him for some hidden purpose she and Fielding had?

The stress of two sleepless nights coupled with his anger over Kate's treachery exploded into rage. Without warning he stomped through the brush, grabbed Fielding by the shirtfront, and smashed his fist into the other man's face. Though Jonathan was over a decade older and Patrick put up a good fight, it wasn't long before Jonathan gained the advantage. He was about to give in to the urge to crush the other man's windpipe when he realized that he was acting like a complete fool.

Jumping to conclusions and allowing his emotions to rule his head were dangerous, in peacetime as well as war. He rolled to his feet and held his hand out to Fielding.

"What the hell was that all about?" Patrick asked, ignoring Jonathan's hand as he got painfully to his feet.

"I want to know what's going on."

Patrick stared at him in disbelief. "You beat the hell out of me for no reason and then ask *me* what's going on?"

"I overheard you and your lover."

*   *   *

"My lov . . . Christ, you're jealous!" Patrick said in disgust as he fingered his bruised jaw. "I can't see why Kate thinks you're so damned intelligent. She isn't my lover, she's my sister."

"Your sister!"

"Hell, yes. If you'd look beyond the end of your nose, you could see it."

Suddenly Jonathan did see a resemblance, especially now that the other man was angry. The stubborn set of his jaw was quite familiar, not to mention the sparks flashing from his eyes. "Then why did you pretend not to know each other?"

"I didn't want her to be in any danger."

"Danger! From me?"

"Hardly," Patrick said. "If I thought you were any threat to her, you could have beat me to death before I admitted anything."

"That makes no sense. Why did you all of a sudden decide it was safe to tell me?"

"I didn't." Patrick's eyes met Jonathan's squarely. "In fact, I'm not sure I should have. I'm banking that Katie's right."

"How's that?"

"My sister is one of the best judges of character I know. God knows why she trusts you, but she does. When the time comes, she's going to need someone who cares enough to protect her." Patrick's jaw hardened. "If it comes to a fight, I'm depending on you to keep her safe."

"A fight? With who?"

"Does it make a difference? Would you shield

her even if it made you look like a Confederate sympathizer?"

"The war is over."

"Not for some people."

"It is for me," Jonathan said. "I walked away from it six years ago, and I have no intention of looking back. People did what they thought they had to do. Too many died on both sides." He paused. "Are you going to tell me what this is all about?"

"Nope." Patrick sat down on his rock again. "Katie may trust you, but I have no reason to. I'm not willing to turn my back to the door unless I'm very sure of the man standing behind me."

Jonathan studied the other man. "I'll keep Kate safe in every way I can, but unless I know what's going on I can't promise to help you."

"Fair enough," Patrick said with a satisfied nod. "At least we understand each other. Better go get some sleep. I'll expect you to relieve me at two o'clock."

Without a word, Jonathan nodded and returned to camp. Although somewhat mollified by the realization that Kate must not dislike him after all, he was still uneasy about what was going on.

As he crawled into his bedroll he decided to write a letter to McNesby, his friend and former superior, as soon as he got home. Though McNesby was no longer the head of American espionage, as he had been during the war, he still had connections in high places. If Fielding had anything to hide, McNesby would ferret it out.

28

"You're going to what?" Jonathan roared.

Patrick and the boys glanced back at the wagon in surprise. Then Patrick grinned, and the three of them rode on ahead, leaving Kate and Jonathan a modicum of privacy as they drove the wagon along. Jonathan didn't even notice.

"I'm going to move into Hofflemeir's cabin," Kate repeated.

"Just like that, you're going to leave us? How am I going to replace you?"

"You won't need to. I'm going to live somewhere else, but I'll still be your housekeeper."

Jonathan gave her a look of disbelief. "How do you plan to do that?"

"It's very simple. I'll be at your house shortly after dawn every morning and won't leave until supper's over."

"Isn't this rather sudden?"

"Not really. I've been thinking about it since we left Cheyenne."

"That was six days ago. Why are you just telling me now?"

"This is the first time you've driven the wagon," Kate pointed out.

"This has something to do with whatever you and your brother are involved in, doesn't it?"

Kate glanced at him surprise. "My brother? What are you talking about?"

"You can drop the wide-eyed innocent look, Kate," Jonathan said. "Fielding and I had a long talk the night before last."

"Ah, the mysterious injuries." She knew something had gone on between the two men when they'd both showed up with various cuts and bruises, but neither of them would tell her a thing. "What did you talk about?"

"After we got our differences resolved, we discussed you being his sister. Mostly he talked about the war."

Kate had a momentary flash of doubt. Patrick had changed his mind and decided to trust Jonathan after all? Then again, maybe Jonathan was just fishing for information. "What did he tell you about the war?"

"People, battles, you know, the usual things."

"He didn't tell you a thing, did he?"

"No," Jonathan admitted after a moment.

She sighed. "Jonathan, please don't ask me to betray my brother. I can't tell you anything. His secrets aren't mine to reveal."

"Not even how you knew he hadn't told me anything?"

"Not even that." She laid her hand on his arm. "My brother has nothing to do with this. He doesn't know what I'm planning and probably won't like it any better than you do. My reasons for moving are my own."

"Am I permitted to know what those reasons are?" His voice was rigidly polite as he stared straight ahead at the team pulling the wagon.

She dropped her hand to her lap. "Clay gave me the notion the other night."

"Oh?"

"When he told me about the women's suffrage bill, I realized that I don't have to have a husband to homestead. I can build the dream Bryan and I had by myself."

"Do you have any idea how difficult homesteading can be?"

"Yes, I do. Maybe it is a ridiculous idea, I don't know. I've never done anything like this before, but the success or failure will be mine alone." She smiled slightly. "And if I do fail, just think how much satisfaction you'll get out of telling me you told me so."

Jonathan ignored her attempt at levity. "November is hardly the best time of year to start a homestead."

"You're probably right, but the house is already there. I'll have a decent roof over my head, and thanks to that early snowstorm there's plenty of broken limbs for firewood. I'll hire the boys to chop me a good supply when they aren't busy elsewhere. Just think of the mischief it will keep them out of."

"I don't see why you're in such an all-fired

hurry," Jonathan said. "Why can't you just wait until spring?"

Kate turned away. "I think you know why," she said quietly. "If we live under the same roof, it will only be a matter of time before we wind up like we did in Chicago."

"You think so little of me that you're afraid I won't be able to control my lust for you? It may surprise you to know I have never slept with an unwilling woman in my entire life. A simple 'no' would be more than sufficient to keep me out of your bed."

Kate bit her lip. "I'm afraid I wouldn't say no."

"Damn it, Kate! You make it sound like I'm planning to spend the winter seducing you. I promise, I won't set foot in your room, especially after dark. You'll be perfectly safe from me."

Kate's gaze dropped to her lap, where her hands were clenched in white-knuckled misery. "But who will protect me from myself?" she whispered. "We both know you didn't seduce me in Chicago. I was the one who . . ." She trailed off into embarrassed silence.

"As I remember, it was mutual."

"You would have stopped if I'd asked you to."

"I'm not so sure about that. Nobility was never my strong suit."

"I never gave your nobility a chance."

"You were drunk."

"Yes, but I knew what I was doing."

Jonathan felt a peculiar wrenching in his stomach as he gazed down at her face, stained with a telltale flush. "What if I promise to yell my head off any time you try to take liberties with my person?" he asked lightly, hoping that a touch of humor would help alleviate her unhappiness.

Kate smiled slightly. "Would you?"

He started to say that he'd shout the rafters down, but something in her eyes stopped him. "No," he said softly, "I probably wouldn't say a word." A feeling of warmth flowed over him as he watched the brown of her irises mellow to green before she turned away.

"This isn't easy for me, Jonathan, and I didn't make this decision lightly."

"What if I refuse to let you do it?"

Kate sighed. "I'm not asking for permission. I'm simply telling you what I'm going to do. You can make it difficult, maybe even impossible, for me to accomplish, but it's still my choice."

"Your mind is made up?"

"Yes."

"Nothing I can say will change it?"

"No."

Jonathan slapped the horses on the rumps with the reins. "Then I guess there's nothing more to say, is there?"

She laid her hand on his arm again. "Please don't be angry. I'm doing this because I need to have something of my own, not to thwart you." Kate smiled. "It may even be my rainbow."

"What the hell is that supposed to mean?"

"My husband was the world's most dedicated optimist. He used to say there was a rainbow after every storm and a pot of gold at the end of it. No matter what went wrong, he always found the bright side. Kate looked out over the landscape. "With almost his last words, Bry told me to look for the rainbow."

"And you think taking out your own homestead might be it?"

Kate shrugged. "That's what we were going to do once we got to Oregon."

A dozen images flooded Jonathan's mind—most painful of all was the memory of Kate after her miscarriage, sobbing in his arms, grieving equally for the baby and its father. From the time she had been forced to work in the saloon right up to the recent strain between the two of them, Kate Murphy's rainbow had been damned elusive.

"Pa!" Levi yelled as he came loping up to the wagon on his horse. "There's some furniture by the road up ahead."

Jonathan pulled his attention away from Kate. "Hmm, kind of late in the year for that. I'll take a look when I get there."

Levi wheeled his horse and headed back up the road.

"Furniture?" Kate asked. "What in the world . . ."

"Happens all the time along here. People traveling west on the Oregon Trail sometimes have to lighten their wagons to get over the mountains. It's usually farther along, though, at the bottom of Block and Tackle Hill."

"What an odd name."

Jonathan chuckled. "Not if you've ever seen that particular hill. It's so steep they have to hook a block and tackle to a tree at the top and pull the wagons up that way. More than one family treasure has been left at the bottom." He shook his head. "Most of it gets ruined by weather, but sometimes you get there before too much damage is done."

"And then what?"

Jonathan shrugged. "Whoever happens by picks it up and takes it home."

"But that's stealing!" Kate was clearly shocked.

"How could it be? The owners aren't coming back after it. I always felt that the settlers who discarded the secretary would be pleased to know it wasn't destroyed."

"So that's where it came from." Suddenly the pieces began to fall into place in her mind. "The hip bath?"

"Yup. The hoosier and the cookstove, too. I've always figured a freighter dumped that, though."

"That's why it was rusty."

"I suppose, although I never really noticed until you pointed it out."

"Is that where you got the windows?"

Jonathan grinned. "No, I had to bribe Ox Bruford to bring those in for me. He always makes a point of reminding me how difficult it was, too."

They reached Patrick and the boys several minutes later.

"It's only a dresser, Pa, and part of a bed," Cole said.

After tying the reins to the brake lever, Jonathan jumped down. "You were hoping for something more exciting?"

"Well, that one time we found the roulette wheel and all those fancy dresses."

"Which we gave to Red O'Leary because we had no use for them," Jonathan reminded his son. "Kate, come look at this."

She clambered down from the wagon and joined Jonathan and her brother. "Oh, how pretty!" she exclaimed when she saw the cherrywood bureau. Leaning against it were the gracefully curved head and footboards of a matching bed. Though the craftmanship was exquisite, it was easy to see why it had been left behind. All three pieces were enormous. The headboard alone was nearly five feet high and probably weighed a hundred pounds. Deep ruts in the road gave testimony to the struggle that had resulted in the abandonment.

"It must have been difficult to leave this behind," Kate murmured, remembering the loss of her own possessions. "It was probably a family heirloom."

"This time of year they were in danger of losing something a lot more precious than a bedroom set," Jonathan said.

Patrick gazed off toward the mountains to the west. "Let's hope they have enough sense to stay in South Pass City for the winter."

"Well, what do you think, Kate?" Jonathan rubbed his mustache absently as he contemplated the bureau. "Shall we try to get it home?"

Kate blinked at him in surprise. "Where are you going to put it?"

"There's plenty of room in the old Hofflemeir cabin. We'd have to build a frame, of course, and find something to stuff a mattress with, but . . . What's the matter?"

Kate was staring at him in astonishment. "Nothing," she said quickly. "Nothing at all. You were saying?"

If he wanted to act as if he'd approved of her decision all along, she certainly wasn't going to complain.

Though Kate's new furniture filled the wagon to overflowing and the added weight slowed them down a bit, they arrived home by midafternoon the next day. Kate clambered down from the wagon and went into the cabin to open the door and windows in an attempt to air it out. Jonathan and the boys were still unloading the wagon when Charlie showed up.

"Dang if I ain't right glad to see the lot of you. I was gettin' tired of nobody to talk to around here but Kate's cow. How was your trip?" Leaning a forearm on his saddle horn, he listened attentively to Cole and Levi's disjointed chatter.

"Our cousin Cassie looks just like Levi. . . ."

"Pa bought these horses for us. . . ."

"They're quarter horses. . . ."

"The bull looks funny, but we named him Sampson. . . ."

"Mrs. Murphy's going to live in Hofflemeir's cabin. . . ."

Grinning at Jonathan, Charlie tipped back his hat. "I see the young-uns ain't changed much. Reckon you don't look none the worse for wear, neither. How's Kate?"

"She survived." Jonathan returned his grin. "I

swear this has been the longest month I've ever spent in my life. How are things here?"

Charlie swung down from his horse and tied it to the corral fence. "Been pretty quiet." He eyed the headboard with interest. "You plannin' on buildin' a bigger house?"

"No, we found this along the trail. Here, give me a hand with it."

Charlie took one end. "Mite big for yer bedroom, ain't it?"

"Yup, but it isn't going there. Kate's been bit by the suffrage bug." Jonathan grunted as he picked up his end. "Thinks she needs to homestead."

The two men carried the cumbersome furniture into the barn a piece at a time and put it in the back by the tack room. When they had finally set the dresser next to the bed both breathed a sigh of relief and stopped to rest a moment.

"How come Kate suddenly wants to take out a homestead?" Charlie asked.

Jonathan shook his head. "She's got some crazy notion she can homestead the Hofflemeir place all by herself."

"Nothin' wrong with that. If any woman can do it alone, I expect it's Kate."

"But she plans to move in as soon as she can get it cleaned."

Charlie frowned. "In November? Reckon you'd best tell her to wait till spring."

Jonathan sighed. "I did, and she informed me it was her choice and she'd do as she pleased."

Charlie was silent for a long moment. "It ain't like Kate to go off half-cocked, Jon," he said finally.

"Is there somethin' more you ain't tellin' me?"

Jonathan suddenly became very interested in the storage bin set against the wall. "What more could there be? You know how women are."

29

Moonflower looked around the interior of the Hofflemeir cabin with disgust. "Charlie say you gonna live here."

Kate looked up from the cookstove in surprise. "Moonflower! I wasn't expecting you."

Moonflower made a face. "I tell Charlie he plumb loco."

As always, Moonflower's unusual speech pattern tickled Kate. The young Indian woman had almost doubled her English vocabulary, but it was liberally seasoned with Charlie's western twang. The result was unique, and Kate found it rather endearing.

"He's right. I am going to move in here." She reached back into the oven and pulled out a mouse nest. With a shudder she dropped it into a bucket. "That is, if I ever get it cleaned up."

"Maybe tipi better way to live. We move camp

before it get this dirty." Moonflower stepped inside. "You show me how, I help."

"Oh, Moonflower, you don't have to do that."

Moonflower shrugged. "I reckon you teach me clean, I teach you dry meat."

"Fair enough," Kate said with a grin.

Within a few minutes Moonflower was attacking the dust and cobwebs as energetically as Kate. "Jon tell you to do this?"

"No. In fact, he's completely against the idea. I think he'd stop me if he could think of a way to do it."

"Then why you leave?"

Kate sighed. "It's difficult to explain."

"He beat you?"

"Heavens, no." Kate was shocked. "He wouldn't dare."

Moonflower shook her head, clearly perplexed. "Why you not do what your man want?"

"Jonathan isn't my man."

"What you mean?" Moonflower looked puzzled.

"I only work for Jonathan. He hired me to be his housekeeper."

"What is housekeeper?"

"I cook his meals, wash his clothes, clean his house, and take care of his sons."

Moonflower nodded. "I do for Charlie, too."

"No, you don't understand. I don't . . ." Kate trailed off.

Moonflower looked even more confused, and then an expression of understanding crossed her face. "You not share his blankets?"

"No." Kate looked down.

"Why? 'Cause baby die?" Moonflower shook her head sympathetically. "Great Spirit make next one strong."

"Oh, no, it isn't that. I'm not afraid of having another baby. In fact, I wish . . ." Kate sighed and started again. "The baby wasn't Jonathan's. It was my husband's."

Moonflower's eyes widened. "Charlie, he think it Jon's."

Kate suddenly remembered the day she'd first told Charlie of her impending motherhood. No wonder he'd wanted to know if she'd told Jonathan yet. "All this time Charlie's been thinking I was . . . that Jonathan and I . . . ?"

Moonflower pursed her lips. "Your eyes say you want him."

Kate started to deny it and then realized she couldn't lie to her friend. Moonflower would never believe her. "Yes," she admitted with a soft sigh, "I do. I want him too much. That's one of the reasons I'm moving."

"I not understand."

"I was raised to believe that people should be married before they . . . share their blankets. Jonathan and I aren't. He isn't my man."

Moonflower gazed at her silently for a moment and then shook her head. "He your man here," she said, touching her heart. "I reckon that where it be important."

"That's part of the problem, you see. He's in my heart, but I'm not in his. Jonathan doesn't love me."

"You are sure of this?"

"Quite sure. I even asked."

Pushing away the bittersweet memory of that night, Kate stood up and briskly shook out her skirts. After giving the stove one last swipe with her cleaning rag, she lifted the lids and proceeded to build a pile of wood shavings and kindling in the firebox.

"Besides, there's more to this move than Jonathan Cantrell. I need to prove something to myself. First my granny and my uncle took care of me, then my husband. Even after Bryan died, I had Jonathan and the boys. I've never had to depend only on myself. Even if I fail, at least I'll know I had the courage to try."

Moonflower slowly nodded her head. "I understand need to prove courage. It is a thing my people admire, too."

Since there seemed to be nothing more to say on the subject, they moved on to other topics as they worked side by side for the rest of that day and all through the next. If the names Charlie and Jonathan came up a bit too often, neither woman seemed to mind, and the time passed swiftly for them both.

Although she bemoaned the fact that there seemed to be no way to clean the hard-packed earth of the floor, Kate nevertheless declared herself satisfied that all the dirt, mice, and spiders had been thoroughly routed by noon of the third day. She had just sat down with Moonflower for a much deserved rest when they heard a wagon drive up outside.

"You there in the house," Jonathan's voice boomed out. "Where do you want your furniture?"

"Where do you think?" Kate called back, too tired to get up from the chunk of wood she was sitting on. It would be nice to have the bed. These improvised chairs were far from comfortable.

"Hurry up, Kate. I haven't got all day."

"Oh, for pity's sake, Jonathan." With an angry swish of her skirt, Kate rose and stomped to the door. "How many different places do you think . . ." When she reached the door, her mouth dropped open.

"Surprise!" half a dozen voices rang out in unison as Jonathan grinned at her. All of Kate's friends from town were there: Rosie, Frenchie, Red, even Silas Jones. As Jonathan helped Rosie and Frenchie down from the wagon, Charlie rode in with Patrick, Levi, and Cole.

"We came to help you move in," Cole said.

Seated on the back of Cole's horse, Levi looked over his brother's shoulder. "Mr. Langton only had one shovel, Pa."

"Silas had three, so we ought to have enough to get the job done." At the back of the wagon, Jonathan started removing shovels and passing them out to the men.

Kate eyed them dubiously. "What are you going to do with those?"

"Well, now, just what do you think we'd be doin' with them, colleen?" Red said with a grin. "We're going to clean your floor."

"With shovels?"

"Relax, Kate." Jonathan casually brushed her cheek with the tip of his finger as he walked past her into the house. "We know what we're doing.

Why don't you and the other ladies look through the wagon so you can decide where you want to put what?"

Kate turned her attention to the wagon for the first time and suffered another shock. It was filled with a wide variety of items contributed by everyone for her new home. By the time she had gone through it all with Rosie and Frenchie, the men had dug up every square inch of the floor.

It was then that Kate missed Moonflower. When she asked Charlie where she was, he gave her a look of mild surprise.

"She went home."

"Whatever for?"

"I don't reckon she thought she'd be real welcome."

Kate was indignant. "Moonflower will always be welcome at my home. She knows that."

"Yup, but most folks ain't like you. All they see when they look at Moonflower is another dirty savage. These folks are fine people, but ain't none of 'em woulda been comfortable if she'da stayed." Charlie gave Kate a lopsided smile. "Don't reckon she woulda been, neither."

"Come on, Charlie," Silas Jones called. "We're waitin' for that harmonica of yours."

Kate raised her brows. "What do they want with your harmonica?"

"That's how we pack down the floor."

"With a harmonica?"

"In a manner of speakin'." Charlie gave an experimental blow on the instrument and then chuckled at Kate's expression. "We're gonna have us a hoedown."

Even though Moonflower's absence took a bit of the brightness from the day, it was impossible for Kate not to enjoy herself. With Charlie on his harmonica and Silas on his fiddle, the music was fast and furious. So was the dancing. In fact, the floor was stomped to a smooth, hard surface in no time, though the dancing continued on until Jonathan finally called a halt.

"Hate to put an end to all this, but if we're going to get everything moved in before dark . . ."

As Kate directed the placement of the furniture, Frenchie and Rosie unpacked a huge hamper of food, giggling about how mad Crabby Abby would be if she knew what Jonathan had done with all the food she'd packed for him.

It was dark by the time the job was done and everyone had finished eating. Kate had tears in her eyes as she bade her friends good-bye at the door. Their generosity had completely overwhelmed her.

At last only Jonathan remained in the cabin with her. She smiled at him tremulously. "Thank you, Jonathan."

He shrugged self-consciously. "It was Silas's idea. He thought of it when I commissioned him to build a metal frame for your bed."

"Maybe so, but I know you're the one who organized it."

"It does look pretty good, doesn't it?" His eyes twinkled as he glanced around the now homey interior of the cabin. "Guess it's time to change the name of this place."

"Oh? I suppose you have something in mind?"

"Actually, I sort of like the sound of Murphy's Rainbow." The warmth of his gaze caused the breath to catch in her throat. "Well, I'd better get Rosie and Frenchie home." He put on his hat. "I'll see you bright and early tomorrow morning. Good night."

Kate closed the door after him and looked around her new home. A table and chairs that could only have come from the Golden Spur sat on the beautiful rag rug Rosie and Frenchie had made for her. Kate smiled as she looked down at the brightly colored braids. When the three of them started on the project back in July, she never would have expected to have it covering her very own floor. It was probably the only rag rug in Wyoming made of silks and satins.

Freshly waxed, the bed and dresser gleamed in the soft lamplight. The stained-glass and crystal opulence of Frenchie's lamp was a bit vulgar, per- haps, but it somehow gave the tiny cabin a touch of elegance.

With a smile, Kate looked over all the treasures her friends had provided. There was everything from pots and pans to dishes and food. Jonathan and the boys had even built a woodbox and filled it with a good supply of wood.

They'd brought over all her personal belongings, too. As she undressed for bed, Kate thought about how wonderful it was that everybody had helped. She hadn't planned on being moved in for another week or so, but thanks to all her friends she was completely settled.

She climbed into bed, blew out the lamp, and

snuggled into the soft feather bed Silas had unearthed from heaven knew where. Everything was perfect in her new home.

So why were tears of loneliness clogging her throat? Why did the big bed feel so empty?

30

"You're sure this will help my sore throat?" Jonathan eyed the steaming cup suspiciously.

"Well, it certainly won't hurt," Kate said. "I still don't think you're well enough to go out on the range today."

"I'm fine." Closing his eyes, Jonathan took a sip of Kate's homemade remedy and made a face at the taste. "It's just a cold."

"Uh-huh, and it's moving into your chest."

"I need to make sure the cows can get to water."

"Why can't Charlie do it?"

"We've split the herd. He's doing the other half."

"What about the boys?"

"For God's sake, Kate, stop trying to mother me. I'm fine!" He swallowed the rest of the medicine and slammed the cup on the table.

"Maybe if you didn't act so much like a child, I wouldn't treat you like one," she muttered.

He stopped winding his scarf around his neck. "I beg your pardon?"

Kate turned away. "I accept your apology."

"That wasn't what I meant."

"I know, but I'll take it that way. I'd hate to think you'd be so ungrateful as to swear at me when I was only trying to help."

Jonathan gave an exasperated sigh. "You never admit defeat, do you?"

"No. Why should I?"

"God only knows. Certainly not because your employer might be offended when you compare him to a child."

Kate smiled. "The truth hurts. At any rate, the fact still remains you're endangering your health. I wouldn't be doing my job if I didn't point that out."

He finished wrapping his scarf and pulled on his gloves. "All right, if it makes you happy, I'll get the cows to water and then come home. You can spend the rest of the day cosseting me if you want."

"I still think you should stay here." Kate poured hot water into her dishpan.

"And I think your brother is right." Jonathan put on his hat and walked to the door. "You are a bully."

"Look who's talking," Kate murmured as the door shut behind him.

As she washed the dishes, she indulged herself by dwelling on the delightful idea of cosseting Jonathan for an entire afternoon. Unfortunately it was only a short leap of the imagination to seduction, and Kate soon found herself in a daydream reminiscent of that unforgettable night of passion in Chicago.

Kate was uncomfortably aware of how many times her thoughts had taken a similar turn over the past three months. Removing herself from Jonathan's house to sleep hadn't reduced the temptation, only the means of giving in to it. She was ashamed of the number of times her dreams had been of him. More than once she'd awakened aching with unfulfilled desire, frustrated to find herself alone in the big bed.

Reminding herself that sleeping alone was exactly why she'd moved to her new home in the first place, Kate pushed aside the enticing thoughts of Jonathan and tried to think of something else.

She glanced toward the open door of her old bedroom. Jonathan had left her bed set up in case the weather ever prevented her from going home at night but he'd converted the room back into an artist's studio. For most of the winter he'd been painting a picture he refused to let anyone see. For Kate, the temptation to peek beneath the cover when no one was around was nearly overwhelming. Today was no different. Angrily scrubbing egg off a plate, Kate wondered if she spent more time each day feeling curious about Jonathan's picture, frustrated that they couldn't be together or guilty for falling in love with him.

The morning seemed endless as she waited for him to return. Charlie and the boys came in for lunch, and still no Jonathan. Telling herself that she was worrying for nothing, she sent the boys to wash their hands, and put lunch on the table. Fifteen minutes later she was promising herself the luxury of telling him off for scaring her like this.

But when Jonathan finally arrived, her anger was forgotten instantly. His lips were blue, and he was shivering uncontrollably.

"Good gracious, Jonathan," Kate cried, jumping to her feet. "What happened?"

"D-damn ice b-broke under my f-feet," he managed to say between chattering teeth. "Y-you were right: I sh-should've stayed ho-home."

Kate looked down and gasped in horror. Jonathan's boots and pant legs were frozen stiff, clear to his knees. "Mercy sakes! Get those wet things off right this minute. I'll put more water on to heat."

While Cole, Levi, and Kate hurriedly set up the hip bath behind the curtain, Charlie cut the frozen boots off of Jonathan's feet.

"Reckon your luck's holdin' out, Jon. It don't look like yer gonna lose any toes to frostbite. Kinda strange how ice'll keep yer feet from freezin'."

"S-some luck. Th-those were new b-boots."

"That's why I cut the seams. Reckon I kin sew 'em back up."

"Better your boots than your toes," Kate said. "Get those pants off and wrap up in these blankets." She set the blankets on the table and turned her back so Jonathan could undress. "I warmed them in the oven."

Jonathan did as he was told, closing his eyes in appreciation as the warm blanket enveloped his frozen legs. He jumped as Kate wrapped his feet in cool wet rags.

"Damn! Did you have t-to soak th-those rags in hot w-water?"

"They only feel hot. We need to warm your feet up some or the bath will be unbearable." She began to massage his legs and feet.

Jonathan grimaced against the pain of returning circulation. "Are you t-trying to take indecent liberties, Kate?"

Kate glanced up, shocked. Even though his eyes were filled with pain, there was a hint of a twinkle in the sapphire depths. How like him try to pass off his agony with a joke. "I might be," she replied. "It seems the perfect opportunity."

"How's that?"

"You can't run away, of course." She looked up at Charlie, who was hovering nearby. "I'm going to fix Jonathan's bath now. Will you help him out of the rest of his clothes and into the tub after I leave?"

It wasn't long before Jonathan was soaking in the tub of warm water, his eyes closed against the discomfort it was causing his frozen limbs. Over the next three-quarters of an hour he gradually relaxed as Kate periodically added hot water. At last, when he was on the verge of sleep, she forced him to drink some hot broth and then hustled him off to bed with Charlie's help.

Jonathan was sound asleep when Charlie took the boys with him to finish checking the cattle on the range. He was still sleeping when they returned several hours later, chattering excitedly about the herd of wild horses they had seen. The three of them played checkers until chore time, and Jonathan slept on. Nor did the noises Kate made fixing supper seem to disturb him.

When Charlie came in to escort Kate home, as he did every night, she said, "I think I'll stay here tonight so I can keep an eye on Jonathan."

Charlie walked to Jonathan's bedroom door and gazed at his partner worriedly. "Reckon he's gonna need you before mornin'?"

"I doubt it. In fact, he's probably going to be just fine." She smiled uncertainly. "I guess he's right. I do try to mother him."

"Could be he needs it. Jon ain't one to take real good care of himself." He put his hat back on and buttoned his coat. "You need anything else 'fore I go?"

"No, but thanks. I'll see you in the morning."

Supper was a subdued meal. Though Cole and Levi were anxious to tell Kate all about the herd of wild horses, they kept glancing toward their father's bedroom. "Is Pa all right?" Cole finally blurted out.

"Your pa's fine," Kate assured him. "He doesn't have a temperature and he seems to be resting comfortably."

"Then why doesn't he wake up?" Levi asked.

"It's not at all uncommon for someone to sleep a long time after they've gotten very cold like your father did today. He'll probably be right as rain in the morning." Kate prayed that she was right.

The sky was just beginning to turn gray the next morning when Kate awoke with a start. Rubbing her eyes, she sat up in bed and listened intently. Unable to identify what had awakened her, she slipped into her dress and tiptoed across the kitchen to Jonathan's room.

The moment she saw his flushed face and heard his labored breathing, she knew that something was terribly wrong. With a cry of dismay she rushed to the bed and felt his forehead. His skin was hot and dry to the touch.

Horrified, Kate sank to her knees beside the bed, tears welling up in her eyes. The deep rattle in his chest confirmed her suspicion. Kate knew this killer well. For nearly two weeks she had nursed Granny through it, and all to no avail.

With a feeling of helplessness, she looked into Jonathan's face and wondered if she'd ever see the beautiful blue eyes open again. She knew the odds were not in his favor. Jonathan Cantrell had pneumonia.

31

Moonflower looked at the dark circles under Kate's eyes critically. "You sure you not want me to stay? Reckon you ain't gonna take care of Jon if you sick, too."

"No, I'm fine. I don't know what I'd have done without you."

"I want to be more help, but he too sick."

"There's not much any of us can do, but if you hadn't been here to sit with him while I got some sleep, I would have collapsed long ago."

Moonflower shrugged. "You do the same if Charlie sick."

"I'm so lucky to have you for a friend."

"You a good friend, too."

"How's Jon?" Charlie asked, stomping the snow from his boots as he came in.

Kate shook her head. "No change."

"Expect we should be glad he don't seem to be gettin' any worse." Charlie looked into Jonathan's room with a weary sigh. "The boys are doin' chores. We went out to see the wild horses again."

"Thank you for keeping them busy." Kate rubbed her forehead. "This is so hard on them. It's almost as if they think they caused it somehow. I don't know what they'll do if . . ." She let the sentence trail off, but they all knew what she meant.

It was a question that had haunted her all week as Jonathan teetered between life and death. Cole and Levi had been perfect angels. Not only had they stayed out of mischief, there hadn't been a fight or disagreement of any sort, and they did everything that was asked of them without complaint. They had been so totally unlike themselves that Kate longed for a little spark of orneriness, just so she'd know they were all right.

How well she understood their fears. Jonathan had been unconscious for the better part of a week, but she had left his side only when fatigue forced her to. Caring for him was a chore she'd accepted gladly, her need to be near him obliterating any fear of catching the disease.

She had been able to get him to drink water and broth at regular intervals. Kate and Moonflower had brewed up every concoction they knew of. His fever was down, but it hadn't broken. Though he hadn't gotten any worse, his condition hadn't improved, either.

Supper was solemn that night, just as it had been every night since Jonathan had taken ill. Kate and the boys picked at their food with little interest. Their ears were all attuned to the heavy breathing in the other room, even though no one spoke of it.

While Kate washed the supper dishes, the boys sat down with their studies. They had accomplished all they could without Jonathan's teaching and were far beyond Kate's ability to help them. But they spent every night poring over their books, as if their diligence would somehow help their father recover. It tore at Kate's heart to see them work so hard.

"I think that's enough for tonight," she said after they'd been at it for two hours. "Charlie said he was going to need your help with the cattle tomorrow."

They both nodded and closed their books. Because she didn't want them exposed to Jonathan's illness any more than necessary, Kate had forbidden them to enter their father's room, but they walked to Jonathan's door as they had every night. Kate fought her tears as they went through their nightly ritual of telling him about their day just as if he were awake.

"Good night, Pa," Levi finally said, turning away.

For once, Cole didn't follow his brother. He was silent for a moment. "We love you, Pa." His voice cracked, and Kate heard a distinct sniff as he stood in the doorway, staring at his father.

"Cole?" Kate touched his arm.

He looked up at her with tears streaming down his cheeks. "He's going to die, isn't he?"

"Oh, Cole." With an anguished cry she put her arms around him. "I don't know, love. I just don't know." Within seconds Levi was there, too, and she pulled him into the circle of her embrace. The

three of them stood together a long time, just holding each other and letting the tears fall.

At last the storm subsided. "I think a glass of
warm milk before prayers might be in order
tonight," Kate said.

Later she tucked Cole and Levi into bed with
good-night hugs and kisses. Because of their ages
she'd never done such a thing before, but they
seemed to take comfort in it now.

The night beyond the curtained windows
seemed darker and more ominous than usual.
Kate shivered superstitiously as she heated more
broth for Jonathan. Telling herself that she had
an overactive imagination, she filled a bowl with
the soup and took it into his room. When she
attempted to feed him, Jonathan refused to swallow, muttering unintelligibly. It wasn't the first
time such a thing had happened, and Kate set
aside the broth, hoping that he'd be more recep-
tive later.

She couldn't seem to sit still. Even her sewing
basket offered no solace, and she was soon wandering around the house straightening and
cleaning. At last even that was finished, and she
went into her temporary bedroom to get the
quilt from the bed. With any kind of luck,
mending the frayed edge would take most of the
night. As she folded the quilt over her arm, she
happened to glance over her shoulder at
Jonathan's easel.

She walked over to it and ran her fingers
lightly over the concealed canvas. She had heard
it said that paintings were a mirror into the

artist's soul. Jonathan seemed so far away tonight, perhaps a peek would give him back to her. Before she could change her mind, she raised the cover.

Kate looked at the landscape in amazement for several minutes before a smile spread across her face. The painting was not what she had expected. Jonathan was the most intelligent man she had ever known—brilliant, clever, successful in everything he did. Except for a bit of a temper and a touch of arrogance, she loved almost everything about him.

Yet here was a side she had never even suspected. Jonathan Cantrell might be incredibly handsome, a wonderful father, a magnificent lover, and a good friend, but he was no artist.

Technically, the painting before her was correct. The trees and the mountains were easily recognizable, but even to Kate's untrained eye the picture lacked feeling or finesse. But there was something endearing about the realization that Jonathan wasn't perfect after all.

As she pulled the cover back down over the picture, Kate was surprised to find that she did feel somewhat better. After she managed to get a little soup down Jonathan, she even felt hopeful. With a sigh, she set to work on the quilt.

Kate awoke with a start. For a moment she was disoriented.

"Where the hell are my glasses?" Jonathan cried out in a raspy voice. "Damn, I can't see a thing."

"Jonathan?" Kate was out of the chair in an instant. "What is it?"

"When that last bomb exploded, it knocked my glasses off. The enemy is advancing, and I can't find them." His voice became frantic as his hands thrashed around on his bed. "There are thousands of them. How the hell am I going to shoot if I can't see the rifle sights?"

"It's all right, Jonathan. The war's over," Kate said soothingly as she tried to hold his hands.

He'd been delirious on and off since the beginning, but this was the first time his words had been understandable. It was obvious that whatever he was dreaming of was distressing him greatly. His breathing became louder and more labored by the moment.

"They'll try to break through the wall here because of the trees. Then they can take the ridge. Damn, we've got to hold it."

Oblivious of Kate, Jonathan continued to ramble, reliving the battle in terrifying detail. His voice rose and fell, sometimes garbled and confused, other times quite clear.

Suddenly he twisted out of Kate's grasp. "Let go of my hands. They're coming over the wall . . . can't see . . . have to shoot. . . . Christ, I'm hurt . . . dead man on top of me . . . can't move. . . . Oh, God, it's Benjamin! *Ben!*"

An odd noise almost like a sob echoed in the small room with agonizing clarity. Kate stared at the tears squeezing out from under Jonathan's closed eyelids. Whoever Ben had been, Jonathan had been devastated by his death.

Suddenly his breathing changed. It became lighter, more irregular, almost as though he had stopped fighting. And then she knew. Death was in the room with them. She could feel its presence. Jonathan was slipping away just as Bryan had. In a few moments he would be gone, too.

"No!" Kate cried. Perching on the edge of the bed, she grabbed his shoulders in panic. "Don't you dare leave me, Jonathan Cantrell. You can't die! Your sons need you. I need you, damn it. I love you. Do you hear me? *I love you!"*

"Kate?" he murmured. "Shouldn't swear. Bad example for the boys."

Kate sucked in her breath. She'd actually gotten through to him! She lifted him so that his head rested against her and smoothed the hair back from his brow. "Then you'd better stay here and protect them, or I'll teach them every bad word I know," she said, fighting the tears that threatened to choke her. "If you aren't around to stop me, I'll let them swear like troopers and act like wild Indians. Cole and Levi are your responsibility, and you'd better live up to it!"

"You're a bully," he mumbled. He put an arm around her waist and settled his head against her chest. "But you're a damn comfortable one."

Afraid to move, Kate leaned back against the headboard and held him tightly. She prayed to every God she knew—Catholic, Protestant, even Moonflower's—pleading, cajoling, begging.

At last, toward morning, Jonathan's breathing began to steady and deepen. Kate could almost feel death withdraw and creep away into the darkness again. With a whimper of relief, she dropped her chin to the top of Jonathan's head and closed her eyes.

She had won.

"Mrs. Murphy?"

Kate's eyes fluttered open. Cole and Levi were standing in the doorway, gazing at her uncertainly.

"I . . . is Pa . . . is he . . . ?"

Kate looked down at the man she held in her arms. He lay sprawled across her, his head leaning on her chest and one arm still around her waist. With hesitant fingers she touched the beads of moisture on his forehead. He was sweating!

"Thank you, Lord," she whispered, tears springing to her eyes. "The fever has finally broken," she told the boys with a blinding smile. "Your father's going to be all right."

When Moonflower and Charlie arrived a short time later, Kate met them at the door with the good news. Jonathan wasn't completely out of danger yet, but he was on the road to recovery at last. For the first time in days, Charlie's face relaxed into a grin.

"Reckon that means he'll make it. Jon's always been a fighter."

Kate returned his smile. "I reckon."

With Moonflower's help, Kate changed Jonathan's nightshirt and his bedding. His breathing was deep and even, the deadly rattle gone with the fever. No longer battling to survive, Jonathan's body had relaxed into a deep, natural sleep. For once, Kate had no problem leaving Moonflower to watch over the patient while she got some much needed rest herself.

It was late afternoon when Kate returned to the sickroom. Charlie and Moonflower had departed for home, and the boys were still outside finishing up their chores. Planning to fill the few minutes before suppertime, Kate settled herself by the bed with her mending.

"Good Lord, Kate. You look terrible."

She looked up, startled. "Jonathan!" She dropped her mending and reached over to touch his forehead. It was cool. "You're awake."

The deep blue eyes regarded her with a mixture of confusion and irritation. "You sound surprised."

She smiled. "It's been a while. Are you hungry?"

"No." He tried to sit up but collapsed in exhaustion. "What's wrong with me?"

"You've been very sick," Kate said, fluffing his pillow and smoothing the blankets around him.

"How long?"

"Six days. I've been waiting all that time to say I told you so."

"Why?"

"You had pneumonia."

He was silent for a moment. "That vile concoction you forced me to drink didn't work."

"It might have if you hadn't fallen in the creek."

"Oh." His eyes traveled over her face, taking in the dark circles under her eyes and the lines of strain around her mouth. "You saved my life, didn't you?"

Kate shrugged. "Moonflower helped." For some

reason she was reluctant to admit that she'd dragged him back from the brink of death, as though her private victory could be snatched away if she told anyone about it.

Jonathan's eyes started to drift shut. "I'm so tired. . . ."

"It's your turn to chop wood!" Cole yelled as he walked by the bedroom window.

"No sir!" Levi bellowed. "I did it yesterday."

"Did not."

"Did so."

"Did not . . ."

Jonathan's eyes popped open. "Damn, are those two fighting again?"

"Yes, I believe they are," Kate said with a smile. "Isn't it wonderful?"

32

"*Well, reckon I'll see* if I can find the boys and go check the south range," Charlie said, rising from the table. "Did they say where they was goin'?"

Kate shook her head. "No, they just said they wouldn't be in for lunch."

"Probably up to some kinda mischief." He gave Jonathan a speculative glance. "I expect we'll be ready to brand in three or four weeks."

Jonathan looked at his partner over the rim of his coffee cup. "And you're wondering if I'll be up to it." He shook his head. "I swear, between you and Kate a person could become a permanent invalid."

"It hasn't been much more than six weeks," Kate reminded him.

"Yes and I'm back to working a full day now," Jonathan said.

Charlie grinned. "And none too soon. I reckon

Kate was about to kick yer backside plumb out the door."

From the moment Jonathan had started to recover he had been less than a model patient. The better he felt, the more restless he had become. Kate had put up with his incessant demands and complaints for only so long and then told him exactly what she thought of his childish behavior.

It had been at her insistence that he'd returned first to his ledgers and then to his painting. The activity had helped his temper, and his convalescence had progressed with few other difficulties. Still, Kate had been as happy to see him go back to work as he'd been himself.

"Anyhow, I wasn't thinkin' about you, Jon. You're practically as good as new. One of us is gonna have to take Kate to South Pass City to file her homestead claim. Might be a good time fer the other to hire a coupla hands for the brandin'."

"That hadn't occurred to me." Jonathan looked thoughtful as Kate refilled his coffee cup. "I'll think about it."

"Let me know what you decide," Charlie said, putting on his hat and buttoning his coat. "I'll see you both later."

"Cole tells me that tomorrow is his birthday," Kate said as the door closed behind Charlie and she began to clear the lunch dishes from the table.

Jonathan gave a noncommittal grunt as he sipped his coffee.

"He said he's never had a birthday cake, so I thought I'd bake him one. Maybe we can have a little party."

"We don't celebrate Cole's birthday."

"Why ever not?"

"Because we don't, that's why."

"Surely not because of something Cole did."

"No, it wasn't his fault. Nevertheless, I'd rather not mark the day."

"And you're not even going to tell me why?"

"No."

"Well, of all the . . ." Kate put her hands on her hips. "It seems to me you're being terribly unfair to your son."

"You know nothing about it."

"Maybe not, but every child deserves a birthday. Unless you give me a darn good reason, I'm going to give Cole one."

"Fine!" Slamming his cup on the table, Jonathan rose to his feet, his eyes shooting sparks as he glared down at her. "Go ahead and bake him a cake, have a party. It doesn't matter what I say, you'll do as you damn well please anyway. Just don't expect me to be there."

With that, he stormed out of the house.

Kate stared after him in amazement. He hadn't had a temper tantrum like that since he'd gotten over his pneumonia. Honestly, the man was impossible to understand at times. It made no sense to deny Cole a birthday party, unless . . . A plate slipped unnoticed from her fingers and splashed back into the water as a thought materialized in her mind. Mary! Could she have died in childbirth?

Kate remembered Jonathan's horrified reaction to her own pregnancy and the way he'd seemed almost to share her suffering when she'd miscarried.

Could Jonathan actually feel that he murdered Mary because she'd died having his child? He might, since he knew how delicate her health was and had allowed her to get pregnant anyway.

Whatever Jonathan's problem, Kate couldn't forget the wistful expression on Cole's face when he'd confessed that he'd never had a birthday. She was going to do everything she could to make it a memorable day whether Jonathan liked it or not.

Though Jonathan hadn't actually forbidden her to have a party, Kate decided to move the celebration to her house. She left the Cantrells' after lunch the next day and spent the afternoon baking the promised cake and fixing Cole's favorite foods. At six o'clock sharp, Charlie, Moonflower, and the boys arrived for supper. The evening was a resounding success, filled with laughter and frivolity.

As far as Kate was concerned, there was only one blot on the festivities: Jonathan never appeared. Her anger at him grew with every passing moment. How dare he ignore his son that way? Cole tried to pretend that it didn't matter, but she could see the hurt in his eyes. It wasn't until everyone got ready to go home that Kate realized she was the only one who had expected Jonathan to come. The boys were spending the night at Charlie's, as they did every year.

"Pa always goes to town on my birthday," Cole said. "That's why we go to Charlie's."

"Why didn't he ask me to stay with them?" Kate asked Charlie. "It doesn't make sense for him to disrupt everyone's life this way."

"I reckon Jon didn't want you to see him when

he came home." Charlie looked slightly embarrassed. "He went to town to get drunk. He ain't never told me why he does it, but every year it's the same. He used to get drunk at home before the Golden Spur opened."

To Kate, Jonathan's behavior made perfect sense. If her suspicions were correct, he thought of the day not as Cole's birthday, but as the anniversary of Mary's death.

Kate didn't notice Levi lagging behind the others until everyone else was already out to the wagon.

"Mrs. Murphy."

She turned in surprise. "Levi?"

Turning his back to the wagon, he lowered his voice so that only Kate could hear. "I think I know why Pa gets drunk on Cole's birthday."

"You do?"

"It's 'cause that's the day our mama died." Levi shivered. "Pa doesn't know I remember, but I do. I was scared because it was so dark and stormy outside, so I went to find my mama. When I got to her room I heard a baby crying and knew it was my new brother or sister. I wanted to see the baby, so I went in." Levi shuddered and looked down at his feet. "Mama . . . Mama was just l-lying there on the b-bed. She looked l-like she was asleep, but there was bl-blood everywhere, and Pa was"—he swallowed—"Pa was crying. He . . . he said he was s-sorry."

"Oh, Levi," Kate murmured in horror, "you couldn't have been two years old."

He nodded. "I know, and that's why I didn't understand. I . . . I used to think Pa had done something to make her die, but Aunt Belle said it was because she'd been sick a long time ago and Cole was such a big baby." He touched Kate's arm urgently. "That's why you can't tell Cole. He might think it's his fault Mama died."

"No," Kate said, nearly choking on the lump in her throat. "I won't tell him. Thank you, Levi." She gave him a hug. "Run along now. You'll want to get to Charlie's before the storm hits."

Glancing up at the fat snowflakes falling from the sky, Levi nodded and ran to the wagon.

Kate closed the door after her guests had driven away, blinking away the tears that formed in her eyes. Poor Levi, so young to carry such a horrible memory. It was as bad as the agony Jonathan had put himself through over the years when he had left his home and his career. He must have gathered up his sons and come west in an effort to escape the guilt. He'd even pulled away from Belle and Daniel.

Then Kate froze in the act of pouring hot water into her dishpan. If Jonathan had come west because of Mary's death, why had he waited six years to do it? Setting down the kettle, Kate thought back to the things Belle had told her. Though Jonathan had made a great deal of money from investments he'd made during the war, he seemed not to care about it. In fact, after Gettysburg he had just walked away—not just from the war, but from everything in his life except his sons. What had happened on that battlefield?

As Kate finished her dishes and straightened her house, she mulled over all the puzzle pieces. Nothing made sense. It was as though something important were missing from the picture.

Baffled by Jonathan's confusing past, Kate gave up and settled down to sew. The evening seemed to stretch on forever as the wind began to howl outside. Kate shook her head. Here it was the middle of March, and there was a full-scale blizzard blowing outside. Thank goodness she had filled both of her water buckets and had a box full of wood for the fire.

It was nearly ten o'clock when she decided to call it a night. She donned her warmest flannel nightgown, took down her hair and was up to fifty strokes when she was startled by a scratching at the door.

Looking over her shoulder at the window, where she could see the storm continuing unabated, Kate decided that her ears were playing tricks on her. She had just resumed her brushing when the noise came again.

"Who's there?"

There was silence. . . . Then the scratching came yet a third time, followed by an odd thumping. Something was out there.

Kate rose to her feet and took a firm grip on the poker. Gooseflesh raised on her arms as she saw the latch lift.

33

Wind whistled through a small crack between the door and the jamb. Whatever was on the other side had stopped. Kate crept forward, her bare feet making no noise on the rag rug. Positioning herself out of sight, she raised the poker over her head and waited. Her heart was pounding so hard, she was sure that the intruder could hear it as the door started to swing inward again.

"Damn it, Kate, open up."

"Jonathan?" Poker lowered, Kate pulled open the door and stood gaping as he staggered in, carrying his saddle.

Dropping the saddle next to the door, he gave her a reproachful look. "Didn't you hear me?"

"I didn't know it was you."

"'Course it's—hic!—me. Who else would it be?"

"You're drunk!"

"Yup. F—hic!—Fielding tried to drink me under the table." He grinned. "He lost." With one large hand, Jonathan swung the door shut against the wind. "Oughtta keep your door closed. It's cold out there."

Kate looked at his shirtsleeves. He was shivering with cold. "Where's your coat?"

"Dunno. Must have left it with my horse."

Kate sighed. "Where's your horse?"

He hiccuped again. " 'Bout half a mile from here."

"What in heaven's name are you doing?" She grabbed the quilt off her bed, threw it around his shoulders, and pushed him over to the stove. "It wasn't that long ago you almost died from pneumonia."

"Couldn't—hic!—help it." He held his hands out to the stove. "Horse broke his leg. Had to shoot him."

"What?"

"Something spooked him 'n' he bolted. Couldn't tell if he slipped on the ice or stuck his foot in a hole." Jonathan glanced down at the mending Kate had left on the chair and then wandered over to her bed and sat down. "My feet are c—hic!—old. Damn hiccups," he muttered, bending over and trying to pull off his boot. "You want to give me a hand here?"

"Oh, I suppose." She moved over to the bed and grabbed Jonathan's boot by the toe and the heel. "Why did you come here?" she asked as she pulled on the heel with all her strength.

"Rosie and Frenchie sent me. Said go home to K—hic!—Kate. Fergot you moved, I guess." He shook his head as he watched her futile attempts.

"Don't you know how to take a man's boots off?"

"This works . . . unh," she grunted as the boot finally came off in her hand, "just fine. Put your other foot up here."

"It'll n—hic!—never work. This one fits tighter."

"Nonsense, I can get it off." She tried jerking the heel toward her to no avail.

"Have to—hic!—use the boot jack on it at home."

"That may very well be." Kate stopped her struggles long enough to glower at him. "But I don't have one."

"Works be—hic!—better if you face the other way."

"It's undignified."

"Who cares?"

"I do." Her face was turning red with exertion.

"Don't think you're making any progress th—hic!—that way."

"Oh, very well," she snapped, turning her back to Jonathan. She swung her leg over his shin and bent down, grasping the boot heel firmly.

For several moments he admired the shapely derriere as Kate continued to tug with no results. Finally he sighed. "Only one way you're going to get it off," he said, placing his stockinged foot on her backside and pushing.

Giving a shocked gasp, Kate landed in an ungainly heap on the floor, the stubborn boot clutched in her hands.

She bounced angrily to her feet, fully intending to give Jonathan a good scolding. She was too late. Her intended target had passed out and lay sprawled across the bed, a victim of the demon alcohol. As she stood there glaring at him, a snore sounded in the quiet room.

Kate shook her head. It was very difficult to stay mad at such a pathetic creature. Besides, she could hardly ignore the fact that he was still shivering. Dropping the boot, she walked back to the bed and pulled off his socks. Jonathan's feet were indeed cold, the skin a mottled blue-and-white patchwork.

The rest of him wasn't in any better shape. She noticed the blue lips and the goose bumps that covered every square inch of skin she could see. If she didn't get him warmed up soon, his weakened lungs could easily succumb to pneumonia again.

With a rapidly increasing sense of urgency, Kate began to strip off his wet clothing. The memory of Jonathan's brush with death still haunted her, and she was determined that it wouldn't happen again. No matter what she had to do, Jonathan was not going to die. When she reached his long underwear, she hesitated only a moment before removing it. The garments were soaking wet, and she wasn't going to lose him because of modesty.

It was difficult to move his heavy, limp body, but she somehow managed to get him under the covers. Even snuggled into the warm feather tick, with the blankets and quilts pulled up to his chin, he continued to shiver. She added more wood to the fire, but that, too, seemed to have little effect.

Kate knew she had no choice. The only way to raise Jonathan's temperature was with body heat. Telling herself that she was doing it only to save his life, Kate pulled back the covers and crawled into bed next to him. Surely it wouldn't take long to warm him up, and then she could leave without him being any wiser. If he was drunk enough to lose his coat and not even notice, the chances of him waking up were minimal.

As she scooted over next to him, she involuntarily sucked in her breath. He was so cold, it was like lying next to a block of ice. Even so, when Jonathan unconsciously cuddled closer to her warmth, she couldn't resist putting her arms around him. No one would ever know, she thought, and she might never get another chance to hold the man she loved.

He was floating on a soft dream cloud, the delicious warmth so pleasurable it was nearly erotic. Or perhaps the delightfully sensual feelings were inspired by the woman who shared his cloud. Though he couldn't see her through the golden mist surrounding him, he knew she was there. He could feel her seductive curves caressing the contours of his own body as her breath fanned his cheek with a feather-light touch. He reached out tentative fingers and encountered the silken strands of her hair. With a satisfied smile, he sank his face into the sweet-smelling mass and inhaled her enchanting feminine fragrance.

The sharp sound of a wood chunk shifting in the stove woke Jonathan with a start. The threads of his dream still lingered in his mind as he tried to make sense of his muddled thoughts. Reality slowly replaced illusion, and Jonathan began to realize that most of the sensations of his dream were still with him. The soft, blissful warmth of Kate's bed was completely real, and so was Kate.

Raising himself up on one elbow, he stared down at her sleeping face in the mellow glow of the lamp. As the blankets shifted around his shoulders, he realized with a start that he was naked. A quick look around the room revealed his clothing draped over various pieces of furniture. With a grimace, he glanced back at Kate.

He had spent five months dreaming of the day he would once more get this woman into his bed, only to be too drunk to remember it when he finally accomplished his goal. In fact, he couldn't recall anything after shooting his horse. Damn Red O'Leary and his whiskey.

Jonathan wondered briefly what he had done to change Kate's mind. She obviously didn't mind his being here. One of her arms was draped across his rib cage, and the other lay curled against his chest. He smiled at the demure ruffle around her wrist. With infinite tenderness, he brushed the backs of his fingers against her cheek. How like her to put her nightgown back on after they'd made love.

A memory of the letter he'd received that afternoon flickered through his mind, bringing a troubled frown to his face. McNesby had found nothing on Thomas or Patrick Fielding. There was no record of his having fought on either side of the war. The letter suggested that the man might be using an alias and had asked for a description.

Jonathan sighed. Perhaps he'd been wrong about Kate and her brother. He knew they were hiding something. They had both admitted as much. Still, neither one had ever really asked him about the war or the gold. Maybe they were hiding their own secrets, not trying to ferret out his.

In fact, he'd never met anyone less like a spy in his life. He leaned down and kissed her slightly parted lips. An unexpected jolt of lightning sizzled through him and brought an involuntary groan to his throat. Suddenly he was rocked by a need so intense that it was difficult to believe his passion had been so recently appeased.

Beneath his fingers the buttons of Kate's nightgown slipped readily through the worn buttonholes as he nibbled at the sensitive skin below her ear. Easing the garment off her shoulders, Jonathan continued his seductive trail of kisses down her neck and along her collarbone. The soft material offered no resistance as he slipped his hands inside to stroke and caress her petal-smooth skin.

Kate came to awareness slowly. She had been deeply asleep, but Jonathan's hands and mouth were creating a whirlwind of sensation that couldn't be denied. The titillating passage of his strong fingers down her back and legs as his lips grazed the delicate skin of her breasts was exquisite torture. Even the tickle of his mustache sent tingles through her. The tumult he created within her was not the gentle breeze of affection, but a maelstrom of ardor that was nearly painful in its intensity.

With a moan, she gave in to the storm of desire

rampaging through her. There was no question of right or wrong as she pulled him closer into her embrace. "Jonathan," she whispered, his name becoming a caress as her lips moved to intercept his.

There was an almost frantic quality to their kisses, as though a tempest were brewing between them. Their bodies molded together, shifting and intertwining as each brought the other to undreamed heights of passion. They came together wildly with a primitive abandon neither had ever imagined. Though both would have liked to prolong the sweet agony a bit longer, urgency drove them to an explosive crest that left them breathless and shaken.

With tremors still echoing through his body, Jonathan rested his cheek against Kate's for a moment. "Good Lord," he murmured as he rolled to his back, his arms still wrapped firmly around her. Closing his eyes, Jonathan savored the weight of Kate's body sprawled across his. He could feel her heart pounding against his own and smiled in utter satisfaction. It was wiped away in an instant when she began to struggle in his arms.

He responded by tightening his hold on her. "Don't, Kate."

"But—"

"You're not running away this time," he said, hugging her fiercely.

"No, Jonathan, you don't understand. You're lying on my hair."

"Oh." Somewhat chagrined that he hadn't even noticed it wrapped around him like a blanket, he rolled slightly to the side so she could pull it out from under him. "Sorry."

"Mmmmm," Kate murmured as she laid her head back on his chest with a satisfied sigh.

Twisting his head so he could look at her, Jonathan was bemused by the glow on her face. It definitely hadn't been there before. "Was the first time like that?" he asked.

She raised her head and looked at him with a mixture of hurt and surprise. "You don't remember?"

"I was drunk," he said with an apologetic smile.

"So was I, but I haven't forgotten one single second of it."

Her words made no sense. Kate didn't drink. The only time he'd ever known her to touch alcohol was . . . All at once he understood her confusion. "No, I meant the first time tonight."

"Tonight?" She stared at him blankly.

"Look, I'm sorry. I probably shouldn't have even mentioned . . . I did make love to you earlier, didn't I?"

"No."

He glanced over at his clothes, then back to her. "So how did I wind up in your bed dressed like this?"

Playfully Kate ran her fingers through the hair on his chest. "I like the way you're dressed."

Jonathan lifted a lock of her hair and brought it to his lips. "Are you telling me I've been seduced?"

She shook her head. "No, it was sort of an accident. You were soaking wet and wouldn't stop shivering. I was afraid you'd get sick again, so I took your clothes off."

"And then you decided to join me?"

"There wasn't any other way to warm you up." She ducked her head but couldn't hide the blush that climbed to her face. "You weren't supposed to know. I didn't mean to fall asleep."

He dropped a kiss on the top of her head. "Don't expect me to be sorry you did."

Kate sighed. "I should have known this would happen." Tracing the line of hair that ran down his belly, she couldn't help wondering if she hadn't subconsciously intended it to. "I told you we couldn't be under the same roof."

"Did it ever occur to you that maybe we should be?"

"What do you mean?" Kate looked up at him in disbelief. Surely he wasn't talking about marriage.

He wasn't. "Who would we be hurting if you came back to my house and we just let nature take its course? We have something very special, Kate. What we just shared . . ." He shook his head. "It's never been like that before. How many people ever find someone who responds to them the way we do to each other?"

"We're perfectly matched, it seems," Kate said with a touch of sarcasm.

"Aren't we?"

"What happens between us is all physical, Jonathan. I told you before, I won't be your mistress."

"But you can't deny you enjoy it as much as I do."

"No, I can't deny it." She closed her eyes. How could such an intense love be so one-sided? "That doesn't make it right."

Silence fell between them for several long

moments. At last Jonathan gently rolled to his side, nestling her securely against him. Propped up on one elbow, he gazed down at her. With infinite tenderness he traced the line of her jaw down her throat to the smooth slope of her shoulder. "I'm sorry, Kate. I guess I was thinking only of myself."

"So was I."

He glanced toward the window, where the blizzard still raged. "No matter what either of us does, we're stuck here until the storm lets up. The way I see it, we have two choices."

"Oh?"

"We can spend that time arguing about which of us is right. I fully intend to keep after you until you give in." He smiled ruefully. "No doubt you'll remain just as stubbornly moralistic about it. Somehow, I doubt either of us will convince the other."

"Probably not. What's the other choice?"

"We call a truce and compromise."

"Compromise?"

"Right. We can stay here in this eminently comfortable bed of yours and indulge ourselves to the fullest."

"I thought you said this was a compromise."

"It is." He touched her nose with the tip of his finger. "As soon as the storm stops, so do we. We can pretend none of it ever happened, and I promise I'll never pressure you again."

"I can go back to being your housekeeper and nothing more?"

"That's right."

Kate bit her lip. It was silly, of course, almost

like a child's game, but it was so very tempting. To spend even a few hours with Jonathan . . . Before she had time to think better of it, she nodded. "All right, but just until the storm stops."

"Agreed!" He gave her a quick, hard kiss and grinned at her with a twinkle in his eye. "I guarantee you won't regret it." His expression was one of smug satisfaction.

"You aren't forgetting that this is only a temporary arrangement, are you?"

He looked shocked that she would suggest such a thing. "Of course not. My word is my bond."

"Then why are you so happy?"

His dimples deepened as he rolled her onto her back. "These spring storms sometimes last for days."

34

"*Want another biscuit?*" Kate asked, sticking the end of her finger in her mouth to lick off a remnant of jelly. Wearing only her robe, she sat cross-legged on the bed with her hair hanging around her in disarray.

"No, but I will take some more wine." Stretched out next to her and leaning on one elbow, Jonathan admired the way the material outlined her full breasts as she leaned over to set the plate of biscuits on the dresser and pick up the half-empty bottle.

"Do you suppose Belle had something like this in mind when she hid this in my bag?" She asked as she filled his tin cup.

"I wouldn't be surprised." Jonathan grinned. "In fact, I have no doubt that Belle would be quite pleased if she could see us right now."

"Probably." Setting the wine next to the biscuits, Kate lay down with a sigh of pure contentment.

The time would probably come when she would regret the choice she had made, but for now all she wanted to do was enjoy. The last few hours had been heavenly. She'd lost track of how many times they'd made love, but every union seemed better than the last. Some had been wildly passionate, others softly fulfilling, but each imbued with the same special magic.

Exhausted, they had finally slept and awakened to find the blizzard still howling outside. Kate had been in the middle of whipping up a meal to satisfy their hunger when she'd remembered Belle's bottle of wine. Suddenly the cryptic note she'd found attached to it made sense. It had said that Kate would know when the time was right to open it. Kate smiled to herself as she thought how right the time was.

She jumped as a cold splash of liquid hit her chest and turned to find Jonathan leaning over her with a gleam in his eye. "How clumsy of me," he said. "I seemed to have spilled my wine on you. No matter. I'll clean it up." Before she realized what he was up to, he bent down and licked the ruby liquid off her skin.

Shocked by such lewd behavior, she gasped, but he only smiled and dipped a finger into his cup. "Ever since I read a description of a Greek orgy, I've wanted to do this," he said, dribbling wine between her breasts and down her stomach. He lowered his head and followed the same path with his mouth as he started to untie the belt of her robe.

"Jonathan, no." She put out her hand to stop him. "I . . . I can't do this."

"You don't have to do anything," he murmured as he parted her robe. "I'll take care of it all." He had kissed his way across her stomach and even sipped wine from her navel before her whimper brought his head up in surprise.

One look at her face and he knew he'd gone too far. Somehow he'd forgotten how prim and proper she was. He had thought that when she'd agreed to his compromise she'd set aside all her inhibitions. Not all, he reminded himself as he saw the mortification on her face.

After he'd pulled the robe closed again, he set his cup on the floor and stretched out beside her.

"Forgive me," he whispered, putting his arms around her and cushioning her face against his shoulder. "I didn't mean to embarrass you."

"I . . . I guess I w-wouldn't have made a very good Gr-Greek." Her voice was shaky, as though she were trying not to cry.

"No, I don't suppose you would have. You'd have probably been beaten for talking back to the men in your life."

"I'm sorry, Jonathan." She sniffed.

"For talking back?" he said, purposely misunderstanding her. "Do my ears deceive me? Could this truly be Kate Murphy asking my forgiveness for all the abuse she's heaped on my head?"

She smacked him lightly on the shoulder. "Don't be silly. You know darn well what I mean."

"See, that proves you couldn't be a Greek. They liked their women meek and mild. An Etruscan, maybe, or an Amazon. Yes, I think an Amazon. They were women warriors, you know. However,

I'm afraid you'll have to give up that notion, too. They cut off their right breast so it wouldn't interfere with the bow string when they were shooting."

"You made that up."

"I did not," he said, running a fingertip down the side of her breast. "Think how bad it would hurt if you twanged it."

"Oh, Jonathan"—she laughed—"now you're being absurd."

"If you say so." With a shrug he got out of bed and stepped over to the dresser, where he picked up her hairbrush. "I still think it would be painful, but I bow to your superior knowledge of the subject." He ran the pad of his thumb across the stiff bristles. "Just as I suspected. All primed and ready to go."

She giggled. "Of course. I keep it in perfect working condition."

He returned to the bed and held out his hand. "Come here," he said softly.

Not quite sure what to expect, she allowed him to help her up.

He looked down at her for several moments and then rubbed the backs of his fingers against her cheek. "Do you realize what an exquisite creature you are?"

Kate knew that she'd never been more than passable, but at that moment she felt truly beautiful. With a tentative smile, she stood on her tiptoes and kissed him.

For a few blissful seconds he returned her kiss, then he playfully patted her on the backside. "Here, now," he said with mock severity, "none of that. Do you think I can't tell when you're trying to distract me?" He sat on the bed, then pulled her down between his knees and began to brush her hair.

Perched there on the edge of the bed as Jonathan patiently brushed all the snarls from her tangled hair, Kate thought her heart might burst from the love she held for this marvelously complex man. The rhythmic strokes of the brush seemed to relax every muscle in her body, and she began to drift in pleasant euphoria.

She was very nearly asleep when he leaned forward and kissed the spot where her shoulder met her neck. "I have something for you," he whispered.

"I know." She smiled drowsily. "It's been a couple of hours already."

A deep chuckle rumbled from his chest. "That too, but it'll have to wait." He rose from the bed and walked over to his saddle. "I did have a reason for coming here last night," he said, flipping open his saddle bag and pulling out what looked like an old sock.

"You said Frenchie and Rosie sent you."

He pondered that. "Hmm. Could be they gave me the idea. I seem to remember your brother being rather heavily involved with one or the other of them, but that's all."

"Apparently you drank him under the table."

"Now, that I do remember. He doesn't hold his liquor much better than you do."

Kate tossed her head. "At least I don't use it as an answer to my problems."

"I know, and that's why I'm here. It's hard to

admit, but you were right about Cole's birthday."
He stared down at his hands. "Mary . . ."

"I know," she said softly. "Levi told me how she
died."

His head jerked up. "Levi? But he was just a
baby."

"Apparently he went into the room shortly after
Cole was born." Kate rubbed Jonathan's clenched
hands. "He has a very vivid memory of it."

Jonathan closed his eyes. "Oh, God."

"I realize how difficult it is for you, Jonathan,
but Cole needs to know why you get drunk every
year on his birthday. He thinks it has something to
do with him."

"I know. All day yesterday I kept remembering
what you said about every child deserving a birthday. I hadn't really ever thought of it that way
before. Even though I've never blamed Cole for
Mary's death, I've been punishing him for it once a
year."

"It's not too late to change," she said gently.

"I realized that, too, about halfway through the
second bottle of whiskey. By then I knew it was too
late to make the party, but I suddenly remembered
the gift I got you in Chicago. I guess I was hoping it
would help you forgive me." He handed her the
sock. "I'll make my apologies to my son as soon as
I can."

Kate looked at the piece of gray wool in her
hand. "You got me a sock?"

Jonathan grinned, and Kate was relieved to see
the pain disappear from his eyes. "What's the
matter? A sock isn't good enough for you?" His

dimples appeared as he shook his head. "Then I guess you'll just have to be satisfied with what's inside. I bought it the morning after Belle's dance, and it's been hidden in my sock drawer since we got home. The sock is just a disguise to fool my snoopy housekeeper."

"Hmph. Snoopy housekeeper indeed." Kate reached inside the soft wool and pulled out a small jeweler's box. With a questioning glance at Jonathan, she opened the lid and gasped in surprise. On a bed of maroon velvet lay a delicately wrought cameo of surpassing loveliness. "Oh, Jonathan, it's beautiful."

He leaned down and kissed her forehead tenderly. "As rare and beautiful as the woman who will wear it."

"I . . . I don't know what to say."

He grinned. "Good Lord, I've never known you to be speechless before!" He lay back on the bed with his hands behind his head. "I'm sure we'll think of some way for you to show your appreciation."

After running her finger over the surface of the cameo once more, Kate set the box on her dresser and then crawled back onto the rumpled bed. With a deep sigh of contentment, she cuddled up next to Jonathan and laid her head on his shoulder. "Thank you, Jonathan. I've never owned anything so nice."

He smiled as he closed his eyes and folded his arm about her.

Kissing the hollow at the base of his throat, Kate slowly ran a hand down his side. Her fingers encountered the vicious inchwide scar just below his left armpit. How well she'd come to know his body, not only during his illness, but during the last several hours.

From the hideously puckered ridge of purple scar tissue to the curiously twisted little toe, she loved his imperfections as much as his beauty. Leaning over, she placed a tender kiss on the scar. "Every time I changed your nightshirt I wondered how you got this."

"Bayonet."

Kate's eyes widened in horror. A few inches to the left and it would have pierced his heart. "How did you escape?"

"He was a little faster than I was."

"Don't you mean slower?"

"No." A muscle tensed in his jaw, and she feared for a moment that he wasn't going to explain. When his voice came, it had a strangled quality. "He recognized me and deflected his bayonet in time." Pulling Kate even tighter against him, Jonathan swallowed hard. "I killed him without even realizing who he was. He saved my life, and I murdered him."

"Benjamin." Kate closed her eyes as she remembered Jonathan's tortured delirium. Well, perhaps today was the day to exorcise all ghosts. Maybe if he talked about all the terrible things that had happened, his healing could begin. "Tell me about the war, Jonathan," she said quietly. "It might help, you know."

With an angry growl, he rolled over on top of her. "The damn war is over. All I want to do is forget it." He brought his mouth down on hers in a searing kiss.

With a few simple words, Kate had shattered his illusion of trust. Jonathan had never told anyone about the death of Benjamin Colburn. The only way she could have known was through the Confederate army somehow.

There were no tender words or touches exchanged this time. Violently, passionately, they clung to each other, knowing that reality was about to rip them apart.

Jonathan knew that he was going to tell Matt McNesby not only what the mysterious Thomas Fielding looked like, but that there was a sister as well. It felt like betrayal, but maybe that was a fair exchange for subterfuge.

Kate was no less driven, for she had noticed what Jonathan had not. The wind had stopped. The storm was over.

35

"Howdy," Jonathan called out as the stranger rode into the barnyard. "What can I do for you?"

"Are you Jonathan Cantrell?"

"Yes."

"Do you have any brass casings?"

"What?" Startled, Jonathan shaded his eyes against the sun in an effort to get a better look at his visitor.

"Do you have any brass casings?"

"Only for the Sharps," Jonathan said. "You'll have to go to supply for the Winchester." It had been a long time since anyone had asked him for a password, and that particular one had always irritated him. The Sharps rifle didn't even use brass casings.

The stranger reached into his pocket and pulled out a folded letter. "Then this is for you."

Jonathan took the message from his hand. "You

look about done in. Got time for some coffee and a bite to eat?"

For the first time, the man smiled. "No, thanks. My orders are to give you the message and leave before anyone sees us together."

"McNesby, huh?"

The stranger raised his eyebrows. "Why do you say that?"

Jonathan glanced down at the note. "Nobody loves cloak-and-dagger intrigue like McNesby." He looked back at the stranger with a grin. "Who's supposed to see us out here, anyway?"

The stranger chuckled. "Good question. Thanks for the offer, but I'll just head back to town."

"You don't need an answer?"

"I wasn't told to wait for one."

"Oh. Well, thanks."

The muscles in Jonathan's jaw tightened as he watched the stranger ride away. Why did I have to be right? he wondered. Couldn't I be wrong just this once? Closing his eyes, Jonathan tried to suppress an overwhelming feeling of dread.

McNesby might love the spy racket and yearn for the excitement he'd thrived on during the war, but he was also an astute businessman. He wasn't one to spend unnecessary money on a private messenger unless he thought it was mighty important.

Glancing down at the paper in his hand, Jonathan sighed. Not for the first time he wished he hadn't let his temper get the upper hand. If he'd taken some time to think about it he probably wouldn't have mentioned Kate in his letter to McNesby. His anger that she'd used their special interlude together to get information from him had remained long enough to post the letter and then had died a swift death. It was impossible to stay mad when she got that hurt look on her face every time she thought he was unhappy with her.

Rubbing his forehead wearily, Jonathan turned toward the house. The last three weeks had been pure hell. Eighteen hours of sex hadn't cooled his ardor for her. In fact, he'd thought of little else since. For a solid week after the blizzard, Jonathan had battled with himself. It was only his promise to Kate that kept him from dragging her off to the bedroom.

When Charlie had taken Kate and Moonflower to South Pass City so Kate could stake her homestead claim, Jonathan had been glad to see them go. He had fully expected his torture to end, but it hadn't. In fact, it had become worse.

Not only did he want Kate just as badly, he missed her like the devil. The kitchen seemed so empty without her, the meals so quiet. It was as if some of the life had gone from his home. All Cole and Levi could do was talk about how much better Mrs. Murphy did things and complain about his cooking. Hell, even he was tired of his own cooking.

It took him nearly five minutes of concentrated effort to locate his glasses in the mess, but at long last Jonathan sat down to read his letter. McNesby's message was straightforward and to the point: Jonathan was to keep his eye on both suspects and under no circumstances mention McNesby, who would be there as soon as he could to act upon Jonathan's information.

Stunned, Jonathan gazed unseeingly at the pile of dirty dishes on the far side of the table. What in God's name had Kate and her brother done? The war had been over for four years, yet these two were still important enough to rate personal attention from the retired chief of Union espionage? With a feeling of helplessness, Jonathan wondered if there was any way he would be able to get Kate out of the mess he'd created.

It was several hours later that Charlie found him in his study painting. Jonathan was so engrossed in his canvas that he hadn't even heard his partner come in.

"Thought I'd stop by and let you know we're back. Kate said to tell you she'll be over in the morning," Charlie said, pulling off his hat and slapping it against his leg.

"Watch that dust," Jonathan said, looking up in irritation. "It'll stick to the wet paint."

Charlie raised his eyebrows. Jonathan was generally pretty casual about his painting and had certainly never complained about trail dust before. He peered curiously over Jonathan's shoulder. If he had been surprised by Jonathan's attitude, he was astonished by the painting. It was obviously Kate Murphy, but it was a Kate Charlie had never seen.

In Jonathan's typical style, the nose was a little off center and the eyes a bit too large, yet Charlie hardly even noticed. Surrounded by a cloud of unbound hair, Kate's face was the epitome of seductive enchantment. Slightly parted lips curved into a half smile, hinting at an intimate secret, while moss green eyes gazed softly out at the world in silent invitation.

The picture ended just below the shoulders, where the naked skin glowed like warm satin. It was the portrait of a woman passionately in love.

Charlie gave a whistle as he watched Jonathan put the finishing touches on the halo of hair. "Reckon you best marry her, Jon," he said at last.

"Who?" Jonathan looked up in surprise. "You mean Kate?"

"It's plain as the nose on yer face you're in love with her."

Dipping his paintbrush into turpentine and wiping it on a rag, Jonathan gave his partner a sardonic glance. "Did you get too much sun?"

"I suppose you didn't mean it to look like she just crawled into your bed?"

"You have a vivid imagination." Jonathan gave his full attention to cleaning another brush. "It's just a picture."

Charlie shook his head adamantly. "Nope. I've seen your paintin's before, and this'n is different."

"Only because I don't usually paint people."

"So why did you do Kate?"

That brought Jonathan up short. Why had he done Kate? He thought back to when he'd started it the day after she'd left for South Pass City. Once he'd begun he'd felt driven to work on it, painting at times when he should have been doing other things.

"'Sides," Charlie said, "if you seen her lookin' like that, I reckon you're sorta obliged to marry her."

"Maybe I just have a good imagination." Jonathan carefully set aside the jar full of brushes and covered the portrait. Suddenly he didn't want any other man to see Kate that way, not even his best friend.

"Could be, but I expect even yer imagination ain't that good. I reckon it'd be near impossible to resist a woman who looked at you that way, 'specially if it was you got her all worked up in the first place."

Jonathan sighed. "All right, I'll admit Kate's gotten under my skin, but she's hardly the first woman I ever slept with. Should I have married them all?"

"I dunno. Did you paint pictures of any of them?"

No, Jonathan admitted to himself, not even of Mary. In fact, he'd never had an image haunt him the way this one had. Of course, Mary had never denied him access to her bed, either. The whole thing with Kate had no doubt been created out of frustrated lust and nothing more.

"I'm not in love with Kate," Jonathan said. "She deserves a man who is."

"You so sure you ain't?"

"Look, Charlie, I do know what love feels like. For almost seven years I was married to a woman I loved passionately. What I feel for Kate is completely different."

"Seems to me, a man loves different people in different ways."

"You didn't know Mary. She was like a delicate little wood sprite, always bubbly and happy, the kind you just naturally want to protect. She always said I was the knight who slayed all her dragons. A dragon wouldn't stand a chance against Kate Murphy."

Charlie frowned. "So Kate can take of herself. You gonna hold that against her?"

"You miss my point," Jonathan said irritably. "Kate is nothing like Mary. I could never find the same kind of happiness with her."

"'Course not. Don't reckon you're much like her Bryan, neither, but that shouldn't stop you from lovin' one another. Mary and Bryan are gone, but I don't reckon that means you and Kate have to live alone forever."

Jonathan rubbed his temples with the tips of his fingers. "I'm not sure I can trust her, Charlie."

There was a moment of stunned silence, then a snort of disbelief from Charlie. "Never known you to be deliberately stupid, Jon. It ain't somethin' you do real well."

"You don't know all there is to know about her, and neither do I."

"I don't know nothing about Moonflower, neither," Charlie said fiercely. "But I'd marry her in a minute if she'd have me. If you had any sense a'tall, you'd realize what's in the past don't make no difference. Life is too short to waste it worryin' about things you can't change. 'Sides, that picture shows what you feel for Kate is deep. A love like that can overcome most anything."

"But marriage—"

"She acts like yer wife in most ways already. The only difference I can see is that you could sleep together all the time." Charlie glanced back at the covered easel and grinned. "Don't reckon that'd bother either of you a whole lot." He paused and ran his fingers through his hair.

"Well, reckon I'd best get to movin', or Moon-flower will be clear home 'fore I catch up with her. I guess I ain't like you, Jon," he said as he left. "I know I got a dang good thing, and I ain't about to lose it."

Jonathan flipped back the canvas cover and stared at the portrait. It was the best painting he had ever done. He had no illusions about his skill as an artist. He painted for the sheer joy of creating, often using a canvas again and again, painting one picture over the other. The best he'd ever accomplished was mediocre, and he'd never liked any of them well enough to keep. Charlie was right, though: this one was different. It had a special quality, a feeling he had never before captured.

Jonathan paced to the window and stared out. Though he couldn't imagine married life with any-one else, Mary was gone, and there would never be another like her. Even Belle, who was her identical twin, was very different. Jonathan realized that he could probably wait his entire life and never find anyone to match him quite the way Mary had.

Restlessly, he wandered back to look at the painting again. As always, the expression on Kate's face caused an odd little twist in his gut. Was Char-lie right? Had he fallen in love?

Yes! The answer rumbled up from deep inside, pushing its way to the surface with undeniable cer-tainty. It was as though he had always known it but had hidden his feelings in a secret corner of his consciousness, suppressed by his guilt over Mary's death. Yes, he loved Kate, with an all-consuming passion, an emotion that seared the soul and practically melted the bed frame every time they made love.

Grinning from ear to ear, Jonathan covered the painting again and headed out to the barn. He'd have to put some thought into exactly how he was going to do this. It had been a long time since he'd asked anyone to marry him.

36

"*What's that stuff* in the kettle outside?" Cole asked, grabbing a cookie from the pan Kate had just removed from the oven.

"It's blue dye. When I was in South Pass City I actually found a peddler who had some indigo." Kate smacked his hand as he started to reach for another cookie. "No more until after lunch."

"I was just going to get one for Levi and Pa."

"They can come in and get their own. Besides, I seriously doubt either of them would ever see any cookie you took out to them."

He grinned. "What's the dye for?"

"I wanted to make blue shirts for you three, but Mrs. Cline hasn't had any blue fabric. She did have some nice white muslin, though."

"So you're going to dye it?"

"That's the plan."

"What happens to the dye when you're finished with it?"

"I'll probably dump it out." She gave him a suspicious glance. "Why?"

He shrugged. "I was just curious."

"Don't even think about it."

His face showed innocent surprise. "What?"

"Whatever it is you think you could use the dye for. It doesn't come out, you know."

"I don't know what you're talking about."

"Humph." Kate turned back to her cookie dough and started to prepare another pan for the oven. "Of course not. You and your brother would never . . . Cole Cantrell!" she yelled as he grabbed two more cookies and ran out the door.

"Those two will be the death of me yet," she muttered, but she couldn't deny the deep feeling of contentment she'd felt ever since she'd returned from South Pass City. Even the satisfaction of walking into her own home with copies of the homestead documents clutched in her hand had paled in comparison with coming back to Jonathan's home yesterday. Though she had grumbled a great deal about the atrocious mess, she'd couldn't help feeling a tiny bit of pleasure that they obviously needed her so much.

Jonathan had said little, but at least he seemed to be over the bad mood he'd been in before she left. In fact, the devastating smile he'd greeted her with had very nearly been her undoing.

Forbidden images of the past had flashed through her head with uncomfortable clarity. It was all she could do not to tell him she'd changed her mind about being his mistress. Not that she hadn't had such thoughts before. Since that unforgettable night in March, she'd thought of little else.

She touched the cameo at her throat. The gesture was fast becoming a habit since she wore the brooch every day, but she couldn't resist the warm feeling it gave her. Jonathan Cantrell was the most handsome, intelligent man she'd ever known, a man who could have almost any woman, and he wanted her.

Though Kate had once overheard Abigail Cline describe her as "plain as dirt and dull as ditchwater," Jonathan thought she was beautiful. It was impossible to think of that and not feel a glow of pleasure.

Kate had known that she'd eventually regret her night in Jonathan's arms, but she hadn't anticipated that her remorse would arise from her inability to think of a good excuse to repeat the experience. Determined to resist such urges for the rest of the day, she went to collect the muslin.

At least producing the exact color of blue she wanted was distracting enough to keep her mind from wandering too far. Satisfied at long last, she hung the fabric on the line to dry.

Kate was just putting the last clothespin in place when a pair of large, masculine hands came from behind and closed around her waist. His long tanned fingers nearly met in front.

"I've always wondered if I could do that." Jonathan's warm breath caressed her ear as his deep, sensual voice sent thrills of excitement through every part of her body.

"Shame on you, Jonathan." Kate couldn't quite keep the smile off her face as she slapped his hands in a halfhearted manner. "Scarin' a body like that."

"Is that why your heart is pounding so hard? Because I scared you?"

"What makes you think it is?"

"I can hear it."

"Horsefeathers!"

"Now I'm wounded," he said in a mournful voice. "What can you do with a woman who won't believe what you say?"

"Stop bedeviling her?" Kate suggested. But she felt strangely bereft as his hands dropped away.

"In that case, I guess I'll have to settle for a cup of coffee and the cookies Cole tells me are cooling in the kitchen." He turned and strode toward the house. "If you care to join me, I have something important I'd like to discuss with you," he said over his shoulder.

"What . . . Jonathan! Don't you walk away from me like that," she called as she hurried after him.

Jonathan grinned in anticipation. For two days he'd waited for just the right moment, and he knew there would never be a better time than right now. Kate was over being mad about the mess the house had been in, and Charlie had just headed out to the range with the boys. They'd be alone for at least an hour. Plenty of time to propose . . . and be accepted.

"Howdy," a voice called out as two unfamiliar men rode into the yard. Covered with dust and sporting several days' growth of beard, they had obviously been on the road a while.

"Lady in town told us you might be lookin' for a few hands." There weren't many men who dwarfed Jonathan, but the one who spoke certainly did.

"That's true," Jonathan said, disappointed at the interference in his plans. As he sized the men up, he knew he'd seen the bigger one somewhere before, though not recently. "Had any experience with cattle?"

"We trailed a couple of herds up from Texas."

"The Iron Brigade," Jonathan said suddenly. "That's where I know you from. Jackson, isn't it?"

"Johnson, Sam Johnson. I was with the Thirty-sixth Wisconsin Infantry. We were part of the Iron Brigade at Gettysburg." He fingered a jagged white scar barely visible under the brim of his hat. "I was wounded. Don't remember much."

Jonathan sighed. "So was I, and I wish I could forget it. Wages are thirty dollars a man for the round-up, with three meals a day," he said, changing topics abruptly. "You're welcome to sleep in the barn."

"How long you figure on the round-up taking?"

Jonathan shrugged. "Probably a little less than a month. We were planning on starting tomorrow around noon."

"Fair enough." Johnson nodded. "You just hired yourself a crew."

"Good. I'll show you where you can bed down tonight."

"There'll be stew for lunch in about an hour," Kate said hesitantly.

Looking directly at Jonathan, Johnson might not have known Kate was there for all the attention he paid her. "It's been a mighty long, dry trip. If you don't mind, we'll stow our gear and head back into town for the day."

"Can't say that I blame you for that. If you want to start down to the barn, I'll be with you directly." As they rode away Jonathan turned back to Kate. "I guess our little talk will have to wait. I'll be back as soon as I can." Jonathan bent over, intending to give her a quick kiss.

Staring after Sam Johnson and his companion, Kate was barely aware of Jonathan's intention. "Are you sure hiring them was a good idea?"

Startled, Jonathan straightened a bit and followed her line of vision. "Why?"

"I don't know." Kate crossed her arms in front of her body and rubbed her elbows. "There's just something about the big one that makes me nervous."

Jonathan smiled. "His size is enough to make you a little apprehensive. Sam Johnson is a bona fide hero. He was an officer whose men obeyed him unquestioningly, and he led them well."

"People change."

"Especially during a war," Jonathan agreed. "And he wouldn't be the first to come out of it a little strange. Still, I'm willing to take a chance on him." He brushed his lips across her forehead and briefly traced the line of her cheek, then walked away smiling.

Actually Jonathan didn't blame Kate. Sam Johnson was one of those individuals who intimidated people without even meaning to.

When Jonathan had been assigned to the Iron Brigade in order to investigate a rash of information leaks to the Confederacy, Lieutenant Sam Johnson had been a prime suspect. Not only had

Johnson been privy to a great deal of sensitive information, he was a natural leader, the kind of man others would follow straight into hell if need be. However, it had become apparent that his loyalties were firmly with the United States of America. If anything, Jonathan had thought Sam a bit overzealous in trying to wipe out the Confederate army.

Sam Johnson was all but forgotten as Kate stared after Jonathan in astonishment. What was the man up to now? If he decided to ignore his promise and seduce her, would she be able to resist? More important, did she even want to? With a swish of her skirts, Kate turned on her heel and went into the house.

The more she thought about it, the angrier she became. Apparently all Jonathan Cantrell thought he had to do was crook his little finger, and she'd come running. What really annoyed her was her suspicion that it would take even less than that.

She was just beginning to stir the stew when a knock sounded at the door. Half expecting Sam Johnson, she wiped her hands nervously on her apron and opened the door.

The first thing she saw was a huge bouquet of wildflowers. Then her gaze traveled up to Clay Langton's smiling face.

"Hello, Kate. Since I'm at least two months overdue coming home, I brought you a peace offering."

With a delighted gasp, Kate took the flowers and buried her nose in them. "Oh, Clay, they're lovely."

"Beautiful flowers for a beautiful woman."

Kate felt an odd dismay. His smooth southern

drawl was no different from before, but today it made her vaguely uncomfortable. Ignoring the feeling, she opened the door wider to let him in. "I see you're still an outrageous flatterer."

He removed his hat and stepped across the threshold. "I only speak the truth, my dear." He held up his hand as she started to speak. "Yes, yes, I know, you don't believe my compliments are real, so I won't mention it again."

"I was only going to thank you for the flowers. Are you home to stay?"

"Yes. We finished up in Cheyenne two weeks ago."

"Were you satisfied with the results?"

"For the most part, though there are some things that didn't quite go my way." He raised an eyebrow. "Aren't you going to ask if the governor signed the suffrage bill?"

"Did he?"

He grinned. "You'll get your first chance to vote next September."

"Imagine that!" She set a cup on the table and filled it with coffee. "Jonathan will no doubt be delighted to see that I get the chance to exercise that right, too," she said sarcastically as she put a plate of cookies on the table and motioned him to sit down. "Anyway, I imagine he'll want to hear all about the legislature and all the other laws that were passed. It was good of you to think of coming over to tell him."

"Actually, I had something of great importance to discuss with you—"

"Clay!" Jonathan burst through the door, with Cole and Levi at his heels. He had been less than pleased to see his sons return home so soon, but the sight of Clay's white stallion outside had been more like a fist in the gut. The thought of Kate alone with the debonair southerner roused feelings of intense jealousy. Leaving Charlie at the barn with Sam Johnson, Jonathan had practically sprinted to the house.

Silently congratulating himself on how well he hid his true feelings, Jonathan gripped the other man's hand and sat down, a smile pasted on his face. No one observing the friendly greeting would ever guess how badly he wanted to plant a boot in the middle of Clay's backside and send his visitor flying out the door. No one, that is, except his sons, who exchanged a look of wary curiosity.

Perched around the table like two small vultures, they listened to their father and Clay discuss the legislature, the winter, cattle prices, horses, even Jonathan's new bull. It was only when Clay gave Kate a warm smile as she refilled his coffee cup that the boys observed a tightening of their father's mouth. Staring at the cheek muscle jumping above Jonathan's clenched jaw, they gave each other a surreptitious glance of understanding.

A moment later all visible signs of irritation were gone as Jonathan seconded Kate's invitation for Clay to stay for lunch. Still, Cole and Levi were aware of an underlying tension in their father that didn't ease even when Charlie came in for lunch.

"You ever see that Sam Johnson handle a whip, Jon?" he asked.

"No, can't say that I have. Why?"

"Just saw him snap the neck of a rat with it."

Jonathan was startled. "What?"

"Dangest thing I ever seen. Didn't even stop talkin' to me, just kinda turned in his saddle and snaked that bullwhip out quick as lightning. Next I knowed, there was a dead rat layin' there next to the barn and he was coilin' his lash up cool as you please." Charlie shook his head as he took his place at the table. "Ain't real sure about that one. Gives me a spooky feelin'."

Jonathan fingered his mustache. "Hands aren't all that plentiful this spring, and I do know the man. Might not be a bad idea to keep an eye on him, though."

Cole gave Charlie a wide-eyed stare. "Do you think Mr. Johnson might teach us how to use a whip?"

"Don't know about that. Reckon it's a mighty hard thing to learn. Dangerous, too."

"How could it be dangerous?" Levi asked.

"I knew a feller once was dang near as good as this Johnson," Charlie began. "Saw him take a fly off his leader's ear without spookin' the team. One day the wind caught the lash and flung it back in his face. Danged if that whip didn't take off the end of his nose clean as a whistle."

"That must have hurt," Levi said, his eyes wide.

"Reckon so. Luckily, this fella had his wits about him. He picked up that little piece of his nose, took it home, and had his wife sew it back on fer him. Healed just as nice as you please."

Cole was all agog. "Really?"

"Yup. Only problem was, his wife was blind as a bat, and she sewed it on upside down. After that, every time the poor feller sneezed he blew his hat off."

Something about Charlie's story niggled at Kate's memory, but it was so fleeting that she was unable to catch it. She couldn't help but smile, knowing how hard Levi and Cole were going to stare at the end of Sam Johnson's nose the next time they saw him.

When lunch was over Jonathan was reluctant to leave, but he finally gave in to Charlie's insistence that he needed help with the heifer he'd brought in from the range.

All too aware of the reason Clay had probably come today, Kate busied herself at the hoosier. "You'll have to come over and see my house," she said. "I've taken out a homestead claim on the old Hofflemeir place, you know. Everyone came one day to help me move in. We dug up the floor, then had a dance and—"

"Kate," he said from directly behind her. He was so close that she could feel his warm breath on her neck. "I think you know why I'm here."

"Well, of course. It's the neighborly thing to do after you've been gone . . ."

With a gentle but firm hold on her shoulders, he forced her to turn and face him. "No, I didn't come to be neighborly." He reached into his pocket and pulled out a beautiful diamond ring. "You were quite right about this, you know. It did make a rather nice ring. What do you think?"

"It's beautiful, Clay, but—"

"I didn't know your size, but we can have it changed if I guessed wrong." Holding her left hand, he stared down at her gold wedding band for a moment. "I think it's time to take that off, don't you?"

"No, Clay," she said as she gently pulled her hand away. "I'm so sorry. . . ."

"I realize how much your husband meant to you, Kate, but you really can't wear his ring and mine, too. It just isn't done."

"Yes, I know. But you see—"

"Kate, I'm asking you to marry me."

"I'm aware of that, Clay, and I can't."

Clay's mouth curved downward into a frown. "What? I thought we had an understanding."

"Not that I was aware of."

"I distinctly remember discussing it last fall before I went to Cheyenne."

"Yes, I know, and I really thought it might work." Kate twisted her wedding ring self-consciously. "I don't love you, Clay, and I don't think you love me. Not really."

"What's that got to do with it?"

It was Kate's turn to be surprised. "If you don't fancy yourself in love with me, why do you want to get married?"

"I think we'll be very comfortable together. We enjoy each other's company, I admire you a great deal, and I don't think you're completely indifferent to me."

"No, I'm not indifferent. I like you very much."

"There, you see? You're exactly what I'm looking for in a wife. There are very few women who even begin to understand the dream I have, let alone are capable of helping me build it. Think of how much you'll enjoy decorating my house." He smiled as he cupped her face with his hands. "We'll go back east on our honeymoon. I've often thought of how much fun I'll have helping you pick out clothing appropriate for my wife and how pretty you'll look."

Kate had a sudden vision of herself dressed only in a ratty old robe and Jonathan calling her an exquisite creature. She pushed the memory away. "Don't you want to fall in love, Clay?"

He shrugged. "People of my class rarely marry for love."

"But people of my class do." With a sad smile, she put her hands over his and turned her head to kiss one lightly before pulling them down. "Clay . . . dear friend . . . I'm not going to marry you, but I will give you some valuable advice. Don't pick a wife because she's comfortable, or because she'll take good care of your house. Find one who makes your heart pound, one who makes you dizzy with lust, and if you're deliriously happy in bed, the rest won't matter. Fall in love, Clay. Be happy."

He was clearly shocked at such plain speaking, and surprisingly angry. "And does Jonathan make you dizzy with lust? That's what this is all about, isn't it?" He dropped her hands and stepped away. "You're only a convenience to him, Kate. He'll never marry you."

He grabbed his hat and slapped it on his head. "I hope you don't come to regret turning away the only respectable offer of marriage you're likely to get out here in the back of beyond."

"Is that why you asked me?" Kate asked, nearly strangling on her anger. "You wanted a grateful wife, and you figured I'd realize no one else was likely to want me?"

He glared at her for a moment. "No. I didn't want a grateful wife, I wanted one I could live the rest of my life with." Then he jerked the door open and slammed it with such violence that Kate winced.

She hadn't even had time to catch her breath when she heard a terrifying roar of pure rage. *"Cantrell!* Goddammit! I'll kill them, I swear to God I will. This time those hell-born brats of yours have gone too far!"

With a feeling of impending doom Kate pulled open the door, then gasped in horror. Clay's magnificent stallion, Gallahad, stood tied to the hitching rack, calmly munching on a pile of oats, apparently oblivious of the fact that his entire body had been dyed a lovely shade of blue.

37

"*You two are a* little late coming back, aren't you?" Kate stopped kneading her bread dough for a moment and looked questioningly at Cole and Levi. "You're supposed to spend an hour cleaning Mr. Langton's barn, not three."

"We did, but he has twin foals that look just like Gallahad."

"Oh?" Kate went back to her task. "So the foals are blue now, too?"

The boys exchanged a look of exasperation. "No, but Mr. Fielding let us help him with them. We thought maybe Mr. Langton wouldn't be so mad if we helped with the foals."

"It doesn't matter what you do extra," Kate said. "Until Gallahad looks like he did before you decided to groom him yesterday, you'll spend an hour each morning doing whatever Mr. Langton wants you to. In the meantime, you still have all your work around here."

"Does that mean we can't work the colts with Mr. Fielding?"

"That's right. And if you're smart, you'll stay away from Mr. Langton. The only thing that kept him from thrashing the daylights out of you two was that your father did it first."

"Pa was pretty mad," Cole said. "I never heard so many big words in my life. That was almost as bad as the belt."

Levi nodded. "And Mr. Langton never made a sound. He just stood there and watched with his arms folded. Do you think Pa really will build a woodshed like Charlie told him to and give us a whipping?"

"Maybe he should. What you did to that poor horse was awful."

"We didn't hurt him."

"But whatever possessed you to do such a thing, anyway? Mr. Langton has never been anything but nice to you."

"Are you going to marry him?" Cole asked.

"No, but I don't see what . . ." Her voice trailed off as the two exchanged a triumphant look. "Oh, no. You did it to drive him away?"

Levi did his best to look ashamed. "We don't want you to leave us, Mrs. Murphy."

"You can marry Pa and stay here and be our ma," Cole said.

"For your information, I refused an offer of marriage from Mr. Langton without your help. You abused that poor animal for nothing. As for marrying your father, that's out of the question, too."

"Why?"

"Don't you like Pa?"

"Of course I do, but people don't get married just because they like each other. Besides, your father has no intention of marrying me." Kate was proud of the way her voice remained steady, in spite of the sting she still felt from Clay's words. "Don't you have something you're supposed to be doing?"

"Nope. Pa forgot to tell us what to do before we went to Mr. Langton's. By the time we got back he'd already left."

"So we stayed in the barn and talked to Mr. Johnson. He was waiting for Pa to get back from town, too."

Levi nodded. "Yeah. Charlie thought he wouldn't want us anywhere around him, but he really likes us. He asked us all kinds of questions."

"Oh?"

"Yup. He wanted to know all about Mr. Langton and Mr. Fielding. He was even interested in Moonflower."

"Are you sure you weren't pestering him? Mr. Johnson hardly seems the type to stand around gossiping about people he doesn't know."

"No, he really does like us. He even told us his nickname."

"Yeah. They call him Bullwhip."

Kate's hands suddenly stilled. "What?"

"Bullwhip. You know, 'cause he's so good with a whip."

"Sweet Lord in heaven!" Suddenly it all came together—Bullwhip Johnson, the vicious killer her brother was hiding from. "Did he say where he was going?"

"No, but I think he was headed to Charlie's," Levi said.

"And that's the way they rode."

"Help me get a horse saddled," she said as she grabbed the boys' hunting rifle and ran to the door.

"What's wrong, Mrs. Murphy?"

"I'm not sure exactly, but Bullwhip Johnson is a very dangerous man. We've got to warn Moonflower and Mr. Fielding."

Within a matter of minutes she was mounted on Levi's horse. "Go find Mr. Fielding," Kate said as she was ready to leave. "Tell him that Bullwhip Johnson is here."

"Where are you going?"

"To Charlie's. Now, get moving!"

The ride seemed to take forever. What did Bullwhip want with Moonflower? Did his hatred include Indians as well as southerners? It all seemed very odd.

Kate could hear Moonflower's screams long before she got to the clearing. Horrified, she listened to them get weaker and weaker until they were only agonized moans by the time she could see the cabin through the trees.

She slid off the mare, tied the reins to a bush, and crept through the trees toward the clearing, the rifle clutched in her hands. The sight that met her eyes made the bile rise in her throat.

Moonflower lay in a crumpled heap on the ground at Bullwhip's feet. She was curled into a protective ball with her arms wrapped around her head, and the calico dress Kate had made was in tatters across her back. Bullwhip Johnson towered over her, lightly tapping a wicked-looking quirt against his leg.

"I told you what would happen if you ever ran away from me, you little bitch. I wasted the whole damn winter in your father's camp waiting for you to show up, and all the time you weren't ten miles from where I lost you." When he drew back his foot to kick the helpless woman in front of him, something inside Kate snapped.

With absolutely no thought of the consequences, she cocked the rifle and stepped into the clearing. "If you touch her one more time, I'll blow your head off."

Bullwhip looked up in surprise. "Well, well, if it isn't Cantrell's little whore," he said with a sneer. "What brings you here?"

"You have no right to treat her like that."

"Who the hell are you to tell me what I can and can't do? I'll treat my wife any way I want to."

"Your wife?" This was the monster who had beat Moonflower repeatedly? Jonathan's hero? Kate remembered the ridges of scar tissue across Moonflower's back, and she thought she might be sick. Those scars could easily have been made with the quirt Bullwhip held in his hand.

"That's right, my wife." He looked scornfully at the heap on the ground. "Not only did she run away from me, she's been sleeping with another man. I just gave her what she deserved, and there's not a court in the country that would interfere. Hell, her own people would have cut off her nose."

"Even if she is your wife, you don't have the right to kill her."

He gave an evil laugh. "If I'd wanted to kill her, I'd have used my bullwhip." Before Kate realized what was happening he'd bent down and scooped his whip from the ground. In one smooth motion the braided leather lashed out and coiled around the rifle barrel. A jerk of his arm sent the gun flying out of her hands.

"Stupid bitch," Bullwhip snarled as he shook his whip free and snaked it toward her once more. "I'll teach you to threaten me."

Kate stood frozen in terror as the lash flicked across her shoulder. She cried out as a ribbon of fire tore through the thin material of her dress and ripped along her skin.

Bullwhip laughed. "Hell, I hardly touched you. Next time I won't hold back. Just remember that." He nodded to his henchman. "Go find her horse. Since she's so concerned about my wife, she can take care of the worthless little slut." After coiling his whip, he reached down and jerked Moonflower to her feet.

Kate's own pain was all but forgotten when she saw her friend's battered face. Moonflower had been beaten almost beyond recognition. Her skin was bleeding in several places, both eyes were swollen shut, and her top lip was split. She wavered back and forth, held upright only by Bullwhip's huge hand. When he suddenly released her she tottered for a moment and then pitched forward.

Kate ran across the clearing to catch Moonflower before she hit the ground, but when her arms closed around her friend, the other woman cried out in agony. Bullwhip laughed uproariously as Kate sent him a glare that should have shriveled him on the spot.

"Well, we've wasted enough time on this," Bullwhip said, sticking the quirt through his belt. "I have more important things to do. Patrick McAnespie will be dead before he even knows I'm here."

Driving the wagon home from town, Jonathan was not pleased when he spotted his sons on the road. After yesterday's debacle he would have thought they'd learned their lesson, but there they were, less than twenty-four hours later, miles from where they were supposed to be.

The punishment that still bothered him apparently had had little effect on the culprits. He'd hated taking the belt to them, but Clay had been so mad there wasn't any other way out. Of course, the little varmints deserved it so much that Jonathan hadn't even felt bad until it was all over.

Though he tried to pretend otherwise, a small part of him had been very pleased to see Clay Langton routed. He'd been worried that before he got to tell Kate how much he loved her, Clay would propose to her and be accepted. There was little chance of the other man stealing the march on him now. Clay Langton probably wouldn't set foot on the place for a good long time.

Jonathan smiled. Surely today he'd be able to find some time alone with her. Then he was lost in a daydream of Kate kissing him passionately and confessing that she loved him madly. It was a scene he'd played over and over in his mind.

"Pa . . . Pa!" Jonathan was pulled back to reality by his sons' desperate cries.

"What's wrong?"

"We're supposed to go tell Mr. Fielding Bullwhip Johnson is here!"

"Mrs. Murphy went to help Moonflower!"

"She says Bullwhip is a dangerous man."

"Now wait a minute," Jonathan said, thoroughly confused. "What did Johnson do to Mrs. Murphy?"

"Nothing."

"Yeah, we were just talking. When we told her Mr. Johnson's nickname was Bullwhip, she turned all white and grabbed our gun."

Cole nodded. "We saddled Lightning for her, and she said we were supposed to go find Mr. Fielding."

"She was real scared, Pa."

Jonathan's mind whirled. What if Charlie was right about Sam Johnson? The man could break Kate in half with his bare hands.

Jonathan grabbed his rifle and jumped out of the wagon. "Give me Thunder. You two take the wagon on home. I'm going to Mr. Langton's. If I don't find Mrs. Murphy there, I'll head over to Charlie's. If you see Charlie, tell him there's trouble and where I'm going." Cole and Levi had barely tumbled off the horse before Jonathan had swung up into the saddle and headed toward Clay's at a high lope.

As he rode, everything began to click together in his mind, and he felt sick to his stomach. Johnson said he'd spent a great deal of time after the war tracking down bushwackers, outlaws who terrorized civilians in the name of the Confederacy. That was obviously how Kate knew the man's name. No wonder McNesby was so interested in Fielding and his sister. In his eyes, they were no better than common criminals.

No, he corrected himself, not Kate. Fielding had made that very clear right from the start. Now everything the man had said made sense. Kate's brother was the worst kind of outlaw, a murderer of innocent people, a traitor to every value Jonathan held sacred. Tom Fielding deserved to die the worst kind of death that man could devise.

When Jonathan finally arrived at Langton's, he realized that the drama had already begun to unfold. Clay lay on the ground, his eyes closed and the front of his shirt saturated with blood. It was impossible to tell if he was dead or alive.

Knowing that there was nothing he could do, Jonathan spared only a single glance for his friend and neighbor before he fixed his attention on the two men facing each other with deadly intent. Neither seemed aware of his presence as they circled each other.

"Come on, Bullwhip," Fielding taunted, keeping a safe distance from the deadly whip. "You must be getting old if you can't even drop a man with that damn whip of yours."

His bravado was at odds with his appearance. Blood ran from half a dozen weals on his chest, visible through the remnants of his shirt. His right arm hung limply at his side, probably broken and almost certainly useless. "Can't handle a man, right, Bullwhip? Your specialty is women and old people, isn't it?"

Though there was a large spot of blood on one of Bullwhip's legs, he seemed completely oblivious of his wound as he continued to advance on the smaller man. It was obvious that Fielding's taunts were getting to him, though. His expression was one of murderous rage as his whip lashed toward his prey again and again, the crack sounding like a pistol shot in the spring air.

The deadly leather seldom connected with any part of Fielding as he danced away from his much larger adversary. When it did, he acted as though he barely felt any pain. "You're a coward, Bullwhip. It must run in your family, because your brother, Frank, was a coward, too."

With a cry of pure rage, Bullwhip put his head down and charged across the ground that separated them. Jonathan realized that that was just what Fielding had been waiting for. Bending, Fielding reached into his boot and pulled out a knife. Clutching it in his left hand, he turned to meet Bullwhip's assault.

In that split second, Jonathan knew that he had to do something or a good man was going to die. Praying he was making the right choice, he raised his rifle and fired.

38

The bark of the Sharps filled the air as Jonathan's shoulder jerked against the rifle's powerful recoil.

"Patrick!"

At the sound of Kate's voice, Jonathan's head snapped up. Until then he hadn't noticed her crouched next to a pile of rags near the stable. Now he sucked in his breath as she flew across the barnyard.

There was a large rip across one shoulder of her dress, and he could see an ugly welt even from a distance. Her hair hung down around her face, and her hands were filthy. She looked as though she'd been dragged through a knothole.

A groan brought Jonathan's attention back to the two men on the ground. With Bullwhip lying on top of the much smaller Fielding, it was impossible to tell which man the sound was coming from. A few long strides and Jonathan was kneeling next to the two. "Are you all right?"

"I will be if you get this ox off of me. He weighs a ton."

Jonathan pushed the body until it rolled over and fell limply to the side. A large bullet hole gaped in Bullwhip's chest, an inch to the right of the knife protruding from between his ribs. He lay perfectly still, his eyes staring sightlessly at the ominous gray clouds building in the sky. The man was quite dead.

"Oh, Patrick!" Kate cried, tears running down her face as she reached them. "You're bleeding." She dropped to her knees and dabbed at the blood on her brother's chest.

"It's not mine—" The sound of a pistol shot cut him off.

All three of them swung their heads around to find Clay propped up on one elbow with a pistol still smoking in his other hand as Bullwhip's companion ran for his horse. The man jerked as Clay's bullet struck his shoulder, but he managed to get onto his horse and ride out. With no time to reload, both Jonathan and Clay were powerless to stop him.

"Damn," Clay said as he watched man and horse disappear down the road.

"How bad are you hurt?" Jonathan called to Clay.

"The bullet went through my side. Hurts like hell, but it didn't hit anything important." He glanced down at his shirt. "It looks worse than it is. You all right, Fielding?"

"I think my arm's broken, but otherwise I'm fine." Patrick took hold of his sister's arm and sat up. "Thanks, Cantrell. That was a damn good shot."

"I'd have done better if I'd had my pistol with me." Jonathan sighed as he glanced at Bullwhip's body. "I was aiming for his shoulder, not his chest. Without my glasses I have a devil of a time using my rifle sights." He shrugged as he stood up. "Besides, it's pretty hard to say whether he died of the bullet or the knife."

Jonathan looked up at the darkening sky. There was definitely a storm brewing. "You'd best help your brother to the house, Kate. I'll get Clay."

"What about Moonflower?"

"Moonflower?"

"She's over there," Kate said, pointing toward the pile of rags. Casting a look of revulsion at Bullwhip's corpse, she shuddered. "He nearly beat her to death. Moonflower was married to him, you see, and he was punishing her for running away from him the last time. What he did to her . . ." Kate swallowed convulsively and shook her head. "I don't know what he was like during the war, Jonathan, but he'd turned into a monster."

Any qualms Jonathan had about shooting Bullwhip disappeared at his first glimpse of Moonflower. No matter what Kate's brother was guilty of, Jonathan knew he'd shot the right man. "Moonflower," he said softly as he squatted down next to her, "you're safe now. No one will hurt you."

"He is dead?" The words were barely intelligible through her swollen, battered lips, but the hope in her voice was unmistakable.

"Yes."

She closed her eyes. "Good."

Jonathan shrugged out of the light coat he was wearing and gently laid it over her. "You just rest now. I'll be back in a few minutes."

"Who is she?" Clay asked as soon as Jonathan joined him.

"Her name is Moonflower, and she was married to our friend over there." Jonathan nodded at the corpse. "Charlie found her in pretty much the same condition last fall. She's been with him ever since. Let's see what this bullet hole of yours looks like."

It took Jonathan only a few moments to discover that Clay had been right about his wound. The bullet had passed through cleanly, without touching any vital organs, but the amount of blood he'd lost was frightening.

"What happened here?" Jonathan asked Clay as he pulled a freshly laundered handkerchief from his pocket and folded it into a pad.

"I'm not really sure." Clay grimaced as Jonathan pressed the pad against the wound. "The big one rode in here asking for some Irishman I'd never heard of. When I said I didn't know him, the man went berserk. Called me a damn southern traitor and went for his gun. I managed to outdraw him, but my aim was off, and I only hit him in the leg. Lucky for me he was a poor shot. He could just as easily have killed me. Damn, Jonathan," he said, sucking in his breath. "You haven't got the lightest touch I ever ran into."

"Be glad Charlie Hobbs wasn't the one to find you. He's downright ham-handed." Jonathan pulled the neck cloth off Clay's neck and tied it to his own bandanna. "What happened after the gunfight?"

"That's the strange part. All of a sudden Fielding was there shouting insults at the man, trying to make him mad. It took about thirty seconds for him to throw down his gun and go after Fielding with that damn whip." Clay shook his head. "I've never seen anything like it, Jonathan. He broke Fielding's right arm on the first crack."

"I've seen what he could do. How did Fielding manage to stay out of his way after that?"

"I don't know. I had just got hold of my pistol again and was aiming to shoot when it felt like my head exploded. Next thing I knew, you were here with Kate, and a stranger was running toward his horse. He must have snuck up behind me and coshed me on the head."

"Too bad he got away." Jonathan tied the makeshift bandage around Clay's middle. "There, that should hold till I get you to the house so Kate can get the bleeding stopped."

"You should have kept her out of this," Clay said. "This is not the sort of thing a delicately nurtured female should be exposed to."

"I didn't have anything to do with it. She was here when I arrived. Can you walk at all?"

"I think so." He grunted with pain as Jonathan helped him to his feet. "Kind of ironic," he said through gritted teeth. "I made it through the whole war without a scratch, and now I get shot in my own backyard."

Jonathan glanced at Bullwhip's body spread-eagled on the ground. "I don't know, your backyard kind of resembles a battlefield today. Here, put your arm around my shoulder and lean as much of your weight on me as you can."

Even with Jonathan's support, they'd have never made it to the house if Kate hadn't run out to assist. Between the two of them, they half carried, half dragged Clay into the parlor, where they laid him on the davenport. Jonathan made sure he was settled and then went back outside for Moonflower.

"You do have medicines and bandages, don't you, Clay?" Kate asked as she stripped away what was left of his shirt.

Clay nodded. "There's a special cupboard in the kitchen."

"I can show you where they are," Patrick said.

By the time Kate had returned with the necessary supplies Jonathan was at the parlor door, Moonflower cradled in his arms. "Put her over there," Kate said, nodding toward the chaise longue.

"I'm sorry I brought this on you, Colonel," Patrick said as he stared down at Clay's bloodied shirt.

"How do you figure this is your fault, Fielding?"

"My name isn't Tom Fielding, it's Patrick McAnespie, and Bullwhip Johnson came here looking for me."

Frowning, Kate looked up from clipping through the temporary bandage. "Now is hardly the time, Patrick. You can make a full confession as soon as I get the bleeding stopped. Until then I'll thank you to stop pacing around. It can't be good for your arm, and it's disturbing for Clay and Moonflower."

"After yesterday, I'm surprised you don't just let me bleed to death," Clay said, "and I guess I wouldn't blame you if you did."

"You don't have a very high opinion of me do you, Clay?"

Clay smiled up at her weakly. "On the contrary, I told you exactly how I felt yesterday. My feelings about you haven't changed, and neither has my regard."

Suddenly Jonathan wanted to be anywhere but there. He wasn't sure how long he could control his intense jealousy if he had to stand here and listen to Clay's flattery. "I'd best get Bullwhip's body taken care of before it rains," he murmured to no one in particular as he turned and stomped out of the room.

Jonathan had barely reached the body when he heard the sound of wagon wheels on the road. He wasn't even surprised to see that it was his own wagon off in the distance. With a cursory glance he noticed a third person riding on the seat with Cole and Levi. Apparently Cole and Levi had found Charlie. Now how in the world was he going to tell Charlie about Moonflower?

Dragging two hundred and fifty pounds of dead weight was no easy task, and Jonathan had just reached the barn when the wagon pulled into the yard. "I thought I told you to take the wagon home," he said without turning around.

"They were going to until I convinced them to help me find you."

Startled by the familiar voice, Jonathan dropped his burden and spun around, feeling as if his stomach had plummeted to his toes. He forced a smile. "McNesby. I wasn't expecting you today."

"I'd have been here sooner, but . . ." The other man stopped cold as he caught sight of the body. "Good Lord, Cantrell, is that Bullwhip Johnson?"

"You know him?"

"Just by reputation, and it's a pretty unsavory one at that."

Jonathan raised his eyebrows. "When I knew him he was a lieutenant in the Union army and something of a hero."

"He was until a bullet creased his skull. Became a complete fanatic after that. His gang terrorized Arkansas, Missouri, Texas, even part of Kansas during the war and long after. It didn't seem to matter if his victims were Confederate soldiers or innocent women and children. As long as they were southerners, they were fair game."

"So that's why he shot Clay," Jonathan said, half to himself.

"Who?"

"Clay Langton, the man who owns this place," Jonathan said as he lifted Bullwhip's shoulders from the ground once more. "He's from Georgia and has a very pronounced accent. You want to give me a hand here, McNesby?" Together they dragged the body through the doorway of the barn and deposited it in a heap near a pile of hay.

"He said he knew you, Pa," Levi said, charging through the door, "and Mrs. Murphy and Mr. Fielding, too."

Cole was right on his brother's heels. "When we

told him you were all here he decided he'd catch
you all together now."

So much for pretending that Kate and her brother
were long gone. "What did you do with the wagon
and the team?" Jonathan asked, stalling for time so
he could think of some way of putting McNesby
off.

"We tied the team to the cor— Pa!" Aghast,
Cole stared at the crumpled body on the floor. "Is
Bullwhip dead?"

"I'm afraid so, son."

Levi swallowed convulsively as he peered over
his brother's shoulder. "Wh-what happened?"

"It's a long story that I don't have time to tell
right now. Bullwhip had become a vicious outlaw.
Unfortunately, the way things happened we had no
choice but to kill him." It occurred to Jonathan that
having his sons around might make it even more
difficult to talk his way out of the tight spot he'd
gotten Kate into. "I'll explain later. Right now I
have a very important job for you two. Moonflower's been hurt, and I need you to find Charlie."

The boys exchanged a look and then nodded in
unison. "We'll take Thunder." With that they were
gone, speeding across the barnyard to where
Jonathan had left the horse.

"Tell Charlie that Moonflower is going to be all
right," he called after them, "and get inside if it
starts to storm."

"Quite a pair of sons you have," McNesby said.

"They're a pair all right." Jonathan pointed to
Gallahad in a nearby stall. "Until yesterday, that
was a magnificent white stallion. My sons will be

regretting their decision to change his appearance for some time to come."

McNesby looked at the pathetic creature. "Good Lord, whatever possessed them to do such a thing?"

Jonathan shrugged. "Near as I can tell, they were mad at my neighbor, though I haven't any idea what he might have done to deserve it."

McNesby chuckled. "Well, at least they're original in their revenge. My nephew was a bit like that when he was a youngster." Then he frowned suddenly. "Where are Patrick and Katharine?"

So much for trying to distract him. McNesby had always been dogmatic. "Look, I don't know what they're wanted for, but I hardly think either one is a dangerous criminal."

"Oh? That wasn't what you thought when you wrote me about them."

"My training, I guess. I spent too long as one of your agents not to wonder about inconsistencies. Fielding represented a lot of them."

"What made you change your mind?"

Jonathan rubbed his face tiredly. What had changed his mind? He'd ridden into the yard convinced that Fielding was the most despicable kind of outlaw there was. Yet he hadn't hesitated to shoot Bullwhip, a man he'd thought a hero, when Fielding was in trouble. "I don't know. It could be because he went up against that monster with only a knife." Jonathan shrugged. "I always liked the story of David and Goliath."

"What about the woman?"

"What about her?"

"Have you changed your mind about her, too?"

"Whatever Fielding was involved in, Kate had nothing to do with it. I never met a more honest, straightforward person in my life." He glared at the older man. "No matter what you decide to do with her brother, she stays here."

McNesby raised his eyebrows. "You're willing to take full responsibility for her?"

"I intend to marry her."

To Jonathan's surprise, McNesby laughed. "Damned if she didn't do it again."

"What are you talking about?" Jonathan asked suspiciously.

"This isn't the first time one of my best men fell for Katie's charm." He raised his hand placatingly as Jonathan took a step toward him. "No, no, don't misunderstand me. I'm not casting doubt upon her, and I agree completely with your reading of her character."

"Then you promise not to hurt her in any way?"

"Neither of them is in any danger from me." McNesby smiled, a bit sadly, Jonathan thought. "They may not be best pleased to see me, but I won't do them the least harm."

"Then you aren't going to arrest them?"

"I don't have that kind of power anymore, Jonathan."

Jonathan rubbed his mustache. "I wonder why you came all this way for two outlaws you can't arrest."

McNesby raised an eyebrow. "I guess you'll just have to figure that out for yourself. Now, are you going to tell me where they are?"

"I don't have much choice, do I?"

"No."

With a weary sigh, Jonathan led his former chief through the light spring rain that had begun as they had been talking. All too soon they were standing in front of the parlor door. Feeling very much like a Judas, Jonathan hesitated a moment before turning the knob and entering the room. Kate and Patrick both looked up when the door opened.

"There's someone here to—"

Identical looks of shocked surprise crossed Kate's and Patrick's faces at the same moment.

"Uncle Matthew!" they cried in unison.

39

"Uncle Matthew?" Jonathan turned astonished eyes toward McNesby, but the other man's attention was centered on Kate's brother.

"It is you. I was almost afraid to hope. . . ." McNesby drew in a breath. "For eight long years I've been waiting for the chance to say I'm sorry, Patrick. I've never regretted anything as much as that argument. When I found out you were in Andersonville . . ."

Kate gasped. "You knew he was in Andersonville, and you never said a word to me?"

"I've known nearly every place Patrick has been for the last seven years, but I could never catch up with him," he said. "I was afraid to get your hopes up." Then he looked apologetically toward Patrick again. "By the time I got someone into Andersonville to get you out, you'd escaped."

"What do you mean, by the time you got someone in?" Patrick asked.

"Your . . . er . . . uncle was the head of Union espionage during the war," Jonathan informed them. "He could get anybody in just about anywhere."

"Uncle Matthew?" Kate exchanged a doubtful look with her brother. "How do you know this when his own family didn't, Jonathan?"

McNesby smiled. "Cantrell was one of my top agents."

Kate's eyes widened. "I thought you were in the line with the regular soldiers at Gettysburg. How can that be if you were a spy?"

"I was investigating an information leak at the time and kind of got trapped in my cover." Jonathan's gaze locked on his former chief. "If Fielding here is your nephew, why didn't you just say so when you sent your messenger?"

"I wasn't sure it was him. As I said, he's always been a step ahead of me. Patrick kept changing his name and always moved on by the time I located him. Last summer I lost him completely. I had people all over Texas looking for him, but he'd disappeared without a trace." McNesby ran a hand through his iron-gray hair. "Even Bullwhip led to a dead end up in Montana."

Patrick's eyes narrowed. "Bullwhip?"

"He was a whole lot easier to follow than you were. Whenever I lost you, all I had to do was locate him and I'd pick up your trail again."

"So that monster really was after you," Clay said from the davenport. "Why?"

"Patrick took exception to Bullwhip's hobby of killing southerners and turned him in to the law," Kate said as she put the finishing touches on Clay's bandage. "He blamed Patrick for the death of some of his men."

"Good Lord." Clay looked at Patrick as though he'd never seen him before. "You stood up to a band of Jayhawkers?"

"And I've spent the last six years running because of it." Patrick's voice was bitter. "The worst part is that I have a price on my head for being one of them."

"Not anymore." McNesby smiled. "One of the first things Grant did when he took office was give you a full pardon."

"President Grant?"

"I'd be interested to know how you accomplished that, McNesby," Jonathan said. "What did you do, threaten to tell everybody his real name is Hiram?"

"Didn't have to. There was no proof that Patrick had ever been part of the gang. Of course, Grant does owe me a favor or two."

"One thing I don't understand," Kate said as she sat down next to Moonflower. "How did you follow Bullwhip here so fast? He only arrived yesterday."

"I didn't," McNesby replied. "I had no idea Bullwhip was even here."

Patrick raised his eyebrows. "Then how did you find me?"

"Last time Jonathan wrote me, he mentioned a man named Tom Fielding and his sister, Kate. The description fit, so I decided to come check it out on a hunch."

Kate looked back and forth between the two men. "Jonathan wrote to you?"

Suddenly Jonathan didn't want to be there to see the look on Kate's face when she realized that he had betrayed her. "I'll go get you some fresh water for Moonflower," he mumbled, picking up the bowl of water she'd used to clean Clay's wounds.

McNesby smiled as Jonathan hurried out of the room. It was quite obvious that he fully expected to be thrown to the wolves. "Jonathan and I correspond on a regular basis. During the war, I discovered he had a knack for making money. I've been involved in a long line of successful business ventures with him ever since."

"So this is the uncle who trained you to be a banker," Clay said to Patrick. "Am I correct in assuming that I'm about to lose my bookkeeper?"

Patrick and his uncle locked gazes, and there was tension in the air as the unanswered question hung between them.

"Oh, for pity's sake, Patrick," Kate finally said. "Six months ago you said you were going to look Uncle Matthew up when this was all over. It seems to me he's saved you the trouble. You're acting like a hardheaded Irishman."

Patrick hesitated for a few more moments. "Oh, hell," he finally said, crossing the room in a few strides. He gave McNesby a quick hug with his uninjured arm and grinned. "It is damned good to see you, Uncle Matthew."

40

Sunlight filtered through the opening at the top of the sweat lodge, dimly illuminating the bodies of the two women who sat within. The cleansing steam, pungent with herbs, surrounded them in a cloud as a companionable silence filled the lodge.

"Moonflower, you ready to go?"

Kate jumped slightly as Charlie's voice came through the animal-hide door.

"I reckon," Moonflower called back. "You go, too?" she asked Kate. "I tell Charlie go away if you want."

Kate shook her head. "No, I think I'll stay awhile. Do you feel any better?"

"I heal fast this time. I expect I be good as new soon. Charlie help."

Kate crawled over to help Moonflower to the door. "Well, they do say love conquers all." Keeping well out of sight, she pulled back the hide so Charlie could reach Moonflower.

She peeked out the door to watch Charlie tenderly wrap Moonflower in a soft quilt and pick her up in his arms. Cradling her against his chest, he leaned down to kiss her. As Moonflower's arms crept up around Charlie's neck, Kate let the hide fall back over the opening and smiled softly.

Kate poured more water on the rocks at the far side of the lodge and settled back with a sigh as the steam curled around her once more. No one would bother her there, and it was the first chance she'd had to really think since Uncle Matthew had walked into Clay's parlor two days before.

Resting her head on her bent knees, Kate grinned as she thought of how shocked her uncle had been to find her working for his friend. She'd been secretly pleased that he had been fooled so completely. It made up somewhat for all the anguish she had suffered because of his attitude toward Bryan and his letting her think that her brother was dead all these years.

Her heart had remained hardened toward him until yesterday, when he had sought her out. For Uncle Matthew, he'd been unusually subdued. They had talked for over an hour, discussing Bryan and Matthew's feelings about his onetime protégé.

In the end she'd finally understood why her uncle had acted the way he had, though it still didn't excuse what he'd done. She'd promised to keep in touch, but it would probably be years before she forgave him completely.

Raising her head, Kate let her hair fall down her back like a damp blanket. Uncle Matthew faded from her mind as whisps of the dream she'd had two nights ago floated through her consciousness. It haunted her, and she'd been able to think of little else. For the dozenth time she wondered if she was crazy to consider changing the whole course of her life because of a dream, no matter how incredibly real. Yet even now it seemed more like a memory.

Bryan held her hands as they stood together beneath the oak tree where he had first kissed her. "Ah, Katie, me love, how I've missed you."

She returned the pressure of his fingers. "I've missed you, too, Bry."

"And now it's time for both of us to let go." He smiled down her. "You've found your pot of gold. Don't let it slip through your fingers."

"You mean the homestead?"

The dearly familiar creases at the corners of his brilliant green eyes tugged fiercely at her heart as he raised a hand to trace the line of her face. "Search your heart, Katie. It's not the land that brings you joy."

Kate stared at him uncertainly. "I'm not sure . . ."

"Just follow your heart. It's never played you false." He leaned forward and kissed her lightly. "Rainbows are elusive, Katie. Grab it while you can."

When she opened her eyes he was standing on a hill, bathed in the golden light of the sunset. As she watched, he blew her a kiss and raised his hand in a farewell salute. "I love you, Katie." The lilting Irish brogue floated to her on the breeze as he faded from sight.

*   *   *

Kate had awakened with a warm feeling, almost as though she really had talked to Bryan. Finding what was in her heart had taken little time, but figuring out what to do about it had taken much longer. After two days of soul-searching, she had come to a decision.

Now, the problem was how to tell Jonathan that she'd changed her mind about having a relationship with him. Behind her closed eyes, Kate conjured a picture of him smiling down at her, twinkling sapphire eyes, dimples, and all. One thing was for sure: he was bound to be pleased.

Lost in a pleasant daydream, she had no inkling that she wasn't alone until a sudden flash of light and cool breeze came in through the doorway. With a surprised gasp, her eyes popped open in time to see a large male form crawl inside the sweat lodge.

"Mind if I join you?"

"Jonathan?" she squeaked. Knowing that it was Jonathan should have calmed her, not caused her heart to lodge in her throat.

"Does that mean yes?" The deep voice held a note of humor as he sat down on the other side of the tiny hut.

"You're naked."

"I thought I was supposed to take my clothes off. Isn't the whole idea to sweat?"

"I . . . I guess so." Kate closed her eyes. Get a hold of yourself, Katharine, she thought. If you're going to be his mistress, you're going to have to get used to this kind of thing. She opened one eye cautiously and could see his white teeth gleaming in the half-light. He was grinning at her.

"What's so funny?" she asked.

"Your sudden shyness. I seem to remember times when my lack of clothing didn't bother you in the least."

Kate was sure that her blush must be lighting up the whole inside of the sweat lodge. "Is that why you're here? So I can seduce you again?"

Jonathan chuckled. "It's strange how you always think you seduced me when I'm positive it was the other way around. No, I didn't track you down so you could have your way with me." He was suddenly sober. "Kate, we need to talk."

"About what?"

"I think it's time we cleared away all the unanswered questions between us."

"Oh."

Kate felt a curious little twist of apprehension in her belly. She hadn't expected him to bring it up so soon. Though she had fully intended to become his mistress, she'd wanted more time to prepare herself. It wasn't easy to cast aside a lifetime of training. No matter how titillating it was to have a man trace erotic patterns with his tongue or sip wine from one's navel, it took some getting used to.

"I . . . I guess now is as good a time as any."

Jonathan's dimples appeared. "All right, what's going on in that head of yours? You look like Joan of Arc headed for the stake."

"I don't know what you're talking about." Kate took a deep breath and forced herself to relax. Perhaps this was the best way after all. From experience she knew that all she had to do was touch him and her embarrassment would disappear. "Why are you sitting way over there? There's plenty of room right here," she said, patting the ground beside her.

His smile deepened. "Forget it. If I come over there we won't get any talking done."

"Oh." Watching him nervously, Kate wondered what this was all about. "S-so what do you want to talk about?"

"Well, to begin with, I'm curious about why you and your uncle are at odds."

Kate shrugged. "He didn't approve of my husband. When he said I had to choose between them, I chose Bryan."

Jonathan was startled. "He told me your husband was one of his best men."

"That's how I met Bry. He worked in the bank, and Uncle Matthew brought him home to dinner one night."

Jonathan smiled. "Love at first sight?"

"Hardly. I was only fifteen at the time, but Granny liked Bry so well she took him in as a boarder. It took the better part of three years for him to realize that he'd fallen in love with me. Even then, I had a hard time convincing him that the ten years' difference in our ages didn't matter. He insisted we wait until I was eighteen before we got married."

"Your uncle thought he was too old for you?"

"That was part of it." Kate hugged her bent knees to her chest. "I didn't really realize until yesterday that Uncle Matthew was afraid that Bryan would eventually leave me."

"Why?"

"Who knows? Uncle Matthew always said you couldn't trust an Irishman."

Jonathan's eyebrows arched in surprise. "McNesby's Irish."

"Yes, but he always points out that he was born in the United States." Kate shook her head. "I never figured out what difference that makes. Anyway, as soon as Uncle Matthew realized we were married, he fired Bryan and made it impossible for him to get another job, by telling everyone about how Bryan refused to join the army."

"Was it true?"

"Yes, that's why it was so effective. You know how touchy people were about the war."

Jonathan frowned suspiciously. Could this be the link he'd been missing? "Why didn't he join up?"

"Why should he? It wasn't his fight. He had left Ireland to avoid a civil war, and he wasn't about to become involved in one here. Besides, he thought both sides had their points. He believed that the federal government should have sovereignty over the individual states, but he didn't like the idea of having to compete with thousands of free Negroes for jobs. Anyway, Bryan wasn't the only man to hire someone to go in his place."

Jonathan could hardly believe his ears. "You actually supported the institution of slavery?"

Kate gave a very unladylike snort. "You just can't imagine a woman having a different political view from her husband's, can you? I didn't take sides, but I was a northerner through and through. I could never abide the idea of slavery. Besides, you forget I had a brother fighting for the Union."

"Apparently against your uncle's wishes."

"Patrick ran away after he and Uncle Matthew had a fight. He lied about his age when he enlisted."

"So I gathered. What in the world did they fight about?"

"Uncle Matthew's name." Kate smiled at Jonathan's astonished expression. "I know, it sounds stupid, but it was the final straw. Our name isn't McNesby, it's McAnespie. Because people always mispronounce it, Uncle Matthew finally had it legally changed. The name McAnespie represented my father to Patrick, and he refused to accept McNesby instead."

"Patrick ran away because of that?"

"Well, not entirely. He got tired of Uncle Matthew trying to control his life."

"I've seen that side of your uncle," Jonathan said. "But how did you and Patrick get involved in the Confederate cause?"

Kate gave him a startled look. "What are you talking about?"

"Isn't that why you and Patrick were hiding here?"

"Patrick was hiding from Bullwhip. It's just a strange coincidence that we both wound up here."

"Then you had nothing to do with the South?"

"I told you, I didn't take sides." She frowned. "What in heaven's name made you think I had?"

Jonathan shifted uncomfortably. He had a sudden image of himself sinking in a morass of quicksand. "You have to remember, I spent three years of my life as a spy. Your uncle trained me to suspect anything that didn't make sense."

"And?"

"And last September I saw you and your brother together. I'd never seen the man before, yet the two of you seemed well acquainted. When I followed him, he led me straight to Clay Langton's. There's never been any secret about where Clay's loyalties lay."

"So you decided the three of us were in cahoots for some reason?"

"I had my suspicions. Later, Frenchie accidentally let slip you'd made arrangements to meet with Patrick at the Golden Spur on a monthly basis."

"But you didn't do anything."

"No. I thought he was your lover. Besides, I could think of only one reason anybody would be interested in me, and that was pretty obscure."

"What's that?"

"At the very beginning of the war, a shipment of gold bullion disappeared. Since I was the only guard left alive, suspicion fell on me."

"What happened to it?"

Jonathan shrugged. "I haven't the faintest idea. We were attacked by men in Confederate uniforms, but intelligence could find no indication that a Confederate force had come north. That's when I met your uncle. He investigated the incident. Once he believed my innocence, he recruited me to spy for him. Since no offcial report was ever filed, there may still be those who think I have it hidden somewhere."

"And you thought Patrick, Clay, and I were after this mythical gold?" Jonathan's distrust hurt. How could he believe such a thing about her? Then her conscience reminded her that at one point she had thought he'd murdered his wife. Suddenly Jonathan's accusations didn't seem so bad.

"As I said, it was a pretty obscure reason. It wasn't until we came back from Chicago that I decided to make inquiries."

"Oh? And why was that?"

Her sharply clipped syllables were the only indication that Kate was upset. Never had Jonathan felt so exposed and vulnerable, and it had nothing to do with the fact that he was naked. He suddenly wondered if it would all be worth it.

Clearing up the mysteries had seemed a good idea. He felt strongly about husbands and wives not having secrets between them. But how was she going to react when she discovered his betrayal? What if he lost her?

"Jonathan, what changed your mind when we got back from Chicago?"

He took a ragged breath and ran his fingers through his hair. "Levi told me that he saw you with a man at the train station, but you denied it. I didn't think much about it until Clay showed up with Patrick in tow. The two of you acted as though you'd never set eyes on each other before, though I'd seen you embracing two months earlier. That night I overheard you telling him about the man at the depot."

"You mean when I said I'd seen Uncle Matthew?"

"It was McNesby?" Jonathan felt a surge of relief. "I'll be damned. Why did you lie to Levi?"

"I disowned my uncle. It's given me a great deal of satisfaction over the years to deny that I know him." Kate suddenly understood. "No wonder you were so irrational and mean on the way back. I thought you were mad because I refused to sleep with you again."

Jonathan was tempted to leave it at that, but an

inner demon demanded to know all. "I wrote to McNesby and asked him to check on a man named Thomas Fielding. He, of course, could find nothing and asked for a description."

"So you sent him one?"

"Not at first. I decided it was all my overactive imagination."

"What changed your mind?"

Here it was, the final question. The chasm yawned at his feet, but he had to know the answer. "How did you know about Ben Colburn's death at Gettysburg, Kate?" he asked softly.

"Benjamin? Why, you talked about it when you were sick. You seemed very ups—" All at once her eyes widened in astonishment. "Colburn?" she whispered. "Good heavens, not Mary and Belle's brother? Oh, my poor Jonathan." Kate never remembered crossing the sweat lodge, only the need to comfort the man she loved, to erase the sorrow from his eyes.

For a brief instant Jonathan flinched from her comforting embrace. The guilt and self-hatred he'd held inside for so long crouched in the corner of his soul, rejecting her sympathy without conscious thought. Then, all at once, something gave way, and he pulled her into his arms with an agonized groan.

His face buried in her hair, he told her the story he'd never shared with anyone before. Her tears mingled with his own as he told of Ben dying in his arms without ever regaining consciousness. As he struggled to explain his single-minded determination to escape, to leave the war and all it stood for far behind, Jonathan's tortured soul groped toward

Kate's understanding like a drowning man for a rope.

"Ben must have recognized me and deflected his bayonet. He saved my life and I killed him." It was the same phrase he'd used during the blizzard, one he had probably repeated to himself thousands of times.

"Maybe not," Kate said as she rubbed his back. "It almost sounds like he tripped coming over the wall. It's quite possible that he didn't see you any better than you saw him."

Jonathan raised his head in surprise. "I never thought of that." Then he sighed. "It doesn't change the fact that I killed Mary's brother."

"No, but you didn't do it on purpose. Besides," she said, caressing his cheek, "you saved *my* brother. Maybe that tips the scales back the other way a bit."

Jonathan stared down at her for a moment and then folded her closer into his embrace. "You're always so damn logical, Kate. I think that's one reason I love you so much."

He loved her? The words sounded incredibly sweet. It made telling him her decision that much easier. There would never be a better time. She took a deep breath and closed her eyes. "I've changed my mind about being your mistress, Jonathan. Of course, I realize there is a great deal to learn, but I'm willing to try. I'll even orgy if you want me to."

The total silence that met her announcement stretched far too long. At last Kate could stand the suspense no longer. She looked up and encountered Jonathan's incredulous expression. "Well, you needn't look like that," she said. "I'm sure I'll learn the proper way of it soon enough."

"Orgying or being my mistress?"

"They don't go together?"

"Rarely."

"Oh." Kate was surprisingly disappointed. "That's really too bad. I thought once I got used to it, I might enjoy orgying."

"What exactly do you think an orgy is?" Jonathan asked, biting his cheek to keep from laughing.

"It isn't what you did with the wine?"

"No, my little innocent, it most definitely is not."

"Well, what is it, then?"

Jonathan told her and then grinned as he watched the color climb to her face. "I love the way you do that," he said, hugging her tightly.

"What? Make a fool of myself?"

"No, blush. It starts on your stomach and works its way up to your face," he said, tracing the path with his hand. "What do you think of the idea of making love in a sweat lodge?"

"I . . . I don't think Moonflower would approve," Kate said, distracted by his lips moving down her neck. "It's kind of a religious place."

"Then we'd better leave," Jonathan murmured against her collarbone, his voice rough with passion, "because in about two minutes one of us is going to seduce the other."

Kate tipped her head back to allow him easier access. "Does this mean I'm going to be your mistress?" she whispered.

"Nope." Jonathan gave her a quick kiss and lifted her off his lap.

"What do you mean, 'nope'?"

"I changed my mind, too. Having you for my mistress isn't what I want anymore."

"Why not?" Kate asked in hurt bewilderment as he crawled toward the door.

"Because I want you for my wife instead," he said over his shoulder as the hide flap closed behind him.

"You what?" By the time Kate had scrambled after him, Jonathan was already in the beaver pond. "What do you mean, your wife?" she demanded, standing on the creek bank with her hands on her hips.

He grinned up at her. "Do you honestly want me to propose to you up there, or are you going to join me here so I can do it properly?"

Before Kate had a chance to reply, Charlie's voice came through the trees behind her. "Where are you two headed?"

"We're going to find Pa and Mrs. Murphy," she heard Levi call out excitedly.

"Yeah, he's gonna ask her to marry him." Cole's voice was closest of all. "We're going to help convince her."

Jonathan laughed as Kate practically dove into the pool. "Don't worry," he said as he put his arms around her and pulled her close. "Charlie and Moonflower will keep them at bay. I posted them as guards in front of your cabin."

"Don't reckon your father needs yer help," they heard Charlie say.

"But what if she says no?"

"I expect the only way that's gonna happen is if she remembers that marrying your pa will make you her sons."

There was a moment of silence. "Maybe we better leave it to Pa."

"I guess so."

"Hey, I know. Let's go cook supper. That'll impress her."

"We'll make biscuits and stew." The voices began to move away.

"We don't know how to make biscuits."

"So? I've watched Mrs. Murphy do it. Doesn't look too hard."

The boys' voices soon faded into the distance.

"Oh, no, you don't," Jonathan said, tightening his hold before Kate could get away. "You haven't answered my question."

"You haven't asked me yet."

"True." Tipping her chin up with one finger, he kissed her quite thoroughly before raising his head and smiling down into her eyes. "Kate, will you do me the honor of becoming my wife?"

With her arms around his neck, Kate snuggled closer in the frigid water. "I don't know. I kind of got used to the idea of being your mistress."

"Oh, you did, did you?"

"Mmmm, and frankly the benefits are better."

"Is that so?"

"Definitely. Wives never get to do anything wild or wicked."

"And mistresses do?"

"All the time." She ran a wet finger down his chest. "Of course, if you were to convince me that I wouldn't be giving anything up by marrying you . . ."

His dimples appeared. "I think I know just the thing to persuade you."

It was a long time before Kate remembered to worry about what was going on in her kitchen.

Watch for

Shadows in the Wind
Book II of the Cheyenne Trilogy

by
Carolyn Lampman

Coming in February 1994
from HarperMonogram

COMING NEXT MONTH

ORCHIDS IN MOONLIGHT by Patricia Hagan
Bestselling author Patricia Hagan weaves a mesmerizing tale set in the untamed West. Determined to leave Kansas and join her father in San Francisco, vivacious Jamie Chandler stowed away on the wagon train led by handsome Cord Austin—a man who didn't want any company. Cord was furious when he discovered her, but by then it was too late to turn back. It was also too late to turn back the passion between them.

TEARS OF JADE by Leigh Riker
Twenty years after Jay Barron was classified as MIA in Vietnam, Quinn Tyler is still haunted by the feeling that he is still alive. When a twist of fate brings her face-to-face with businessman Welles Blackburn, a man who looks like Jay, Quinn is consumed by her need for answers that could put her life back together again, or tear it apart forever.

FIREBRAND by Kathy Lynn Emerson
Her power to see into the past could have cost Ellen Allyn her life if she had not fled London and its superstitious inhabitants in 1632. Only handsome Jamie Mainwaring accepted Ellen's strange ability and appreciated her for herself. But was his love true, or did he simply intend to use her powers to help him find fortune in the New World?

CHARADE by Christina Hamlett
Obsessed with her father's mysterious death, Maggie Price investigates her father's last employer, Derek Channing. From the first day she arrives at Derek's private island fortress in the Puget Sound, Maggie can't deny her powerful attraction to the handsome millionaire. But she is troubled by questions he won't answer, and fears that he has buried something more sinister than she can imagine.

THE TRYSTING MOON by Deborah Satinwood
She was an Irish patriot whose heart beat for justice during the reign of George III. Never did Lark Ballinter dream that it would beat even faster for an enemy to her cause—the golden-haired aristocratic Lord Christopher Cavanaugh. A powerfully moving tale of love and loyalty.

CONQUERED BY HIS KISS by Donna Valentino
Norman Lady Maria de Courson had to strike a bargain with Saxon warrior Rothgar of Langwald in order to save her brother's newly granted manor from the rebellious villagers. But when their agreement was sweetened by their firelit passion in the frozen forest, they faced a love that held danger for them both.

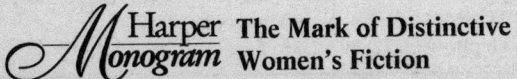 **Harper Monogram** — **The Mark of Distinctive Women's Fiction**